ADVANCE MAN

STEVEN JACQUES

CALUMET EDITIONS

Minneapolis, Minnesota

FIRST EDITION OCTOBER 2014

Printed in the United States of America.

10 9 8 7 6 5 4 3 2 1

ISBN: 978-939548-20-7

Advance Man

Steven Jacques

CALUMET
EDITIONS
Minneapolis, Minnesota

To my parents, Frances and Clemens Jacques. Despite their concerns about the nature of politics and their worries about the rationality of dedicating long stretches of my life to it, their unconditional love and support remained constant.

Special thanks to Antonia Felix, the brilliant and talented bestselling author, opera singer, arts entrepreneur and educator. Without her wise counsel and coaching there would be no book, only a pile of words taking up space on my hard drive.

With grateful appreciation to my wife Christine Colby, who had me at "who the hell are you and why are you talking to me?"

"Advance Men — the small teams of political operatives who arrange the tours of major presidential candidates—are practitioners of one of the most complicated skills in American politics; a good advance man must combine in himself the qualities of a circus tout, a carnival organizer, an accomplished diplomat and a quarter-master general."

—Theodore H. White, The Making of the President

"One constant in the world of advance men is redundancy, over-planning. There is a presumption of possible disaster. Nothing can be left to chance. . . . In the world of modern politics, advance men are somewhat like secret agents—people whose existence is best concealed for the sake of the mission."

—Los Angeles Times

"It was February 2008 and we were one year into an almost two-year presidential campaign. It was the longest campaign I've ever done, except for the weekend I did an Advance trip for Howard Dean in 2003."

—Bix Benjamin, Senior National Lead Advance

1

"I should shut this rally down," the fire marshal yelled at Bix over the din. "You've got at least four thousand people in a gymnasium that's rated for three thousand, and look at all the space you've taken up for the press area, the lighting trusses, the stage, and the ten-foot buffer zone around it. Look at it." He pointed back inside the gym as if Bix had never seen the site before.

It looked gorgeous to Bix.

The double crash doors closed behind them as they walked out of the gym into the secured hallway where it was quieter, where Bix hoped that cool reason would salve Fire Marshal Fierro's worries, but the man remained strident. "The stage and press areas are completely encircled in bike rack, and you've got rope and stanchion everywhere else. If there's an emergency, those are all barriers. I should really shut this down."

Bix could see that Fierro was serious but seemed to be searching for a way out of the dilemma. Luckily, calm was called for; Bix had no energy left for any other emotional state. The unintended benefit was that his vocal cords were as tired as he was, and he sounded like Gregory Peck playing King Solomon—a helpful affectation, he thought, as he tried to reassure the fire marshal. "It is certainly an unexpected crowd, but my counters tell me there are just a few more than three thousand people coming through the magnetometers," he said, stretching the truth a bit. "We actually left a lot of people outside," he summed up, stretching the truth a bit more.

Mike Pitcher, the team's Site 1, walked over and interjected, "And every single body in this room has gone through security, so none of them could be carrying any hazardous materials," which was absolutely true, but completely meaningless. They were the most convincing facts that Bix and Mike could muster for an argument they didn't have.

"Absolutely," Bix concluded authoritatively. "That's an important point. And in case of an emergency," he continued, "Mike and his Site 2, Ron, have volunteers posted at key positions along the bike rack and rope lines, so it can all be de-coupled and moved out of the way or dropped. The same crowd-control measures we deploy to move people into the rally site would be implemented in reverse to facilitate a quick evacuation, with the exception that we won't make people go through the magnetometers again as they exit screaming."

With one look at the fire marshal, Bix knew he shouldn't have mentioned the screaming part, especially at the moment that his Solomonic assurances were beginning to have an impact.

"What if there's a panic?" the fire marshal asked, sounding panicked.

"We're very good at dealing with panic," Bix said. "We're in a constant state of it. And if we lose all ability to control our bodily functions, we've got the Secret Service here to tell us what to do, so we have nothing to worry about." He said it loudly enough for the Special Agent standing post nearby to overhear. The agent smiled.

Mike pointed to the agent. "See, we have adult supervision."

"And—," Bix was the first to notice a gaggle of bodies walking toward them, "we have the next President of the United States coming down the hallway towards us as we speak." As The Candidate drew close the fire marshal was taken aback. His reaction was money in the bank; Bix seized the moment.

"Senator, this is Fire Marshal Fierro," he said, "and he has been more than kind in working with us on our unexpectedly large crowd."

"Good to meet you, sir." The Candidate reached for the fire marshal's hand and flashed his million-dollar look of sincerity. "So, does it look like we're gonna need a bigger boat?"

Fierro's tenor changed dramatically. "It's pretty crowded out there, but I think we can manage."

"Well, I appreciate you working with us. Bix is the best advance man in the business. He's been doing this since Harry Truman and I don't think he's lost a voter yet."

"To be honest," Bix told the fire marshal, "I've never lost a *supporter*, a record of excellence that I will endeavor to maintain."

"Good man," The Candidate laughed. "I respect that level of commitment, and that level of honesty."

The fire marshal laughed, sort of.

"Bix, are we ready to go?" The Candidate asked.

"Yes sir." Bix sent Ron out to cue the soundman and start the music at the right moment. Then he looked over at Mike and told him to cue the Voice of God. Mike loved doing the VOG. He quickstepped over to a wireless microphone lying on a stool in the hallway near the double doors and turned it on.

In his deepest voice, with a bold but not triumphant inflection, Mike boomed, "LADIES AND GENTLEMEN... (pause)... PLEASE WELCOME THE NEXT PRESIDENT OF THE UNITED STATES... (pause)," and then bellowed The Candidate's name in the stentorian drawl of a ring announcer. Site 2 Ron cued the soundman to start the entry music, which was one of the pre-approved pieces that Bix didn't recognize on the music CD sent out by Headquarters to Site Advance staff.

The Candidate walked out, enthusiastically but not triumphantly, because it was impossible to overstress the non-triumphant nature of his campaign, and entered through the double doors, past the pipe-and-drape curtain and into the gymnasium. Deafening noise that could only be described as thunderous greeted his arrival; the building quaked as if it might collapse. Every square inch of the room was occupied with enthusiastic supporters. Massive bleachers holding more than fifteen hundred bodies towered over stage left, exactly opposite the press cutaway riser on stage right, providing the perfect location for five fervent, animated supporters holding seven foot-high letters of The Candidate's last name carved out of two-inch thick white Styrofoam insulation panels. It was a Bix thing; he'd carved them himself.

There were no looky-loos in the audience, no objective observers who attended to make a dispassionate assessment of The Candidate and his message. It was an historic campaign; the first African-American who could, and might, win the White House.

The Candidate quickly shook hands with a few dozen people who were reaching over the bike rack-lined path as he rushed to the stage trailing a trio of Secret Service agents. He bounded up the stairs and when he reached the summit, where the entire crowd could see him, the noise level increased past seismic.

In his previous experience with presidential candidates, not going back quite as far as Truman, Bix usually had crowds this size only in the final weeks before general elections. This time was a phenomenon. They had been producing large crowds since Day One, when Bix produced The Candidate's announcement tour of Iowa almost a year before. The crowds were constrained only by the size of the venues available, or by the intent of the campaign to do smaller events for specific purposes, such as "meet and greets," "town halls," or "round tables."

Every once in a while the director of Advance would call with a new directive. "We're catching heat in the press because we're always doing big crowds. We gotta take it down a notch, make it look like we're connecting with 'real people,' so we're gonna do some smaller events."

Hearing that was like a slap in the face to Bix and every real Advance Lead. It was an unalterable tenet of Advance that Advance people love big crowds. Big crowds were exciting, measurable, and they compensated for a lot of screw-ups, in case there happened to be any.

With four thousand people in a gym rated for three thousand, The Newton High rally was a rock and roll show. The people all looked "real" to Bix, and he assumed they looked real on television.

When The Candidate started his speech the fire marshal resumed his diatribe, but the rally had passed the point of no return. Bix was amazed that the Secret Service hadn't entered the fray, so he was happy to take the heat as long as the fire marshal was talking and not taking action. Bix invited him to have his picture taken with The Candidate along with members of local law enforcement after the rally; the fire marshal graciously accepted and continued the harangue for another ten minutes—as long as The Candidate's speech—and the rally rallied on without a hitch.

This one last act of local diplomacy allowed Bix to fulfill his singular mission as Lead Advance: crafting national media coverage that would dominate the day's news cycle, and along the way controlling everything that might have an impact on that outcome. For the sake of the cause—saving the world for democracy—he stood there and took one for the team.

The dinosaurs, the old guys, Bix's mentors when he started in national politics, all said that Advance was about "control." "Control" was the mantra. Like them, Bix had grown wise enough to accept that there would be situations over which he had no control at all. That acceptance was still hard fought, only the last option after he'd exhausted all others, and fire marshals always ranked high on the list of things that could not be controlled. He knew he'd gotten lucky. The stars happened to align at that moment and Bix knew he had dodged a bullet, although he kept such figurative mixed metaphors to himself around the Secret Service.

* * *

Once, a long, long time before, up until about five hours earlier that morning, Bix had clung to the hope of a better tomorrow. The future he envisioned involved having the next day off after more than a month of no sleep and bad fast food. A week earlier, the director of Advance had personally promised Bix he could take a day off on Primary Day to rest and recreate. But soon after he got out of bed that morning, Bix already knew that his dream of eight hours' sleep, a civilized brunch, then an afternoon nap followed by a trip to the Laundromat, would remain just that—an exotic, unachievable dream. He even had a book that he planned to read at the Laundromat, a three-pounder by Robert Caro that he had been toting around for months, *Master of the Senate.* In retrospect he realized he was only deluding himself.

The day started normally; he woke up exhausted. Even then, one spark of optimism still smoldered under the rubble of his ravaged countenance. The prospect of twenty-four hours' R & R, beginning immediately after the day's events ended, remained very real. He should have guessed that his last grain of hope would soon be stolen, along with what was left of his innocence, which wasn't much.

Nothing surprised him anymore, but he never ceased to be amazed. He was only moderately amazed to find, just after being jounced out of a short night's sleep, a voicemail on his phone from Egan, his boss, asking him to call as soon as his rally ended because "there are rumors circulating that might have a negative impact, and we're gonna need you in South Carolina pretty soon." In a profession where nothing is more brutally evident than the adage "no one is indispensible," he knew he was about to get the "you're indispensible" speech from a guy who wasn't old enough to know better. Bix should have known better, but it was one of those valuable lessons that he had to re-learn at length: in Advance, the promise of a day off isn't really a promise so much as a way to get someone off your back. He knew he would have to wait a little longer—or forever—before getting a day off for good behavior.

The waxen image looking back at Bix in the mirror that morning reminded him of a statue he'd seen of Charles DeGaulle in Madame Tussauds after a fire. He thought of the first rule of Advance—Advance men are supposed to be invisible—and it seemed like a good day to make a special effort in that regard lest he frighten the volunteers.

Game day ticked ahead, the culmination of seventy-two hours' intense preparations for The Candidate's final rally of the New Hampshire primary, the last chance to influence voters before Election Day. It was only the second contest of the primary season and The Candidate's nomination was by no means guaranteed, adding a little extra edge to every Advance trip. Bix was already suffering from chronic road ravage after seven months of constant travel, in addition to his daily caffeine deficit disorder. It wasn't as if the fate of the presidential campaign, much less the fate of the free world, depended on his work that day, but, as always, one mistake could cost The Candidate the election, so in a sense—it did.

Advance was a conundrum; always an unequal set of rewards and punishments. If all went well and several thousand people all did exactly what they were supposed to do at exactly the right moments, and any surprises were handled deftly, and all the media coverage was stellar, Bix could take satisfaction in controlling the news cycle for a day. On the other hand, one mistake, or one oversight, might be enough to make everyone go home permanently. Bix was especially concerned about the poor journalists who would have to find another assignment if The Candidate's campaign went belly-up. That concern—that passionate, burning, emotional concern—gave him the strength of purpose to carry on. "Save the journalists!" echoed in his head and pounded in his heart when he awoke every morning in another barely familiar hotel room.

In a few hours he would walk up a set of portable stairs into the front cabin of The Candidate's campaign plane to give his initial briefing, and for the next twenty hours perform his role as impresario of the presidential candidate's public persona despite having so little left of his own.

His cell phone vibrated on the bedside table that morning at 5:31 a.m. with the lilting sound of a hand grenade. It was Mike, no doubt, politely waiting until at least 5:30 to report, as instructed. Mike Pitcher, old friend and Site 1 on the Advance Team, was last seen at Newton High School outside Nashua where Bix had left him three hours earlier. Bix walked back to the bed as fast as his stiff legs could carry him to answer the call. He heard himself groan as he sat.

"This is Bix."

"Good morning, sir," Mike said. "We've got a couple of problems."

Bix mumbled as he rubbed his eyes. "Take it as a good omen. If everything seems to be going well it means you've overlooked something. Who is this?"

"Your worst nightmare, your trusty site guy who has had even less sleep than you. The magnetometers that were supposed to show up last night so the Secret Service could start setting them up at five a.m. still haven't arrived. No one seems to know where they are."

"I'll call Bill," Bix told him, referring to Bill White, the Lead Secret Service agent for the Advance trip and Bix's counterpart. "I'm sure he's aware that our Candidate has been known to spontaneously ask his Detail Leader to throw open the doors if there are still people waiting outside when he arrives. The agents dislike that almost as much as they dislike surprises, but not nearly as much as they dislike advance guys who cause surprises. What's the other problem?"

"Not so much of a problem, really, more of an ominous probability. Dick O'Malley from Max News showed up a few minutes ago trying to get into the building before pre-set so he could set up his cameras, plural."

"The last time I saw O'Malley out on the road he was trying to do an exposé on Democrats stealing Christmas from orphans. How many cameras did he have?"

"Three."

"With three camera crews?"

"And two producers and a huge truck," Mike said.

"That's ambitious. He's probably investigating allegations that The Candidate is an admitted heterosexual, or that his sister is a practicing thespian; stuff his audience would appreciate. How is it you refer to O'Malley's audience again?"

"Pre-Homo sapien."

"Yes. Well, the man's got to make a living somehow. Given his skill set, it's either a show on Max TV News or working on the stun line in a meatpacking factory. I'll email Rachel and copy the press office. Is that it?"

"For now," Mike said. "Other than that, everything seems to be going well."

"You keep thinking that, General Custer, and I'll get in touch with Bill."

An involuntary political knee jerk reaction caused Bix to conjure potential story lines the eternally indignant O'Malley might be pursuing, but it wasn't worth considering hypotheticals. It was enough to know that O'Malley believed that he was on to something sufficient to warrant a small army of Max News employees.

It was then that he noticed the voicemail that had been left on his phone at five a.m. by the director of Advance. When he heard "call me as soon as your rally is over," he knew his R & R was a fantasy. Another involuntary muscle movement caused him to grin broadly, as if trying to fool his brain into believing that it was a good thing. "It's good to be needed," he thought, after his initial, more visceral reaction. It crossed his mind there could be a connection between Egan's phone call and O'Malley's arrival with half of the Max News division.

He decided to send Special Agent White an email about the magne-tometers rather than attempt to engage him in conversation at that early hour, and then emailed Rachel, the Advance Team's Press 1. He also shot a note to the campaign's press office about O'Malley. He averted his eyes from the incoming emails on his BlackBerry as he did it, then summoned his energy to start the coffee maker, shuffle back into the bathroom and survey his face once again in the mirror. If not for the lack of sleep, he was certain he could be mistaken for someone much younger who had simply lived a very hard life in a gulag.

Standing in his skivvies in a hotel room in New Hampshire for the umpteen millionth time, he definitely felt older, though he refused to succumb to the full Methuselah pity party. His brown locks, while a little thinner, were still brown, and his six-foot-one inch frame bore the years unbowed. It was his eleventh presidential campaign and he was determined it would be his last, just as he had sworn during the previ-ous two. Like the Mafia, they kept pulling him back in, and they used a pressure tactic that was as ruthlessly diabolical as it was brutally effec-tive: they asked. He could not withstand the weight of such unrelenting coercion.

Out of perverse habit, he was compelled to check his BlackBerry be-fore completing his morning routine. Most of the emails could wait until he made another cup of the fine in-room cappuccino, but one caught his attention. The campaign manager, Bob Peem, pricked him with the subject line, "S Carolina." Bix looked to see how many recipients were on the email and found he was the only one. A layer of dread suddenly descended upon the dismay he'd felt after the voicemail from Egan. He felt compelled to read it the same way a crowd is drawn to look at a car crash. It took him a few moments to translate: "Bix, nd tlk w/u 2day. Issues in S.C. Am in meet all a.m. Wil cal soon. Bob"

He wondered if Peem was channeling a Western Union operator. He replied immediately with all the concern he could muster: "Bob, lk frwrd tking wt u. Bx." He felt it would be courteous to acknowledge re-ceipt, but the word "issues" stood out. The only "issues" that concerned Bix were the ones he could see looming on the horizon threatening to decalibrate the finely honed instrument that was his mind. Combined with the voicemail from Egan, he sensed some matter of importance had achieved gravitas in Headquarters' collective imagination, and maybe in reality. Who knew? It was important to remind himself, for the umpteenth million time, it didn't matter which.

Bix's irritation turned to pique, but really bad pique, as he re-read the email. Too often "issue" was a euphemism for "crisis," and he had never seen an exception to the rule that political campaigns sprouted crises like mushrooms, in vast numbers out of manure in the cavernous recesses of peoples' heads. Bix hadn't grown so cynical as to believe that political staffers purposely cultivated crises to feed their self-importance, although he very recently acknowledged to himself it might be possible. He was precious in that way. There were enough real problems to go around, but Bix was from Missouri and he had seen too much of politics to waste all of his good angst on something that turned out to be insignificant. He needed a day of rest; *that* was significant. Almost biblical.

As if Big Brother was monitoring his emails in real time, Bix's cell phone rang again. It was Peem, and the early hour of the call underscored his concern.

Bix did his best to sound coherent. "Bob, this is a somewhat terrifying honor. What can I do for you?"

"Good morning Bix. Thanks for taking my call this early. I know you've been on the road for a long time without a rest, but we have a tough situation in South Carolina and, as much as it pains me to say it, you are uniquely qualified to engage on this issue."

"That must have been distasteful," Bix said. "Would you like some Listermint?"

"I'll be fine. I'm stuck with the realization that's it true. We need a combo on this one, Advance and ultimately foreign affairs."

"Ultimately foreign affairs? That sounds much more enticing than it's probably going to end up. What do you need?"

"When you were a DAS at the State Department, did you know an Iranian-born gentleman named Jamir Parviz who used to work there, too?"

"I know him. We did a couple of projects together when he was the desk officer for the Near Eastern Affairs Bureau. He's a good guy. Lovely wife. What about him?"

"He was a college friend of The Candidate's," Peem said.

"That should raise suspicions immediately."

"It's more than that. There are reports from the university where he now teaches in South Carolina that he and our Candidate participated in Iranian-inspired anti-American activities in the early 1980s when they were undergraduates. There's a rumor that they wrote a manifesto calling for jihad against America."

"It's a little early for jokes, Bob. I've got a lot of—"

"Apparently there's enough substance to the rumor that the Wall Street Review and two major network news organizations, if you include Max News as a major news organization, have sent investigative reporters to South Carolina to find out if it's true. Also, the Republican National Committee and The Opponent's campaign have their own investigators looking for Professor Parviz. If it *is* true, everyone will be looking for that manifesto. I just received the email you sent to the press office about Dick O'Malley. We think his appearance at your event may be tied-in."

"You're actually serious.

"The rumour is out there. We can't ignore it."

Bix walked over to the window and looked down at the hotel parking lot, where lamp posts made a few circles of light in the darkness. "It sounds like we're the last to know about this," he said calmly. "To ask the remarkably obvious, what did our boss have to say about the manifesto?"

"He doesn't remember anything that could be damaging," Peem said. "He and Jamir were friends and were active in campus politics together. He said they co-wrote articles on a lot of topics, but didn't get many published. He doesn't think any of them could have been construed as radical or inflammatory, certainly nothing calling for jihad."

"Any idea of the source of these reports?"

"It's supposedly students or fellow professors, people from Eliot Stearns College, the school where Professor Parviz teaches, saying they had seen it or he had talked about it."

"What would be Jamir's motivation to claim such a thing?" Bix asked. "I recall that he was very conservative on the topic of American-

Iranian relations, certainly not a left-wing radical, and not outside the mainstream of policy options. He's more of a hard-liner about Iran than The Candidate, but if they were friends, why would he try to damage his candidacy?"

"I didn't know he was a conservative, but maybe that's why," Peem said. "Professor Parviz may be trying to force The Candidate into taking a more hawkish stance toward Iran by suggesting that he was radically pro-Iran, or pro-terrorist, during the height of tensions between the two countries."

"Bob, that's a stretch. It's five a.m. and I've had two hours' sleep and even I am more lucid than that," Bix said.

"We've got two problems anyway. One, he can damage The Candidate just by claiming it's true without any evidence. Two, if they did write something together that can be construed as suggesting that jihad against America might be a good thing, even if it was never published, it will destroy the campaign."

"Has anyone tried calling Jamir?" Bix asked.

"He's disappeared," Peem explained. "He took a sabbatical at the beginning of the semester and then when reporters started calling him, he vanished completely. His cell phone doesn't respond."

"What would you like me to do while I am relaxing in the sunny state of South Carolina?" Bix asked. "It sounds like Egan wants me to do an Advance trip there as well."

"Actually we both want you to do the Advance. We have some events we'd like you to do, and we were hoping that while you were there you could track down Jamir and talk with him."

"In my spare time?"

"Sort of."

"These 'events'—may I assume they will be simple and relatively easy to produce?"

"Not really."

"Good to know. Is there any reason to believe Jamir is still in the state, much less the country?"

"Well, we think he's in South Carolina. That's where the reporters and investigators are looking for him," Bob said.

Bix sat down on the edge of the bed. "As long as we're operating on such reliable intel, then I'll totally go tilting at windmills," he said. "Why do you think I'll be any more successful than trained investigators other than my incredible powers of deduction, and my pipe and deerstalker hat?"

"For one, you know Professor Parviz," Peem replied, "and for another, your extensive roster of international contacts and acquaintances. You know people he knows. You know his professional colleagues from government, and more importantly, you have credibility with the people who would be most likely to share confidences. And we wanted you to do the South Carolina trip anyway. It's critical we get this one right. We need the full Bix treatment."

Bix winced to hear Peem lay it on so thick. "Good grief, Bob, extensive roster? Full Bix treatment? Come on, I believe my own PR more than anyone, but hearing it come out of your mouth sounds weird. Why the snow job?"

"We think you can find the guy, that's all, and you can do the media event we need."

"Uh-huh. What if I find Jamir and it turns out to be true, what then? Are you suggesting I commit an act of incivility? And speak up so I can get you on tape."

"We want you to determine his intent. Find out what he is claiming and how far he intends to take it. If he has a document he claims was written by him and The Candidate, try to get a copy. If he seems open to reason, try to reason with him."

"You're assuming I have any left myself. Manifestos are usually cumbersome things, difficult to hide, and we're going to race the news media to see who gets to him first?"

"That's essentially what I had in mind. So, can we count on you? The Candidate needs you, the campaign needs you, Lady Liberty needs you."

"Bringing up old girlfriends will get you nowhere."

"Speaking of that," Peem said, springing to life, "I hear that Storie Toller is the Regional Political Director for our Opponent in that area. Does that name ring a bell?

"Of course," Bix said.

"She's been spending a lot of time in South Carolina and you may run in to her. They want to win South Carolina badly and they're going all-out. Thought you'd want to know."

"It's not surprising. Good heads-up."

"That's why we need you in South Carolina. We could lose the primary and the nomination. You know all the players. Can we count on you?"

"Can I count on some support from headquarters? I could use an intern or two to do research. It may be difficult tracking down some of the people I have to find and some of the information I'll need. At this moment I can't even predict."

"Absolutely. Whatever resources you need."

"I just want someone who will respond quickly when I call, who can be creative in ferreting out information. Someone you trust. Better yet, someone I trust."

"You can work with my assistant, Sophie," said Peem. "She's much better than you deserve. I know that because she's much better than I deserve. She'll be able to handle anything you throw at her."

"Thanks. Sounds good."

"I don't need to tell you how much is riding on every aspect of this. Everyone here is concerned. We can't appear to be freaking out, especially since it looks like the vote tomorrow in New Hampshire may not go our way. We'll need to regain our momentum in South Carolina, we need to figure out how much of a problem we face with Parviz, and we need to do it quietly."

"In that case I'll cancel the press release announcing my arrival. And the marching band to greet me at the airport."

"Bix, you are the soul of stealth," Peem said.

"The sultan of *sub rosa*?"

"No, but when we win we can have you appointed ambassador there."

"I've already got that job," Bix said. "I'll get in touch with Sophie as soon as I can after the rally. Can you send Kate Hillhouse to do Press?"

"I'll find out. If I can I will."

"That would be good. Let me know."

"Thank you, Bix. I appreciate this."

Bix noted that it was the second time Peem thanked him, which was two times more than he had ever thanked him in the past, a campaign's generous equivalent to the warm gratitude a spy receives when he's being sent on a mission from which he may not return.

* * *

Special Agent White responded quickly to Bix's email about the lost magnetometers, writing back: "Sorry about the confusion. Just found out the truck transporting the mag's to the site hit a deer and all of the equipment had to be loaded onto another truck. They will be there within the hour."

"Republican deer probably," answered Bix. "Thanks for the info." He cc'd Mike at the site.

He tried to focus on the issues at hand while he dressed. There was the small matter of the presidential campaign rally he was producing that day, two motorcade movements, three newspaper interviews, The Candidate's previously unplanned airport arrival and an overnight with two busloads of traveling press in tow. He scrolled through the checklist in his head, which he knew was a poor place to keep it, and everything seemed to be going well. It concerned him. These were the times when mistakes could easily occur, when he was awake. The cumulative effect of seven months on the road and the anticipation of nine more months until the general election were taking their toll, as was the lack of decent barbeque. He referred to it as "the paucity," as if it were a plague.

He gathered his stack of notes and schedules and tried once again to organize his wits, thinking they might come in handy. He wondered if he would have thought himself capable if, seven months prior, someone had been able to predict how intense the campaign and his schedule would become, but he realized it was a stupid question. Of course he would have. Addiction robs one of rationality, particularly an addiction disguised as a calling. It was insidious.

Lurking behind each blinking synapse in the still-functional portion of his mind was the awareness that one error in judgment, even one bad visual, could irrevocably damage the campaign. Bix only had to think back to the photo of the little professorial Democratic presidential nominee wearing a big helmet, riding around in the big tank. It wasn't difficult to recall, since the photo was known to the entire country as the self-inflicted wound that helped kill the diminutive Democrat's presidential aspirations. Bix also remembered that the Advance Lead on that trip, an officious young fellow with the light touch and good taste of a kazoo player in a grade school production of "HMS Pinafore," was summarily promoted. Failing-up was a not uncommon method of getting ahead in the Democratic Party. Bix thought he might get a chance to see if it worked for him on the upcoming trip.

He scrolled down through the volume of emails from headquarters as he drank his coffee. All the young staffers in the various offices—Press, Communications, Political, Field and "Skedvance," cleverly jargonized from the Scheduling and Advance Office—were professional, hard working, and surprisingly talented. The downside was there were at least a half-dozen offices at HQ that attempted to supervise aspects of Advance that had always been the purview of the Lead.

None of the headquarters staff had ever done Advance, which added to the indignation, and certainly none appreciated the skill it took to control the actions and reactions of hundreds or thousands, or tens of thousands of people, including the press, the public, the pols, the pals and The Candidate, without them feeling as if they had been "choreographed," as Bix described it. None could conceive the artistry of it, the essence of capturing lightning in a bottle and making it reappear on the evening news in a manner that closely, or even exactly, resembled a non-paid political advertisement.

He likened it to conducting the orchestra and directing the ballet at the same time, while stage managing, coordinating the grips, writing the music, and, in his youth, which at the time seemed inexhaustible, trying to get lucky with the ballerinas. He led trips for presidents, vice presidents, and presidential candidates over three decades, and he believed he started to get really good at it just about the time that technology and human nature combined to make Advance a committee process. Simply because cell phones and emails and jpegs allowed anyone or everyone at headquarters to crawl up his pantaloons any time the emotion moved them didn't mean they should, he thought, but inevitably they did, as he knew they would. The few dinosaurs who were still doing Advance always demurred when asked what they did for presidential campaigns or for the White House. "I'm just the guy who moves the furniture around," was the coy response they had coined many years earlier. Cycle by cycle, presidential campaign bureaucracies were slowly trying to make that a reality. Bix hoped the same scourge afflicted Republican Advance people, but given their regimentation, they probably wouldn't notice anyway.

He continued his mental checklist as he prepared for the drive to the airport for wheels-down that morning. Airport arrival, local press, greeters, motorcade, site, national press, press pre-set, crowd, arrival, site greeters, VIPs, his own luggage—the day's first act of physical labor. His own not-unsubstantial baggage needed to go to RON hotel, a Secret Service-ism meaning Remain Over Night, where Bix and his team were being forced to move for the night because The Candidate would RON there. Bix was so *not* looking forward to it because it was *so* much nicer than the hotel where he and his team had stayed for the previous three nights where breakfast had been free, coffee was always available and parking was just outside the front door. Not so at the fancy RON hotel.

In the previous month he had led six Advance trips involving twenty cities and towns in Nevada, Iowa, and New Hampshire, produced eight rallies, ten "Meet the Candidate/Town Halls," one Economic Round Table, and a Canvas Kick-off, all of them covered by the national press, most being The Candidate's "event of the day," and worst of all, no place on the schedule with good barbeque. The incivility of it pushed him to his breaking point. If all he had to deal with was the stress, and the pace, and the media scrutiny, and the travel and the unrelenting pressure, he could handle it. He was cranking out media events every two or three days with no smoked meat or sauce fit for human consumption in sight, and it was beginning to wear on his delicate sensibilities.

Before leaving for the airport, his last order of business was to check in with his team: Mike, at the site, and Rachel, the Press 1.

Mike was standing in the lobby of the high school gymnasium when Bix called to ask for an update. Good friends since the previous presidential campaign when both worked for the same candidate, Sen. James Curley, they had Advanced enough trips together to develop a rhythm.

"Michael, are you having fun yet?"

"The fun never ceases in Advance world."

"Good attitude. What happened, did you start smoking cigarettes again?"

"Nope. Something even more soothing. The truck arrived with the mag's and the Secret Service is setting them up now, but they're still missing one. We'll be ready to open the doors in less than an hour. I estimate we have about three thousand people already waiting to get in."

"Another full house. Imagine my surprise."

"It'll be overflow," Mike suggested, "and I'm too tired to deal with another irate fire marshal."

The Advance team was confident of the crowd despite the fact that it was midday on a Monday. Crowd building for The Candidate's events was never a problem—the problem was crowd management. Many months before, during the dog days of the previous summer, long before the Iowa Caucuses when most presidential candidates were happy to meet with fifteen people in someone's living room in towns such as Cherokee, Estherville, Spirit Lake, LeMars, Greenfield, and Harlan, The Candidate was drawing crowds in the hundreds or thousands.

The Nashua high school gymnasium Bix chose for the rally could hold more than 3,000 people. If Mike shoved hard enough, he could make it 4,000. It was a big space. If Bix could have found a larger one, he would have chosen it.

"How much sleep did you get last night?" Bix asked.

"Less than two hours. We stayed a little later than you to deal with the lighting guy, who didn't seem to know the difference between an HMI and a PAR can."

"You're telling me that we have a lighting contractor who doesn't know the difference between a hydrargyrum medium-arc iodide spot light and a parabolic aluminized reflector spot?"

"That's impressive," Mike said. "I bet the ladies love it."

"They do. How have the site agents been? Any problems with the rope lines?"

"Not bad. We had a little disagreement about the buffer zone around the stage, but we worked it out."

"Is that where we needed to shrink the width of his pathway between the stage and the bleachers?" Bix asked.

"Yeah, I told them we needed to cheat the bleachers to the south a little to accommodate the cutaway riser and ensure the visual. I convinced them that having the main stage close enough to the cutaway riser that the press could jump to it was not a good idea. Basically, I laid on the floor and screamed and kicked my arms and legs until they gave me my way. It was all very professional."

"Good job. This is why I see you in a senior administration position after we win, possibly something in international diplomacy." Mike was the only person Bix ever met who held dual citizenship in the U.S. and New Zealand, and it was the only thing Bix didn't trust about him. How could Mike be loyal to America, Bix asked him, and our arch nemesis, New Zealand, bent as they were on a marmite-fueled quest for world domination in rugby? Mike admitted his role in the conspiracy but showed no remorse.

Mike spoke English like a Midwesterner but with a vaguely inscrutable New Zealander accent that women found attractive. Other than that, Bix liked him. The feelings of respect were mutual. They were both tall, imposing figures in the sense that they both enjoyed their work and it showed, and they did their best to impose that positive attitude on everyone involved with their Advance trips, whether or not said attitude was welcome. Mike, like Bix, clearly understood the advantages of projecting pleasant enthusiasm and unflappability at all times, which was no mean feat under the constant stress of a presidential campaign. Both had a keen eye for visuals that defined and punctuated The Candidate's messages, and Bix respected Mike's opinion despite his relative youth. He was thirty-two, young enough to be Bix's younger brother.

It stuck with Bix that when he started working in politics, lo those many decades before, he worked with a guy who was thirty-two years old and that guy had seemed unapproachably old. Damn.

"Bix, what's your assessment?" Mike asked. "Are we ready?"

"We're ready," Bix said. "The event is solid, and we have the two main ingredients to fight what I call 'the dreaded Candidate quiescence' during down time. We have a gym where he and the boys can shoot baskets, and cable television in the Hold where they can watch either A, professional basketball, or B, college basketball. In this case, we have achieved nirvana. If the gym and the sports networks aren't enough, I'll get out my Dan Quayle/Lloyd Bentsen hand puppets and recreate scenes from the eighty-eight vice presidential debate. He could stay occupied with that for hours."

"Speaking of being occupied for hours," Mike asked, "did you ever hear why he changed his schedule and went back to Chicago yesterday?"

"He hadn't been home since he won the caucuses last week and I think he wanted to go back and bask in the glow of spousal approval. I swear he is the first man in history to run for president to impress his wife."

"That would be one of the nobler motivations I could imagine," said Mike, "but you and I both know that she was part of the plan, not the cause of it."

"You're right. He's Machiavellian, but small 'm' machiavellian. He actually seems to have good intentions.

"Grandma always said 'the streets of hell are paved with good intentions.'"

"So are the streets of heaven, but not the streets of Washington. By the way, the word from headquarters is that he is running on-time this morning, which means he'll be a half hour early."

"We'll be ready a half hour early and have ESPN cued up in the Holding Room," Mike promised.

"You're the best site guy in the business," said Bix, who, like most of the Skedvance staff at headquarters, truly thought so. Bix was also well aware of what Mike thought of the compliment.

"Thank you," Mike said, "and up yours."

As Bix and everyone else agreed, Mike was also good enough to be one of the best Leads, but he was too valued as a Site 1. The campaign wouldn't assign him to do many Leads, but promised to slate him on

Bix's teams whenever possible, which made up for it somewhat. Bix wasn't a pain to work with for a man who thought himself to be a creative genius. Sometimes he was, and his sites usually ran like clockwork.

Bix asked one more question. "Before I forget, how are Ron and Billy working out?" referring to their young Site 2 and Site 3. Whenever Bix and Mike worked together, it seemed their penance was to be assigned the greenest novices available. Their current director of Advance told them what they already knew, that the only way to learn how to do Advance was to *do* Advance, and he wanted his staff to train at the feet of the masters. They marveled at how something could be both complete B.S. and true at the same time.

"Ron is great," said Mike. "I've got him doing the rope-line music cues with the sound guy, but Billy could use some work. He must be the son of a major fundraiser or someone incredibly powerful. He's been fairly useless the entire trip. I've got him moving the VIPs into place."

"Don't let Billy touch anything. His mother and I worry about him constantly. Call me if you need anything."

"If he is the product of your loins, please have yourself fixed before it happens again," Mike told him.

"I would, but it's unnecessary at this point, even redundant. I'll call you when we have wheels down. Break a leg, sir."

"Back at ya," Mike replied.

Bix called to check in with his Press 1, Rachel Lindstrom, another old friend from the previous campaign. He had encouraged and helped train her on her first few trips early in that campaign and watched her blossom from a reticent neophyte Press 2 into a self-assured and inquisitive professional who would keep a room full of burly staff and security guys answering questions for two hours during a countdown meeting. She would consume every detail of every potential site that Bix considered using, no matter how long it took or how many people needed to be involved. He admired her grit and determination, and she appreciated his support. Once she stuck her nose to the grindstone she worried every issue until it bled, but could never tell when she was prepared enough or when she had done a good job. So she never quit and drank far too much Mountain Dew.

Bix loved and respected Rachel as a friend with every fiber of his being. She bore a striking resemblance to Zasu Pitts, which, as an old movie buff, Bix found endearing. But he promised the director of Advance that he would strangle himself with his own shoelaces and relish the sweet release that death would bring if he ever had to work with her again. Sometimes he was afraid to engage her in substantive conversation for fear that he would not have enough time left to live the rest of his life. But she worked herself harder than anyone else, and Bix thought it was a testament to this presidential campaign's character that they searched for the right fit for her.

"Rachel, Bix. Just checking in. How's pre-set?"

"Bix, thank God it's you," she said quickly. "We are a little late getting started because I wanted to rearrange the tables in the filing center so it would be easier for the national press to get to the food tables for the lunch we're having brought in after the rally and I couldn't have the local press sitting there with their laptops plugged-in while we were moving everything. Then we knocked out some of the power cables that are running under the tables, so that took some time, and after we got them all plugged-in again it took a little more time to figure out that it had triggered a circuit breaker on our generator outside. Then we started letting the press in. It's all going well." Her pace quickened. "Except for the guy with the knife."

"The knife?" Bix asked. "I hear a commotion in the background. Is someone raising his voice at you, or attacking you?"

"Mostly he's yelling at the uniformed Secret Service agents. He's with the press. They found some kind of knife in his bag as he was being screened, and they don't want him to bring it in. He looks like he's about to start a fight. OK, this is beginning to look serious. What should I do?" The slight quiver in her voice undermined, for an instant, her 'press pro' deportment.

Bix wasn't worried that she would lose control of the situation, but that she might think she was. He tried to get her to relax. "Is it Dan Rather?" he asked. "I swear he lunged at me in a dark alley behind the United Center during the two-thousand Democratic convention. I heard he bit a press person on The Opponent's staff a few months ago, which is a terrible place to be bitten."

"No, it's a camera man for one of the local TV stations. But thanks for the story. I'm sure it's all true."

"I'd stake your life on it."

Rachel finally laughed. "And to think he used to be one of my heroes."

"Then my work here is done. And don't worry about the guy with the knife in his bag. If he calms down and you think he won't cause another commotion, let him in. If he continues to be a problem, Service will probably ask him to leave. Your media advisory specifically reminded the press not to bring sharp implements, or something to that effect, so let him explain *that* to his news director if he gets kicked-out. Did you get my email about Dick O'Malley?"

"Yes, thank you. He's up to something, I think."

"Try to chat up his producer. It should be fairly unsurprising to ask why they have so many bodies here to cover a rally. Please let me know if you hear anything. And by the way, please be aware of the fact that you've done a great job putting the press piece of this together in a very short time. You've done everything you could possibly do. Hang in there and call me if you need me. I'm on my way to the airport. You don't have to be there until about forty-five minutes before wheels-down, so don't feel like you have to rush. It should just be a matter of finding the press busses before the sweep. Once they're swept we can line them up in the motorcade. "

"Thanks, Bix. I'll leave here in an hour then. We should be set, and I'll leave Anna here to deal with local press. I'll see you at the airport."

He hung up and took one last look to see if he'd forgotten to zip his pants or shave half his face or apply his morning squirt of Rogaine, and he was pleased to see he had managed to pull himself together. A quick glance in the mirror and he couldn't help but remark, "Bix, ole boy, you have to admit, you've still got it, the looks of Cary Grant and the moves of Rocky Graciano." Both had been dead for decades.

2

On the seventh floor of campaign Headquarters, where senior staff cloistered in beige in cells surrounded by the photographic evidence of their talent for clutching VIP's—personal shrines to Narcissus known as "ego walls"—Larry Drule walked into Bob Peem's office with a look of concern pasted on his pasty beige face.

Contrary to Drule's own constant admonitions to those beneath him on the food chain that they "need to stay in their lane" and remain "inside their wheelhouse," the deputy campaign manager for Field felt no compunction about critiquing the decisions that Peem and Skedvance had made regarding the Charleston/Scepter Advance trip. Drule underscored his sincerity with the dire language of *political ramifications* that such *outcomes* might have on Field operations in the region and the *sensitive issues* facing his Regional Field Director.

They were his first maneuvers in an attempted character assassination. He opened with an unassailable statement of an unalterable fact of politics, wherever it is practiced. "The politics down there in"—any place one chose to name, in this case it was South Carolina—"are complicated, and we're at a delicate point in the campaign." Ipso facto, he posited the problem. "We can't afford to have an Advance team blundering around getting in everyone's way." Therefore, he concluded that he "needed to discuss the events in Scepter and Charleston."

"The events or the Advance?" Peem said.

"Well, the Advance. I heard you're sending Bix. Is that wise?"

"Why not?" Peem said. "What's your problem with Bix?"

"He's arrogant, and I'm worried he'll try to fuck up our political operations in the state."

Peem shrugged. "Of course he's arrogant, he's an Advance guy. I'm not all that fond of them either, but when we have an Advance trip, we have to send an Advance team. Why do you think Bix would try to fuck up our political operations? Is he a double agent?"

Drule sniveled slightly, then condescended. "He may not do it intentionally, but my Regional Field Director tells me it's not a situation that Bix can walk into and do whatever he wants without doing major damage to our politics in the region. He's heard about Bix's reputation."

Drule's portents were political code for "I think he's an asshole and I hate him." He neglected to mention that his Regional Field Director, or RFD, had "heard about Bix's reputation" from Drule himself, a person who never allowed facts to stand in the way of a good grudge. He helpfully offered a solution. "Why not just send somebody else? Isn't there someone else we could send?"

"You know the situation in Scepter," Peem said. "The mayor down there owns the place. Intimidation is his *first* tactic, and his second and third ones, too. Bix won't let the guy roll over him, and he's got enough connections to mitigate Mayor Bacon's pain-in-the-ass-ness."

"My RFD, Don Shaunesy, has control of the situation. Bix can only fuck things up. Shaunesy has worked hard to keep the mayor neutral and Bix is gonna piss him off," Drule said.

"*Neutral? Mayor Bacon?* That guy's not neutral. He's completely in our opponent's camp. Bacon's concerned about what's good for Bacon and I don't think your RFD has done anything in the two weeks he's been on the ground to change that. Right now all I want is to ensure that the good mayor doesn't do anything embarrassing for us when the senator's in town."

Drule made his barely-veiled power play. "Then why don't I at least go down there to oversee things? I'm just concerned about Bix making a mess of things we've been working hard to control. He's gonna butt heads with the mayor, and we can solve this problem before it starts."

Peem remained unmoved. "You don't have enough to do here? This sounds personal. What's your real problem with Bix?"

"I don't have a problem with him. He's got a problem with me. He physically assaulted me at an event during the last campaign. He literally shoved me against a wall because he said I was about to walk into his visual. All he's concerned about is his precious media coverage and the events and not giving a shit about the politics or our organizing efforts and he doesn't care who he antagonizes because just wants to *own the evening news,* or something like that, so fuck him and winning the news cycle because we can't take any chances in South Carolina. It's too important, and when he leaves we'll have to clean up after him."

"That's bullshit," Peem said, "take a breath. He may be an arrogant son of a bitch and he pushes the envelope from time to time, maybe too often, but he knows his politics and he doesn't leave blood, I'll give him that. I've seen him leave some people wondering what the fuck just happened, but not pissed off. At least no one who matters." Peem eased back in his chair and relaxed. He'd convinced himself with his own argument. "Why don't we watch him for the next day or two? In addition to this being one of the shortest Advances on record, Bix's skills match up with our needs on this trip."

"Yeh, I know, the Arab college buddy who is trying to screw us. So let Bix take care of that part and send another Lead and let me take care of the local political situation because in two days this thing will be over and Bix could do some *real damage.*" Drule's voice squealed over the last two words.

Peem could see Drule hyperventilating and it irritated him. His voice raised an octave. "The guy is freaking Iranian, which is not Arab. And *you're* not hearing me. I've asked Bix to accomplish a shit load of stuff in two and a half days, and he's the most experienced political operative we've got, and whether you want to admit it or not, he gets results. *Despite* the fact that he might think he's God's gift to whatever, he's good at what he does. "

Drule wiped the right side of his mouth, the side that drooped a little, with the back of his hand. "I don't have to admit that. And even if he is,

you could send an Advance woman. Send Kate Hillhouse—she's great."
He played the gender card. What Democrat could argue with that?

"Kate *is* great, but she does Press," Peem said.

Drule wouldn't let it go. "I want my RFD to be in every meeting Bix
has with the mayor, and I want him to be consulted before Bix chooses
a Site. I intend to tell Shaunesy to monitor him closely, and if he gets out
of line or causes any problems to let me know," Drule said. "We can't let
any problems fester. If he makes Mayor Bacon angry I'm gonna suggest
we pull him from the Advance. We need to show the mayor who's in
charge in this campaign, and it isn't Bix."

"It isn't Field operations either. Your guy has to learn to work with
the Advance team, and if you've got a bigger personal beef with Bix I
want to know about it."

Drule also didn't mention that he had several reasons to make Bix's
life as miserable as he could.

Nor did Peem mention his own cynical reasons for placing Bix in
the middle of a maelstrom from which it would be difficult to emerge
unscathed. It was a win-win situation as far as he was concerned.

* * *

Bix's half-hour drive from Nashua to the Manchester Regional Airport
was a sentimental journey. He had worked a half dozen New Hampshire
primaries, and his mind wandered back to his first presidential campaign in the snows of New Hampshire and his first boss, Jim Kane, the
legendary Advance man from south Boston who had started his career
working for the Kennedys. It was Kane who said that the best Advance
men were invisible, and also a bit neurotic. Apparently it was a good
fit, Bix thought, but he couldn't decide if he became a good Advance
man because he was neurotic or became neurotic because he kept doing
Advance.

Bix witnessed the last vestiges of buccaneer Advance, as Kane
called it, during his first campaign four years earlier, in 1976, as new
federal election laws and local pols began to wise up to Advance men's
more adventurous and bohemian practices. Bix remembered the dictate

that Kane famously handed down to all of his Advance protégés in the very first Advance Seminar that Bix attended: "The days of buccaneer Advance are over," he told them. "We *cannot* leave blood. We will have to go back to that town, whether it is you who does the Advance or not."

There were Advance men who worked before the advent of campaign regulations in the 1960s and early 70s, when it was still an all-men's club, who could never go back to some towns for fear of being strung up by the locals. Advance men had developed a reputation for making promises that weren't kept, incurring debts that weren't paid, and breaking local ordinances with abandon, particularly those regarding public gatherings, construction, noise, speed limits, pilfering, and corrupting the morals of fair maidens, legal though they were. There were stories of Advance men who stole cars to use in their motorcades.

"Advance men are invisible," was only the second-most memorable line that Kane spoke during that mid-August day in 1976, Bix's first Advance Seminar, because he followed it with, "We don't get our pictures or our names in the press, and if you have to brief the candidate in public, drop back and brief him, and then get out of the way. Do not clutch. If we see a photo of you standing within ten feet of the candidate in a major national publication or on national television, *we will guarantee you a bus ticket to within fifty miles of your home.*" Bix believed him; he was very young and very intimidated, and he believed in the candidate and the cause passionately, without reservation. It was "the good old day" in his memory because that was about how long his innocence lasted.

Bix couldn't remember the last time he'd believed in the political process, or a candidate, with such passion, but he could remember when he last felt that way about a woman.

It was precisely the wrong time to be thinking of Storie every few seconds and wondering if they would see one another and worrying if she would be happy to see him, but it was too enticing not to. She crowded his mind.

* * *

He arrived at the airport that morning an hour before wheels-down to find that his motorcade Advance guy, Hornig, had risen to the last-minute challenge of procuring the volunteer drivers, rental cars, vans, and press buses. They were lined up along with two black Secret Service SUVs, or OVs, one of which would carry The Candidate; several support vehicles, including the one known as the "War Wagon," packed as it was with multiple and various lethal means of protecting the protectee; a few state highway patrol and local police cars and an EMT truck—all in the process of being swept by the Explosive Ordnance Disposal team.

A heavily armed gentleman was slowly circling the Staff 1 van with his German Shepherd, directing the dog to sniff under and inside every inch of the vehicle as a half dozen volunteer drivers stood watching at a distance, rapt with interest, huddling in the cold next to the chain link fence separating the parking lot from the tarmac. All of the doors to the rental cars and vans stood open awaiting inspection. Milling about were a dozen Secret Service agents tastefully attired in dark suits, dark overcoats, dark glasses, black shoes, white shirts, subdued ties, and squiggly wires running out of their ears and under their coats. Another two dozen uniformed members of local and state law enforcement, along with a couple of camouflage-bedecked combat-ready gentlemen holding small but menacing MP-5 automatic rifles, clustered in a few small groups near the vehicles and out on the tarmac.

It was a "Closed Arrival," meaning no press were allowed on the tarmac to watch the plane pull up. A lone camera crew stood in the parking lot facing the fence, feeding images to a nearby satellite truck. A reporter clutching a microphone in his mittened hand was doing a stand-up in front of the fence with the empty runway stretching out behind him.

"Slow news day," Bix thought as he drove past and parked at the end of the line-up of cars, vans, and busses soon to be The Candidate's motorcade. His rental car would be used as the Straggler, driven by a volunteer who would follow the motorcade after it was determined that no one had been left behind at any site. He moved his luggage to the Staff 1 van, turned on his BlackBerry and watched as another stream of emails flowed onto the small screen. Two were voicemail messages from Mike.

Bix called him immediately. "Michael, I'm back on the air. What's up?"

"It's a good problem. We're definitely going to have an overflow crowd, but there are a lot of people still outside waiting to get in because that one mag never made it to the venue. They're hand-wanding to make up for it, but it's going slower than we need."

"Ask the agents at the VIP entrance to start wanding general public, then send as many people as you can to that entrance. Maybe we can get everyone in before the fire marshal puts a stop to it."

"The old VIP entrance gambit. Slick."

"What about O'Malley?" Bix asked. "Is he big-footing everyone?"

"He's here. He's got a camera crew and a producer on the main press riser and two cameras on the cutaway, one on a tripod and one hand held that appears to be attached to some kind of chest harness."

"Sounds like he's either shooting a docudrama or he plans to go mobile. Be prepared to do a Loftus," a reference Mike would understand regarding the removal of a member of the media by force.

"I'm serious," Bix repeated the warning to Mike. "You should expect the worst. O'Malley is like the international press—he has no standards of behavior. Double-check the bike rack surrounding the press areas."

"Will do, boss. And I'll see if anyone has any extra barbed wire to wrap it with."

"See if our electrical contractor can run a current through it, too. I'll call when we have wheels down." He hung up and had started toward the FBO when a call came from Rachel.

"I'm running a little late," she said. "I just left the school. I wanted to let you know that I talked with O'Malley's producer. She told me they're doing a retrospective about The Candidate's life going back to his college days."

"Retrospective? Is this for 'American Experience'? Did she mention anything in particular or use the words investigative report?"

"No. She clearly had her game face on. She wasn't about to give up any information and O'Malley wouldn't speak with me at all. He must believe he has some good dirt from The Candidate's youth. They've dedicated a lot of assets to whatever he's working on. The question is whether he's traveling in his usual alternate universe."

"That's very perceptive. You're probably right." Bix didn't feel it was appropriate to mention the conversation he'd had with Peem. "He can travel wherever he wants with all those cameras and people and that big Max News satellite truck. It's huge."

"I hear they can reach a hundred twenty slanders per hour in that thing," said Rachel.

Bix laughed out loud. "I'll send an email to Philpot and the press office to let them know about the Max News retrospective. Obviously Philpot is on the plane and doesn't have his BlackBerry on—you may want to take a moment to brief him when he arrives. I have a friend who's a producer on another Max News program and I'll see if he knows anything. I appreciate your information—good job." He thought he heard her smiling. "Wheels-down is now a half hour early and there's only one camera crew out here in the parking lot. You might want to head straight to the press busses when you arrive."

"If I hear anything else, I'll call you," she said. "We have a full contingent in press world on this trip, so I'll be busy."

"Let me know if you have trouble with the indigenous population there. If they get rowdy, just remind them we can have gruel catered for lunch."

"Good threat. See you soon."

Bix emailed the press staff, his scheduling desk, bcc'd Peem about Rachel's findings, dug out the email address of his friend at Max News and wrote an email as he walked slowly to the motorcade.

* * *

He stopped to hit "Send," looked down the row of parked cars and spotted Hornig, his Motorcade advance, walking toward him decked in sartorial splendor, cleaned up for game day in his best dark suit, dark overcoat, black shoes, white shirt, and subdued tie. Hornig was framed on either side by two Secret Service agents. At his left was Special Agent Bill White, Bix's counterpart, and at Hornig's right Special Agent Art

Mose, the Transportation agent and the only person in the assemblage older than Bix. It could have looked ominous, but all three were wearing smiles to complement their official attire.

"Bix, you remember Special Agent Mose," Hornig said.

The two reached out to shake hands while they were still several feet away from one another. "Remember? He's one of my cohorts in crime. Sorry, poor choice of words. Art, it's good to see you again." Bix turned to Hornig and White. "I've annoyed Art on many trips over the past hundred years, and he's been very tolerant with things like this last-minute change to the schedule. How have you been, sir?"

"I'm still having fun." Mose then explained why the fast-forward schedule wasn't a big deal. "We've done this airport so many times we know the motorcade routes, local train schedules, railroad crossings, that type of thing. We already had all the technical information we needed. We didn't need to advance it."

"I know it still adds a lot of extra paperwork for you," said Bix, "and I hope Hornig hasn't caused too many headaches."

"I just blamed everything on you," Hornig said.

"As well you should," Bix told him. "You know I'm there to take the bullet for you and for you two gentlemen as well, of course." The Secret Service sometimes joked that the real purpose of the Lead Advance was to act as a human shield for the agents. Bix always assumed it was a joke.

"Art," Bix said, "didn't you tell me some time ago that you were going to retire soon?"

"I'm leaving at the end of this year, right after this campaign season."

"You enjoy this that much?"

"I don't mind it," Mose replied, "but it had more to do with getting in thirty years of service. If I'd reached that mark last year I would have left, but then we wouldn't be able to enjoy these golden moments together one last time on the campaign trail. The question is, why are *you* doing this again? I thought after the last campaign you'd had it. You were on the road for an entire year, if I recall correctly."

Mose then turned to Hornig. "Did you know that in the last campaign Bix took one day off in the middle of an Advance trip to Cincinnati, checked-in to a hospital, had his appendix removed, and then came back to work the next morning?"

"I didn't know that," Hornig said. "Why in the world did you do that, Bix?"

"Just for the fun of it, or maybe I lost a bet. I can't quite remember. In any case, it was actually easier than having a bad cold, except for the initial excruciating pain."

Art pushed the question. "Why *did* you agree to subject yourself to another campaign? It's crazy."

"Clinically, it's delirium tremens. I agreed to serve because I believed in The Candidate's ability to be a transformative figure, because we didn't win last time, and mostly because I knew that everyone else on the campaign staff was pubescent so the health insurance premiums would be cheap. I'm taking advantage of it by having all sorts of work done—you can probably tell I started by doing some lipo on my frontal cortex."

At that moment Bix heard a familiar booming voice in the ether. "You seem just as normal today as you did when I first met you, which has me worried," the voice said.

Bix turned to see another old friend, Gary Howell, the Special Agent in Charge, or SAIC, or "sack," of the Boston field office.

"This *has* turned into a geezer convention," Bix said. The two shook hands warmly. Bix introduced his friend and "legendary Secret Service agent" to young Mr. Hornig.

"Bix and I have known each other since before the White House had a fence around it," Howell told Hornig.

"Gary," said Bix, "you're radiating happy, you've got iridescent sparkles glinting off your teeth. Boston obviously agrees with you. You have the look of someone who has been away from Washington for a long time."

"Nothing against DC," Howell said, "but in Boston I have more of a home life, and everyone I meet doesn't instantly assume that I must be a Democrat because of my accent."

"When did you two first work together?" Hornig asked them.

Howell responded quickly, as if he was on a game show.

"1979. It was an international trip to the Netherlands for the vice president."

"Good memory!" Bix said. "How do you remember that?"

"Because it was epic," Howell said.

"Good answer," Bix said,

"Someday you'll have to get him to tell you what he did to the Dutch deputy foreign minister on that trip to the Netherlands," Howell told Hornig.

"That's never going to happen, Mr. Howell," said Bix. "You know the motto of Staff Advance Black Ops: 'If I killed you, I'd have to kill you.'"

"I thought the Staff Advance Black Ops' motto was, 'Send the bill to headquarters,'" said Gary.

Bix laughed. "Well, it was in Latin, so I probably mistranslated. I've never been strong in the romance languages. At any rate, we don't have to tell everything, just the complimentary stuff. And the 'Junkeer' had it coming to him." Bix pronounced the word with the Dutch inflection, "yun-kier." "The man was a burr under our saddles for two weeks, and I was young and impetuous, not that that's any excuse."

"Right," Gary said, smiling broadly. "If we didn't already have US personnel stationed on Dutch soil, there could have been an international incident."

They all smiled and nodded like friends whose bonds had been forged in the trenches, with insights about which only they were qualified to see the humor.

The cold air started to bite. "Bix," Agent White asked, "shouldn't you tell your drivers that they can go inside and get warm?"

"You've grown cynical, Bill," said Bix. "You know the volunteers would rather be out here where all the action is. We're the sideshow of the big show. When the newness wears off and the numbness sets in, they'll go inside on their own." He slapped Bill's arm. "Thanks again for all the last-minute hustling. We know it causes you extra work, and you know the boss is aware and he appreciates it."

"Not a problem. Really, this was easy," White said. "Any predictions about tomorrow?"

"It's completely serendipitous at this point," said Bix. "The independently minded denizens of New Hampshire are contrarians to their core. If they don't believe our Candidate should be anointed on the morrow, we may have an unpleasant surprise."

"Is that what you expect?"

"It's my job to expect unpleasant surprises, just like you guys, and is there really any such thing as a pleasant surprise at our age?"

There was much harrumping in agreement among the long-in-the-tooth crowd. Hornig, who was in his twenties, had no idea what Bix was talking about.

Bix's phone rang. It was Rachel, and he paused before answering. "Hornig," he said, "our VIP greeters should be arriving any time. Would you please escort them to the FBO if they show up while I'm on the phone? And by the way, you clean up real good."

Hornig grinned and agreed to watch for the greeters. Bix excused himself and walked a few feet away.

"Hi Rachel." Bix listened closely to the voice in his ear.

"Just reporting in," Rachel said. "I'm here at the airport and headed directly to the press buses to make sure they're stocked. Other than that, press world is a 'go.'"

"Thanks. Wheels-down is now confirmed a half-hour early as usual. If you finish with the buses and feel like it, come up to the FBO. I'll introduce you to our greeters."

"I'd like that. Hopefully the buses won't take me too long."

* * *

Bix thought it important to participate whenever possible in the pre-event care and calming of the motorcade drivers. As he walked to meet the group still standing next to the chain link fence, he motioned to Horning to join him.

"Hi, everyone," he said. "My name is Bix. I work with Mr. Hornig on the Advance team and I want to thank all of you for doing this. We appreciate it, and the next president of the United States appreciates it, too, and since you're not getting paid, that will have to do. I want you to have fun today." He reminded them that as a way of saying 'thanks,' the campaign wanted them to get a photo with The Candidate, which would probably happen at the end of the trip, and asked how many of them had brought along a digital camera. They all raised their hands and cameras.

"Splendid," Bix said. "This might be the most intelligent and best-looking group of motorcade drivers we've ever had on this campaign, and we've had some great ones. Now, there's no fee for us taking the photo. However, we do require a small handling charge of fifty dollars per picture that you can pay to me personally in cash before wheels-down. I am happy to take multiple photos as I'm financing a vacation to any place with palm trees."

They enjoyed it. "We'll go with you," one called out.

"That's what I was planning. Everyone goes. We'll motorcade everywhere."

Bix watched Mose walk up to the group to do his official Secret Service motorcade briefing for Hornig's drivers, another highlight of their day. Bix was mindful that everything about game-day was exciting to people who had never seen any of it before, and that it might very well be a life-long memory. He wanted his drivers to be as un-nervous as possible, and it was not inconsequential to the campaign that these volunteers would talk about their experiences to everyone they knew, and possibly the media, for many weeks to come. He wanted those experiences to be positive.

"Cheese it," Bix said. "It's the cops. Ix nay on the onny-may." He then introduced his friend. "Ladies and gentlemen, this is Special Agent Mose, who is our Mr. Hornig's official Secret Service counterpart."

"Is he trying to squeeze you guys to pay him for motorcade photos again?" asked Art. "Bix, have you ever gotten anyone to give you money?"

"You remember—there was that guy in New Jersey. He volunteered to drive the staff van, then you ran his name check information and found out he had two outstanding warrants for felony assault with an illegal concealed firearm. You made us get another driver, which I thought was very judgmental. But I made up for it by selling bathroom breaks to the site volunteers. Those go for big money. I think I made about twelve bucks."

"It went to a good cause, I'm sure," Art said.

"That's how I bought this beautiful watch. Which reminds me," he addressed the drivers, "the building at the far end of the parking lot is the FBO, or Fixed Base Operation, where we can go inside and get warm before my watch freezes and breaks. Art, would you care to give them your briefing indoors?" Bix asked.

"That seems like a quality idea," Mose said. The drivers agreed.

Bix and Hornig led the assemblage indoors to a far corner of the FBO lobby where they gathered around Mose to receive their instructions for driving in an official Secret Service motorcade. Art proceeded with the ceremonial handing-out of the Secret Service day pins—small, square, tin pins marked with the letter "A" in white against a red background, with tabs that bent over to attach to the drivers' lapels, or blouses. The pins, Art explained, needed to be worn where the agents could see them, so that any Secret Service agent could immediately identify them as motorcade drivers and avoid gunning them down in the street. Having seen their name check information, Bix knew that the drivers ranged in age from twenty-three to sixty, but they were all as enthusiastic as school kids.

Bix excused himself from the group. "I have to brief our greeters, but I wanted to thank all of you again. Seriously, have fun today."

He found his greeters, retired General Jim Johns and his wife, Janet Townshend, sitting on a low couch at the far end of the FBO lobby. They were there because Bix had strongly suggested to headquarters that they be invited. Johns was the first retired general to endorse The Candidate and served as a surrogate for the campaign and The Candidate occasionally. He and his wife, a professor at the War College, lived near Nashua, and after the last-minute schedule change created the need for an airport arrival, Bix thought it might be appropriate to invite them to come and greet just for the sheer sociability of it. It took headquarters a few hours of intense assessment to approve his suggestion.

He strode toward them and shook their hands. "General, Janet, it's good to see you again. Thanks for coming."

"Bix," Johns said, "please call me Jim. It's good to see you again, too. Thank you for inviting us. It's the first time we've been asked."

Bix wasn't surprised to hear it. "It's an honor to have both of you here."

"I found out after the last time we met that you know my wife," Johns said.

"Not only do I know her," Bix said, "I quoted her. She gave me more than an hour of her time and a book's worth of intellectual capital for a strategic communication plan I wrote for the Secretary of State on the eve of the war in Kosovo. Janet made me sound as if I knew something. When my colleagues at State saw the attributions to her, they were impressed. I told Janet there was an ambassadorship in it for her, but I haven't made good yet."

"Please, don't hurry," Janet said. "We like living here."

"It's just as well. They only ask my opinion on ambassadorships in places where the mosquitoes are as big as vultures."

Bix briefed them on the arrival procedures and excused himself to find Rachel at the motorcade. He found her helping her volunteers stock the Press buses with non-alcoholic liquid refreshment, much to Bix's surprise due to certain time-honored assumptions that he had about the press corps riding on common carriers past noon. Then he remembered that the Press charter didn't enforce TSA restrictions on carrying liquids. The traveling press would be well self-stocked.

He found Rachel in the first Press bus organizing beverages for easy access. She seemed relaxed and smiled pleasantly when she greeted him.

"Should I be concerned?" Bix asked. "Everything seems to be going well and you look happy."

"For once I actually feel we're prepared," she said. "But if it will make you feel any better, I promise to have at least one emergency before the day is over."

"I'd prefer to keep the stress level at adequate, not all the way to emergency," Bix said. "You can have either two minor issues or one major concern."

"Deal," Rachel said.

"What's the latest from Anna at the site?" he asked.

"I spoke with her a few minutes ago. She tells me that the local press is set, no issues with Dick O'Malley, the gym is full and the local TV news crews tell her the stage looks beautiful on camera."

"It's the Boston ferns," Bix said. "When you can't do anything else, line the stage with a lot of Boston ferns. They offend no one, look vaguely presidential, and they're often surprisingly affordable to rent."

She laughed. "Another good tip. I've got a question about our press coverage. Tell me how the local press will cover the event differently than the national press at this point?"

He mapped out the kind of coverage their rally would garner over the next twenty-four hours before primary election-day coverage made it yesterday's news, but cautioned, "I should warn you that I don't have any idea what I'm talking about. The moment I say the press will zig, they will almost as certainly zag. All we can do is try our best to lead them down the path we'd like them to go. Ultimately, we control the environment, and especially the visuals. It would be nice if we could create more distinctive ones so the vast majority of Americans who get the vast majority of their information from TV images will remember something, or anything, about The Candidate's message. But such is life in an over-communicated society."

"You sound cynical."

"No, just realistic. We're not only competing with the other candidates for a piece of peoples' minds, we're competing with taking the kids to soccer practice, holding down two jobs, and sitting down at the end of a long day to just veg-out and watch a 'Dukes of Hazzard' marathon. We're also competing with McDonald's and Nike and Cap'N Crunch and all the other thousands of marketing messages that assault us every day. Most voters make their decisions based on emotion, not on information, and most of them decide how they feel based on the images they see on TV. First comes the emotional reaction, and then they rationalize the decision after the fact, the same way most people decide what kind of car or beer they want."

"Is that true?" Rachel asked.

"Sadly, it is. But at the same time, it provides us with a mission, and the challenges have only become greater since the dawn of the twenty-four hour news rectal exam. It takes a lot more effort to have an impact on voters' minds, unless the story is bad news or a major screw-up. Then everyone in the world knows about it in nanoseconds."

"But you have to admit that you enjoy the challenge of trying to control the news coverage, and you *have* to enjoy the political theater of these big events. There's so much energy."

"Don't try to put me in a good mood." Bix laughed, amazed that he was doing all the talking. "Yes, of course, these are fun. You'd have to be dead not to love big rallies, but more importantly, I love my ability to remain behind the rope lines during them. I get claustrophobic in crowds. For the life of me I cannot understand why people attend these things."

"For a guy who doesn't like crowds, you picked an interesting avocation."

"I love crowds, as long as they're my crowds, and they're on the other side of the rope line, over there, like the press, especially the international press."

"They're awful," Rachel said. "Truly mean and nasty."

"They're generally ruthless all the time. They know no bounds other than physical force."

"Talking about it reminds me why I got into all this," Rachel said. "When we win, I can't wait to do international trips for the White House, despite the press."

"I love the international trips too, but only to Miami or Hawaii." Bix looked at his watch. "Wheels-down is in five minutes. I will retrieve our distinguished greeters and see you down at the site. Have fun today. Remember to brief Philpot about O'Malley. Do you have time to come up and meet our greeters?"

"I'd better not at this point. Too close to wheels down. I'll see you when we get to the site."

Bix found Janet and Jim once again and escorted them out the security door to the tarmac as The Candidate's plane touched down, taking a few seconds to call Mike with 'wheels-down.' As he walked out to the arrival point, he looked down the line of motorcade vehicles that were parked next to the runway with all their engines running and their drivers at the wheels. He saw Hornig standing a hundred feet away next to the Guest van and flashed him an inquisitive thumbs-up. Hornig responded with an affirmative one.

"I keep forgetting to tell you," General Johns said to Bix enthusiastically, "we found out that you Advanced the rally that we attended for Senator Curley four years ago in Topeka for the fiftieth anniversary of the Brown versus Board of Education decision. It was the most dramatic event we've ever seen. You must have had thirty thousand people there, and the news coverage was incredible."

"You were in Topeka that day?" Bix asked. "I thought it was more like fifty thousand."

"I was working in Wichita at the time and we decided to go. It was an historic moment, and we wanted to see Senator Curley in person. You had giant fifty-foot banners hanging lengthwise between the columns of the state house that read "EQUALITY," "EDUCATION," and "OPPORTUNITY." When we saw the news coverage that night, it seemed almost poetic. They showed amazing overhead shots that I'll never forget. You made it poignant and celebratory at the same time," she said. "We came away from the event thinking that the senator would win the election in a landslide. Don't take this the wrong way, but it reminded me of *Triumph of the Will*."

"And we all remember how that turned-out," Bix said. "Maybe I should tone it down a little to avoid the Riefenstahl references."

"The difference is that you're doing it for the good guys," Johns said.

"I'll take that as an endorsement."

They stood on the lip of the tarmac and waited while two sets of stairs were rolled into place under the front and rear doors of the jet and the motorcade drove up. The first limousine stopped directly to the front set of stairs, where The Candidate would exit, blocking the view of any would-be evil-doers, and Bix escorted his guests around it to take their place between the stairs and the car. Once the greeters were in place, Bix walked up the stairs and into the front cabin to brief The Candidate, trip director, and press secretary.

* * *

"Good morning, gentlemen," Bix said as he entered the cabin. He could see through the window that the press was beginning to disgorge from the rear exit.

"Bix!" The Candidate said. "Good to see you. How long has it been? Seventy-two hours?" He laughed. "You look terrible. What fun do you have in store for us today?" He then stood up and, turning away from Bix, walked to the back of the cabin to retrieve his overcoat.

"Lovely to see you, too, senator," addressing him loudly enough to be heard. "Our fun begins with two contestants at the bottom of the stairs vying for the grand prize—a chance to shake your hand upon arrival at Manchester Regional Airport. I'm certain you'll recognize contestant number one, retired Brigadier General Jim Johns, and contestant number two, his lovely wife, Janet Townshend, who in her spare time likes to be a professor at the War College. Then, after we arrive a half hour early to our site, beautiful Newton High School, we will be greeted by another three to four thousand contestants who have won the privilege of hearing you speak in person."

Merle, the trip director, craned his neck to try to see the greeters from the airplane window. "How does the rally look?" he asked.

"Do you remember the six hundred rallies you've done over the past year? It will look just like that, only this one will have enthusiasm," Bix said.

"I'm glad to hear that," The Candidate said, looking over his shoulder at Bix as he put on his coat. "Our previous six hundred rallies have been kind of a downer."

"And we have a bonus round," said Bix. "Our special guest is canard-wielding journalist Dick O'Malley along with three Max News camera crews, a couple of producers, a very large satellite truck, and a band of technicians. They'll be playing for their own grand prize, which is The Candidate's head."

"Do you know what they're up to?" Merle asked.

"Our P1, Rachel, reported that O'Malley's producer characterized it as a retrospective of your life going back to college."

"What does *that* mean?" Merle asked.

Bix looked at The Candidate. "Our candidate may be in a better position to answer that."

"I'm innocent," The Candidate protested as he slid a few papers into his briefcase, which he handed to his personal assistant, the body guy, Peaches, a former college basketball player who apparently once was known for his sunny disposition.

"We're ready to go whenever you're ready," said Bix. "I should mention that while it is a Closed Arrival, there is one camera crew for a local station in the parking lot shooting what appears to be a live shot. Merle, let's talk by phone during the motorcade. I'll call you in a few minutes. If there's nothing else—" He started to exit the cabin.

The Candidate spoke up. "Bix, I'd like to talk with you later, after the rally. I'd like to discuss one of your non-Advance-related areas of expertise."

"That sounds ominous," Bix said.

"We'll talk after the rally. I know you like challenges."

The Candidate's last three words rang in Bix's ears. They sounded like the bells of Notre Dame Cathedral, the big ones, and Bix felt like Quasimodo must have felt standing next to them as they clanged—nauseous. "I'd like to know where you heard *that*," Bix said quietly as he walked out of the cabin.

"Didn't you say that?" The Candidate yelled.

"I was misquoted," Bix yelled back.

As Bix reached the bottom of the stairs, The Candidate followed quickly behind. The two spoke briefly with the general and his wife before Bix excused himself and walked ahead to his car in the motorcade, the Lead Marked car. The Lead car was a State Highway Patrol cruiser in which he rode with Special Agent Bill White, Bix's counterpart, and Special Agent In Charge Gary Howell, who chose to go along for the ride. Bix reached in through the front window of the cruiser and shook hands with the man at the wheel, an affable New Hampshire Highway Patrolman, Lieutenant Don Miller.

"My name's Bix, and if it's all right with you, I'll be riding in your car today."

"Yes sir, we've met before, on your visit to Nashua last summer." Miller looked pleased to mention the connection.

"I thought you looked familiar," said Bix. "Have you been stuck doing a lot of these for the past six months?"

"No, not that many, but I enjoy doing it. But you must be riding in motorcades all the time."

"Every few days I get the pleasure of being flipped-off by members of the general public who are stuck in traffic because of our street closures. It makes me feel like I'm accomplishing something."

Miller laughed. "I know the feeling. I'm used to getting the warmth of their love."

"Sometimes we lose more votes than we gain on these trips by causing traffic jams. Boston is the worst, but luckily they have no choice but to vote Democratic," Bix said. He refreshed Miller's memory about his procedure. "Lieutenant, just like last time, I'll stand here outside my door while everyone finishes loading into their cars. When I get the word from my motorcade guy that we're good to go, I'll get in."

Special Agent White walked over to the cruiser and took his place on the opposite side, urging Bix to "hurry it up."

Bix opened the door behind the driver and waited another fifteen long seconds until he could see that every car, van and bus was loaded. Hornig flashed another thumbs-up and Bix gave The Candidate the high sign and waved goodbye to the general and his wife. The Candidate got in his limo, Bix and White climbed into the cruiser, and the long line of vehicles took off slowly. They passed through a gate in the chain link fence on to the two-lane highway en route to Newton High School, twenty-two minutes away.

Bix called Mike to let him know they were on their way and to get an update on the crowd.

"We'll get everyone in the building, I think," Mike said. "It looks great. Get here before the fire marshal starts finding fault with our numbers."

"I'll see what I can do. I'll call you at 'Bravo.'"

Bix asked White if he would bump-up the speed a notch, but he knew the constraints. The Service wasn't fond of going much faster than

the speed limit, especially in the dead of winter—the two armored limos in the motorcade were heavy and slow, and the press busses lagged
for the same reason. Barring an emergency, motorcades didn't hot rod
around much. He settled in to enjoy the ride and the conversation.

Exactly seventeen minutes later, Bix called Mike to tell him they
were at "Bravo," Secret Service code for "five minutes away." The
Secret Service had a reason for using the code, but for the staff it was
just so much easier to say "Bravo" than "we're five minutes away" with
all those extra syllables. It was a real time saver.

3

The motorcade arrived at Newton High at 10:45, a half hour early, as Bix predicted. They drove around the back of the building to their arrival point near the loading dock, away from the general public, where Mike and Special Agent Cole, Mike's counterpart, met them curbside. Anna, the Advance team's Press 2, and a handful of volunteers stretched out along the length of the motorcade to guide the national press and traveling staff through their assigned entrances to their appointed destinations inside the building. "We're still holding the fire marshal at bay," Mike whispered to Bix, but I don't know how much longer we can."

"Let's talk about it when we get inside."

Bix and Mike led The Candidate to his Holding Room, briefed him about the crowd, told him they could start the program in approximately ten minutes—twenty minutes early, music to everyone's ears—turned-on the TV to ESPN and walked out with Merle, the trip director, to do a final check of the site.

They walked through the secured hallway past the classrooms and lockers to the double doors at the far end that led into the gymnasium. Bix walked through, then out of the pipe-and-drape curtain they'd set up a few feet in front of the doors, and gazed with wonder at the huge gym lined with tall bleachers on three sides, with another set of portable bleachers behind The Candidate's stage. It was packed wall-to-wall and floor-to-ceiling struts with a diverse spectrum of white, middle-class, LL Bean-wearing New Hampshirites for whom this was an historic moment. The crowd was pumped and the energy level was, as always, very high. Bix's wonderment stemmed from the fact that he hadn't yet heard directly and fervently from an official on the federal level who wished to voice his or her concern about the size of the crowd and its ratio to the number of square feet being inhabited.

Bix turned to Mike as they walked into the gym through the backstage area where The Candidate would soon enter. "Where do we stand with the fire marshal?" he asked.

"I told him we couldn't make any decisions until you arrived," Mike reported, "and he bought it. But he's looking for you, and he seems miffed."

"Miffed? How miffed?" He knew the answer.

"Miffed as in there's fire shooting from his eye sockets," said Mike. "I think that's where he got his title, and his name. He's threatening to shut down the rally."

Just as Bix was about to retrieve The Candidate and start the rally they spotted their Site 2, Ron, behind them. He was escorting the fire marshal in their direction.

As Fierro walked through the double doors, Bix sensed intuitively that the situation may have been direr than he thought. The marshal's eye tick was a subtle 'tell,' along with his snarl. Through long years of devoted, almost scientific observation, Bix had learned to read such subtle gestures and others as well, such as having guns pointed at him and being punched.

"Why don't you go get the senator and I'll talk with Fire Marshal Fierro," Bix told Mike. He then ushered the fire marshal aside to deflect any bile that might start to spew.

"Sir," Bix said, "thank you for working with us on this." He tried to steer the conversation toward happy highway. "This was completely unexpected." He didn't specify just what was unexpected—the size of the crowd or the fact that Mike was able to get most of the people inside the gym before the fire marshal or the Secret Service began to object.

"I should shut this rally down," the fire marshal said between what appeared to Bix to be clenched teeth.

But for some reason he didn't.

Even the most ardent, liberal, mathematically challenged Democrat would have admitted that the gymnasium was packed with too many bodies and too much equipment, but Fire Marshal Fierro hesitated. Mike, Ron, and Bix managed to keep him occupied long enough for Bix to insert The Candidate, and then overwhelm him with the momentum of the event itself. Before Fierro could react, The Candidate was on stage.

"Come, watch from here. You'll be able to see the entire scene." Bix ceremoniously ushered the fire marshal toward an opening in the curtain, a move that appeared to have the desired effect of making the man feel like a VIP being singled out for a once-in-a-lifetime glimpse of history. He interjected running commentary for the fire marshal to annotate The Candidate's speech. The fire marshal stood mostly motionless, as if peering at the lid of the Ark of the Covenant and both fearing and willing it to be flung open at the same time. At odd intervals he abruptly craned his head as if it was on a gimbal, and his eyes darted around the auditorium searching for signs of anarchy.

And the rally rallied on.

* * *

Bix's interlude with Fierro was interrupted by a call from the director of Advance, who wasn't waiting for Bix to call after the rally. It was an unneeded distraction. Given a choice between the fire marshal's brow beating and more bad news from headquarters, he preferred the brow beating.

The only calls Bix usually received from headquarters during events were from friends in Skedvance, who often watched the live television coverage of his events and called to shower him with compliments. The director, Egan, wasn't that kind of guy. He was not likely to be wasting time watching live coverage of Bix's events, nor was he the warm and fuzzy type who would call Bix in the middle of a rally to tell him how good it looked on CNN. Egan assumed that Bix's events and consequent media coverage would be successful. A very serious young attorney, it was Egan's second presidential campaign and he trusted Bix as much as he was capable of trusting anyone, so he tried to restrain himself from practicing his usual micromanagement style that had made him such a hit with the other Advance Leads.

Bix answered calmly, "Trixie, I thought I asked you to never call me on this number."

He heard the director's voice, in dulcet tones, "Hey buddy, your event looks great on CNN. I haven't seen that much excitement since the last time I watched 'The Price is Right.' Congratulations."

The word "crap" flashed through Bix's mind. The final destination of the conversation was someplace he was not going to like.

Inside the gymnasium The Candidate was concluding his remarks.

"Thanks, Egan," Bix said. "I appreciate it. Can you give me a second? The boss is finishing his speech and I need to take a look inside."

Bix walked out of the double doors leading into the gym as The Candidate walked offstage to begin shaking hands with the hundreds of people jammed along the front rope line. He heard the music kick in right on time as Ron cued the soundman. Everything appeared to be concluding well until Bix looked over to the cutaway press riser.

"Egan, I need to call you back," he said at a staccato pace. "Dick O'Malley and one of his camera crews from Max News just jumped the barricade around the cutaway and they're sprinting through my secured area behind the stage to accost our candidate."

"Please call me as soon as you can," said Egan, "maybe from the motorcade when you leave the high school. We need you to go to South Carolina first thing tomorrow morning. We may have a problem on our hands down there." He sounded uncharacteristically plaintive.

"Peem told me earlier," Bix said, "unless, of course, you have something else on your mind, which would come as a huge surprise."

"This is in addition to what Peem discussed with you," Egan explained. "It's about the Advance trip itself, about the town where we need you to do a rally, and it's serious."

"When is it not serious?" Bix said. "I'll call you ASAP." He hung up.

By that time another two camera crews had taken O'Malley's lead and were all dashing behind the stage in an effort to get an angle close to The Candidate along his exit route. In the spirit of having backups to his backups, Bix had personally moved a second row of bike rack metal barricade into place during the site build to secure The Candidate's walking path in and out of the gym. But behind stage left, at the back of the bleachers, The Candidate's walking path narrowed to eight feet.

Bix called Mike and Rachel to alert them to the breach. He told them that O'Malley was sprinting around the back of the stage to pounce on The Candidate in a manner that Bix referred to as "shock and paw." It was a dime store version of ambush journalism. Rachel, whose job was, in part, to control the press, saw her press area disintegrating and rushed over to stem the exodus.

O'Malley dragged his crew along as he maneuvered to a spot where he could pop out unexpectedly, stick a camera and a microphone in his victim's face, and bark the most controversial question of the moment in the most unsettling terms possible. While the tactic was effective in creating a usable quote on some occasions, mostly with inexperienced politicians, The Candidate had proven long before that he was adept at dealing with such reporters, especially O'Malley. Bix wasn't overwhelmingly concerned.

Despite his confidence, Bix moved quickly to secure the left side of The Candidate's walking path from further incursions. He directed his staff and a few volunteers to arrange themselves along the stretch of bike racks where O'Malley could reach out and touch The Candidate, and told them to face inward with their backs to the camera crews that were lining up. He grabbed Merle, who was six feet six inches tall, and asked him to stand in the middle to block O'Malley from jumping the barricade and stepping into The Candidate's path.

The agents standing post nearby were aware that the 'newsies,' as they referred to them, had intruded back stage, but were unconcerned because the second line of bike racks secured The Candidate's path. Service didn't see them as a security concern unless they tried to jump that barricade as well.

O'Malley saw the Secret Service agents but he knew that no one was likely to drag him away. He took a position along The Candidate's exit and skulked to the point where the crowd stopped and The Candidate finished shaking hands at the end of the bleachers, immediately before the exit.

Merle's presence, in addition to blocking O'Malley from climbing over the second line of barricades, also—and completely coincidentally—blocked the Max News cameraman's view of the scene. As the cameraman maneuvered to get a shot, Merle moved ever so slightly into his line of sight. It might have coincidentally happened three or four times.

At the moment The Candidate finished working the rope line and walked around past the stage, just before he walked into view of the jostling camera crews, Bix looked over to see O'Malley punch Merle in the back.

He saw Merle first stagger forward, then regain his footing and look back at O'Malley with a wide grin. O'Malley raised his arm as if he was about to hit Merle again and screamed eloquently, "You punk, get the hell out of my way!"

Agents standing nearby moved in to break up the fracas. Merle seemed unfazed, but everyone else in the vicinity reacted as if a fight had broken out. It was beautiful. O'Malley was screeching as if he was the one who had been punched, the Secret Service was restraining him, Merle continued to bob back and forth into the cameraman's line of sight, and The Candidate walked by on the farthest side of his walkway looking quizzical.

O'Malley was apoplectic. He managed to bark lamely at The Candidate, "What about coming on my show?" The Candidate shrugged him off with a "when this is all over" and continued to walk through the pipe-and-drape and out the double doors leading to the Holding Room. Bix led him out past the Holding Room to another small gym, which was empty.

* * *

The Candidate was pleasantly surprised. Basketball standards were lowered into place and Mike had ensured an ample supply of properly inflated basketballs. Few things were more disappointing to The Candidate and his crew than a good basketball court with flat basketballs.

"We've got twenty minutes of down time for the press to file their stories and grab some food," Bix reminded The Candidate.

"OK," The Candidate said as he picked up a ball. He bounced it a few times and tried a bank shot, which he missed. Merle and the other two members of the traveling staff—Philpot the press secretary, and Peaches, the body guy—sauntered in.

Bix asked Merle if he was all right. Merle seemed unaffected but concerned about the media impact of what just happened. Bix reassured him that it was a tempest in a teapot.

"Are you going to shoot some hoops?" Merle asked Bix.

"I'll be back in a few minutes. I'd like to see if O'Malley has shed the blood of any innocent bystanders. On the positive side, the fire marshal should be happy that we didn't have mass casualties."

Bix went back to the site, which was emptying quickly, and walked into the press area behind the main press riser where eighty members of the national and local press were buzzing with news about O'Malley's altercation with Merle.

Among the wires and cables lying everywhere and the camera equipment and long tables of journalists working devotedly at their laptops on their stories or playing solitaire, Bix found Rachel. Bix thought he already knew the answer to the question, but he had to ask. "Did we get any blowback from the incident with O'Malley?" In most disagreements between members of the press and the campaign staff, the press would usually side with their own. Bix had no doubt that the traveling press corps regarded O'Malley in much the same way he did.

"None," said Rachel. "They hate that guy. This is only the second time any of them have seen him on the road. They don't consider him one of them, or even an actual journalist. On background, one senior political columnist for a nationally recognized daily newspaper called him an oozing human pustule."

"Those veteran print journalists have such a wonderful way with language, don't they?" Bix said. "It would be a pleasure to be insulted by a person with such talent. So, what happened to Mr. O'Malley?"

"He climbed back over the bike rack and stormed out of the building, cursing the entire way," said Rachel. "He left in a Max News van."

"Are any of the press siding with O'Malley?" Bix asked. "Do they blame Merle at all?" He assumed the answer to those questions as well. Merle had a good reputation with the traveling press. He was friendly and straightforward, and he always lost at poker, or any game of chance.

"No, they liked Merle before and they like him better now."

Bix was satisfied. The traveling press would file their stories about the rally, and the O'Malley dust-up would become merely fodder for gossip among the press corps.

"Call me when the press is ready to start loading into the motorcade," Bix reminded Rachel. "Don't rush, we're running a few minutes ahead of schedule."

When Bix returned to the small gym, the talk was about Merle's clash with the fourth estate. The Candidate threw Bix a basketball and told him to relax for a few minutes, so he put down his notebook, took off his sport coat and enjoyed a few recreational moments. Everyone was ribbing Merle, all good-natured banter, about what Philpot coined "The Smack Down between Madman O'Malley and Merle 'The Hammer.'" The nickname "Hammer" stuck with Merle the rest of the day and inexplicably seeped out to the traveling press corps.

Merle still seemed cautious, reluctant to yuck it up as much as the rest of the boys. Rachel called. "The press is ready whenever you are."

"Give them a few more minutes and then you can start moving them. We still have to do the photos with local law enforcement."

Bix informed The Candidate that they would be ready to leave in a couple of minutes, but rather than his usual "OK," he took Bix aside. "I heard from Peem that you know Jamir Parviz. Is that true? "

"Yes," Bix said, surprised both by the question and the source of it. It almost sounded like the beginning of an actual discussion. "We worked together at State during the last administration on a couple of projects."

"We were friends in college back in the early eighties," The Candidate said.

"Bob mentioned that."

"The campaign is concerned, overly so in my view, about a potential situation with Jamir in South Carolina. People I've spoken with tell me that you're the person we should send," he paused and searched for the words, "for a local appreciation on the ground."

It seemed to Bix a strained attempt at a complimentary-ish request. "So you're not particularly worried about it?"

"I don't really know. I'm letting Peem deal with it. You'll need to coordinate with him."

The answer came as no surprise. It was increasingly apparent that The Candidate preferred to discuss substantive matters, meaning anything longer than two sentences, with only a few senior aides. One question, however, occurred to Bix that he wanted The Candidate to answer directly. "Let me ask you this. Do you still consider him a friend?"

"Yes, well, sure. We were friends in college. He's a smart guy. He was a Foreign Service officer at the State Department when I was still a law clerk."

"Do you think he may have a motive to cause problems for the campaign?"

"That's not something I'm thinking about. Talk to Bob. He'll tell you all about it."

"OK," Bix replied, sensing that their exchange of words imparting information was concluded. After eight months and hundreds of events, it was as far as they had ventured into that dangerous, unexplored territory of human interaction known as "conversation."

Bix called Rachel and Mike to make sure they were moving the traveling press to the motorcade, and then led The Candidate out into the hallway to a waiting lineup of six local police officers and the fire marshal. The Candidate positioned himself at one end of the line and they walked by one at a time to shake his hand as Ron clicked their pictures using one of the police officer's cameras. After the photos, Bix led him out to the motorcade and they departed en route the RON hotel.

* * *

As the motorcade lumbered off and everyone settled in, Bix took a few minutes to catch up on the latest scuttlebutt with his car mates. Their conversation was entirely about the altercation and Dick O'Malley's meltdown. Bix noted that even law enforcement professionals disliked O'Malley with an intensity that combined the very best elements of disdain and contempt. Gary Howell, the SAIC, showed Bix a photo on his BlackBerry that revealed Merle grinning ear-to-ear and O'Malley's taut face, wild-eyed and open-mouthed, resembling an astronaut in a ten-g accelerating centrifuge.

All four men in the Lead Marked car were laughing. The Secret Service Detail Leader riding in The Candidate's limo directly behind the Lead car saw the scene in front of him and called Agent White to ask for a report. White briefed the Detail Leader about the photo, and then the Detail Leader briefed The Candidate.

After things settled down in the car, Bix called Egan.

The Director was relieved to hear from him. "Can you leave tomorrow morning for South Carolina? We kind of need you there."

"That sounds kind of urgent, Egan, and you know I will kind of be there for you, but I want you to remember I requested twenty-four hours for some R & R, which you agreed I needed after I told you that I had started talking to the television, and I assumed you knew I meant that those twenty-four hours should be contiguous. Well, now the television has begun talking back directly to me and it's telling me to become an Independent, and it's quoting scripture. Very convincing."

"We really can't wait. We need a kick-off rally for the last two-week push leading into the South Carolina primary, and we need you to work your magic in three days. The Opponent is doing a kick-off rally in Columbia that day and we have to compete. We're down in the polls by eight points and twelve percent are still undecided." Bix knew that Egan knew that Bix loved to go head-to-head with the competition. "It doesn't have to be massive—you could do it indoors in a big gym, like today, with a lot of high energy. You can make a couple thousand people look like a million."

"I appreciate your confidence," said Bix, "but you've got two or three other Leads who could handle the Advance, and at this point they are probably less likely to be found following pigeons around in the local park."

"We have those other issues in the state that are tangential but related, which Peem spoke with you about. I don't know if he mentioned this, but this is a personal request from the very top." Egan's tone was the soul of gravity.

"You sound like you swallowed a government spokesperson," Bix said. "Yes, the boss spoke with me a little while ago. He mentioned someone's name, which, I believe, is the party of the first part affecting said issues to which you refer obliquely?" Discretion was the byword—the walls had ears, and so did the people in the car.

"Yes, that's it, and Peem needs to speak with you about it again. He has some new information to share. It's above my pay grade."

People in Washington loved that expression. Bix thought The Candidate should have used the same line.

"That's the second time I've been told that in the last half hour," Bix told him. "When do you expect this will happen?"

"Bob is in a meeting at the moment, but he'll come to my office and we will call you together as soon as he's out. Within the next half hour."

"I appreciate it. That timing should work."

Bix hung up and enjoyed the remainder of the journey. After another several minutes of pleasant conversation about the campaign, The Opponent's campaign, and a few horror stories about The Opponent's treatment of agents on that detail, Bix called his RON advance, also known as the Staff RON, Becky Carmillo, to tell her the motorcade was at Bravo.

* * *

Five minutes later the motorcade arrived at the grand Montrest Hotel in Nashua, where Becky stood curbside in her high heels with her clipboard and Secret Service counterpart, the RON agent, at a secured arrival point in the rear of the hotel at the loading dock, which was also the location of the hotel dumpsters, as fragrant as Calcutta in spring.

Becky and the RON agent led the usual gaggle—The Candidate, Advance Lead, Lead agent, and Detail Leader—through the bowels of the hotel to a service elevator and up to The Candidate's suite on the sixth floor, which was secured and posted with Special Agents and a couple of C.A.T. members in full urban combat gear. Along the path they passed and greeted several agents serving as post standers with whom they had developed friendships during the long campaign.

Once inside The Candidate's suite, Bix briefed him and coordinated timing for the remainder of the day. The Candidate walked around slowly and fiddled on his BlackBerry while Bix spoke.

"You have a little over an hour for prep time before the three print interviews, which we've set up in another suite one floor down. I will come back at that time. Do you need anything from Becky or me?"

"No, I'm great," he said, looking up from his device, "but tell me what happened in the gym with O'Malley after the rally? Did he really punch Merle? What was Merle doing?"

Bix thought, "Three questions in a row. This could set a new record."

"Merle was standing there because I asked him to," Bix explained. "O'Malley and his crew jumped the barricade around the cutaway riser and ran around behind the stage to ambush you. Then two more camera crews followed. In addition to a cameraman wearing a chest harness, O'Malley had a sound guy with a boom mike, all of which indicated some premeditation to me. It also meant they could stick it in your face as you rounded the bleachers. I placed a couple staff and a few volunteers along the bike racks lining your walkway to prevent him from going any farther, and Merle *just happened* to be directly in front of O'Malley and his cameraman." Bix flashed his best look of faux sincerity. "But he was facing away from the guy. O"Malley was angling for a confrontation of some sort."

The Candidate noted dryly. "O'Malley, confrontational?"

"I know I may have judged the man too harshly. But in the heat of whatever kind of heat he was in, I opted to take the safe route and secure that side of the barricade. Next time I'll carry a taser. The Hammer is worried that he may have caused some bad press."

"It wasn't his fault," said The Candidate. "If O'Malley hadn't jumped the barricade into an area where he knew he wasn't supposed to go—"

"And then reached out and physically assaulted a man who was facing away from him..."

"Yes, and that too," The Candidate said.

"I'm sure Merle is outside—I'll go out and find him." Bix noted the time. It had been a record-breaking conversation, involving dozens of words spoken in a nearly continuous flow. It was worth logging the exact time and place.

* * *

Bix headed back down the service elevator to find Merle, who was still outside at the arrival point, as expected, smoking a butt. "Gimme a cigarette," Bix said.

Merle passed him a cigarette and lighter. "When did you start smoking?" he asked.

"Just now," Bix said, "and just one. When I started doing Advance the drugs of choice were caffeine, nicotine, and aspirin. I'm just keeping a tradition alive."

"Did he say anything about the O'Malley thing?" he asked Bix. "I feel badly about what happened."

"Yes. We talked. He and I agreed that you should be blamed exclusively. The boss wishes you could be a better person and he hates you. On the other hand, if it turns out to have been a good thing, then it's agreed that I get all the credit, as usual."

Merle's mood lightened.

"Honestly," Bix continued, "he asked me what happened and I told him. He views you as the victim of O'Malley and probably me. He was definitely amused."

"You don't think it will get us bad press?"

"I've taken a poll, and within a margin of error of plus or minus zero, ninety-nine point nine percent of press and general public surveyed think you rock just for getting punched by O'Malley. I wish I'd known it was that easy. The traveling press corps is taking up a collection for your defense, which in this case is a large bodyguard. You could be elected king of the Zoo plane." He figured using the old term for the press charter would put the situation in a perspective.

Merle was reassured. They finished their cigarettes and Bix recommended they stop in the hotel restaurant for coffee before heading to the staff office, which was outfitted by Becky with the latest in high-tech equipment that the Advance team and traveling staff could use to create and receive more emails, jpegs, Skypes, faxes, and photocopies. Lots of copies.

They walked around to the front and entered through the lobby where they saw that most of the traveling press had taken up residence in the lobby bar. "Shocking," Bix said, "there's something you don't see very often or more than two or three times a day." Upon seeing Merle, some thirty or more members of the group broke into spontaneous applause accompanied by numerous rhythmic guttural chants of "HAM-MER! HAM-MER! HAM-MER!" Bix couldn't imagine how they found out Merle's nickname. He wondered if it might have been the blast email he sent to his "friends in the media" list serv.

Merle acknowledged the accolades in his usual manner, with the appearance of appropriate head-shaking humility.

They sat down at a tall bar table to order coffee and Bix's cell phone rang. It was Egan.

"Bob needs to talk with you again," he told Bix. "He is on his way to my office and I wanted to make sure you were available. Before he gets here I wanted to tell you about the South Carolina trip. Obviously it hasn't been announced to the press."

As the Director started telling Bix the details of headquarters' yet-to-be-announced plan for a major media event, members of that specific profession who would have been most interested in the topic were walking up to his table to congratulate Merle and shake his hand.

"We need you to go head-to-head with The Opponent on Friday, my friend," Egan continued. "Our tracking numbers for the primary there in New Hampshire don't look encouraging, and given the demographics in South Carolina, the expectations in *that* state are high. We need this rally to push our momentum heading into the last two weeks, and we need you to do the job."

Egan was seldom so solicitous. More journalists, photographers, crew members, videographers, and on-air talent wandered over to the table to pay their respects, and Merle obviously loved the attention even though he was maintaining his best 'aw-shucks' routine.

"That goes without saying," Bix told Egan, "and it's beside the point. How about a compromise? Let me sleep in tomorrow and I'll go tomorrow night. Who else is on the team? Who are my back-ups? Can't they start without me?"

"We thought we'd let you pick your team for this one," Egan said. "And we have you in the best hotel in Charleston."

Bix felt the gentle sensation of something being inserted into a portion of his anatomy into which he preferred not having something inserted.

Merle was enjoying the attention so much he ordered a gut-buster burger with extra cheese and bacon, which required him to sit and wait a little longer. Bix ordered a club sandwich. A few more happy journalists, including a couple of the more well-coiffed and high-heeled national correspondents, meandered by and struck up conversations, all of which began with some variation of, "Hey, good job with O'Malley."

Bix tried his best to be discrete among all of the interested parties and Merle appeared to be perspiring.

"That's code for 'It's going to be a RON,'" Bix whispered back at Egan. "The only time you put us in the best hotels is when The Candidate is going to stay there, too." He raised his voice again. "And that means I have to deal with those voracious predators we charitably refer to as the national press corps for another entire day and night." The two correspondents who were standing at the table heard the remark and laughed appreciatively.

"I'm changing my title on my business card to that," one of them said.

Bix looked at her and raised his right eyebrow. "Make that Senior Voracious Predator."

She looked at Bix and threw him an air kiss. He didn't know if it was a good or a bad thing. It took him a second to re-focus on the telephone call.

"And I get to choose my team? " Bix asked quietly. "Your tangential issues must be doozies. Where would you like me to do this?"

"That's one of the tangential issues I can discuss," Egan said. "We want to do it in Scepter, outside of Charleston. It's an historic town in a medium size county that is still mostly undecided, and we have a little situation with the mayor."

The two lady correspondents finally left Bix and Merle's table and returned to their own.

"Yes, I've met the mayor. Can I put you on hold for a moment?" Bix put the phone on mute and took a bite of his club.

Merle leaned over to him and whispered, "Some of the on-air talent is very talented."

"I wouldn't know," Bix said. "I left my hormones tied up in a closet at home. You have fun."

"I'd like to ask one of them out. Do you think I could trust her to keep things off the record?" Merle asked.

"Unless she finds you hiding in her footlocker and calls the cops, you probably have nothing to worry about. It's your wife you should worry about."

"You know I'm not married," Merle said.

"That's not what they think. They think you have a wife and kids."

"Why would they think that?"

"Someone must be spreading the rumor. I've had several people tell me they already heard it when I was repeating it to them, so it must be out there in the ether."

Merle laughed. "Must be."

"Next I'm going to start telling 'em that you're a grandfather." Bix took another bite of his sandwich. "I have to get back to this call."

"Egan, sorry, we had journalists at the table. Where were we? Yes, you want me to go to a town that is ruled with an iron fist by a mayor who has, because of his long-term ties to the Democratic establishment, probably already endorsed The Opponent. Am I right so far?"

"He's officially neutral, but he's with The Opponent. Do you know him?"

"His name is Bacon, which I remember for obvious reasons. I met him once at a fundraiser in DC for Senator Fritz Hollings, who was thinking about running for president in 1984. Bacon has been the mayor of Scepter since before Millard Fillmore. He's essentially the county boss. He was one of the first white city officials in the south to support the Civil Rights movement when he was a Scepter city councilman in the 1970s and was rewarded with a mayorship for life. He wins all the demographics. He's the Stalin of Scepter County, without the labor camps. He runs the third largest county in the state, they vote in large numbers, and he controls a lot of those votes."

"Do you think he's corrupt?"

"I'll ask some friends who would know better than I, but I don't think so. He's close to Senator Hollings, which must speak to his character, and from what I remember he stays in power because he plays it straight with his constituents, but he can be an overwhelming pain in the ass with outsiders."

"We've heard he can make your life miserable if he wants to," said Egan. "His brother-in-law is also the chief of police. He likes his perks, and one of his perks is to do things his way in his town."

"Thanks for your candor. Any other shoes to drop? Has there been an outbreak of ambivalence in the area, or maybe the Air Force is practicing urban bombing runs over town that day? Why me? The other Leads are diplomatic. They could handle him."

"Not this guy. That's why we wanted you to do this trip all along. Bacon would harass the hell out of the other Leads. He can kill us in the statewide media and he'll go out of his way to do it. And you have the Hollings connection. Come on, you love making those guys dance at the end of your string."

"Yes, I do, except for those times when they don't. Then they do their best to run riot through my carefully crafted media events. You're setting me up for four days of hell. Now that I think of it, it's actually two and a half days of Advance hell from the time I arrive until wheels-down, then another day and a half of constant worry that hell will be unleashed. Why do I get these trips?"

"'A, because we've never had a trip like this before, and B, because you'd complain if you didn't," Egan said.

"There is that," Bix said.

"And there are those other issues we are working on that may have greater impact than the mayor, Bix. These could potentially affect not just the outcome of the South Carolina primary, but also possibly the entire campaign. Bob just walked in. I'm going to put you on speaker."

"Bix, are you on your cell?" Peem asked.

"Yes."

"Can you get to a hard line?"

"I'll go up to the staff office and call you in ten minutes."

"Great."

Bix wrapped his club sandwich in a napkin as Merle's second gut-buster was being delivered to the table. They laid down their tips, picked up their food and headed upstairs.

Bob Peem and Bix had known each other for years, although Peem was originally a Field organizer and there was an historic, and not completely unfounded, dislike of "Advance" by "Field." While the two men were cordial, and Bix's relationships with local field office staffers around the country were positive, there had always been a slight chasm between the two men, especially in the way they approached campaign crises.

In Bix's experience the differences in temperament stemmed from the fact that Advance was consistently high-pressure and fast-paced, and Advance people were accustomed to crisis management on a daily basis for weeks on end. Field organizing was more plodding, and as a result, Field organizers were usually more methodical . . . slower . . . less accustomed to crises, and therefore less likely to take them in stride.

The rift between Advance and Field, Bix had found, also may have had something to do with the fact that Field organizers in major presidential campaigns were sent to a town or region for weeks or months at a time. They had to find a place to sleep, often on someone's couch, spend their own money for rent and food, use their own cars, find volunteers and train them, and scrape to find office equipment and supplies. They seldom met, much less hung out with The Candidate. During the primary season, once their primary or caucus was over, Field organizers had to scramble for new jobs in other primary states, and once again during the general election.

At the opposite end of the spectrum, Advance staff blew into town four or five days before a candidate's big local appearance. They flew in on the campaign's nickel, had rental cars waiting at the airport and hotel rooms reserved and paid for by the campaign, received per diems and were provided cell phones and laptops and almost all the other resources they needed, including a budget and a credit card. They came to town and stole all the volunteers, commandeered all the resources, took over the local headquarters and sucked the energy out of the entire town. Then, when The Candidate arrived, the Advance team had all the fun, took all the glory and the gals, and then blew out of town at their earliest opportunity, leaving behind whatever detritus that may have resulted. Presidential candidates continued to do public events throughout the primaries, then, with success, through the summer and the general election, and Advance staffers worked steadily throughout.

This was Field's perception of Advance, unfair though it may have been, and these things colored Field organizers' opinions of Advance people, as Bix understood. He had met a thousand Field organizers who told him they wanted to do Advance, but he had met only one Advance person who said he wanted to do Field . . . and *that* guy was still doing Advance four years later.

Philpot greeted Bix and Merle when they arrived in the staff office, "Bob called and asked me to sit in on this call with you, if you don't mind."

"Please, participate," said Bix. "Two sets of ears are better than one, and you have a perspective that I don't." Merle excused himself to go to his room and consume his side of cow.

Bix called Egan's office number from the office phone and pushed the speaker button. Egan answered.

"Bix, hi. We've got a couple of issues to discuss. Bob's are up first."

"Egan, no one's issues come before yours in my mind. By the way, Philpot is here with me."

"Hi Bob and Egan." Philpot said. "You guys should see Bix. He looks like what we used to say on the farm, like he's been rode hard and put up wet." It sounded mean-spirited.

Bix was surprised to hear the negative comment about his appearance coming from Philpot, a man who made the Pillsbury Dough Boy looked swarthy and slim by comparison, but he refrained from making the pithy response.

"Bix, here's the new thing," said Peem. "After you let us know that Dick O'Malley was at your event, our Press Office contacted his executive producer. He told us that O'Malley will run with the story about Parviz and the alleged manifesto one way or the other on Friday as part of his show, which airs immediately after your kick-off rally in Scepter. If he can confirm the story, he will run with it as an expose. If he can't confirm the story, he'll report the rumors and the controversy. Either way, we're screwed. The only way this doesn't turn into a story suggesting that The Candidate is a closet terrorist is to find the truth, and find it to be exculpatory."

"O'Malley never allows facts, or metal barricades, to stand in the way of a good rant," Bix said. "We had a little run-in with him today at the rally."

"What happened?"

"He jumped the barricade and ran up behind Merle and punched him in the back of the head. I thought you would have heard by now."

"He did WHAT?" Bob yelled.

Philpot interjected. "That's essentially what happened, but it wasn't quite that bad. No one has photos or video. O'Malley will probably scream about it on his show, but none of the other press is making a big deal out of it, and there aren't any pictures."

"Except for the Secret Service," Bix said. "They've got some great photos, real action shots. If I can get the SAIC to send me copies, I'll send them to you just after I sell them to Max News."

"There's that initiative we all admire," Peem said sarcastically. "Now we need you to use your skills to make this thing go away by Friday."

"Oh, you mean this Friday?" He decided it was the moment to mention his Advance team. "Can you send Mike Pitcher to do site at my event in Scepter?"

"We'll call him as soon as we're off the phone," Egan said, "but he has already been slated. You guys will travel together tomorrow."

"Good. Is Kate Hillhouse available to do Press?"

"She just left for vacation, but we'll tell her you asked for her."

"Please do—we need an adult on the team. Ask her who she wants as her P2. Her choice is good enough for me. And I would appreciate having Thigpen for Crowd, Ben Oliver for Site 2 and Henry Benton for Motorcade."

"Done."

"Something about this smells suspiciously unscandalous," Bix said. "At the risk of seeming cavalier, I would suspect a fraudulent document before I'd suspect either our Candidate or Parviz of doing something cripplingly stupid, even in their late teens or early twenties in a liberal college. First of all, The Candidate has known that he wanted to run for office since he was old enough to think, and B, Parviz's family left Iran because of the revolution. They were royalists. He still has family members there who could be threatened by the regime. And he and his wife love musical theater—they go to Broadway shows. I've never heard of a jihadist who loves Rogers and Hammerstein. Now that I think of it, I've never heard of a right-winger who loves musical theater, either. There's something telling in that."

"Bix," said Peem, "this could kill us! Please be serious." For a moment he sounded like a nine-year-old girl.

"I am serious, but I'm not worried yet. I'll save my anxiety for a better moment, such as the second I know we have something to worry about. Until then, I'll hold off expending my limited and rapidly receding store of energy, thank you very much."

"Jesus, Bix, you're cold," Peem said. "Your friend Jamir could destroy the campaign, and you've got a sonofabitch of a local mayor who controls the entire county and wants us to lose. I don't see how you can be so unconcerned."

"I promise I'll start working on finding Jamir as soon as I hang up. If I can't find him, I'll try to get him to come to us."

"Please be careful," Peem said, still tense. "Don't fuck this up."

"Bob, despite the poor judgement of your last comment, just to prove to you that I understand the enormity of our situation, when The Candidate arrives I'm going to have some adorable child give him the most attractive local cultural headgear I can find and force him to put it on in front of the press corps."

"We owe you for this," said Peem. "I promise we'll make it up to you."

"I'll add it to the list. And I'm serious about the hat. You know the local Pee Dee Indian tribe just received official recognition from the State of South Carolina, and they have some very distinctive traditional head gear that I'm certain would be most appropriate on the occasion of this rally."

Then it occurred to Bix that Egan said they were working on two issues. His heart sank to his ankles. He thought how nice it would be if he enjoyed drinking. "Egan, you said at the beginning of this conversation that you were working on a couple of issues. I've only heard one. What else would you like to share?"

Peem stepped in. "It's an endorsement, but we can't tell you anything more right now."

"Great. I hope it's with Seagram's or Budweiser, both of which are products I would like to sample. We could be the first campaign in history that winds up in the black, or on the carpet."

"Hardly."

"What you're telling me is that I will have another event to produce, therefore, the overnight in South Carolina. OK, I'm slow, but I eventually catch on. Am I going to have to sail an aircraft carrier into Charleston Harbor to deliver the Dalai Lama, or the Pope, or the ghost of Mickey Mantle, so they can endorse The Candidate on the ruins of Fort Sumter?"

"Something like that," Egan said. "We're not sure yet. I'll let you know the minute I can."

"We're Democrats. The only minute we acknowledge is the last one, which seems to align perfectly with the minute we get around to doing most things. Can you send JD Ebsen for the second site?"

"Done," Egan said.

Bix asked to be switched over to Egan's assistant, Sophie. He immediately began asking her to find phone numbers or emails for a few former ambassadors and a half dozen Foreign Service officers with whom he remembered working on the policy review committee, along with former White House and Defense Department appointees who may have known Dr. Parviz. He also asked her to find out if there was a Young Democrat organization in the university where Parviz worked.

Bix pictured the next four days hovering over his head like a twenty-pound pigeon, and then derided himself for thinking of such an over-used and trite metaphor. Then he thought, no, it's apt. He called Mike, who had just left the site after cleanup and was on his way to the Montrest Hotel.

"Don't expect any sleep for the next four days," Bix told him, and explained the situation as well as he could. "For the fiftieth time you've been given a once-in-a-lifetime opportunity to serve your candidate, sacrificing your health and potentially your political career."

"There's no upside to things like this," Mike said. "There are a thousand land mines planted all over it, and the half-life of appreciation in Washington is about a nanosecond. Even *I* have been down this road too many times to have any illusions. If it goes wrong, we get blamed. If it goes well, no one remembers who made it happen."

"We're supposed to be invisible," Bix said.

"They expect us to handle anything and everything, but I have the feeling that Peem and even the senator just think of us as the guys who move the furniture around. You're in a different situation because you've already worked in two previous administrations, but not me. If this goes badly they can send me home and no one will ever hear from me again."

"It's the same for any of us. We're dispensable. You knew that Advance was extreme politics when you signed-up, and it beats jumping out of airplanes for thrills. Besides that, if it goes badly, there's a good chance that all of us will go home anyway no matter *who* does it. Who would you trust more, us or someone else?"

"Let me think about it. Let's see. I'd say *anyone* else," Mike said.

"Exactly. Me too. But sometimes I have to admit, in moments of candid reflection I still have illusions of adequacy, but they're fading faster than my six-pack abs, which I also still have. I keep them next to my truss in my overnight bag. Look at this as a fun challenge."

"Sure, but just like skydiving, there's always the chance that our parachutes won't open in time," Mike said. "The difference is that in Advance the pain lasts a lot longer."

"Yes, but we'll have the comfort of a lot of company on the way down."

* * *

The remainder of that icy Monday in Nashua was a model of efficient media output. National broadcast news that evening produced the coverage Bix expected, positive but unremarkable. Bix sent emails and made phone calls until past midnight, ensuring all of the trip's morning preparations were in place, and began his outreach to former colleagues who might have known of Parviz's whereabouts, his thumbs flying across the keys of his BlackBerry until they ached. He had become one of "those people," hunched over his tiny black brick, and he did not like the picture. Mercifully, Morpheus soon took him, still clutching the device, and he slept the sleep of the innocent or the heavily medicated.

4

High in the lofty environs of Max News headquarters, Dick O'Malley was finishing his day with a late-night harangue at his exhausted production staff. The camera crews, too smart to hang around, had left two hours earlier when the news trucks arrived back in New York, leaving a handful of captive staff—producers, assistant producers, a researcher, and a couple of unfortunate interns—to bear O'Malley's high-decibel diatribe in the empty news room. He wasn't a pleasant man to be around under the best of circumstances, and he'd come away from his field trip to campaign-land with nary a piece of embarrassing video or one-day manufactured news scoop. As a result, the moment was far from being "the best of circumstances."

He saved his blackest bile for The Candidate and Merle, who, as The Candidate's trip director, was the best-known member of the traveling staff and therefore an easy target, just as he had been when O'Malley cold-cocked him in the back of his head earlier in the day. O'Malley was still unaware of the puppet-master role that Bix played in the Punch and Judy show, because he assumed that Advance staff were on hand at presidential campaign events for the sole purpose of absorbing his abuse. Bix was, as always, invisible, especially to Dicks of the O'Malley variety.

O'Malley's feelings were unambiguous to his tiny troop of bleary-eyed underlings.

"What the hell is wrong with you people? We didn't get shit today," he bellowed. Then it occurred to him that he still needed "those people" tomorrow, and he feinted to a contrite pose. "OK, OK, I take some responsibility for that. However, we all know those sons of bitches fucked with me," his pitch and volume rising once more, "and we can't let them get away with it. I want their fucking heads on a silver plate. I can't allow *anyone* to do this shit to me without *divine* retribution." He stuck his index finger into the air, pointing straight to God. "Especially a bunch of amateurs on some shitty little presidential campaign. WE are the professionals, and WE will always be here and WE are going to take this guy out," accentuating each point with the same index finger pointed toward himself. "I don't care *what* you have to do, but we are going to take his campaign *down*. They're dirty!"

Ali, one of the young assistant producers, a three-year veteran of national and local news reaching back to her junior year in college when she produced the Soccer Roundup at MUTV, saw her opportunity to be tough, too. "What do you want us to do, Dick?" She always called him by his first name.

O'Malley's suddenly blank face belied his lack of prep for the follow-up question, but he recovered quickly. "It's all hands on deck to find that Jamir Parviz. I don't care what you have to do, as long as you do it. I'll discuss it with Adam."

It was the second time he'd mentioned his lack of concern about their methods, as long as results were forthcoming.

After another two minutes of obscenities interrupted from time to time by words, once even he realized that he was "beginning" to ramble, about ten minutes past the time he first opened his mouth, he finished on a softer note. "Adam, stick around and we'll let these nice folks go home for the night." He asked his senior producer, Adam Strayberg, to remain behind.

"Shit," Strayberg thought.

The two then wound their way through the maze of desks to O'Malley's corner office, closing the door behind them.

O'Malley took out a bottle of single malt whiskey and two glasses from his desk drawer. Strayberg always hoped they were clean glasses when O'Malley and he sat down for their late-night tete-a-tetes, which had happened only three times in the three years that he had been the senior producer of "The O'Malley Intrusion" on Max News. It wasn't that Strayberg wasn't still in the newsroom until quite late on most nights, but O'Malley never stuck around after his show aired. When he did, drinking was involved.

O'Malley poured liberally, appearing refreshed merely at the thought that whiskey would soon wet his lips. "What's the latest report from your technical boys, your geek squad? Have they found out anything about this Parviz *gentleman*?" He said the last word with a sneer.

It occurred to Strayberg that this conversation could go on for a while. He took a long drink and swallowed it, then a half of another long drink. He wanted to go home, and he didn't want to provide O'Malley with details, knowing that O'Malley really *didn't* want to know what his senior producer's outside consultants were doing to harvest political intelligence from so-called "public sources." He made a semi-conscious decision to be brief and sufficiently vague as he began to feel the effects of the bender he'd embarked upon a minute and a half before.

"We know they are planning a big rally around noon in a small town called Scepter, outside Charleston. And we know who they're sending to do the Advance."

"Why do we give a shit about that?" O'Malley seemed irritated.

Strayberg, having gulped another drink, got a little irritated at O'Malley's irritation as well as his ignorance. "Why do we care who they're sending to control this shit show in South Carolina? For a couple of reasons." He looked straight into O'Malley's eyes and did not smile. "For one thing, the Lead Advance controls the show, wherever the show is. A good Lead controls everything—everything you see and everything you don't see. Who do you think set up two lines of metal barricades between us and The Candidate today, and who do you think created that impromptu crowd in front of our camera crews when we got past the first line?"

O'Malley listened and tapped his fingers against his glass.

"And who," Strayberg continued, "created extra space on the opposite side of that rope line so their guy could veer right just as he reached the point where our camera crews were located? Their Lead Advance. His name is Bix, and frankly I don't know his last name, everyone calls him Bix. Either way, he's the guy who cleaned our clocks today. He's the senator's Senior Lead, and let's face it, he controlled his environment and his news coverage. And he prevented us from turning it into the Dick O'Malley show."

"Yeah, well, I think he's a prick." O'Malley was drinking a little faster than Strayberg. "So fuck him, too. What else you got?"

Strayberg continued his train of thought as if O'Malley hadn't spoken, and he continued to look directly into O'Malley's eyes. "The other reason it's important to know that Bix is doing the Advance to Charleston is that he knows Jamir Parviz. Bix was a senior official in the State Department in the last administration. He apparently worked with Parviz and he knows a number of the players in this scenario. He'll probably lead us to the guy. *That's* why it's important. He knows people. And now we have him on our radar." He didn't explain what that meant. O'Malley didn't want to know, and Strayberg assumed that even O'Malley was smart enough to know that "radar" didn't mean actual, physical "radar."

O'Malley assumed it was some sort of bugging operation but as long as he didn't know about it, it tickled him to think that they were listening in. As far as he was concerned, they were bugging people who were so "dirty" that they would do anything to win, so he had to stop them by any means necessary, and he wasn't clever enough to see the irony.

Strayberg had assured him when he hired the geeks that they were simply trolling the Internet, and O'Malley was happy with that explanation. He never asked how they were able to discover information that wasn't public yet, like events, and information that would never be public, like internal discussions and decisions that had been made only minutes earlier. It was a mystery, that new-age technology stuff. "Things happen in real time on the internet," is how Strayberg explained it.

O'Malley was taken with a great new idea, and it came forth from his lips as a commandment. "In that case I want all of you down in Charleston as early as you can make it tomorrow. Your team should fly in, and I'll send the Max News truck first thing in the morning to meet up with you. You can take your computer geeks if you want to."

Strayberg demurred. "That's a good offer, Dick, but they can do what they do pretty much from anywhere, and making them travel only diminishes their resources. They're happy where they are." He was still irritated that O'Malley was so clueless that it was easy to keep him more clueless, and by then he was a little drunk. He was happy where *he* was too, back home in New York, and he didn't want to go to South Carolina. "Are you sure you want to send another team? You know that Max News already has a team down there and they're working on this story."

O'Malley was resolute, as men are like to be when their courage has been supplemented with alcohol. "Yeah, I know Max News sent a team, but it's not *my* team, and I want the 'A Team' down there. So fuck 'em. I need you down there to find this guy Parviz and his manifesto, and prove that he and his friend Senator Osama Bin fucking Laden were fucking college radicals."

"Got it, chief." Strayberg knew that O'Malley liked being called chief in moments of high dudgeon. He called the car service for O'Malley's trip home, and figured "what the hell" and ordered another car for himself.

5

Bix reveled in the four-and-a-half hours sleep before his wake-up call at 5:00 a.m. on what he hoped would be the last brittle cold morning he'd see for a long time. He felt refreshed in comparison to the day before, he thought. One lesson he had learned from doing vice presidential Advance was not to set the "expectations" bar too high.

After a thirty-second pep talk, he found the testicular fortitude to drag his carcass out of bed and downstairs to the hotel gym for a half-hour of moderate to unenthusiastic exercise before dragging it to Boston Logan Airport for a 9 a.m. flight to Columbia, South Carolina. Mike Pitcher would be traveling with him. Consequently, Bix planned to start his first "team meeting" the moment they drove away from the hotel in Nashua. It would last, no doubt, until they arrived in Columbia.

He walked down the fire escape stairs, past the Secret Service agents standing post at the first landing down from The Candidate's floor, and compulsively looked down to check the front of his sweatshirt for his hard pin, the security pin or "S" pin that labeled him as clearanced for any location, in case the same two agents weren't there when he wanted to return to his room.

"Good morning, gentlemen," Bix greeted them as he continued down the stairs. "Just making sure I can get back up if you're not here when I return. Thank you for your service at this unholy hour of the morning. Care for some breakfast tea and some lovely homemade scones when I return?"

"That would be great," the one in the dark suit responded, "but make mine a beer. I'm about to be off-duty."

"How about you?" Bix asked the other agent. "Beer and scones?"

"Make mine a martini, stirred not shaken, and a steak."

"Done deal. I'll charge it to the senator's suite, because if we can't earn your affection we'll buy it," he shouted up the staircase.

The next face Bix saw in the staircase was that of another agent, Al Caputo, The Candidate's Detail Leader, climbing the stairs on the way to the command post. He was freshly attired in a dark suit, white shirt, understated tie, squiggly wire, etc.

"Al, you didn't get the wardrobe memo? Everyone's wearing exercise attire all day today," Bix told him. "It's The Candidate's fun fitness day."

The agents didn't *always* have to wear the dark, unspoken, regulation Secret Service uniform. They tried to blend. If the protectee dressed casually, they dressed casually. The problem, or convenience if you were a Secret Service agent, was that this protectee always wore dark suits, white shirts, understated ties, black shoes, ad infinitum.

"I wish." Caputo reacted in mock seriousness, although it may have been real seriousness. "I could use a 'fun fitness day' and a 'fun-by-the-swimming pool day with a piña colada' day after that. Could you work on that with your scheduler?"

"Absolutely. I just promised the two agents standing post that I'd bring them aperitifs. Next trip I get to Hawaii I'll work on the pool and piña colada schedule for you."

Caputo changed the subject and the expression on his face turned to that of a concerned but friendly law enforcement official. "Speaking of fun times, I hear you're slated to do the trip to Charleston and Scepter. You realize we're arriving on Thursday night?"

"That's a whole two-and-a-half days from now," Bix said. "Do you have a concern?"

"This trip will be tougher than usual," Caputo said. "We see red flags all over the place down there, and you'll have to deal with more than your usual share of logistical and political challenges, including a bully of a local mayor who will be just as difficult for us as he will be for you. He's already caused problems for a few of our folks when we were in Scepter with your Opponent. He can be recalcitrant."

"I don't think there's any reason to use that kind of language," Bix told him. "He's probably a sweetheart."

Caputo laughed. "I coulda said worse. And we will also have a larger than usual footprint on this trip because of…well, it's South Carolina."

"I get your point," Bix said. "Do you know who the Service Lead is?"

"Yes, it's Shane Emory. You'll like him. He's a good guy, one of the next generation of leadership in the Agency. I'll let him know about you," Caputo promised.

Bix smiled. "That's my greatest fear. I'm sure he'll reach out to me by phone and email before I arrive in South Carolina and I'll plan to touch base with him as soon as I get there. As for Mayor Bacon, Shane and I can show a unified front on any unreasonable demands. If the mayor's smart, he will keep his posturing and political games somewhere between bad judgment and an outright security risk. That's what I worry about. You and I both know Shane can't help me there. The mayor is probably bright enough not to cross that line, but if he does, we can take the opportunity to put things in perspective for him. When I'm dealing with big shots like that, I've found that if you rattle their cages, shake their self-confidence a little before game day, they are less likely to cause a problem once The Candidate arrives. But as I said, the mayor's probably too smart to open that door."

"Let us know if there is anything we can do to help. Also, it's my understanding that there may be another event scheduled for Friday morning, so if you could let Shane know about that as soon as you can we'd appreciate it.," Caputo asked.

Bix grinned. "Is that the type of thing he might want to know?"

"Just a little."

Bix knew that the entire Advance, no matter how quickly he made his decisions or how cooperative he tried to be with the Secret Service, would be a bitch for everyone involved, and a little sensitivity outreach never hurt anything. "Let me apologize in advance for what I'm certain will be a last-minute decision for that event, and I'll express the same to

Shane. But I think I know what kind of event headquarters will want. I'll begin looking for a generic site and a generic crowd to fill it the moment I arrive, at the same time we're looking for the rally site for Friday. I'll try to keep it small and manageable, and I'll do my best to pick a site quickly so Shane has as much time as possible to do what he has to do," Bix told him.

"That sounds great. It looks like you're going downstairs to work out, so I won't hold you up, but I'm glad you're working this trip. We're going to have some real issues to deal with," Caputo said.

There was that word again. "Issues."

Bix jogged down the rest of the fire escape stairs to the basement gym and found an unoccupied treadmill. He started the machine at a slow pace, then slowed it down a little more, and started to think about his Scepter Advance game plan. There were less than three days until wheels-down in Charleston on Thursday night and he hadn't left New Hampshire yet, and as he thought about the totality of it, for a brief instant it startled him as if he had woken up at the wheel of a car going down the highway at 70 miles an hour. There was a lot to accomplish before The Candidate's arrival, and the traveling staff's, and the traveling press, on Thursday night, and foreboding would do him no good, but he did it anyway.

"Relax, enjoy this, go to a happy place in your mind," he thought. He pictured the lovely environs of Charleston, warm air, coatless mobility, jogging along the Battery, lovely people, his favorite antebellum heroine Scarlett O'Hara. Bix loved the accent of South Carolinian ladies, and Vivian Leigh's too, whatever hers was.

As his muscles lubricated he took the opportunity to search his BlackBerry for a weather report in South Carolina. It elicited something roughly akin to a sensation of enthusiasm, if he remembered the emotion correctly, when he saw that the temperature would be 73 degrees on that very day. He hadn't experienced the sensation of feeling in his toes for over a month and the prospect of outdoor warmth was too enticing to even consider. It posed a real danger that he might skyrocket into mild eagerness. Once again he thought of Storie, as did every point of reference by then.

In Bixworld, where no future prospect of "good" could occur without an equal and opposite prospect of "not good," he worried that the climate and Storie's presence in Charleston might combine to cause him to feel a sense of unwarranted optimism, and he worried that it would be shattered ultimately. It concerned him that she might sense he'd grown cynical past the point of retribution; she knew him better than he knew himself and she was never fond of cynics.

He clicked to his emails and scrolled down to two marked "Charleston/Scepter, SC, Schedule Draft I" and "Team C/S," which contained not only the slate of his team members but also the team's travel plans, and saw that most members of his team were scheduled to arrive at the Columbia airport around the same time, 11 a.m. "Perfect," he thought. He would gather them at the airport for his second team meeting of the day, brief them on the trip and task them before they picked up their rental cars and drove to Charleston and Scepter to begin the Advance. He would discuss the entire Advance with Mike as they travelled and devise their plan of action, and then Mike could focus on the one event for which he was responsible. And maybe another.

Bix noticed some empty time on the schedule, from 8:30 p.m. Thursday until 11:00 a.m. Friday, when The Candidate would be in town but there would be no media coverage, other than the fact he had arrived, and no video, no pictures of any kind in the media. There would be no coverage with any meaning—no additional coverage to hype the rally, no positive images emanating from the state, no evidence of contact with the people of South Carolina. "This calls for an OTR," he thought. An open scheduling window that wide was begging for an off-the-record event.

Bix cross-matched his thumbnail review of each Advance person's strengths and weaknesses against the first stirrings of his imagination, envisioning game day for the first time, conjuring the visuals he wanted to create. The thought of an indoor event left him cold. If Scepter was warm, Bix was determined to do an outdoor event to take full advantage of it and avoid the constraints of walls and fire marshals.

If they didn't win the New Hampshire primary today, Bix reasoned, the coming contest in South Carolina would loom larger, with a direct impact on the expectations placed on Advance and Bix's kick-off rally. As a starting point, he knew he needed to create a rally that exceeded everyone's expectations, and when he thought of "everyone's expectations" he was thinking solely about the media's. He could phone in a three-thousand-person crowd in the local gym and make it look like ten thousand, but it wouldn't have the resonance, the aura, the impact that a real show of force, a massive event, would generate. Bix wanted to elevate his rally to the level of an electoral touchstone, an exhibition of strength, a spectacle, and he wanted the media to portray it as such. He wanted the whole enchilada—including genuinely enthusiastic reporters offering excited commentary, as well as the requisite incredibly dramatic pictures—the audio as well as the visual. Despite the news media's well-known cynicism, it was still possible to impress them on occasion.

At Headquarters, the offices were still dark. It would be another couple of hours before the staff started arriving, but their creative juices had begun to flow and the wish list for the Scepter/Charleston trip had begun to grow. Soon, another cadre of interested individuals—local civic leaders and Pooh-Bahs who called Scepter and Charleston home—would swell the ranks of those with wish lists. Most had only honest, if self-serving, intent. Predictably, there was at least one individual, likely inhabiting the darkest office with the biggest ego walls on the upper floor of Headquarters, whose intent was both self-serving and self-aggrandizing.

One of the emails, from Sophie in Peem's office, provided the name and contact information of the campaign's regional field director for the Charleston/Scepter area, a Mr. Don Shaunesy. With it was a cryptic note that read "Let's talk about this. I'll fill you in." She put a little "frownie face" emoticon after it.

Bix pocketed his Blackberry and dialed-up the treadmill and finished off his last twenty minutes at a jog. After a set of push-ups and some weights, he headed back upstairs.

He met Mike in the lobby at 6:45 for the drive to Logan. Mike brought along the national and local morning newspapers, and the pictures looked good. So did the headlines. Almost great. Their conversation quickly segued to the rally in Scepter.

Mike asked a question to which he already knew the answer. "So, how big should we make the Scepter rally? Should we do a monster blow-out spectacular, or a colossal monster blow-out spectacular?"

"They're definitely going to get the colossal version," Bix said. "Headquarters just doesn't know it yet. There is almost no benefit in producing another event that essentially looks like all the other rallies the press corps has been forced to endure. If we can pull off a thirty-thousand-person rally on a Friday for no special reason other than to see *The Candidate*, and I believe we *can* get at least thirty thousand, even the press will be impressed. Thirty thousand is less than a third of the population within a half-hour radius. When we get to the airport, let's go on-line and check out the Scepter city website, if they have one, and see what visuals they're using to promote their town. I want a site that screams South Carolina."

"We'll have him speak from a palmetto tree," Mike said.

"That might be a little extreme, but I'd be open to finding a palmetto tree-shaped podium," Bix said. "Although that might look a little 'Ricky Ricardo.' Then we'd need to get him a back-up band."

"I love it. So you think we can get thirty thousand at noon on a Friday? These people work for a living," Mike said.

"Yes, absolutely. At least I think so. What do we have to lose if we build a huge site and it's half empty?" Bix asked.

"The election," Mike suggested.

"Exactly. That's why they'll show up. But just in case, let's find a local marching band, or two or three, to play at the event. They take up a lot of space and make a lot of noise. We can always tighten an outdoor site before the build if we think we won't get the crowd, but I think they'll come."

"Me, too," Mike said with a large smile. "Thigpen may actually have to do some work on this trip."

"It'll be good for him. He can learn some crowd-building skills."

"What size crowd do you think our Opponent will get for her rally in Columbia?" Mike asked.

"They'll go conservative, despite the fact that her event is in a larger metro area and her Advance team can tap twice the number of bodies living within a radius of ten miles. They wouldn't have the balls to try to fill Williams–Brice Stadium. That's seventy-two thousand seats—if it were us, I'd try it. They'll do an indoor event, so they'll have to use a gym and will be limited to two or three thousand people."

"What about our budget?" Mike asked.

"Headquarters will give us some latitude on this trip. I'll request enough to pay for real crowd building, even if we have to rent busses and haul people in. In terms of the production, go for it. Time is too short and the need is too great for Egan to quibble over a few dollars."

"You haven't spoken to Egan or Peem about what you're thinking in terms of crowd yet, have you?" Mike asked.

"Tonight, after we've done our due diligence, and after several more hours have passed and they have less of an opportunity to express their penury, I'll fill them in on the plans. Or I might wait 'til tomorrow morning. It depends on what we can accomplish today."

Just after 7 a.m., Bix's cell phone rang. It was Sophie. Bix was impressed.

In the spirit of a socially conscious Democrat, aware of the dangers of driving and talking on the phone, Bix thought about pulling over and letting Mike drive, but the urge lasted only for a moment. He reached over into the backseat and pulled out his notebook from his bag, then opened it on the console between the front seats and kept on driving as he backed off the gas a touch.

"Sophie," Bix answered. "This is impressively early."

"Good morning, Bix. Did you get my email about Shaunesy, the Regional Field Director, with his contact information?"

"I did. I'll contact him as soon as I hit the ground and try to go meet with him immediately."

"Which is good. You need to do that, but I want to caution you. He's only been down there about two weeks and already he has kind of a bad reputation with the local Field staff. I have a friend who's been working there for almost two months and they are *not* at all happy that this is the person who's been put in charge for the last three weeks of the primary."

"Interesting."

"The Field staff couldn't wait for the new big shot Regional Field Director to get there," Sophie said, "and now they can't wait for him to leave. Apparently his people skills are as developed as his political skills, which is not at all."

"How did he get the job?" Bix asked. "Who put him there?"

"Here's the thing—he's friends with Drule. Drule got Shaunesy the job."

The unfortunately monikered Larry Drule, deputy campaign manager for Field operations, who personified his name. Every photo and video of him that Bix had ever seen looked as if he would begin oozing saliva out of the corner of his mouth at any moment. Bix realized that he might have had a bias; he knew that Drule had a reputation for being ethically challenged when the guy was a Hill staffer. Drule's superiors seemed blithely unaware of his proclivity for duplicity as Drule was uniquely adept at the old Washington two-step, kissing up and pissing down. Bix assumed that Drule had been bullied as a child by people wearing political campaign buttons.

"Good to know," Bix told her.

"Shaunesy has a personal agenda, according to my friend, and his priorities don't seem to have a heavy emphasis on winning the primary. He spends all of his time with a few wealthy business leaders in the area or in the office on his phone. Nobody can figure out who he's talking with, but it doesn't sound like it has anything to do with the campaign. And his only staff meeting was nothing more than an hour-long diatribe about what they should and shouldn't be doing with their time, despite the fact that their responsibilities have already been designed and approved by Headquarters. He apparently also has a thing about not sharing information, and he gets openly hostile when he's asked anything."

"Would you call him a ticket-puncher, someone who's just putting in minimal time on the campaign so he can get a job in the administration?"

"Absolutely, first and foremost. But he's also not doing much to ensure that there will be an administration in which he can get a job. The morale in the Charleston and Scepter field offices is very low. A lot of those people have been there for many weeks and they know their jobs. He's got them doing stuff they shouldn't be doing."

"It sounds like he's beaten Drule's world record for the fastest time from introductions to animosity. Do you have any suggestions on how to work with him? Does he have a gate keeper?"

"His administrative assistant is a Laura Ratchel, affectionately known as Nurse Ratched. No one gets past her. She literally fills the doorway to his office. Apparently she's built like a retired linebacker. My friend told me last night that both of them have made some snide remarks about the Advance team and told the Field staff not to lift a finger to help you guys."

"Don't you love politics?' Bix asked. "We have a Regional Field Director who is committed, motivated, and energetically pursuing an agenda that is aggressively unhelpful to the campaign."

"And he's being a jerk about it. When you get there you will recognize him immediately. Apparently he looks like Napoleon Dynamite, red hair and all. My friend thinks that might be the root of his problems. The only difference is that Shaunesy has a slightly better haircut."

"They say that Washington is Hollywood for ugly people."

"Well, now the guy is making South Carolina ugly," Sophie said. "Be careful down there, and please keep all this under your hat. The Candidate's visit is Shaunesy's big chance to do something, and you know he will try to take advantage of the situation."

"I appreciate your help, Sophie. You are a great American."

"Yes, but I'm not a legend like you."

"A legend in my own mind. It must have leaked out—my mind, not the legend."

"Go leak it on Shaunesy. He's making everyone miserable."

"Tell your friend that salvation arrives today, or at least a brief distraction. We'll do our best to make sure that everyone there has a good time while we're in town, and promise your friend that the Field operation will benefit from the rally. There is a lot of organizing you can do if you've got thirty thousand people in one place."

"Thirty thousand!" She seemed startled. "I didn't know it was going to be that big."

"It will be, but please keep *that* under *your* hat. I'm not telling Peem or Egan until I've scoped some sites. But yes, we're going to do an outdoor rally with all the accouterments."

"Good luck. I'll email you more contact information on the people you've asked me to track down as soon as I get it. Let me know whatever you need." They said their goodbyes and hung up.

Bix turned to Mike. "Shaunesy, the Regional Field Director?" He paused.

"Yeah," Mike said. "What about him?"

"He doesn't get an 'S' pin," Bix told him.

"Got it."

* * *

They arrived at the airport and made it through ticketing and security with relative ease, ignoring the strip searches and cavity probes that always resulted from the fact that their tickets had just been purchased the night before, an automatic red light for the TSA. After settling in at the gate a little past 8:00 a.m., Bix's digital portal opened with a vengeance, both outgoing and incoming.

Bix emailed his entire team instructing them to meet with him on arrival at the airport, then began emailing and calling friends and colleagues, current and former officials at State, the White House, and Defense who might have known Dr. Parviz on a personal level. He emailed the president of the college Young Democrats at Eliot University, Parviz's school, and replied to an email from Special Agent Emory to let him know when he'd arrive and arranged a time for their first countdown meeting that night. In his emails and voicemails to those who still held government jobs, he was careful to ask them to contact him regarding a "personal matter." They would understand not to use a taxpayer-funded method of communication.

Mike started researching visuals and found an image of Scepter's favorite landmark, an ornate Corinthian column thrusting majestically into the air, flanked on two corners at its base with clustered sculptures of square-jawed men in uniform, armed to the teeth with muskets and knives. Situated in front of the county courthouse, it was the focal point of town pride, a monument to Scepter County's Confederate dead.

Mike offered his opinion of the scene as a potential rally site. "It certainly screams South Carolina, although it may be more of a rebel yell. The weapons are a nice touch."

"It's lovely," Bix said, "but it might not be the most appropriate visual for the rally."

"Unless the message is about safe sex and we cloak the whole thing in a giant condom," Mike suggested.

"The local folk may take umbrage. I've gone to some disturbing lengths to cover up unwanted visuals, but that would be a new high in low. You *are* thinking outside the box, though. How about we keep looking. Do they have a local college?"

Mike clicked on the image of a large Greek revival building with very tall columns across the front. The caption read, "College of Scepter." With another click Mike enlarged the image, and he and Bix looked at each other and smiled.

They spoke in unison. "Banners."

Tall, vertical banners: Bix's trademark. The taller the better. At one rally they had spanned a height of fifty feet. His philosophy was simple: When you are outdoors, go big. Dr. Janet Townsend's observation about *Triumph of the Will* had been incredibly perceptive—Bix's visual role model, for banner size alone, were those used as a backdrop for the 1934 Evil Party Congress rallies in Nuremburg. And one of his role models for production, and just production, was Riefenstahl's film. While the Nazis were degenerate criminals of the lowest order, they put on a hell of a rally, literally. Bix bemoaned the fact that he'd never be able to march Americans into his rallies in neat rows, legion standards held high in the air the way that Romans used to do it, lined-up in perfect order. It was a shame, but it was a trade-off in his mind. "You give up a little in spectacle but pick up democracy and freedom," he noted, "which is a good thing." He was a very deep thinker on these matters.

Bix had witnessed an evolution over the past twenty years, as television news became warier and warier, and warier, of being manipulated into shooting video that looked like campaign advertisements, and they began framing their shots tighter and tighter. Ultimately all that was seen on TV news was the candidate's head and a few inches around it. But Bix found that if he gave the press a visual so dramatic and different they could not ignore it, they would use it. "They can't not use it," was his rationale. Once news cameramen and women opened the frame of their shots, they couldn't help but show more of the rally, and then more of the crowd, and the enthusiasm played out on-camera for the enjoyment and edification of the viewers at home. Usually the "still" photographers, the good ones, captured images that were equally dramatic, i.e. edifying, and even iconic—sometimes "good" iconic and sometimes "bad" iconic.

"Is that the college's administrative building?" Bix asked.

"It looks like, and it appears to have a large courtyard or campus quad in front of it," Mike said. "If it doesn't have palmetto trees we can plant some."

"Or if they're in the wrong place we'll move them," Bix said. I think we found our site. We're going to need to find a banner maker."

"I'll start on that as soon as I get to town," Mike said. "What do you want them to say?"

"Don't know yet, something memorable. Find contact information on the college president and we'll go there when we get to town. I want to show up on their doorstep."

Bix had enough time to cram in another series of emails before they boarded their flight and he saw that Sophie was still sending him more contacts before he was forced to turn off his phone. He and Mike had arranged seat assignments next to one another so they could continue their conversation, and were pleased to find a lovely young woman and her beautiful baby, who must have had a terrible earache, sitting directly behind them. The screaming lasted throughout the flight. There was no conversation and no sleeping.

6

Strayberg was up early talking with his "tech contractors" on his disposable private cell phone, not the one that Max News provided and not the iPhone he kept as his official personal cell phone. The disposable cell was an extra layer of privacy between him and foes, friends or law enforcement, as much as any cell phone could be. He maintained a semi-cautious approach when he used it, knowing the capabilities of people who, when very motivated and well-funded, could easily find a way to listen-in, watch, hack, tap, bug or spy on anyone with the click of a mouse. It was remarkably easy. It was also remarkably easy to hide that kind of activity under the guise of "oppo research" which used only "publicly available sources," because everything was available over the web now anyway. Once the conservative geek squad locked themselves in their office, who knew what they were going to wind up with? He assumed they could write an algorithm that could predict exactly what The Candidate's Deputy Press Secretary was going to say in a private email even before he pushed "Send," or what voicemails people would be leaving for him even before he knew, and they could do it with consistency with many of The Candidate's press staff, then eventually Scheduling and Advance. Those tech guys, with their metadata, were geniuses at analysis, at drilling down.

Out of a minimal abundance of caution, Strayberg told his outside research contractors, incorporated as TechTeam08Vision, not to gather the same "data," as he called it, on The Candidate's senior staff. He assumed that their communications would be monitored more diligently for external threats, such as his "metadata gathering," and less likely that Press and Skedvance would be as cautious in guarding their own communications.

It was amazing what the tech guys could do, including the man on the phone, Darryl, one of the managing directors of TechTeam08Vision. TechTeam, located in Arlington, consisted of thirty-three individuals— two administrative assistants, both female, and thirty-one managing directors, all male. Very egalitarian, very horizontal, every man a king, or queen, in his own cubicle with his own desk and his own computer, every woman perfectly free to accept the status quo or leave.

Darryl was managing director of the O'Malley account, or as TechTeam08Vision referred to it, "Account 21." He was a strapping young zealot, twenty-three years old, with close-cropped hair and a closetful of plaid madras short-sleeved shirts. There was a bit too much white around the irises of his eyes during normal conversation, including when he talked with Strayberg and stared at his 24-inch flat screen.

"Mr. Strayberg," Darryl said when he answered his headset, as if to I.D. the client for documentation purposes.

Strayberg stayed light. "Darryl, I knew you would be there. You probably didn't leave last night."

Darryl didn't claim it. "No man, I wanted to get here early to work on a new algorithm. South Carolina is lighting up like a Christmas tree."

Strayberg wasn't surprised by anything, primarily because he didn't question too deeply. "Have you been able to get a geographic on our primary potential source?" It sounded vague enough in his mind to be inscrutable if he was being taped.

Darryl's answer was equally felonious and equally faux vague. "We are monitoring public statements and watching public means to track the individuals, friends, who are working to find him. Those avenues of finding your primary potential source are the best metrics we have. They are multiple and appear on several operational platforms."

Bullshit, Strayberg thought. He couldn't determine if Darryl was being ambiguous because he was trying to be legally vague, or if Darryl sounded like a bad impression of a civil servant because he wasn't accomplishing shit and this was the best explanation he could think of. Same answer, different meanings.

"Darryl, I'm going to need regular updates today and tomorrow. Constant, hourly, at minimum. I'm taking the production team to South Carolina this morning and we can't waste a minute in finding this guy and his publication. If we don't get intel from you, we're going to be cooling our heels, shooting lots of B-roll, stumbling around looking for *the* story or *any* story. So you've got to have my back on this. We need real-time intel, and we need to find my potential source first. If he's on this continent, I need to get there first."

"We'll have your back, Mr. Strayberg." There was that I.D. again. Irritating.

"Thanks, Darryl. I appreciate it. Email me as you get a grip on this situation." Strayberg realized as he said it that it might sound pejorative, but he decided he was OK with it.

Darryl reacted surprisingly, with an upbeat promise. "I'll stick with you on this until the situation is resolved, and I'll email you hourly updates if not more often."

Strayberg gave Darryl the benefit of the doubt. The young man was a young right-wing ideologue who looked strikingly similar to Lee Atwater in his youth; a geek with a blond buzz cut and a conviction that his belief system, ingrained since youth, was absolute in its perfection. Among the many convenient rationalizations by which he lived his life was one that perfectly suited the occasion.

"Since the left-wing liberals and left-wing liberal press do anything they want to suppress Conservatives in this country," Darryl said, "it's OK to do anything necessary to fight back. The only way to fight fire is *with* fire. 'Nuff said." The future cult member needed no more justification.

He apparently wasn't aware that there are other ways to fight fire, with water for instance, or a fire extinguisher. It wouldn't have made a difference. He was a crusader with a laptop and a mission to burn left-wing heretics, so Strayberg decided to give him the benefit of the doubt, and he knew that O'Malley would consider the kid to be a "fucking genius.

* * *

Another flood of emails and voicemails greeted Bix once he touched down. He started replying before the plane pulled up to the terminal.

To Special Agent Shane Emory: "On the ground in SC; will call you when I'm en route Charleston. How about a countdown meeting tonight at 7 p.m.?"

To Sophie: "Thank you for the hunting down my contacts. Great job! Here's another—can you find R. Clayton Baycroft, former career FSO and ambassador to the OSCE, now retired. He lives in Maryland but his phone is unlisted. Thanks again."

To the RFD Don Shaunesy: "I would like to introduce myself and talk about the event in Scepter…will call when I get to town and plan to drop by your office in Charleston later this afternoon. Will you be available? My cell phone: 312-555-2076."

To Kate Hillhouse: "No, I'm neither a sadist nor a masochist. Trust me, you'll have fun. (And your check is in the mail.) Meet at baggage claim carousel 3."

Down the list he found an email from Alecia Fortunati, his Scheduling Desk, subject lined "fyi." She wrote: "Drule just came in here and yelled at me for 'giving a couple of Leads too much leeway' as he described it. By 'a couple of Leads' I think he meant you. He told me the RFD in Charleston wanted to go with you to choose the rally Site and should have final approval. I told him we don't do things like that. He said it was a politically sensitive region of the state, and that I wasn't acting like a professional, not like Headquarters staff ought to act."

Bix hit Reply. "Drule said what? That's the oddest thing I've ever heard. Never let anyone tell you you're not perfect. Never let anyone tell you the Advance team isn't perfect either. Whenever Field staff wants to involve themselves in Advance it's a bad sign. I've emailed and voice messaged Shaunesy; happy to bring him along if he wants. He hasn't responded yet." Bix lied about the "happy" part.

Bix and Mike took their time exiting the plane and ambling through the concourse to baggage claim; their team members would take another half hour or more to arrive. They planned to sit somewhere and relax with a cup of the precious brew; a special moment they could remember for the next seventy-five hours of total, unmitigated, nerve-grinding, hard-nosed politeness and diplomacy.

They stopped at a coffee stand, dropping their heavy carry-on bags on the floor. "When do they plan to announce this visit?" Mike asked.

"Just as soon as we pick the site I'm sure we can get them do to a press release within an hour or so, hopefully. We, on the other hand, should start announcing it the moment we step foot on the campus of ol' Scepter U. Start the word of mouth. When anyone asks why I'm there in a situation like this, I tell 'em. I don't wait for headquarters to put out a press release, but I don't talk to the media, either. Just to regular people… they'll spread the news."

"I'm down with that. Why keep it a secret?"

"Unless the media *happen* to be there, in which case I tell them on background, with the agreement that the source is identified only as 'a campaign field organizer,' Bix said.

Mike loved it. "I'll remember that one. Technically it's true. We're organizing in the field."

"Trying to explain what Advance is to the local press would only confuse them. Trying to explain the difference between Advance and Field would confuse them even more, so I just use the technically correct dictionary definition of our activities, on the ground, per se, as it were."

"Don't mention it to Kate," Mike said.

"She knows. She knows not all rules apply in every single circumstance."

"What you're saying is she won't rat us out to HQ."

"Exactly. But she'll let us know when we're about to cross the Rubicon. Thankfully she suffers fools, but she doesn't suffer much foolishness."

As Bix spoke his phone rang again. "Egan," Bix answered, "I feel like we're bonding on this trip."

"Bix, Peem wanted me to let you know that the college Young Republicans at Stearns U where Parviz teaches have put out a press release calling on him to come forward with his manifesto. O'Malley and the right wing press will use that all day long."

"They put out a press release? That was my back-up plan. Have any real media outlets picked it up yet?"

"Not really. It's localized and too unsubstantiated so far, but for O'Malley this is substantiation enough. We'll hear about it at length on his program today. The rally in Scepter this Friday will be a trigger for the main stream press to start paying more attention if Parviz hasn't shown up by then," Egan said. "By the way, Peem doesn't want you to mention this to your team. There's no reason they have to know you're working on it."

"I can't promise that," Bix said. "They're here, it involves the press, and I'm not comfortable keeping my team in the dark, especially the senior team members."

"I'm just passing it along."

"Please pass along to Mr. Peem that I will give his suggestion serious consideration," Bix said.

As they spoke, they spotted Kate walking briskly past the coffee shop, well-dressed in a tweed sport coat, dark vest and pressed blue jeans, pulling her carry-on bag from which were hanging a dozen colorful, laminated bag tags from foreign trips she had done for the White House during the Clinton administration. It was one of the few status symbols that Bix found tasteful, unostentatious. The tags all read "Trip of the President to…" whatever exotic geographic location they had traveled and the date.

Bix jumped up from the table and hustled out to intercept her. They hugged and laughed and looked at each other with the expressions of a couple who were about to jump off a bridge tied to a bungie cord. She and Mike had the same sort of greeting and the same look on their faces. They all had an idea of what awaited them.

"Gentlemen, are we ready to scale this mountain?" Kate's voice was a sonorous rasp. She sounded like Lauren Bacall after a night of heavy smoking.

"We were just about to get up and start climbing," Mike told her, "but now that you're here why don't you sit down and have a cup of joe?"

"That's not what I need to drink right now," she said. "I'll wait until later when I can have something with an umbrella in it. My last couple of trips have had a surplus of national-class assholes, and the next one that shows up may have his head chewed off."

"Coming from you that's quite an indictment," Bix said. "The greatest oath I've ever heard you swear was something like 'by Saint Aloysius.'"

"I've finally realized that an asshole's an asshole," she said.

"You have my word that we will encounter no miscreants, misanthropes, jerks, or low-lifes on this Advance trip," Bix said, "except for the two low-lifes you've already run into. This will be fun; you will thank me for roping you into this."

"And you'll respect me in the morning too, right?"

"Absolutely, every bit as much as I do now. Also, I'm from the federal government and I'm here to help you."

The three headed to baggage claim and along the way Bix told Kate about his concerns regarding Shaunesy, the Regional Field Director. "We will have to work around him to the extent possible. I don't want any of us to use his office space in Charleston, and we will have to decide whether we want to do any work out of the district office in Scepter. I'll ask Missy Bellew to set up the staff office in the hotel immediately when she arrives, and you can take it for your press operations."

"I understand completely," Kate said. "If Shaunesy has only been there for a couple of weeks he won't be able to do us much good anyway. And if he screws with us, we'll kill him."

"He's a friend of Drule's," Bix told her.

"Then we'll wound him."

Bix grinned. "Proportionality. Works for me."

They found three of their Advance team waiting at Carousel 3— Thigpen, Henry Benton, and Cornelia Underwood, a tall, somewhat gangly and reticent young woman who would serve as Kate's Press 2. Bix immediately wondered whether she was up for the pressure of dealing with the national and local press corps.

Man hugs all around ensued, except for Cornelia, to whom Bix introduced himself and Mike. Kate had worked with Cornelia once one month before, and it was obvious to Bix by their greeting that Kate had a good impression of the young lady.

The RON Advance, Missy Ballew, was scheduled to arrive mid-afternoon. The only things Bix knew about her were that she had only done a few previous RONs as a trainee. JC Ebsen's arrival time was still unknown.

Dan Thigpen, Crowd Advance, was the biggest character of the group, although not in an especially attractive manner. Bix felt the need to mention his appearance when he saw him. "You look like you spent the last two nights sleeping on a park bench."

"Hey, I got stuck doing the fucking RON hotel arrangements for fucking staff and the fucking press when they went back to Chicago at the last fucking minute. I don't fucking *do* RONs, and I was up all fucking night." Thigpen was, as always, a victim, and a profane one.

"You will be happy to know," Bix reassured him, "that you will have ample opportunity to do what you're best at on this Advance—I'm referring to your enchanting elocutionary skills—and you'll get to do a lot of crowd building too, with even less sleep."

Most of the Advance team knew Thigpen's reputation for excessive and unimaginative epithets; they nodded appreciatively.

Bix liked his Crowd Advance guys and gals to be a little nuts, and Thigpen fit the bill. His eccentricities tended toward the juvenile. He dressed in frat boy grunge most of the time and cursed like an adolescent longshoreman for no apparent reason, and wasn't especially creative about it. Every fourth word in every sentence was the f-bomb or some variation of it. Sometimes there were multiple variations of the same epithet in the same sentence. But remarkably he cleaned up his act, both physically and verbally, when he was working with his volunteers, particularly the large groups he gathered on Game Day eve.

Thigpen loved being the center of attention when he conducted his volunteer walk-thrus on-site the night before big events. He could keep two hundred volunteers rapt with attention for a two-hour meeting as he described the event to come and the various roles they would perform to manage the event site, tasking them with their duties—crowd directors, site decorators, VIP check-in tables, press area volunteers, clean-up crew—and dividing them into their subgroups for additional briefings, with nary a curse word to be heard. He even wore long pants with no holes in them for those moments. Bix was confident that Thigpen's eccentricities were affected, not ingrained; he proved he could affect normal behavior when it was absolutely necessary. The boy was certainly frenetic, and Bix calculated that about twenty-five percent of the effort and nervous energy Thigpen expended achieved meaningful results, but usually that was enough.

"I'm not taking you out in public looking like that," Bix told him.

"I'll shave when I get to the hotel," Thigpen promised, "and put on a better pair of pants."

Bix noticed he hadn't said "a good pair of pants."

Henry, Motorcade Advance, was actually Henry Benton V, great grandson of the late Senator Henry Benton from Michigan, but everyone called him Freeway after Bix gave him the nickname. Henry was six feet three inches tall, sandy-haired, and pie-faced. One of Bix's older Advance buddies started calling him The Aryan, but that nickname didn't have a good-natured feeling about it. Bix settled on Freeway after he and Henry did a trip together to Lansing, Michigan, where part of a highway that runs through downtown was officially named the Henry Benton Freeway. The moment Bix saw the first "Benton Freeway" sign, a dim light bulb went off.

At first Freeway wasn't thrilled with the appellation. Bix convinced him that it could have been something worse, like Stinky or Horn Dog, which have a tendency to defile as well as stick like glue. So Henry accepted his fate, secretly pleased that he had a nickname conferred by Bix, to whom he was devoted. Bix had rescued him from a Field organizer position in Western Iowa at the beginning of the campaign, for which Freeway would forever be grateful, or until he secured a job in Washington, whichever came first.

Intellectually, Freeway was what Bix had heard described once as "more think-telligent than intelligent." He was comfortable planning and implementing tangible details of motorcade operations, and his commitment manifested itself in 24-hour workdays and excruciatingly exact logistics. The poor boy would have thrown himself in front of a bus for Bix or The Candidate, and on a few occasions Bix had to do interventions to keep him from working himself to a frazzle. People like Freeway made great cannon fodder for causes and candidates who would take advantage of that level of commitment. Given a few colored ribbons, Freeway would have been one of the first over the top at Gallipoli.

Last to arrive was the team's Site 2, Ben Oliver, with whom Bix had worked once in 2004 when the young man was an intern in the nominee's campaign office and he had been allowed to do one Advance trip. Ben graduated from college the next year and managed to find a job at Headquarters compiling briefing books for The Candidate, but he still wanted to do Advance. Born and raised in Boston, he grew up surrounded by the lore of Democratic politics, and Bix saw in him a natural ease with people and uncommon good sense, all but two of which were attributes Bix had at his age. Unfailingly polite, Ben's specialty was coercing elderly ladies into performing unspeakable amounts of hard work. He was also unfailingly appropriate in his standard uniform—khaki pants, navy blazer and dress shirt, with a tie stashed in his coat pocket just in case. Ben was always street-ready for any Advance circumstance.

"Good morning sir," Ben said. "Thanks for getting me on your team. I really appreciate this."

"Let's see if you're still so appreciative Friday afternoon," Bix said. "You never know, I may have done this to you out of spite."

Kate spoke up, "Bix has been telling me this is going to be a vacation excursion, a highlight in my otherwise dreary life."

"That's the adventurous part," said Bix. "There is a very good chance that this Advance will be the most fun we've ever had, or, a complete embarrassment depending on whether you're a glass-half-full or half-empty kind of person. I know *my* entire team has the right attitude, that 'can do' attitude 'because-Bix-will-freaking-kill-me-if-I-screw-this-up' look of fear that I want to see in all of your eyes. And Thigpen, notice I said 'freaking' and 'screw' instead of 'fuck.'"

"Absofuckinglutely, Bix," Thigpen said.

"I knew I could count on you. Before we get our rental cars and head to Charleston we need to get our act together. Let's find a quiet place to talk for few minutes so we can hit the ground running," Bix said.

The group found a deserted corner of the airport near a glass display case with musical instruments and artifacts from a local jazz museum. Bix was able to get in a few seconds of enthused inspection of an old saxophone reportedly used by Charlie Parker before starting the meeting. "We have a little more than two days before wheels down if we don't include sleep. We've got two crowd events to produce—an as-yet-unnamed media event and a rally, in addition to the overnight. Thigpen." Bix looked at his Crowd Advance. "I'm going to be searching for a site that will require at least thirty thousand bodies."

"Thirty thousand?" Thigpen asked. "At noon on a fucking Friday? In fucking podunk?"

"You can do it, I have faith. And we will be doing this in Greater Podunk, so it will be easy. As soon as you check in and perform whatever acts of personal hygiene you require, you're going to need a printer who can produce large quantities of flyers and posters by tomorrow morning. Good luck finding a union printer in South Carolina. Don't even waste your time. Let's get a design started where we can fill in the blanks. Also keep your eyes peeled for a printer that can do large banners. Obviously, we will need to organize a full-blown crowd building effort for this event. Blast emails alone won't cut it here. The digital divide is alive and well in these parts. Contact the president of the Y.D.s at Scepter College first. I'll email you his contact information."

"Not our Regional Field Office?" Thigpen asked.

"Not yet. I'll let you know. You'll need volunteers to canvass and hand out flyers, staff a phone bank, and do outreach to local schools. By the way, if you can, get a marching band or two or three. If we get more than one, we'll have the band directors coordinate a pre-rally musical program. And find any kind of transportation you can lay your hands on—buses, trucks, organize car pools, sign-up sheets and staging locations. Freeway can help with that. My guess is that all of your volunteers can be rolled into your site management plan for game day. Working the site on game day can be their pay-off, their reward, for busting their butts for two days beforehand."

"Got it."

Bix thought of a reference to Tom Sawyer and whitewashing a fence, but he stuffed a sock in it.

"And, Thigpen—because I enjoy making your life complicated, we're going to need a second crowd for another small event on Friday morning."

"A second fucking crowd? How big, for what kind of event?" Thigpen asked.

"Just a hundred and fifty bodies. Headquarters told me we're doing an event, title yet to come, and I plan to keep it intimate. I'm taking a bit of a leap of faith, but I think you can focus on finding military veterans for this one. Contact veterans' organizations regionally and promise them transportation and seating in the V.I.P. section of that event *and* the rally. Freeway, we'll pay for some over-the-road buses to cart these people around, so add those to your list of rentals."

"Cornelia, I am going to ask Kate to accompany Mike and me to our first meeting with the mayor. While we're doing that, I need you to help Thigpen. He has to track down a lot of resources and bodies. Thigpen, Cornelia can start by finding your phone bank resources. Ben, once you've checked into the hotel I need you to start searching the internet for a small venue in the Charleston area, a place that will hold a couple of hundred people where we can do the event that shall not be named. Then you can organize your old lady brigade like you did for us in Philadelphia in '04. We all know that the women do all the work in the Democratic Party. Let's get Charleston's Democratic doyennes working for us. Right now I will need you to drive me and my rental car down to Charleston while I make phone calls."

"Will do," Ben said.

"Mike, I'd like you to swing by Scepter College and take a look at the site we're thinking about *before* we meet with the mayor. I don't want to waste our time hashing it out with the mayor if the site sucks. If you think it'll work go ahead and ask Scheduling to vet it."

"Happy to," Mike said.

"Also, drive by our Field Office in Scepter and scope it out. Let me know if it's big enough for Thigpen to use for crowd building and volunteer operations."

"Happy to."

"Kate, I'll get headquarters to spring for some paid radio advertising, but I want to talk with you later about working with one of the local radio stations to promote the rally. We'll also need a place to cut our radio spots, and I don't want to pay for production, but we should have the budget for a decent time buy. We're going to need market penetration, if only because I enjoy saying market penetration."

"Penetration, got it," Kate said, "a de facto radio sponsor. Are you planning to mention this to the press office?"

"Totally de facto. No fingerprints, just local enthusiasm. We need this to be something that the locals did spontaneously. And obviously we will need a media advisory the moment we secure a site, but if you could also place some local media interviews for whatever news programs exist, radio and television. I would prefer to identify a beloved and revered local civic leader who supports us to do the interviews, rather than paid staff or elected officials, if you catch my drift."

"Drift caught," Kate said. Bix loved that voice; everyone noticed it immediately everywhere she went.

"Freeway, you may as well come with us to the mayor's," Bix continued. "I'd like you to drive Kate and me once we get to the hotel, and you can be my muscle if things get out of hand with the mayor and his boys."

"Would you like me to stop along the way and buy a baseball bat?" he asked.

"Yeah, but a small one, something tasteful."

"You got it, boss. I'll see you at the Hotel Marianne."

"Speaking of the Hotel Marianne, it looks like a *lovely* hotel, so you can expect to have to pay through the nose for *everything*. I will spring for a coffee maker for the staff office; I'll ask Missy to pick one up when she arrives, but until then you're on your own for your five-dollar mocha latte double grande espressos in the lobby coffee shop. Freeway, I'd like you to find a place for us to park our own cars on surface parking near the hotel so we can come and go at will, without the valet. Go see the hotel management when we get back from Scepter. Tell them it's for us and the Secret Service, which will make it sound less like something they can say no to."

"Got it."

"Plan on a 6 p.m. staff meeting," Bix said. "We have a 6:30 conference call with headquarters and a 7 p.m. countdown with Service at the hotel tonight."

"We'll be there," Mike said.

"And one last point, young comrades. We have an opportunity to do something extraordinary, for a change, and we need to be up and running full-force before the campaign finds out and attempts to squash it into a mediocrity. If the New Hampshire primary doesn't go well for us today, we are our campaign's first and best chance to regain the momentum, to show that New Hampshire didn't have a lasting impact. We could literally change the national conversation from here on out. Let's don't let the moment pass. Remember, it's carpe that per diem. Unless you have any questions, let's head to Charleston and create history."

* * *

Bix, Kate, Mike, Freeway, and Thigpen picked up their mid-size, four-door, so-called American-made rental cars. Ben took the wheel of Bix's car and Bix, sitting shotgun, dove into his list of phone calls for the Advance. The "Manifestogate scandal" would have to come second.

Mayor Bacon was at the top of his call list, first on his list to visit, and first among those potential rapscallions who would, he was certain, require a management plan, but he called his Secret Service counterpart first out of professional courtesy.

"This is Emory," he answered.

"Mr. Emory, this is Bix. I just arrived in Columbia and I'm on my way to Charleston."

"Bix, thanks for calling, please call me Shane. I wanted to touch base to find out what you know about sites, and to set up a time for our first countdown meeting. Do you have any ideas where you want to do the rally and the other media event we've been told about?"

The Secret Service *always* asked that question as soon as he arrived in town, and his answer was always no. "Honestly I have an idea where we might want to do the rally in Scepter from a photo I saw online, but

I want to look at it before I mention it in case the site isn't viable," Bix said. There were a hundred reasons why any potential Site might not work no matter how badly anyone wanted to an event there. Also, and more importantly, the moment Bix told Emory that he was thinking about using the College of Scepter as a site, Emory would tell his site agents, who would then, in unbridled conscientiousness, swarm the College, probably with local police in tow. It was an exceptionally unsubtle thing, having a gaggle of gentlemen in dark suits and dark glasses and driving dark sedans show up "just to look around," and Bix wasn't prepared to announce his intentions to the world before he met with the mayor.

"I understand," Shane said, "but as soon as you can."

"Shane, the moment I know I'm close to locking-in a rally site, I will let you know. Same for the second event—it will be tomorrow before I have a venue for that, but I promise it will be much smaller and, ideally, more manageable. One commitment I *can* make to you right now is that we will only need one mag at the second Site. My rally Site will be much larger."

"How much larger?"

"Thirty-five thousand," Bix told him. He always used his maximum number, or larger, when estimating crowds for the Secret Service to encourage them to bring enough magnetometers. It was a constant ir- ritation. Service estimated that six hundred people per hour could go through each mag, a number Bix found laughable. He had heard that number for years and years and he always had the same response: They'd have to sprint to go through that fast.

"That's a large crowd. I don't know if we can get the assets,' Emory told him. "You know your Opponent is in Columbia that day."

"Yes, but she will have a *much* smaller crowd," Bix said. It was meant to sound as if he was looking down his nose. "I'm just giving you the heads-up. The politics of this visit are crucial, and headquarters asked me to produce a rally that will jump start the last two week push." Bix was not shy about invoking, when necessary, the untouchable 'poli- tics' in which the Service should do their best not to interfere.

"I understand—we'll do our best," Emory told him. "Thanks for the heads-up. We'll see what we can get."

"Sorry to do that to you." Bix had a bad habit of feeling responsible for the inconvenience his decisions caused the Service.

"It's not like it was totally unexpected. Mr. Caputo mentioned that your campaign sends you to do their big events. May I safely assume there isn't an indoor venue in Scepter with that kind of capacity?" Emory asked.

"That's a very good question. I haven't asked but I will have to check that out as soon as I arrive in town." Bix wasn't lying. Both he and Shane knew the answer, but honesty, whenever unavoidable, was always the best policy. "If it's going to be warm, I will be looking to see if I can do the event outdoors." Bix knew that an outdoor rally posed different challenges and risks for the Service, and Emory would appreciate knowing as far in advance as possible.

"Let me know what you find, and we'll see you at 19 hundred."

Bix's next call was to Mayor Bacon's office. "Hello, is this the mayor's office?"

"Yes, suh," the southern lady said quietly. "Are you the Advance gentleman we've been told to expect?" she asked.

"Yes ma'am," he said. He loved working in small towns. It was like he was bringing the circus to town. "My name is Bix, and I just arrived at the airport in Columbia. I'm on my way to Scepter and I wanted to touch base with the mayor first before I spoke with anyone else." He made it point of pointing out his courtesy. "Would he be available before I get started in Scepter, either in person or by phone?" It was the nicest way he had of telling her that he was starting his work in town with or without the mayor's input.

"Of course, suh. May I put you on hold for a minute?" A few seconds later she came back and said the mayor invited him to come by as soon as he arrived in town.

Bix was encouraged. "Thank you ma'am. May I ask your name?"

"I'm LuAnn, the mayah's administrative assistant."

He was already on a first name basis, another encouraging note, but he was cautious. They suck you in with niceness down here, he thought. "LuAnn, it's nice to talk with you. I look forward to meeting you in person."

"I do too, Bix." Her voice was the soundtrack of his cinematic fantasies, but they were costume dramas and far too difficult to stage in his distracted imagination, so he stuck to his knitting.

"See you in a couple of hours," he told her.

The other most important person with whom Bix needed to talk was one of his best sources, an insider's insider on the subject of South Carolina. Charlie Quick was Senator Hollings' chief of staff, an old acquaintance and a man who would definitely remember that Bix had organized two fundraisers for his boss. Quick's insights were the best hope Bix had of minimizing the impact of local politics on his events and on his nerves. Quick gave him the ten-minute version and it was, as Bix hoped, insightful. In the short briefing Bix was reminded of South Carolina's political players, most of whom had crossed his path at some point, as well as their passions, motivations, prejudices, strengths, weaknesses, and a vulnerability or two. There were never enough of the latter.

Post-Quick briefing, Bix felt prepared to navigate the treacherous waters. Quick pulled him back down to reality. "They'll still eat you alive down there if you don't watch yourself. But don't back down either, you've got to do your job. Everyone you meet will sure as hell be trying to do theirs."

It sounded ominous, but by then Bix had grown used to the feeling and his BlackBerry was lighting up with emails and missed calls, the first wave of responses to his and Sophie's discrete inquiries about Jamir Parviz's whereabouts.

After having several hours to contemplate "Manifestogate," and dedicating at least five seconds of those hours to intense reflection, neither the concept that Jamir or The Candidate could have written a pro-Iran, anti-U.S., jihadist manifesto while they were in college, nor the idea that Jamir was attempting to influence The Candidate's campaign by remote control seemed any more likely. But, he had seen other presidential campaigns wilt for flimsier reasons, and as always, he was compelled to avoid the negative.

Four of his State Department friends emailed through their private accounts, as did two former officials from the White House. Bix used his campaign account; he wanted no question about who was employing his services in case anyone had reservations about helping his presidential campaign, although he found it easy to be forthright. He was confident that all of his contacts were supporters or supportive, and he was confident that none would question his motives, although he did constantly.

He responded to each person individually, in an effort to avoid the appearance of spam panic, and after appropriate thanks he wrote "I'm looking for Jamir Parviz, currently on sabbatical from Stearns College. Do you have any idea where he might be, cell phone, email, cables from Tel Aviv, postcards from Paraguay? Thanks for your help. Bix." He didn't explain why.

By the time Bix sent the sixth email he received a response from the first, from a genial gentlemen who still worked at State in the Bureau of Diplomatic Security, Matt Crowell. Under Subject Line "Jamir," he wrote "Bix, good to hear from you. I've been following your adventures on the campaign through a friend who covers it for the NY Post... says you're kicking ass. I don't know where Jamir is, but I think Bob Baycroft might be able to help you. He knows Jamir's family. Here's his phone number. Good luck on the campaign. MC."

Kismet. The number had a Maryland area code, a good sign. Bix replied, "Matt, next time I see you I'm going to kiss you on the lips." Others on his contact list were slowly responding but this was his only lead so far, and it was a good one. Baycroft reportedly had the biggest Rolodex in the State Department.

Crowell replied quickly, with the subject line "Lip kissing." He wrote, "Next time you ask for help I'll think twice about giving it."

"Then I won't have to worry about brushing my teeth," Bix replied.

Bix couldn't wait for a private moment to call; he turned to Ben, who was intensely making his way down Highway 26. "Ben, pardon me for a minute, I have to make a phone call. If it starts to sound interesting, please ignore it. I'll explain things later."

"Yes sir," Ben said.

Bix called Baycroft. "Mr. Ambassador, this is a blast from your recent past."

"Bix, I recognize your voice. How *are* you," Baycroft crooned with enthusiasm. He was an amiable man, and brilliant.

"I'm fine sir. So you're saying I shouldn't consider a career as a phone stalker?"

"Probably not, but you might want to think about hosting your own radio talk show."

"I've certainly got the face for it."

"I haven't seen you lately Bix, but that was never your problem. Are things heating up on the campaign trail?" Baycroft asked.

"You knew I was with the campaign?" Bix asked, surprised.

"Of course, I read the papers, and every once in a blue moon I see you on television, standing off in the distance keeping watch over everything. You must be working long hours these days. Is there something I can help you with?"

"I make the kids on the Advance team do all the heavy lifting, and yes, I could use your help. I'm looking for our old friend Jamir Parviz and it seems logical that you may have some special connections, as you have special connections with the entire planet."

"As a matter of fact I do, and you do, too," Baycroft said. "His brother-in-law is Hani al-Saleem, the deputy foreign minister in Jordan. We worked with him on your POTUS trip in ninety-five."

"I remember him. Good guy, tennis player, University of Georgia. He's Jamir's brother-in-law?"

"Yes, and I have his email. Would you like it?" Baycroft asked.

"Bob, there's an ambassadorship in this for you," Bix said.

"I've already had one of those, thank you. Your good will is the only payment I need. And make sure your guy wins." He gave Bix Hani's email address.

After they hung up Bix immediately started writing an email to Hani as he spoke to Ben. "Did you hear anything?"

"Nothing, nothing at all, Bix. Even if they hooked up electrodes to my genitals, I heard nothing."

"Good attitude. I appreciate your zeal."

Bix finished his email to Hani, requesting any information he may have on the whereabouts of his brother-in-law, Jamir Parviz. It was before midnight in Jordan and Bix was hoping Hani would get the email before bedtime.

"I'm honored that you thought of me," Ben said, eyes on the road. "The people in Skedvance all told me that this trip is critical for the campaign, and when everything is on the line they turn to you."

"Yeah, to move the line."

"No, to make things work."

"That's nice to hear, but it's also a metaphor for the way they view Advance these days. From their perspective we're the political adaptation of *Modern Times*, all of us Little Tramps on the road, making the gears and sprockets turn more and more quickly. It's our job to make the machine work, and if we avoid getting chewed-up in the cogs and spewed-out as corrugated waste, it was a good trip."

"From what I hear, none of your teams have met that fate, but it's going to be interesting to see how you pull off a thirty-thousand-person rally in a couple of days."

"I'll be interested to see how we do it too," Bix said. "It's always an education. Truthfully, the rally is the easiest part. Not that it will be simple to produce, but at least we know what we have to accomplish once we choose the site and design it."

Bix's BlackBerry was going off almost constantly with new emails by that point. All of the responses about Parviz were a variation on the central theme—"I wish I could help...have you tried so-and-so." He was beginning to think that Hani might be his only hope, but two degrees of separation were still two too many. All he could do was wait.

7

Drule was on the phone to Shaunesy early, before Bix touched down in Columbia. Even at altitude, Bix's ears should have been burning.

"I wasn't able to get Bix thrown off the Advance," Drule droned. "We've got to control those Advance assholes. We have too much to achieve on this trip to allow Bix to fuck things up. I told Peem that we need to approve the site before Bix commits to it."

Shaunesy, committed as he was to the status conferred upon him as an RFD, or as a caricature of one, was most receptive to Drule's observations.

"Other than approving the site, what can I do to control the Advanceholes?" asked Shaunesy. It was cute, but he hadn't invented the term. It had been coined by another bitter, insecure, victimized Field guy who felt overwhelmed by an Advance team that had come to his town to do its job, with cars and hotel rooms and all the bells and whistles and a budget, and stole all of his volunteers for three days (mon dieu!), and stole all of the pretty girls, then didn't give him an "S" pin so he couldn't hang out in the Holding Room with The Candidate…which is why they didn't give him an "S" pin in the first place.

That anonymous pubescent Field organizer cleverly coined the term "Advanceholes" because the Advance team was doing its job, *despite* the fact that they'd gotten the Field organizer a grip with The Candidate *with* a photo, which was *all* that really mattered after the encounter concluded no matter *how* long the encounter lasted. As far as encounters with self-absorbed Field organizers were concerned, briefer was better.

It was an indication of Shaunesy's bias that he had adopted the term "Advanceholes" as his own.

Drule waxed vitriolic. It was personal. He had too much skin in the game to be completely rational, and he had conviction. "You have to exert control over all the local aspects of this trip," he told Shaunesy. "Get one of your people on the inside of the Advance operation, insist on your choice of location, and attend all the meetings that Bix has with your key political leaders. Call your local contacts and let them know that should talk with you if they want something from The Candidate, and not to trust the Advance guys because they will promise them anything, and then not deliver."

Shaunesy agreed in a studied fashion, stroking his chin with his thumb and forefinger as if he could be seen over the phone. "That makes sense. I should be the one who provides access, not Bix."

"You don't have to be available to Bix at his beck and call. You call the meetings, and you pick a site that you're already familiar with so you'll be on your turf."

Shaunesy kept his mouth shut. If Bix's options were restricted only to places that Shaunesy could call "his turf," he would have to hold the rally in Shaunesy's office.

Drule already knew it. "Ask around. Find out if there's a location for this rally that your local leadership contacts recommend. It's an opportunity to tell people you're bringing The Candidate to town. If you get any solid recommendations, maybe go take a look at them and introduce yourself to whoever is there, that way they meet you first."

Shaunesy stepped over the reference to his local leadership contacts, of which he had added exactly zero since he'd arrived. The few major local supporters who already existed when he blew into town were slow to return his phone calls after his second attempt to talk with them ended uncomfortably. He'd summoned them as a group to his small office and then lectured for an hour about their role in achieving the campaign's goals. He provided "no courtesy, no interest in their opinions, no coffee or water, no comfortable chairs, no freaking cookies, no damn local sensitivity," as Sophie had explained to Bix. The entire seven-member local

Charleston regional steering committee decided en masse that they had better connections at the national Headquarters, and decided to maintain those avenues of communication to the exclusion of Mr. Shaunesy.

Shaunesy had pegged this visit as his opportunity to show the locals that he had clout. "I'll call the steering committee and tell them about the visit, and tell them I'll arrange a meeting with The Candidate."

Drule sensed that maybe the Charleston area steering committee had already heard the news from their connections at Headquarters. "Go careful, Don. They may already have been told. But you can take control of arranging a grip with The Candidate. Keep the number in Charleston as low as possible so we can supplement with our own people."

He didn't have to explain to Shaunesy what he meant by "our own people."

8

Kate and Freeway left their cars at the Hotel Marianne and, with Freeway at the wheel, sped off with Bix to Scepter, while the others checked in and started work. As they drove, Bix received a call from his RON, Missy Ballew. She'd missed her flight and wouldn't be in until after 11:00 p.m.

"What's going on?" Kate asked from the back seat.

Bix turned around to look at her. "Missy Ballew missed her flight. She'll be here later tonight."

"Missy's establishing a pattern," Kate said. "She missed her flights on her last two trips. Now she's late for her first Advance as the only RON? Skedvance won't do anything about it because her father is Tommy T. Ballew, a big-time bundler in the Boston area."

"Should I be worried about her?"

"It would be wise to keep an eye her," she said. "She was on this last trip with me, and I intend to pay extra attention to the press corps' RON accommodations to make sure nothing goes wrong. We have a pretty good reputation with the traveling press—things usually go pretty smoothly, but we had some problems last time. A few of the press didn't have rooms reserved at all. We fixed it, but it took some time and the journalists were annoyed as hell. To me she seemed more interested in her relationship with the hotel management."

"Do we have a budding hotelier on our team?"

"Maybe," Kate said. "The other day, first thing in the morning, without coordinating with anyone, or *asking*, she decided to bring several of the hotel staff members up to The Candidate's suite to have him thank them personally for their hard work. She said she viewed her role as that of an honest broker—an impartial middle-man between the campaign and the hotel."

"Impartial? Are the hotels paying half her salary? I'll ask Thigpen to identify a few good volunteers as soon as possible to help her with the hotel, and I'll talk with her about the 'middle-man' concept."

Bix mentioned to Kate that he had an idea he wished to discuss later, after the countdown meeting. She told him it sounded as if he was going to "go creative" on her again. He assured her that there was nothing creative about his ideas, just simple math.

"The law of multiple positive media exposures and its relationship to market penetration is immutable," he opined, "and good Advance should always search for natural opportunities to amplify The Candidate's message through the media. Or in lieu of a message, pretty pictures of his face will do, preferably surrounded by adoring throngs."

"You just like thinking up more creative shit to get press coverage, and you like saying market penetration. I'm surprised you haven't put a press riser in The Candidate's bathroom."

"You want me to nix the privy press riser? You'll probably be against asking The Candidate to wear a forehead cam for the day so the public can see his perspective of the campaign."

"That one I actually like," she told him, "as long as you're the one who asks him."

After a twenty-five minute drive they found Mike Pitcher standing in front of Scepter's City Hall, a dingy gray stucco two-story building at the north end of Main Street. Built in the 1930s as a WPA project, it was apparently the newest construction in downtown. It had no Southern, or even architectural, charm, like much of the remainder of town. It was as if South Carolina had been allotted a finite amount of beautiful historic quaintness and Charleston had been given the lion's share while Scepter was still waiting in the queue. But Bix enjoyed seeing the small number of Victorian-era—which is to say post-General Sherman—buildings that set Scepter apart, including its impressive and beautiful county courthouse down the street from city hall, selected swaths of late nineteenth-century private homes straight out of *Southern Living Magazine*, and several old churches. The late eighteenth-century College of Scepter Administration building was the crown jewel.

Bix turned to Mike. "Did you see the Scepter college campus?"

"It's perfect," Mike said. "There's a large open space in front of the Admin building. It will hold thirty thousand, but we can make it look good with twenty thousand. We can secure the perimeter, and it has good access for trucks and equipment."

"Did you talk with anyone on campus?"

"No, I just walked around noting which palmetto trees I will want to have moved to our site."

"Did you have a chance to see the campaign Field Office in town?"

"I did. It's a large storefront operation. It's huge, and there's a loading dock in the rear. We could run all of our crowd and volunteer operations out of it," Mike said.

"Great work. Then we're off to meet the mayor," Bix said, and he led his entourage through the metal doors.

The receptionist lit up at the sight of them. "You must be the folks from the presidential campaign," she cooed. She was seventy years old if she was a day. She was wearing a floral print dress and sporting a short-bangs Mamie Eisenhower haircut atop a tiny little face adorned with a sincere smile. "The mayor's office is right up those stairs. You can go right on in."

"Thank you ma'am. Very kind. I'm Bix and this is Kate, Mike and Henry, but we call him Freeway." It was Step One in Advanced Advance 401—Be courteous, especially in the South and especially to old ladies, and make everyone feel they're part of the team.

"It's lovely to meet all of you. I'm Mary Ann. I bet I'll be seeing a lot of y'all for the next couple of days."

Bix hoped not. Long hours at City Hall weren't a part of his dream schedule. "Ma'am, you just let me know if you get sick of us and we'll get out of your hair." Damn, he thought, he couldn't help mentioning the hair. "We will do our best not to be a nuisance."

After other pleasantries, they went upstairs, through another drab hallway with offices subdivided by old wood and frosted glass walls.

Over the doorways were office signs as old as the building, reading "Assessor," "City Clerk" and "Director of Revenue," and one newer sign which read "Chief of Police." Duly noted, Bix thought. Kate and Mike noted it too. The Chief's got an office in City Hall.

At the far end of the hall stood a large edifice: an intricately-carved, oversize door surrounded by an equally oversize, and carved, door frame, both made from sumptuous dark faux mahogany, on either side of which hung five-foot-long shiny brass and glass wall sconces. Above the door was mounted a large-but-tasteless oval ebony sign which read "Office of the Mayor" in raised gold letters.

"What do you want to bet there's a couple of sphinxes on either side of the door when we get inside?" Bix asked beneath his breath.

"That's not the question," Kate whispered. "The question is, how big will they be?"

"And whether he has a Praetorian guard," Mike said.

"And how big they'll be," Kate said as they walked through the heavy door.

Bix entered the inner sanctum, but it turned out to be the outer sanctum. More dark wood, finely figured paneling with faux columns and chair rails covered the walls, and heavy dark furniture filled the floor, which was covered in maroon shag carpet. Enlivening the environment was one entire wall of photos of Mayor Bacon with every major political figure who had passed within fifty miles of Scepter, and another wall dedicated as a shrine to a sole, poster-size photo in an ornately carved gold frame. The photo, with faces retouched to angelic perfection by an airbrush artist, was of Mayor Bacon with Pope John Paul, posed as if they had just left the bingo parlor. There were so many shiny plaques and golden tchatchkies in glass cases cluttering the office it looked as if his interior decorator had chosen exclusively from the Looted Contents of Saddam Hussein's Villa Collection.

LuAnn, the mayor's administrative assistant, was sitting behind a large mahogany desk in the middle of the large room. She rose immediately when she saw him and held out her hand. "You must be Bix. It's so good to meet you. Welcome to Scepter. Who are your friends?" She was southern grace personified, an attractive woman, also well into her seventies. Bix assumed she'd worked for Mayor Bacon for decades.

Bix introduced his group to her, and she showed them through another gigantic door.

Bix's smile widened as he walked into the mayor's innermost office. The mayor, a stout churl with a potato nose, an oversized suit coat and a lit cigar clenched in his teeth, remained seated, unsmiling. A massive crystal chandelier hung over his head, hung from a spot in the ceiling that looked like it had been raised five feet for the sole purpose of accommodating the light fixture. It was definitely a statement piece.

Bacon sat stiffly and watched them as they entered and didn't offer his guests a seat.

* * *

Bix loved it. There were very few of this species left in the world, the authentic political boss. Here was a man who wanted to show 'who runs things around here' and Bix was happy to let it be thus.

"What can ah do foah you folks?" Bacon asked, unsmiling.

Bix kept his wide grin and walked up to the edge of the desk, leaned over, and looked down into the mayor's eyes as he extended his hand. "Mr. Mayor, my name's Bix," he said forcefully, for effect.

The mayor, being a politician, reflexively shook his hand.

Bix took the mayor's hand and kept talking. "My friend Charlie Quick tells me that you know more about politics than anyone in South Carolina, and that if I cross you you'll cut out my guts and feed them to the catfish you have in the pond in your back yard."

The mayor wasn't expecting Bix to be an old fart with mutual connections. He also wasn't expecting his own intimidating pose to be so ineffective.

"Am I right so far?" Bix asked, then let go of Bacon's hand.

The mayor tried to force back a smile, but his persona began to crack. "No, suh, I nevah resaht ta vilence unless it's absolutely called fah. So how d'ya know Charlie Quick?"

"From D.C. We were both in the Carter Administration, and I did a couple of fundraisers for Senator Hollings when he was thinking about running for president back in the eighties. One in Washington and one in St. Louis. You and I actually met at the one in Washington."

The mayor was stuck. He couldn't play his role as a hard ass with someone with whom he already had a history, a person who had been around almost as long as he.

"I remembah the fundraisah," Bacon said. "It's good to meet ya again. Usualla they send me neophytes. Youah wah in theh Cahter Minstration?"

"Yes, Mr. Mayor."

"Youah don't look old enough."

"I was a kid."

"Youah must 'a been. How'd youah get that?"

"By knowing what to kiss and when to kiss it."

Bacon laughed immediately, , genuinely, with a warmth approaching, but not quite achieving, friendliness. "Have a seat and introduce me ta ya friends," he said.

"This is Kate Hillhouse, Mike Pitcher and Henry Benton," said Bix.

The mayor looked at Henry and asked, "Just like *Senatah* Henra Benton?"

"Yes sir, he was my grandfather," Freeway said.

That factoid seemed to count as important. Bacon sat back in his chair for the first time and seemed to be either impressed or dismissive. Bix couldn't tell. The mayor didn't explain himself.

He looked back at Bix. "Why were yuh doin' a fundraisah for Senatah Hollin's in St. Louis?"

"I'm from that neck of the woods," Bix said, "and I had some friends there who were also old White House Advance guys who could raise some money and help produce the event. The line we used when we were hitting-up people for money was 'Even if Senator Hollings isn't elected president, he will still be the next Chairman of the Senate Commerce Committee, and *you* know what *that* means.'" Bix smiled broadly. "No one ever asked, 'No, what does that mean?' We couldn't have answered—we didn't have a clue."

The mayor laughed loudly. "That's jus great."

The warm camaraderie was beginning to flow.

"Ah was one of the people tellin' him he should run fuh prezdent," Bacon said. "He would have been a great prezdent. Ah didn't know he had help from folks like you. So, Bix," the mayor asked, "what cannah do for ya?"

It was a reasonable question, asked in a sociable tone by a guy whose look still said, *What can I do for you if I feel like it?*

"Mr. Mayor, the campaign sent us here to put on an event in your fair city this Friday." Bix kept it vague. "We will bring the next President of the United States and the entire national traveling press corps, not to mention news media from around the entire region. If we do our jobs right, the whole thing turns into one giant Chamber of Commerce video for your town."

The mayor may have been warming to Bix but he still had an agenda and it was still his town. "I got a call from yua office this mornin' tellin' me you wuh comin'. They asked me ta host yua Candidate."

Bix could see where the mayor was headed. "Yes Mr. Mayor, as the host city."

"Well, usualla candidates who come through mah town ask me what they need tah do tah appeal to the votahs. I made up a little schedule that yua Candidate can do whahl he is in ma town, one that ah believe will get him tha most votes." The mayor handed Bix a sheet of official stationary on which was typed "Mayor's Schedule" at the top, followed by a list of activities.

Bix read through them while Kate, Mike, and Henry waited. Mayor Bacon wanted The Candidate to come to his home for breakfast, take a walking tour of downtown Scepter, then speak at a local senior center which happened to be named the Eugene V. Bacon Activity Center.

"Mr. Mayor," Bix said, "these are wonderful suggestions and I will immediately pass them up to the big thinkers at headquarters who make those decisions, but so far I have only been asked to put on one event, a speech." Bix couldn't tip toe around reality. "I am happy to do anything else that they tell me to do, but in the mean time I have to focus on the one thing I've been tasked with."

The mayor smiled. "What do ya have in mind?"

"Sir, our Opponent is doing a rally in Columbia that same day, as you probably know, but she is there and we are here, and we are bringing the national media with us. I am looking for an outdoor location that is quintessentially Scepter, a venue that makes it clear we are in your lovely town, where our Candidate can give a speech." Bix wouldn't call it a rally, and he definitely wouldn't tell the mayor how important it was to the campaign, although the mayor already knew.

"Yah ah natural diplomat," Bacon said.

"Nothing natural about it, Mr. Mayor," Bix deadpanned.

Bacon laughed out loud. "Do ya have enneh place in mahnd?"

"I'd like to look at the College of Scepter first. I saw a picture of the administration building, which says 'Scepter' right on it, and it has a quadrangle in front of it. I'd like to ask for your help."

"Ah know the prezdent of the college," Bacon said.

"I thought you might."

"Let's go there now. Ah'll drahve," the mayor announced. Bix was surprised.

"Perfect," Bix said. It was, sort of, but the mayor would have his finger in it and Bix doubted the man had good finger hygiene.

The mayor led them outside and Bix was invited to ride over in the mayor's official car, a robin's-egg blue 1970s vintage Cadillac Fleetwood with a white vinyl top. Bacon plopped his ample girth behind the wheel, leaned over and opened the glove box, grabbed an electronic device and stuck it onto the center of the dashboard and turned it on.

Bix didn't ask. He found a seat belt after some effort, a lap belt, plugged it in and pulled it snug.

They drove around to the front of City Hall, where Mike and Freeway fell in behind and the three-car motorcade chugged ahead, slowly at the beginning. Soon the mayor was moving along smartly, just a little faster than the speed limit at first, but enough to cause concern through the better-populated areas of town where there were street lights almost every other block and tidy little two- and three-story red brick buildings to obstruct the line of sight at every corner.

The mayor turned to Bix and tapped the device on the dashboard. "Watch this," he said. "It changes the lights to green."

Bix watched as the street lights magically changed from red to green as the car entered each block, and he began to see cars traveling on the intersecting streets screeching to a stop as *their* lights changed from green to red after only brief seconds. As the population density dropped the mayor's speed increased and the space between his car and the streetlights as they changed to green shortened to the point of being dangerously close, and Bix's sphincter muscle was getting a healthy work out. They careened around one corner and Bix looked back at Mike and Henry trying to keep up, and the look on their faces was priceless, assuming abject fear can't be purchased. Bix thought this would be a stupid way to die.

Bix could see that the Mayor had switched intimidation tactics. When Bacon couldn't play hard-ass, he had decided to play Lyndon Johnson, riding around the LBJ ranch at eighty miles an hour in an open El Dorado convertible with a group of terrified ranch guests, and Bix was playing the part of Hubert Humphrey wearing a ten-gallon hat.

"We got this d've vice fuh the police and fiah depahtment," Bacon said.

"But don't they have sirens on their vehicles?" Bix asked.

"I thaht that would be too ostentatious. Evr'yone knows ma cah. If thah's an emehgency they get outa ma way." He sounded like every actor who ever played a small town southern mayor in every movie that had one, and in every movie, the small town mayor was corrupt. Bix tried to guard against stereotyping, but these were powerful stimuli.

Bix's cell phone rang. It was Mike, and if Mike thought it was important to call at that moment, Bix thought he should answer it. "Yes, Mike."

"Where the hell are we going? This isn't the way to the college."

Bix turned to the mayor. "Mike wants to know where the hell we're going."

"Ah thaht we'd drav past thuh senia centa that ah was talkin' about, it's on thuh way."

"Mike, did you hear that?" Bix asked.

"Yes, I heard it. So he's kidnapping us."

"Yes Mike, he's kidnapping us." He said it loud enough for the mayor to hear clearly.

"No, no, no. We'll jest drav by. We're goin' to the college.I just want ta show you whea the senio centa is in relation tuh thuh college."

Bix decided to hold out a carrot. "Mr. Mayor, I promise to go look at it after we've found a site for the rally. Then I can let Mike and Kate go do their jobs. And sooner or later you're gonna want to slow down anyway so I can see the place, so why don't we do it now in preparation."

Bacon just smiled and held his cigar tightly between his teeth as he barreled through light after light. He did slow down considerably when they drove past the Eugene V. Bacon Activity Center and Swimming Pool complex on the north side of town, but he didn't stop, true to his word. The place was attractive; it could have worked as a venue for several different kinds of events, just not Bix's event. *Too bad The Candidate won't see it this trip.*

"Mr. Mayor, you have every reason to be proud of it," he said. "It's a great building, it's serving the community and it's beautiful. I'll report that to headquarters."

"It's a great lookin' place, idn't it?" Bacon said.

In the next moment Bacon's conversation altered direction and shot off at an obtuse angle like a UFO in the night sky. "Do yah know a laydah bah thuh name of Storeh Tollah?"

"Storie Toller?" Bix asked. He wanted to confirm that there might have actually been a person whose name was Storeh Tollah.

"Thas correct."

"Yes, Mr. Mayor, I do. The Democratic party is a small universe, but not highly evolved."

"She's the depuddy national field directa fa yuh Opponent."

"That's what I understand."

"She's vera good at huh job."

"That's what I understand." Bix also understood what the mayor was really telling him.

"She's smart, like you," Bacon said. "She was in Chaaleston a month ago to meet with local political leadas and I couldn't make it to the meetin', so she took huh time to drahve all the way out heah to Scepter ta meet with me, which I vera much appreciated." Mayor Bacon was in full flower. "She spent a good paht a' the day heah and I showed huh Sceptah. She's vera pretta, and she's pretta young, but not like all those *neophytes* I have to deal with all the time. "

"I think she's been around for a while," Bix said.

"She uses huh Midwest chahm to buffa what Ah considah ta be an *encyclopedic* knowledge of pahty politics, and Ah bet anathing she *is* relentless. You must know that she will make yuh Opponent moh fomidable. Miss Tollah has been workin' South Carolina pretta hard. She has a lot of thuh Democratic leadaship sewed-up."

"Including you, Mr. Mayor?"

"Ah have made it clea that Ah will remain neutral in this prahmary. Ma concehns are foa the citizens of Sceptah County, and I will provahde any and all candidates in thuh Dem'cratic prahmary with all of thuh kuttesies and resohces that ma office has to offah, and Ah will let the citizens decahde with theah voices and votes."

This was a character out of a Faulkner novel, and Bix was enthralled. "I appreciate that, Mr. Mayor."

Bacon then embarked on another line of conversation, his impressions of the campaign's RFD. "Who is that *neophyte* ya'll have runnin' ya Regional office in Chahston, that Mista Shaunesy?" He snarled when he said it. "That po New Yahk boy don't know his butt from his button holes. I wouldn't trust him to wash my spats."

"I haven't met him yet. You still wear spats?"

"It's a metaphoa son, a metaphoa. That New Yalk boy is not doin' yua campaign ana good around hea. But I have to tellya that Miss Tollah is achievin' good results for yuh Opponent hea in Sceptah County. She wuks vera hahd and she's *vera* pretta." It sounded both less sexist and more lascivious in a polite southern drawl.

"I heard she beats her grandmother and steals her Social Security checks and spends the money on designer clothing for her Shih Tzu," Bix said. "That's what I heard."

"Is that true?" he said, straight faced. Then he got the joke, laughed and slapped Bix on his leg. "Thaht's a good 'un."

"We're in different lines of work," Bix said. "She does Field organizing and I do Advance. My concern is the media coverage we will get *today*, and she's building an organization for election day and for early voting. Our jobs are apples and oranges, separate worlds."

"Ah was just wonderin' if you knew huh. She's shahp, and she's vera good lookin.'"

"Then I'll ignore the rumors to the contrary," Bix said.

"Storeh" clearly had Mayor Bacon sewn up and wrapped around her finger, which was to Bix the least revelatory news of the day.

After wending their way through more streets than Bix thought could possibly exist in a town the size of Scepter, the Baconmobile pulled up into a horseshoe drive on the back side of Scepter College's Administration building. Mike and Freeway had already arrived.

Bacon moved slowly to extricate himself from the car seat and Bix was out the door as quickly as he could move. "I'd like to see the front of the building first," he said without waiting for an answer. He walked quickly around toward the front as Mike, Kate, and Freeway caught up. They talked as they walked and admired the building. "Can you imagine, this was built soon after the Revolutionary War. If only it could speak to us," Bix said.

"I'll speak to you," Mike said. "That guy very nearly killed us. Did you see—a couple of times cars didn't see the light change and almost t-boned us. That's why I eventually dropped back and let you guys go ahead."

"You chose well," Bix said. "That Mayor Bacon is a scamp. We can expect him to have more surprises up his ballot box. He's definitely *not* one of our supporters. The last thing in the world I want to discuss with him at this moment is the size of the crowd we want to build, so let's keep that to ourselves. If he asks, it's his town. He knows how many people are likely to show up at noon on a Friday."

"Do you think he'll try to mess with us?" Kate asked.

"With us or on us, TBD, but my sense at the moment is that he won't do anything overt—we won't find ourselves in the Scepter County calaboose on a trumped-up charge. I kind of like the guy. He's actually fairly up-front about things, and there's a slim chance he has some respect for us. Maybe it's Freeway's grandpa that did it. At any rate, he *will not* want to make his town look bad to the national media—*but* he's not going to mind so much if *we* do."

"What can he do to us?" Mike said.

"The only subterfuge I can imagine at the moment is that he might try to suppress the size of our crowd, but I'm certain he has many hidden talents," Bix said.

"The like of which we cannot foresee," Mike said.

Freeway spoke up. "We're paratroopers, we're always surrounded. Isn't that what they say?" Every once in a while he'd throw in a military simile as dramatic haiku. He liked to compare Advance to the armed forces.

"Very romantic, Freeway, and not completely inaccurate," Mike said.

They rounded the far corner of the Admin building and walked into the quad directly in front of the columned front edifice. Bix beelined to the middle of the open space, not looking up or around until he reached his destination, at which point he raised his eyes and absorbed the entire scene. He then slowly turned around three hundred sixty degrees. It oozed South Carolina. There was even moss in the trees that bordered the expansive lawn, although they weren't palmettos.

"Mike, I agree this is perfect. And we can save a ton of money on our moss budget. It's freaking perfect. Pardon my language," Bix said.

"No offense taken," Kate said.

"I was talking to Freeway."

A giant oval grassy mound edged with an ancient two-foot high brick wall rose up directly in front of the building. "What is that, and can we build our stage and some bleachers directly on top of it?" Bix asked.

"It's the old cistern, as old as the college, and I don't know yet if we can build on it." Mike said.

"The site has great access on two sides for trucks and equipment," Bix said. "If we can put the stage on the cistern with low bleachers behind, main press riser head on, cutaway riser on left, we can provide an over-the-shoulder angle from behind The Candidate, and we need a cherry picker behind the main press riser. This will look spectacular from twenty-five feet up."

"The press will love this," Kate said. "It reeks character, a sense of place."

"We can put the mag's outside the main gate, stick our VIP section in front of the cutaway, and funnel our crowd along the perimeters of the site," Bix said.

"We can fit twenty thousand in the cutaway angle alone," Mike said. "What do you want the vertical banners to say?"

Kate laughed. "So you're going do your trademark enormous vertical banners?"

"That's why they built this building, isn't it?" said Bix. "I don't know what they'll say yet, if anything. I'm thinking generic symbolic imagery."

At that moment, they spotted President Gerta Gilliman storming down the outside Palladian staircase that curved down from the second floor portico, with Mayor Bacon puffing along behind. Grim countenance carried her swiftly along the seventy-five yards across the lawn to her destination—Bix's face. Large, square, thick-lensed glasses rested on her fleshy nose, giving her eyes the appearance of arriving several feet ahead of her head. It was obvious that Southern fried food agreed with her.

"This is my campus. You should talk to me before you start making any plans," she said sharply, with no discernable accent. She obviously wasn't from around these parts or any parts south of the Mason-Dixon.

"President Gilliman, it's so good to meet you." Bix smiled and reached out his hand and she reciprocated out of reflex. "We wanted to view this lovely scene before we took up any of your valuable time, just in case for some reason it wasn't as perfect as we thought it might be, but it is. The national press would love this."

Gilliman softened slightly. "Thank you. We should sit down before you go any further. I want to find out what you want to do here."

Talking ceased, Gilliman's face tightened once more and she led the troop back across the lawn and up to her office, the walls of which were lined with pictures of Gilliman posing with B-list famous people, including several Republican office holders, no Democrats. A Presidential certificate appointing Gerta Gilliman, PhD, to the Federal Commission on Maritime Mining hung among the photos. It was dated 2005, a bad year for presidential appointments.

"So tell me what you're doing here," she said. "And let me add that you made a big mistake coming on to my campus without telling me first."

Bix stopped and looked at her. "This *is* us telling you first, Doctor Gilliman. I certainly haven't told anyone else other than the Mayor, but as I explained I wanted to see the area of your campus that appealed so much to Mike and me when we saw it on-line. There can be a thousand logistical reasons why a possible site might not work as a location for a speech, *despite* its beauty. I didn't want to waste *your* time discussing the subject if the campus was simply inappropriate for our logistics." Bix wanted to establish that there was a precedent. "You've probably had politicians on campus to speak to the students. This is just another one of those, although we bring national and international press with us and therefore, as we say, we bring the world."

Kate leaned over the Mike. "I've never heard us say that."

Mike whispered back, "We do now."

"Not coincidentally," Bix continued, "it's a great thing for your students to see."

"I would have to get this cleared through my Board of Regents," Gilliman said. "We've never had a presidential candidate speak here in the three years I've been president. We don't like to get involved in politics."

Bix reminded himself that snarkiness would get him nothing, but he couldn't contain it. "Unless my math is wrong, I don't think we've had that many presidential elections in the past three years."

She stuttered a bit. "Yes, well, that's true. But you know what I mean. "I'm beginning to," he said.These kinds of things stir up controversy, and I'm concerned about violence."

"Violence?" The word discharged from his mouth faster than he could control it. "People come to these things for a good time, and there will be more cops here than you can shake a stick at, not that I'm suggesting you'd shake a stick at a cop. It'll be the most secure place on the face of the planet! There's *never* any violence. This isn't Berkeley, and it isn't the 1960s."

Mike looked at him. "You probably Advanced that."

"Good times, great press," Bix said. He took another breath and regained his diplomatic footing. "Madam President, I hate people who say things like this, and I apologize in advance, but time is short, so I'm going say it. I have done hundreds of these events at colleges over the past thirty years and they have always turned out well, the schools always look good on TV and in the newspapers, everyone has a good time and everybody is happy afterward. Colleges and universities, even high schools all over the country and throughout the world *universally* agree to allow major presidential candidates to speak at their institutions. The point is that the school is simply providing a forum, serving as a marketplace of ideas. It means you're open to any of the major candidates who ask if they can speak here, and, if, by chance, a major Republican presidential candidate asks…you won't be in a position where you have to say no. Everyone is welcome." He was tapping his last reserves of subtlety and scraping bottom.

"You make a good pawnt Bix," the mayor interjected. "Prezdent Gilliman, as a memba of thuh Boad of Regents, Ah can say that as long as weah fay-uh about it, thah should be no problem with allowin' ana majah presidential candidate ta speak hea if they ask. It's a good oppohtunity foa thuh students, and it's good pee ah foa thuh college."

Bix could have kissed the guy. He looked at Bacon. Bacon looked at him. Being a bit slaphappy from lack of sleep, his ability to self-censor diminished, Bix was momentarily whelmed, not overly, with the feeling of brotherly affection. "Mr. Mayor," he deadpanned, "did I mention that I think you're the best mayor in the entire country?"

The mayor belly-laughed. "You ah a pistol, son."

"President Gilliman," Bix said, "I promise you that your college will look not just good but great in the national media, and I will do everything to make that happen. You have my word. The publicity value to your college—before, during and after the event—is worth tens of thousands of dollars, if not hundreds of thousands." He spoke from his pea-sized heart. "To be honest, I kind of need to know now whether we can do this or not." He avoided calling it a rally, and he steadfastly avoided any mention of crowd size.

"How many people do you expect to bring on my campus?" Gilliman asked.

There it was. Crap, he thought. "Well, we would hope that most of your student body will attend, but you would be a better judge of that. You've got fifty-five hundred graduate and undergraduate students." Bix wanted her to know he'd done his homework. "So maybe four thousand of those I'm guessing, and I can only guess how many general public would want to come at noon on a work day. People have to dedicate at least three hours to stand in line and go through the magnetometers then watch the speech. It's a long time."

"You think maybe another three or four thousand?" she pressed.

"I really can't predict. Naturally we'd love it if a million people showed up, but I don't think that will be the case. The mayor is a more reliable source than I on that topic."

Gilliman counter-offered. "We could have your Candidate speak as part of our convocation series, and do it in our auditorium."

"That's very kind, but how many people can your auditorium hold?" Bix asked. He knew the answer. God bless the World Wide Web.

"I think it will hold most of the student body," she said.

Mike leaned forward, raised his index finger and spoke up quietly, "It's a twenty-five-hundred-person, fixed-seat venue, and then we would have to take up a lot of room with press."

"Don't you love the internets," Bix said, looking at Gilliman.

Gilliman was stuck. "So you want to do this in front of my administration building?"

"Yes ma'am. If the cistern will take the load we'll put the stage right on top of it." Again, he made no mention of accessories and accoutrements, such as several sets of tall bleachers to enhance the visuals, banners, placards, bunting and miles of bike rack. "We'd put the main press riser directly facing the main stage so most of the press would be shooting at your signature building, and we'll position The Candidate far in front of the building for visual perspective, that way most of it will be seen on television. We will credential your college videographer and a still photographer and they can stand on the press riser. I guarantee you will use those images, *and* the press coverage, for years to come."

He had her flatfooted.

"What'schall think, Gerta?" the mayor asked.

"I think the board needs to be told," she said. "Does your campaign have insurance?"

"Yes ma'am. We can fax you an insurance rider that names the College of Scepter as co-insured. And I need to pay a rental fee for the space and time we're using, which will hopefully be nominal, so we are legally responsible for the space." Bix's definition of "legally responsible" meant he could establish a "First Amendment Zone," actually a pen, for protestors, somewhere off-site, closer to Cleveland.

"I'll have to let you know after I talk to the Board of Regents," she said.

There was no method of determining whether her tepid response was evidence of decision-phobia or Democrat-phobia. Based on the evidence staring at him from her wall of shame, Bix knew she had no political-phobia.

"President Gilliman, you'll forgive my concern, but this event is scheduled for Friday at noon, I have two-and-a-half days to pull it together and I need to find a site if for no other reason than out of courtesy to the Secret Service." Republicans couldn't resist that line of reasoning; he played the *law enforcement* card. "They are waiting to begin all of their preparations based on the site that I choose."

"Gerta, this is good fah the school and good fah Sceptah," the mayor was taking a strong advocacy position and would no doubt expect recompense. "*Ah'll* talk with the boad."

"I see your point. I suppose we could do it. You must assure me you won't leave my campus a mess," Gilliman said.

"Mike will have plenty of trash receptacles, port-a-potties and a clean-up crew," Bix assured her. "Your campus will remain bucolic, your board will have V.I.P. seats and we will take good care of you and your campus." He consciously mentioned "your campus" again in deference to her need for ownership, and then decided to do it again for punctuation. "*Your* campus will be lauded for its uncommon beauty and historicity, and I'll bet *your* campus will even see a spike in interest from college applicants."

"OK, I will approve it, barring any negative feedback from the Board," Gilliman said.

"We are very grateful, ma'am, and I want no misunderstandings. The moment I leave your office I will contact my office and tell them you have agreed to let us use your campus, and they are going to tell me they need to see a signed agreement with your college for the use of the space and any fee that we'll need to pay. Then I will call my Secret Service counterpart, Special Agent Shane Emory, and tell him that we have a site, at which time he will deploy his agents who will descend on you like a swarm of polite locusts. Are you all right with that?"

"Mayor Bacon, if you speak for the board, then I'm all right with it," Gilliman said.

"Thank you, President Gilliman," Bix said. "Mike Pitcher here will be in charge of the site from our staff, and soon you will meet Special Agent Emory, who is my counterpart from the Secret Service. Now, if you don't mind, we'll spend a few minutes walking around the site now to fine-tune our logistics, and naturally we'd like you to greet the senator when he arrives here on Friday."

"I will be happy to," Gilliman said.

"You and the mayor are welcome to come outside and walk around with us," Bix said. "We have to figure out precisely where we want to place all the nuts and bolts, because I want to have a well-thought-out concept when we meet with the Secret Service." He was pleased to find another opportunity to speak the words "Secret Service" again.

If Gilliman had heard the words "site diagram," her next request would have been "I want a copy." He had learned the hard lesson in his first presidential campaign: "Never share the site diagram with anyone except the team and the Service." The visual stimulation sets off a chain reaction, a powerful process that begins with small dreams and ends in explosively bigger dreams, with the inevitable fallout: critiques, wish lists, or demand lists. Bix preferred to delay the inevitable as long as possible, or at least not provide additional food for thought.

"Thank ya fuh th'invitashun," Bacon said, "but Ah'll be getting' back to ma office. Bix, let's you and Ah talk lata this evening about th' remainda of yuah schedule." It was clear that Bacon wouldn't let Bix forget the favor nor the debt that Bix owed.

Gilliman, satisfied for the time being, also politely refused the invitation for a walk-thru. "You and your staff go ahead, but keep me informed about what you're doing. I'm sure we'll be talking regularly."

"I look forward to it," Bix said, hoping it sounded authentic.

Both Gilliman and the mayor politely refused the invitation for the walkabout. As they rose to leave, Gilliman asked bluntly, "So what kind of name is Bix?"

"It's a nickname," Bix said, grinning.

"What kind of nickname is that? Is your first name Bixby or something?"

"No, ma'am. My father said that when I was a baby my crying sounded like a trumpet. And he was a fan of Bix Beiderbecke."

"Who?" she asked.

"Bix Beiderbecke. He was a trumpet player in the jazz era."

"Never heard of him," she announced proudly. "So do you play the trumpet?"

"No ma'am. The cimbalom."

"The what?"

"The cimbalom. It's sort of a dulcimer that you hammer," Bix said. "It's from Hungary."

"Never heard of it."

"It's a country in Eastern Europe. Just joined the NATO Alliance in nineteen-ninety-nine."

"No, I mean the instrument." She was serious.

"It's gaining in popularity," Bix said as he walked to the door then stopped to look back at Gilliman. "Just one thing." He decided to it was the time to push his luck. As we looked up at your beautiful building, it occurred to us that we could hang some very dramatic long banners and create a really unique visual. Something very tasteful—completely non-political. I have an idea for something you could use later in your marketing as well."

"Let me see what you have in mind. We can't put up anything political," she said.

"Yes m'am, I understand."

As Bix led his team out onto the campus lawn, Kate noted their success. "When Gerta goose-stepped down here to confront us I thought it was all over, and when she force-marched all of us into her office I *knew* it was all over. Then when you told her she was an idiot for saying they hadn't hosted any presidential candidates, I thought she might pull a Lugar out of her desk and plug us all. But that's exactly what she wanted to hear."

"It was the mayor. He sealed the deal," Bix said.

"And what the hell is a cimbalom? Do you really play such a thing?"

"As I said, it's a hammered dulcimer. I saw one played at a concert of Hungarian folk music once, so yes, you could say I'm a virtuoso. I wanted to give her something else to say she never heard of. It's rare to see an academic so proudly declare ignorance. Thank goodness for the mayor."

"No, Bix, dude, you overwhelmed her," Freeway said. "She attacked and you stood your ground, then you snuck-up on her flanks. It was like, improvise, adapt and overcome."

"That's a creative analysis Freeway, but don't repeat it to anyone," Bix said.

"I noticed you didn't mention that we're going to shut down her campus for most of Friday," Mike said. "She doesn't have a clue what's about to hit her."

Kate sounded a note of caution despite her lack patience with local big shots. "Let's be sure we tread lightly here. We need to turn up the heat as slowly as possible so by the time the water is boiling it will be too late for them to jump out of the pan."

"Did you just equate our local hosts with amphibians?" Mike asked.

"Yes, but in a good way."

Team Charleston/Scepter walked the grounds for another fifteen minutes, creating Draft I of the site diagram and coming to grips with the grand vision.

"What do the banners say, and are we putting up three or five?" Mike asked.

Bix just looked at him.

"I guess that means five," Mike observed. "It looks like we have about forty feet of height to play with."

"President Gilliman is going to crap if we try to put up anything that might cause a controversy," Kate said. "Maybe they should just be generic red, white, and blue swirling flag-ish looking banners like we did in Baltimore."

"Keep in mind," Bix said, 'we're in South Carolina and you're talking about red, white, and blue *American* flag-ish representations. Given the circumstances, the fact that our candidate isn't the whitest looking Yankee they've seen run for president, it might be looked upon negatively by some of our Southern brethren. It's not *their* imagery, unless they see hippies burning it, in which case they'll defend it by beating the hell out of 'em."

"Good point. What are the alternatives?" Kate said.

"We almost can't *say* anything that won't be inappropriate on some level," said Bix. "So how about we make the banners solid blocks of different colors? Nothing controversial there—we could say it's a tribute to Mark Rothko."

"That's fantastic!" Kate said. "It's got style and culture. I vote for that one. We can *not* put up generic Confederate flag-ish looking banners."

"What would you think about flying five banners," Bix suggested, "with the four to the right depicting forty-foot palmetto trees, and the fifth banner, on the far left, showing a crescent moon in the upper quarter—all in off-white against an indigo blue background. Just like the state flag. It screams South Carolina, but tastefully."

"I love it," Kate said. "The press will love it too. It will force them to take the widest possible shot, and I get to call the fifth one the Rothko banner."

"Let's do it," Mike said. "It will look dramatic as hell on TV. Now we need to find a banner-maker who can produce them in less than thirty-six hours. We'll need to hang them late Thursday night. I'll keep looking."

The gaggle of strangers began to draw the attention of some students, several of whom finally approached the Advance team as they were about to leave. One of them, a young woman wearing a tatty white tee shirt, dark tweed sport coat, black short shorts, black leggings and platform sneakers, took the lead. Bix turned to Mike and whispered, "These *have* to be Young Democrats."

She approached Kate. "Are you guys with one of the presidential campaigns?"

"Yes we are," Kate answered. "Are you all interested politics?"

"We're with the college Young Democrats and we were wondering if you were thinking about doing something on campus. We'd love to help."

Bix told them they were more than welcome to volunteer, that they were now his favorite people on the planet, and that the whole thing was hush hush. He raised his voice to address them all. "It's wonderful to meet you, and whatever you do, please do not tell anyone about this. You're the first to know about it and it has not been announced publicly. And if you *do* tell anyone about this please don't mention that it will be a public event, and please don't send any emails to people you do not trust to pass them along to others, or to friends in the media, or the entire student body of the College of Scepter. If this gets out we're likely to have a huge crowd on our hands, and it might turn into a rally. It is just a rumor at this point and I trust you to act appropriately. If we end up with an enormous crowd I will hold you responsible and force you to work your butts off throughout the event, then make you meet The Candidate so he can berate you personally. Understand?"

The six students jumped up and down and hugged each other.

"I think they understand, Bix," Kate said.

The team moved on, but Freeway tagged along only after he tarried to talk with one of the female students a while longer. Freeway quickly rejoined his team. "You didn't see that," he told Bix.

"I didn't, but Kate did. She takes notes."

"Don't worry about it, Freeway," Kate said. "I only use it for blackmail. Purely profit incentive, nothing political. You've got no problem as long as you can pay."

"I have only the most honorable intentions. You guys know I'm a gentleman," Freeway said. "I'm just a soul whose intentions are good."

"Despite the pithy Animals reference," said Bix, "may I remind you sir that you have a tradition to uphold, and if you're not willing to act in a completely despicable manner we can still get another Motorcade Advance. Now get in the car and drive. I don't even want to look at your face. Kate, let us sit in the back seat where we can do our work in private without the disturbing wholesomeness of this *gentleman*."

"Really, Bix, where do you find these guys?" Kate said as she got in the back seat. "You seem to have a penchant for people with ethics. How do you expect to accomplish anything?"

"Indeed," Bix said. "It's as if 'ethical' has become the new radical extremist counter-culture form of protest. In the seventies we dressed like slobs, grew long hair and mustaches, those of us who could anyway, and rolled over guys like Mayor Bacon without a thought…very counter culture. Now that the politics has devolved into an especially *nasty* version of Cutthroat Island, the only way to protest is to act ethically. It's radical."

"That's OK," Freeway said from up front. "I'm willing to work harder at my debauchery."

Bix patted him on the shoulder. "Just drive, for now," he said.

9

Peem talked by phone with The Candidate three times before 3 p.m. to discuss Jamir and the South Carolina situation. Each time they seemed to raise one another's stress level a notch, as many of the questions Peem was asked had no answers and many of The Candidate's concerns had no basis in fact. Being stressed was unfamiliar emotional territory for both, and each handled it in his own way. The Candidate became more sullen and Zen. Peem became more animated. At 4 p.m. the phone on Peem's desk, the direct landline, rang again, and he saw an unfamiliar number with a Las Vegas area code. He assumed it was the number for a Holding Room phone along The Candidate's scheduled path that day. He quickly checked his copy of the daily schedule and found it listed. As a former Field organizer, he imagined himself flipping the electronic switch under the top left drawer of his desk and lowering the dome of silence.

"This is Bob."

"Hi, Bob," said The Candidate. "I've got a minute in between events. Is there anything new?"

"No boss. Our people are still looking for Jamir, and Bix still hasn't reported any results in South Carolina." Peem was beginning to sweat out some of the garlic he'd had on his Chinese take-out lunch. "I'm beginning to think that there's no other explanation for Parviz's disappearance than he has something to be embarrassed about. I think he *jimmied* something up with your name on it to impress his students and now it's coming back to haunt him. I don't know. Why else would he vanish?" He squealed the word "jimmied" as if he'd been poked in an uncomfortable place when he said it.

"You may be right. I hope not, but I've seen some people I thought were friends do some strange things during this campaign. Nothing would surprise me."

"You're right," Peem agreed. "As we've seen, there's no way to predict the bullshit that people will pull." In his mind he'd already condemned Parviz to the junkheap of unavoidable bad PR, the severity of which was the only outstanding issue. "We need to be prepared to respond on Friday when O'Malley throws his best punch. Our problem is that it will be late on Friday afternoon and no one will see our response except on MSNBC, and Max News could ride the story for several days."

The Candidate grew quieter. "Is this about the other day with O'Malley?" Then his voice rose. "Is he pissed that he was frozen out and didn't get a quote?"

"I think that was a symptom and not the cause," Peem said in a rare nod to cogent analysis, but he couldn't help himself. "But Bix didn't do us any favors with that stunt of his."

"I don't know what his options were. It was O'Malley who hit Merle. Bix didn't make him do that."

Peem backed away for the moment. The time wasn't ripe for a bash Bix moment. "That's true. And if Bix finds Parviz and neutralizes the threat he poses, then it won't have made any difference."

"Is he going to find Jamir?" It wasn't the first time The Candidate had asked him the question.

"We hope so. We think he's the best chance at this point. I'm sending Sophie down there to help him and keep an eye on things."

"I suppose that's a good idea. It will help to have Sophie's eyes and ears on the ground."

"Yeah," Peem said, "to watch Bix."

"What do you think he's gonna do, Bob?"

"I don't know. That's why I sent Sophie to keep an eye on him."

The next President of the United States didn't respond. Peem took it as an approval.

* * *

Once Bix and Kate pulled out their BlackBerrys, it was total immersion. Dozens of emails awaited them. Among the onslaught from various offices at headquarters and a few more from his friends who might have known Jamir Parviz's whereabouts, Bix searched for a response from Hani Al-Saleem, Jamir's brother-in-law. He found none, and still no response of any kind from Shaunesy, the Regional Field Director, which was, by that time, odd.

He emailed Special Agent Emory. In most cases he would have waited until headquarters officially signed-off on a site before giving his Secret Service counterpart the heads-up, just in case headquarters said no. He didn't want to send agents off on wild goose chases, and often he wasn't ready to inflict a horde of dour law enforcement officials in dark suits upon his unsuspecting hosts. But with the power he had to unleash a small army of Special Agents, who would probably tote along a couple of uniformed state highway patrol officers for good measure, Bix felt that an armed onslaught at that moment would be just the thing to seal the deal with President Gilliman.

"Shane, I'm confident the rally site will be the College of Scepter, in front of Admin building. HQ has not approved yet, but I think it's a go. See you at countdown." He gave the same message to Alecia Fortunati, the Scheduling Desk; Egan, director of Advance; and Sophie.

Freeway dropped off the team at the Hotel Marianne and as they walked into the lobby, the grand room reminded of the old Guthrie Hotel in Savannah, ornate but subdued, with tall ceilings supported by long thin columns topped with robust ionic capitals. It was tastefully decorated, an ever-present reminder of how much it was costing his team to live there, if only for three days. He was sensitive to the issue; once a young team member accused him of being "an expensive Lead" because he suggested the team go to Olive Garden for dinner.

Before heading their separate ways, Kate and Bix were set upon by a man who looked like Napoleon Dynamite, but with a better haircut. His upper lip was perpetually curled to hold up his glasses, which kept slipping down his nose as he loped over to them slowly.

Kate whispered "Another one?"

"Apparently," Bix said.

"Are you guys the Advance team?" the man asked.

"Are you Don Shaunesy?" Bix asked.

"Yes, yes I am. I'm the Regional Field Director."

A rational person might have assumed that if Bix knew his name he probably knew his title, but Shaunesy was on a mission.

"Hello Don, it's nice to meet you. This is Kate and I'm Bix. I was wondering when I would hear from you."

"Well I've been very busy and I thought you'd wait to talk with me before you got started with your Advance," Shaunesy said.

"In an ideal world that would have been great, but we've been compelled to begin finding a site where The Candidate can speak because he's showing up here in about forty-eight hours, and we had a good idea where we wanted to look first."

"Well, I'm responsible for everything that goes on in this region and the next time you need to talk with one of my political contacts, I'd like you to let me know."

"Let's find a quiet place to talk for a moment," Bix said. "Kate, I know you've got a ton of press things to do, so if you need to leave, go ahead."

Kate didn't require a second invitation to jump ship.

As they looked to find a private place to talk, Bix asked, "So, how have you been enjoying Charleston?" It seemed like a question guaranteed to get a positive response.

"It sucks," said Shaunesy. "These people don't have a clue about how to do politics, and they think their town is so charming, but it just looks old. I think they're all still bigots. And the food sucks."

Once they found a niche off the main lobby, Bix tried to explain his job to the constipated little fart with the curled upper lip. "As I said, in an ideal world it would be great if I could keep you informed before I talk with anyone here, but I hadn't heard from you and Headquarters has tasked me with producing a major rally in just two days. They've been keeping me updated about the political situation in the region, which I assume is coming from you, so please forgive me if I miss a few of the political niceties. I promise that Field will benefit from it. You can use this as an organizing tool."

"Well, you don't have to tell me how to do my job." He sounded more and more like Mr. Dynamite. "For one thing, I wouldn't pick Scepter. We already have that town wrapped-up. You should do this in Charleston, where there's more people. You Advance guys can't just come in here and take over. You shoulda talked to me before you started making decisions."

"And that would have been great in an ideal world, but HQ had some peculiar ideas about where they wanted me to do this event, and they were so specific that I couldn't really ignore them.

"If you believe that they've made a mistake or you have a better alternative, you have to send it up the food chain at Headquarters and have them send it back down to me to digest." Bix was thinking, "thank God for bureaucracy."

"Well, you met with the mayor without me. What was that about?" Shaunesy whinnied.

"It was about doing an event in his town. But we waxed philosophic about *many* subjects as he drove me around Scepter and he showed me all of the lovely sights, sounds, and smells that grace his bucolic village." Bix smiled at the thought of using "bucolic" twice in one day.

"You drove around with the mayor?" Shaunesy blurted.

"In his beautiful blue Cadillac Fleetwood, with the traffic light changer on the dashboard, and he did, in fact, speak of you—prominently."

"Well, we have a good relationship. He's being lobbied hard by our Opponent, but I've talked him into remaining neutral," Shaunesy said.

"Quite an achievement." Bix said. "My immediate concern is that he doesn't do anything that would compromise the integrity of our event."

"Well, I don't think he'd do that," Shaunesy said.

Bix drew upon every ounce of civility he had left. "As unlikely as it is that someone in politics might act in a self-serving way, it would be good for me to have a relationship with the man. He will certainly have an agenda of his own."

"Well, I can stay in touch with him about that. If he needs something, I think I should be the one that interacts with him."

"I think so, too. But once again, I have Headquarters telling me to do my job the way I normally do it. It's a tough position for me, but if you can get the National Field Director to tell the Director of Advance to make you the Advance team's liaison with local officials, and get my boss to agree, I'm happy to have that off my plate," Bix said. He wondered if Shaunesy was going to say "well" again.

"Well, I wasn't talking about all that. This is just about Mayor Bacon."

"Well, then," Bix said. "Well, well, well. Well, I will keep you informed about key aspects of the trip, and let you know where you need to be on game day. It's likely that you'll get to choose a few people to greet on arrival somewhere. If you really want to help, we could use some space in your Scepter Field office to serve as a meeting point for our volunteers. I understand you've got a lot of room there."

"Well, uh, I dunno. That's gonna disrupt their activities."

"Don, here's the thing. We need a location from which we can work in Scepter. It's either our own local Field office or I go back to Mayor Bacon and ask him if he has any space we can use for a few days. My guess is he can find someplace appropriate if I ask, but I know what Headquarters will say about that, if you have space you won't allow us to use. It's up to you."

"Well, just make sure you don't take any of the volunteers we have working in Field operations," Shaunesy said.

"Don, you realize of course that you can identify *dozens* of new volunteers and *hundreds* or *thousands* of new supporters with this event as your organizing platform?" He emphasized metrics, thinking Shaunesy might respond to that perspective, but he had lost hope. "We'll do our best to help you and your staff take advantage of that. But now, as much as I would love to stick around, that would prevent me from leaving. How about if we meet at your office early tomorrow? Ten a.m.? That will give me some time to get organized tonight. Will you be in your office?"

"I'm not really sure at the moment. My assistant, Laura, has my schedule. She'll let you know."

"That would be most excellent, Don. Thanks for coming by to meet me. By the way, who's in charge of your Field office in Scepter?"

"Well, that's Nora Jankowsky. She's the district manager," Shaunesy said.

"Don, take my word for it. You're gonna love this. Work with us, let me know what you need to help you organize and I'll do my best to make it happen." Bix said it and he meant it.

"Well, if you need anything politically, come to me first." Shaunesy's mission to confront Bix apparently included a limited number of talking points; once he ran out he could only repeat himself.

As Bix walked away he looked back to see Shaunesy pulling out his Blackberry and beginning to type. "Let the sniping begin," he thought.

Ben Oliver walked out of the elevator just as Bix headed toward the front desk.

"Who is that guy?" Ben asked.

"That's our Regional Field Director, Mr. Shaunesy."

"He has a weird expression on his face. Is he going to be a problem?"

"A problem? Not the noun I had in mind. The mayor of Scepter and the president of the college—they will be problems. This guy? Nostradamus predicted his arrival specifically by name. It's in like the fourth quatrain, something about a 'red-haired Shaunesy spawning pestilence.'"

"What's he want?"

"What he wants most is not to let the moment pass. When he heard The Candidate was coming to town his first thought was, 'What can I get out of this?'"

"What are you going to do?"

"I'll let him have as much as I can within reason, with an eye to any point along the path where *his* benefit and the campaign's diverge, at which point the campaign's interests take precedence."

"What if he tries to screw you?"

"Then he better kiss me on the lips first."

"That's gross," Ben said. "I got a meeting room for countdown. It's the Stonewall Jackson Room on the mezzanine level and the staff office is room 725. There are a few extra keys in the room."

"Mr. Oliver, you are a great American. See you in the staff office in about a half hour," Bix said as he arrived at the front desk.

After the usual formalities, the front desk manager handed Bix his key card. "Here is your room key, sir."

It was room 723.

"Is this room attached to room 725?" Bix asked.

"Yes, sir, they are adjoining."

It was the last place Bix wanted to attempt to sleep. "Room 725 is serving as our staff office and there could be activity there at all hours of the night," Bix explained. "Usually the person on our Advance staff who is working with the hotel stays in the room next to it. Her name is Missy Ballew and she should be checking-in later this evening. Can you put me in another room, preferably on another floor?"

"The seventh floor is the one the Secret Service will secure on Thursday night," the desk manager said. "Don't you want to stay there?"

"You're right, I forgot. In that case I definitely want to be on another floor. If you've got one on the sixth floor it would be perfect."

"I will put you in the mini-suite on the sixth floor that I was going to put Miss Ballew in. You were originally supposed to have the mini-suite, but she has apparently already been in contact with the hotel manager and switched rooms," he told Bix.

Bix had to give Missy an "A" for effort, but an "F" for trying to stick her Lead in the loudest room in the hotel. A big "F." Plus an "F" for missing her flight. Bix felt he was being "F'd" to death by his RON.

Bix quickly looked at the desk manager's nametag. "Thank you, Todd. Let's switch them back, and when Miss Ballew checks-in, if she has any questions, you can refer her to me."

He walked up the six flights of stairs to his floor, entered his sumptuous digs, and was greeted with the sight of a beautiful gift basket on the dining room table with a card addressed to Missy Ballew, signed "Arhen Mondi, hotel manager." An assortment of five beers, cold somehow, surrounded a variety of fruits, cheeses, crackers, and a small salami torpedo. Bix put the beers in his refrigerator, washed his hands, grabbed a grape, and sat down on his comfy couch.

Among the new messages on his Blackberry was an email with an odd address that looked like spam. It was from Hani. "Bix my friend, it is so good to hear from you. This is my wife's email. What can I do to help you? I am traveling to Washington tomorrow and I will call when I arrive. I am happy to do whatever I can. Hani."

Several thoughts raced through Bix's mind. "Tomorrow? When? Where is he traveling from? Amman? Sheboygan? If he's coming from Amman, how long is the flight? Didn't I ask him if he knew where Jamir was or if he had a phone number? Is he incommunicado already? Crap."

He replied: "Hani, Thank you for getting back to me. Sorry to trouble you with this, but I need to find your brother-in-law Jamir as quickly as possible. If you haven't left yet, or you get this while you are traveling, please email or call me. Bix"

Bix finally opened the last in a series of emails from Peem: "Nd updat asp. fone tonite pls." Bix wondered why the man didn't have the time to type another "a" into "asap"?

He replied: "Wil cal aftr cntdwn, aftr 8 estrn."

As he did, another email from Alecia popped onto the screen, subject line, "WTF" It read "WTF did you just say to the RFD? Drule just came in here. Call me before countdown."

Bix called her immediately. "Alecia, is Drule being mean to you or me again?"

"He just stormed in here and told me that you're messing around with local politics down there and that I should warn you to not stick your nose into things. He said that's Shaunesy's responsibility down there. What did you do?"

"I met with the mayor of Scepter."

"Wasn't everyone telling you to be sure to do that before you did anything else in town? Isn't the mayor the county Democratic boss?"

"Yes, and yes. It was Politics 101."

"Then why is Drule so upset?"

"Maybe he didn't get the memo, or maybe because Shaunesy's upset and they have something a little deeper going on under the surface. Doesn't Drule understand the role of Advance?"

"He came from the Hill, so, no. He hasn't been exposed to presidential Advance in his career. He thinks our national television coverage and those huge media events just happen because The Candidate showed up. He was a state Field guy before."

"Even if I wanted to appoint that two-week wonder Shaunesy to be the team's political liaison, which I don't, we don't have the time to waste. It took him more than six hours to contact me after I emailed and called him, then he accosted me in the lobby of the hotel. He's not making a positive impression."

"I told Drule that you had to do your job the way you always do, and that everyone else seems to get along fine with you, so maybe Shaunesy was the one with the problem."

"God bless you. Seriously. That took cojones, which means some guy is walking around without a pair at this moment. I appreciate it, but I don't think you've heard the end of this. Shaunesy's likely to keep carping, and I expect he'll have *lots* of things he'll want to accomplish on this visit, so sit with your back to the wall."

"I've already turned my desk so I can see who walks in the door," Alecia said. "I'd only spoken to Drule once before, and that was just an introduction. He's been in here twice in one day and he's also not making a positive impression."

"I'm sorry you have to endure that."

"It's not your fault, don't worry about it. By the way, I just got word that the College of Scepter passed vet."

"Great. Thanks. I'll ask about when they plan to announce it to the press on our conference call, but obviously if we can send out a release tonight we can make it into the local morning papers and TV," Bix said. "Talk to you in a half hour."

Bix stuck the phone in his pants pocket and began to gather his notes for the staff meeting when the hotel phone, on a wall jack next to the bar, rang. It was 5:58 and he had a thing about being late for meetings, but it was probably the front desk calling and it would only take a minute. He answered despite his reservations.

"This is Bix."

"This is Storie."

"Storie who?" he said.

"The one you're still madly in love with."

"Could you be more specific?"

She laughed that hearty laugh he hadn't heard in more than ten years.

"The one who beats her grandmother and steals her Social Security checks. The one who isn't completely repulsed by your obnoxious and annoying presence."

"So this is the one who is only partially repulsed by my obnoxious and annoying presence. Has the honorable Mayor Bacon been sharing confidences?"

"You knew he'd tell me. I knew it was your way of saying hello."

"Hello."

"Hello."

"Where are you?" Bix asked.

"Two floors down from you. Meet me for a drink later."

"You know I don't drink."

"Then come down and watch me drink."

"That I can do."

"How about ten-thirty in the hotel bar? We can watch the results of the New Hampshire primary," she said.

"Sounds good."

"How will I recognize you?" she asked.

"I'll be the one wearing a lime green double-knit leisure suit and white patent leather shoes with a matching belt."

She laughed that laugh again. "Hot! In that case I'll be down there at ten-twenty-five. See you then."

They hung up and Bix gathered the rest of his notes, put the beer bottles back in the goody basket, and removed the note card to Missy. Then he turned on the TV picked up the hefty basket, and left for the staff office.

* * *

Cornelia and Ben were already in the makeshift office, which he expected to be empty except for some chairs. Instead there were three eight-foot tables covered in white tablecloths and a laptop computer with a printer/fax/copier attached.

"Where did all of this come from?" Bix asked.

"Cornelia got it done," Ben said.

Bix looked at her and smiled. "Thank you Cornelia. This is excellent. And because, as the old saying goes, 'no good deed goes unpunished,' Excellent. And could I ask you to print seven copies of Draft III of the schedule for the team?"

"They're sitting over there, next to the copier," Cornelia said.

"And she got a coffee maker for the room," Ben said.

Bix held out his arms. "What, no deli platter or cocktails?"

"The kitchen is delivering those in a few minutes," Cornelia laughed. "It looks like you already brought your own."

"This is from the hotel management, welcoming us to their humble establishment, Bix said, as Kate and Thigpen walked in. Everyone may feel free to partake, except for the five beers, which Kate will want all of."

"That's correct," Kate said. The rest of you can gnaw on that salami."

"Really?" Ben asked, looking heartbroken.

Thigpen reached over Kate's shoulder and grabbed a bottle from the basket. "Gimme a fucking beer." He walked around Kate and plopped in a chair, his knees sticking through the holes in his khakis.

"That's how he lost his job as the sommelier at Sans Souci," Kate said.

Mike and Freeway soon arrived, and happily for team morale, neither Cornelia nor Bix wanted a beer, which enabled everyone who wished to become impaired to do so.

They sat in a loose circle and handed out copies of the schedule. Bix opened the meeting with kudos to Cornelia for setting-up the staff office. Everyone applauded. Kate looked like a proud mother.

"Our RON Missy Ballew will be joining us later this evening, and I still don't have an ETA on JD," Bix said. "Let's work from the schedule. 'Draft Three' now shows wheels-down at 8:30 p.m. on Thursday at the Charleston Airport. It's a closed arrival, no press, no greeters. Kate, Freeway and I will be there to do site, it's a simple 'load and go,' with 9:15 p.m. arrival at the Hotel Marianne for the RON. Mike and Ben, if you're not already down at your site starting the build by that time, I'd like you to be at the hotel for arrival. "

"We can do that," Mike said.

"Kate, do you have a preference whether you do the press check-in on arrival at the hotel, or hand out the room keys on the buses?" Bix asked.

"Either one is ok with me, if you have a preference," Kate said.

"We'll talk," Bix said. "I might want you to hand out room keys on the buses."

"Are you going to get creative on me?"

"I might. Once we arrive at the hotel they're down for the night. Are there any questions so far?"

Freeway spoke up. "Thigpen, do you have leads I can call this evening to find motorcade drivers?"

"Yeah, I've got a contact with the Charleston County Democrats who can get you drivers. I'll send you his contact information," Thigpen said.

"We'll hold off on discussion of hotel preparations until Missy arrives," Bix said. "The next morning, Friday, The Candidate will probably go to the gym around seven-thirty a.m., and we depart the hotel at nine-thirty a.m., depending on drive time, en route an unknown destination for an as-yet-undefined event. Ben, have you had any luck finding any potential venues?"

"Yes, I've got two potential sites so far. One a small gym at a junior college and the other is a VFW hall."

"Can we go look at them tonight, just casually?" Bix asked.

"I think so. The VFW hall is definitely open, and we should be able to see the gym. I'm checking."

"I think the VFW hall would be a perfect venue for political reasons, but their ceilings are usually too low for our needs. We'll check them out tonight. Thigpen, any luck with finding veterans groups?"

"Yes, we've made a contact with the VFW hall's membership, and I've got a contact with a local Vietnam Vets group. We'll find a hundred-fifty bodies," Thigpen said.

Bix returned to the schedule. "After our morning event, we are scheduled to depart at eleven a.m. en route to the rally, which will be held at the College of Scepter in front of their Administration building. It's been vetted and approved by headquarters. Mike, did you have any luck finding the facilities manager and starting on a contract?"

"I should have a signed contract first thing tomorrow morning."

"Did you see any agents while you were there?" Bix asked.

"Yeah, a couple of sedans and a black Chevy Suburban rolled-up, then a state highway patrol car. I'd say about ten guys went into the Admin building," Mike said.

"Good. I'm hoping the intimidation factor will etch this thing in granite in Gilliman's mind even without a signed contract."

"Or it might scare the hell out of her and she'll renege on her commitment tonight," Mike said. "You're gonna love this, the Mayor's brother-in-law showed up."

"Chief Bud Fry?"

"The one and only."

"Did you talk with him?"

"Absolutely. I wasn't going to pass up that opportunity. I introduced myself and told him what I was doing there, and he was definitely concerned about what we were trying to accomplish. He kept asking how I was going to do it in two days, and asked a couple of times if we had 'jes desahded' to hold the event here or if we've known about it for some time and didn't tell anyone. I reassured him that campaigns always make these decisions at the last minute, unless they can wait even longer. He didn't look like he believed me."

"Did he strike you as someone we can work with?"

"He called me 'boy' a couple of times, which didn't sit well, and he looks like a bad caricature of a southern sheriff, but more rotund. He mentioned that the college sits within his 'jurisdicshun' several times, and kept saying 'we'll jes' have ta see 'bout that' every time I said anything, or 'the Mayah may have somethin' to say bout that.' And he kept eyeballin' me like I'd just stepped off a spaceship. Other than that, I'd say he'll be ok."

"We'll have to call you Klaatu from now on. He sounds like Sheriff Buford T. Justice."

"If Sheriff Buford T. Justice mated with himself, that's what you'd get, along with the usual genetic defects one might expect. He's Buford Justice squared. Naturally, he walked around looking as if owned the place, and he always kept his hand rested on his gun, which was the biggest freaking pistol I've ever seen."

"What is it about this trip!" Bix lost it for a second. "It's *nice* that people feel a sense of ownership, but its rampant here. Did all these people have deprived childhoods?"

"Let's get down to the real issue, Bix," Kate said. "You promised me there would be no assholes on this trip and I'd say so far you're batting zero."

"That's because you're a glass half empty kind of person. I would say I'm batting a thousand. They're just normal people caught up in unfamiliar territory. They're frightened and confused, and it's our job to lead them to happy land, where they will all be...happy." Bix shook his head. "Although I have to admit, for the first time in my career I'm beginning not to care whether we leave blood. Maybe we hand everyone over to Klaatu here and let him melt them with his laser eyes."

"That was Gort, the robot," Mike said. "I'll get his name check information in case we need him later."

Bix ran through the remainder of the schedule for the rally, Kate's press needs, Mike's efforts to find contractors, Thigpen's first foray into crowd building, Cornelia's first contact with the Laborer's Union in Philly, the Advance team's access to the Scepter Field office and the Field Director, Nora Jankowsky, and Freeway's flirt with Miranda, the student from the college Young Democrats. Freeway, fresh-faced and age-appropriate for the young lady, turned beet red at the mention of it.

Bix pressed on. "After countdown I'd like to look at Ben's potential sites for the event which cannot be named, and take another trip back to Scepter to see the local Field office and meet Ms. Jankowsky. Anyone else who wants to go is more than welcome, except for Mike, Ben, and Thigpen, who are required to come along."

At 6:30 they gathered around one of the tables and Bix called into the teleconference with headquarters, putting his BlackBerry on speaker.

At 6:32 Alecia, the Scheduling Desk, opened the inquisition on Team Charleston/Scepter.

"Bix, are you there?"

"Team Charleston/Scepter is here," Bix said.

"Good, then let's go through the schedule." Alecia walked through it minute by minute, asking Bix questions along the way.

Bix presented an anodyne report, all business, nothing that might spark serious questions from the assembled masses on the other end of the call. There was no way of knowing exactly who, or how many, had logged-on to the conference call, but he assumed Drule would be lurking on the line with his phone on mute.

The Scheduling office, Press office, Political office and Advance office representatives were merciful questioners during this, the first of only two conference calls that would occur during the truncated Advance. It was too early for very many questions from Headquarters staff, and Team Charleston-Scepter would have had very few answers, anyway. There would be plenty of time by Wednesday for everyone at H.Q. to think of anything they needed from the trip.

Alecia made a final point. "Bix, I have to stress how important it is that we have wheels up by two-ten p.m. on Friday. We've got a five-hour cross-country flight and he has to be in Los Angeles by four o'clock for his speech to the International Relations Council. This is a hard deadline. We can't be late."

"We understand," Bix said. "Before we wrap up, is Egan on the line?"

"I'm here," Egan said.

"You got my email about doing some radio spots," Bix said. "Given the time constraint and the fact that the rally's on a weekday at noon, we could face some real challenges in getting more than a few hundred people to show up." Bix felt a little alarmism was justified. "Send me the disclaimer and I'll produce a radio ad locally and do the time buys. I'll have them on the air by tomorrow afternoon."

Chad Cora, the young deputy Press Secretary, sputtered, "Can he do that?"

"We've never done it on this campaign," Egan said, "but they used to do it in the past. I suppose he can. "

Bix wasted no time exiting the call on a high note. "Thanks, Egan, in that case we'll follow-up with you on the particulars. We've got countdown meeting in five minutes, so if there's nothing else Team Charleston/Scepter will sign off."

"Go ahead Bix, we'll talk later," Alecia said, equally happy to let sleepy dogs lie, or at least obfuscate.

"Thanks, all." Bix said.

"You made it out of that unscathed," Mike said.

As they prepared to leave, Bix scanned the new emails that flooded his screen, searching for another contact from Hani. It was there, from a half hour before, once again from his wife's strange email address. He clicked on it as they walked down the opulent hallway to the wood paneled elevator, hopes high.

Hani wrote: "On layover in Paris. Arriving in DC Wednesday noon. Jamir and Abia rented a cabin in the middle of the state, she's writing a doctoral thesis. I don't have address but was there last summer. They don't answer their phones. I'll call you when I arrive. Hani."

"Another mystery," Bix thought. "What state, and when is he arriving?" Bix convulsed verbally, "Got dandruff and sumofit itches!" startling his elevator mates.

"Something wrong?" Kate asked.

"Oh no, the usual. Wheat futures down in the Hong Kong market."

Ben led the team to the Stonewall Jackson Room on the mezzanine level overlooking the lobby and Bix took a moment to stop at the railing to enjoy the architecture. He noticed a group of people walking beneath him and brilliantly concluded it was a television camera crew because one of the men was carrying a large professional video camera in his right hand, at knee level, with a Max News logo sticker on the side. Bix motioned to Kate to take a look. "Let's talk later," he said.

* * *

The team entered the meeting room at exactly 7:00 p.m. to find the full contingent of Secret Service Advance personnel already there. They had arrived at 6:50 because "on-time" in Secret Service parlance is ten minutes early, as compared with Republican time, which is "on time," and Democrat time, which is "any damn time we feel like showing up."

Three agents in the room who knew Bix from previous trips greeted him enthusiastically. They were young, in their thirties and forties. When Bix started doing Advance in 1976, all the agents were much older—old guys in their thirties and forties. A tall athletic young man with graying temples and a college face walked up. "Are you Bix?"

"Shane, it's good to meet you," Bix said.

"It's good to meet you too. I've heard a lot of good things."

"I just got the word that the college site has been vetted and approved," said Bix.

"Great. Any idea about the second site?"

"Do you mean for the event which shall not be named?" asked Bix. "No, but we've got a couple of possibilities. We'll take a look at them tonight after countdown."

Bix and Shane took their seats at a table in the front of the room, facing forty chairs set-up conference style, twenty on either side of a center aisle. The agents, along with two Counter Assault Team members wearing dark fatigues, occupied all but a few of the seats on the left side of the room; the staff Advance team, minus Bix, populated six on the right side. All the people on the left carried weapons. None of those on the other side did, except for Bix, who, according to Mike when they discussed the meeting later, carried his rapier wit wherever he went.

Bix opened the meeting by asking everyone to introduce themselves. The agents spoke up row by row with their names and functions—Transportation, I.D., Airport, RON, Counter Assault, Site—followed by the Advance team. When Henry Benton, Motorcade, introduced himself, Bix pointed out that he was also known as "Freeway."

Both Bix and Mike noted the slight man with a persimmon puss and flat-top crewcut seated in the front row. He identified himself at Kurt Rudd, site agent for Scepter College, Mike Pitcher's counterpart. He appeared to be about thirty years old and Bix could see the veins in his forehead. Bix looked at Mike; they knew what each other was thinking.

Bix went through the schedule point by point. He didn't mention that he was having creative thoughts about The Candidate's arrival at the hotel. HQ dictated that the airport arrival was "closed" due to the late hour, but they hadn't said anything about the hotel arrival.

"The next morning, Friday" Bix said,"I expect The Candidate will want to go to the gym, and I expect that Merle, our Trip Director, and you, Shane, and the Detail Leader will work out the timing Thursday night after they arrive. Am I correct?"

"Yes. We have that planned, we'll discuss timing that night," Shane said.

Bix went over the details about finding a location for sweeping the press corps' luggage, and allowing hotel employees and law enforcement to get their photos taken with The Candidate.

"I have a question," Special Agent Janice Meyer said. "I will be doing the second site. Shane told me you're looking for a small venue, possibly a hundred to two hundred people in attendance. Is that correct?"

"Yes."

"In that case, I would suggest you take a look at the Red Schoendienst Gym at Madison Junior College. It's small, and they have good parking."

Ben spoke up. "That's on our list."

"In that case, it's a great suggestion," Bix said. "Thank you. We'll go look at it tonight." It got a decent laugh.

Bix liked to be a step ahead of the Service, whenever possible, because it imbued the Advance team with the appearance of competence. "Moving on with the schedule, at this time we have departure from Site One at 11:15 a.m. en route The College of Scepter. At the moment I'm assuming a half hour drive time, although that's TBD, and I have arrive at 11:45. The college president and some local politicos will greet, and we will find a location indoors to do that. Any questions so far?"

Special Agent Rudd raised his hand. "I've been to the college this afternoon," he said, "and I would recommend not using it as the location for the rally."

Several of Rudd's fellow agents looked at him quizzically. Bix thought maybe Agent Rudd's barber had cut a little too much off the top.

Bix looked at Shane, who seemed surprised but willing to let the Rudd continue. "Why do you say that?" Bix asked.

"Unless you do the event indoors. It's an outdoor location, and it will take a lot of assets to secure a three-hundred-sixty-degree perimeter. You probably don't understand the size footprint we have or the amount of assets we need to deploy." He was schooling Bix, who had been doing Advance since before Special Agent Rudd was a zygote, and several agents in the room knew it, so Bix thought it would be tacky to mention it. Mike looked at Bix; Bix smiled slightly and said nothing. He was interested to see how far Rudd would go.

"Besides that, the president of the college tells me that those kids don't vote, and they're mostly kids with from wealthy families so they probably vote Republican," Rudd said. "And the Chief of Police says there's a history of trouble in that area and doesn't think you should do it there. Maybe tone it down a bit."

Shane appeared a bit stunned. "So what do you think, Bix?"

Bix was amazed but refused to look it. He was also tickled but tried not to show it—this wasn't a fight that Rudd could win under any circumstance, unless he could prove Al-Qaeda dug a tunnel beneath the quadrangle. Bix remained straight faced.

"Kurt," Bix said, "You're telling me that the Chief Bud Fry, the Mayor's brother-in-law, the same mayor who supports our Opponent, is advising us to make our event smaller and move it to another part of town?"

"I didn't know he was the brother-in-law, but he did say there was a history of violence there," Rudd said.

"The Chief is absolutely correct, and 'history' is the correct word too because he's referring to the nineteen-sixties when they had civil rights demonstrations on campus. I'd be happy to go on the record about my lack of concern that civil rights demonstrations will break out on the Scepter College campus while we're there."

"But it's still an outdoor venue, and you have the weather to consider," Rudd said.

"True, but I've got a weather forecast and The Candidate's back against a huge building, which cuts down your three hundred and sixty degree perimeter to a hundred eighty degrees. And as far as the political affiliations of the student body, I think I'll take that chance too." Bix thought Rudd might shut up at that point.

"This will take a lot of assets," Rudd said. "You don't seem to be very concerned about your Candidate's safety."

"Here's the thing." Bix raised his sternness level a touch. "You haven't told me anything that will have an impact on The Candidate's safety." Then he raised it a notch higher. "You've expressed concerns

about your assets, which is basically about your access to magnetometers and extra post-standers and a Counter-Assault Team, the students'
voting record, the mayor's politics, the police chief's proclivities and
the weather. And while I am certain that both my team and I will come
to appreciate your remonstrations in the fullness of time, as I am equally
certain that your perspective is born of caution, not prejudiced by perfidy, I must cleave to the plan as we have conceived it." He looked at
Shane. "You good with that?"

Shane nodded, Rudd looked confused and the Advance team smiled,
as did a few of the agents.

Mike leaned over to Kate, "Perfidy?" he asked in a whisper.

"Perfidy," she whispered back.

"Villainous perfidy?" he asked.

"Is there any other kind?"

"Let's move on in the schedule," Bix said. "At eleven-forty-five
a.m. we arrive, do a short greeting line then go to Hold. I'll get you the
names of the greeters ASAP. We are in Hold for ten minutes while the
national press sets up, then we move to the speech site. We all good so
far? Any questions?"

Rudd spoke again. "What are you going do about any demonstrators
who show up? You know we can't help you there."

"We know that, Kurt; we'd never put you in such a position. We'll
set up a First Amendment Zone outside the secure perimeter for those
who want to demonstrate, as we always do. And we'll hire our own
muscle with cattle prods and attack dogs. Thank you for reminding me.
Mike, be sure to get some quotes on thug contractors." Bix didn't smile
when he said it.

"We have an hour on the schedule for The Candidate's speech and
working the rope line," Bix continued. "We are expecting a crowd up-
wards of thirty-five thousand, so he will take some time to shake hands
afterward. Then we go back to Hold for a half hour so the press can file,
and we'll do lunch while we're there. Any questions?" Bix and everyone on the Advance team looked at Rudd, who remained silent.

"Good. We will also need to feed the press lunch after the speech,
and arrange the logistics of said food, just so you're aware of that," he

said to Shane and Rudd. "The motorcade is scheduled to depart at thirteen-thirty en route for the Charleston Airport. Once we arrive at the airport at fourteen hundred hours, it's a simple load and go, no greeters for departure, with wheels-up scheduled for fourteen-ten. Any questions?"

Special Agent Gus Burnett, another friend of Bix's who was serving as I.D. agent, spoke up. "Are you thinking about any OTRs?" He knew Bix's tendency to become inspired when unforeseen opportunities presented themselves. "I know how much you enjoy Off-The-Record movements, and Charleston is a lovely place to go site-seeing at the spur of the moment."

"Why, Special Agent Burnett, whatever do you mean?" Bix said, emphasizing his rising inflection. "You know I am a strict adherent to the schedule as written. If it isn't on the page, it isn't on the stage."

Burnett laughed. "Right, and you've got some costume jewelry you'd like to sell me. So, no OTRs?"

"Headquarters has said absolutely nothing about any OTRs, and I don't believe we have any time on our schedule on Friday to even contemplate it."

"I agree, but what about Thursday?" Burnett noticed the specificity of Bix's answer, and he wasn't stupid.

"My plan is to take The Candidate directly from wheels-down to the Hotel Marianne with no stops in between, and I promise not to deviate from that."

What Bix was contemplating wasn't really an OTR so much as a spontaneous gathering of supporters. The Candidate wouldn't have to go anywhere—Bix was thinking about bringing the crowd to him.

"Just thought I'd ask," Burnett said.

Shane ended the countdown meeting with a boilerplate admonition, aimed at the Advance team, about operational security. "A reminder about 'Op-Sec': please don't leave classified materials such as old drafts of the schedule lying around in your hotel room or in the staff office. If you want to throw away old schedules, feel free to use the shredder in our command post. And be careful who is around you when you're discussing details of the trip on your cell phone. If something seems suspicious to you don't hestitate to voice your concern with us."

They ended the meeting and Shane leaned over to Bix. "I'll talk to Kurt. It's his first time as a Site 1."

"I'd appreciate that," said Bix.

Bix and Mike made a point of shaking hands with Rudd before they left. At five feet six inches, the stubble of Rudd's flat top almost reached the stubble on their chins.

"Kurt," Bix said, "I realize an outdoor site is a lot more work for you guys, but we're going to need a few more hours to plan the site before we're ready to do a final walk-thru. Give us until eleven a.m. and we'll have a site diagram we can share."

"That's too late," Rudd said, his face taut. "We have a lot of arrangements we have to consider if you're not going to take this thing indoors, which I still think you should do."

Bix allowed his inner-wise guy free rein. "If I take this thing indoors, we don't achieve our political goals, and if we don't achieve our political goals, my guy isn't elected president, and if he isn't elected president, there will be no Christmas. Children will starve and the world will be thrown into turmoil. Since I don't want that to happen, I'm going to produce this rally in the quadrangle of The College of Scepter." Bix maintained a passionless mask in contrast with Rudd. "You can safely assume we will put the stage on the cistern in front of the Admin building, with the main press riser facing it about sixty feet away, with a cutaway riser on the left side as you face the stage."

"Yeah, but that doesn't tell me everything I'm going to need to know—"

Shane broke in and spoke directly to Bix. "We can get by for the time being with the information you've given us. As soon as you can finalize the logistics, please let us know."

While subtle, it was the most overt public diss Bix had ever seen one agent give another.

They all agreed to meet at the college for a walk through at 11:00 the next morning. Bix shook Rudd's hand, smiling kindly as he did it. He meant it as a slight and was certain Rudd would take it as such. The young site agent had his undies in a bunch about something, and he seemed set on an unalterable course of conflict with the Advance team whether the situation called for it or not. It was never necessary, as far as Bix was concerned. Being mean to Bix was like being mean to a puppy, in his opinion.

A few minutes later, as the Advance team walked through the lobby, Mike said, "Seriously, Bix, in the four hundred years you've been doing presidential Advance, have you ever heard anything like that?"

"Gotta admit, that was a first," Bix said. "Don't worry about him; Rudd is his own worst enemy. If he keeps saying silly stuff like that he's only going to shoot himself in the foot, in a manner of speaking. Also, in the four hundred years I've been doing this I've never heard anyone refer to the four hundred years I've been doing this and live to talk about it."

Mike looked at Kate, "Has he tried to drink your blood?"

"No. You?"

"No," he said.

"It's only 'cause I like you guys. The jury's still out on Thigpen," Bix said.

"Fuck you," Thigpen said. "I'm already one of the undead dude."

They parted ways. Kate and Cornelia returned to the staff office to write a media advisory and dive into preparations for the press and Bix took the Testosterone Squad to see the VFW Hall and Madison Junior College. Madison Junior College had the advantage in Bix's mind since he was a Cardinals fan.

* * *

Mike couldn't contain himself once they'd exited the hotel. "I've never said this about an Agent, but he's an asshole. It's like he watched an Internet video on how to be a secret agent. He thinks we're the enemy."

"When we've gone to such lengths to hide it," Bix said.

"He's gonna be a pain in the ass," said Mike.

"It's rare," said Bix, "but when it happens it helps to remember that we control the body, within the boundaries of good taste and The Candidate's desire to do whatever the hell he chooses, *we* control the body, not the Service. And they know that. The only time *they* control the body is when shots are fired, and at a moment like that we *want* them to control the body, and we want to help make it easy for them to ensure his safety. The difference is that guys like Agent Rudd ask for the sun and the moon, and we can't simply put The Candidate in a bullet-proof Plexiglas ball and roll him around like a hamster. At some point it becomes a question of who is controlling the protectee's inter- action with his environment. Is it the protectee and his staff or is it the Secret Service? Who is controlling access to the protectee? Who's con- trolling his public image? Then you get into questions about the slippery slope into a police state, yadda yadda yadda. Special Agent Rudd hasn't crossed that line, and maybe he just doesn't like us, but he was definitely showing some sort of extreme bias."

"When they've gone to such lengths to hide it," Mike said.

"Let's go by the VFW hall first to get it out of the way," Bix said. "I love VFW halls, but they're usually too small."

Freeway took the wheel while Ben navigated and Bix took up res- idence in the back seat for more electronic sleuthing. Another couple of dozen emails crowded the screen of his BlackBerry as he did his primary scan. The few from personal email accounts interested him most.

One last name he recognized on a private account was a friend he'd known since college, John Garianni, the producer at Max News whom Bix had emailed the day before. He left a New York phone number.

Bix called immediately.

"Bix," John said. "How the hell are you?"

"Personally I'm groovy. Professionally I haven't a clue. How about you? Is everything good with Mary and the family?"

"We're all good. Say, it was interesting that you should email me because your name has come up here in the newsroom at work. They know you're in South Carolina and they know why you're there."

"Why do they think I'm here?" asked Bix. *Do "they" think I'm in South Carolina for an Advance or for Manifestogate?*

"They say you've been sent there to find a man named Parviz who used to work at State, and that he's got dirt on your boss. And I've heard you're doing a rally in Scepter, too. I assumed it had been announced."

It was a fairly comprehensive intelligence report. "Do you know where they got this information?" asked Bix.

"Nope. But they've got it."

There were very few ways that Max News could have known. The Candidate's trip to Charleston and Scepter hadn't been announced to the press, much less the specific details, and Bix's undercover secret mission should never have been known by anyone outside the campaign until he wrote a roman à clef about it years later.

"What are they doing about it?"

"They're bird doggin' your trail down there and it sounds like they're keepin' a close watch. O'Malley is back in the studio today after his run-in with you guys yesterday, and I heard him mention your name. He said you'd lead us to Parviz...unless he was talking about another Bix."

"That's creepy, and yet flattering in a way. John, I can't thank you enough. Is there anything else you think I should know?"

"Yeah, watch your back."

"Thanks sir, I'll try to do that. Tell Mary I send my regards, and tell her she can send me some of her peanut butter brownies."

"She would if you'd stay in one place long enough."

If Garianni's tip explained the Max News crew's presence in the Hotel Marianne, Bix thought, it was certainly brazen. They weren't skulking in the shadows.

More emails demanded attention, including two from Peem pressuring Bix for updates. He called Peem and asked that they keep the call brief, then told Peem about Parviz's brother-in-law Hani's arrival in the U.S. the next day and the news about Max News. Bix knew that tidbit would go off like a bombshell.

It did. Peem bounced off the ceiling. "O'Malley knows about you being in Charleston to find Parviz? How the fuck did he find out about that?".

"My friend at Max doesn't know how. How many people know about this at headquarters?"

"Just me, the senior staff, Sophie, Egan, and the traveling staff. How the fuck could he find out? Who have you told?"

"I've told Mike, and I'm going to tell Kate tomorrow."

"We're screwed—we're absolutely screwed," Peem said. "Max News is starting to pound on it. We've got to do something, anything," Peem said.

"That's exactly what I plan to do, Bob, anything. I'll do some of that and get back to you tomorrow when I know anything."

"Call me in the morning," Peem said. "We've got to stop this thing in its tracks."

"Don't lose sight of the fact that I've got a thirty-thousand-person rally to produce." Bix thought it might be good moment to mention it while Peem was distracted with manifestogate.

"What do you mean, thirty-thousand? Is that possible?" Peem said.

"It better be—that's what I'm planning. You wanted an event to kick-off the last two-week push, and it's either that or a twenty-five-hundred-seat auditorium."

"We're teetering on the brink of disaster and this feels like you're pushing us closer to the edge. What are you thinking?"

"I'm thinking that we'll need some shiny object to distract the press if Manifestogate isn't resolved one way or the other and O'Malley reports the rumors alone. If the rally is unexpectedly large, and exceptionally well-produced, I might add, *it* will be the news of the day, not some right-wing putz standing in front of a camera reporting that a few students are saying bad things about our Candidate. And if the worst happens and Manifestogate blows up in our faces, a show of force is the best shot we have at overcoming the problem. Don't you agree, Bob?"

"I don't know. You just better pull this thing off. We can't look like we're pro-terrorist and overly ambitious, too. Don't fuck this thing up."

"So it's OK to be pro-terrorist as long as we're humble about it?" Bix asked.

"Huh?"

"Nothing. Thanks for the support, Bob. We'll talk tomorrow. I gotta go."

The fun continued. Next on his to-do list was an email from Shaunesy that Bix didn't want to touch, as though it were hot. Under the subject line "Advance" Shaunesy wrote, "I understand you're looking for more sites for another event. Please discuss with me before you do anything." Drule was obviously Shaunesy's mole.

"Gentlemen," Bix announced to the Advance team in the van, "Please do not under any circumstances discuss any aspects of the trip with our Regional Field Director, Mr. Shaunesy. Either he believes he should have the power of pre-approval of all our activities or he is Caligula."

"I thought it was Caligula Dynamite," Mike said.

"Good point. And Shaunesy doesn't get an 'S' pin, he doesn't go anywhere unescorted, we don't let him near the Hold on game day, and we don't put him in a room with a mirror—it's too upsetting for him. If I were you, I wouldn't let him near your livestock, either. I think he might do bad things."

He replied to Shaunesy's email: "Still developing prospects for site visits. Would love to hear if you have any recommendations."

Freeway pulled into the parking lot of VFW Post number 37 in a middle class neighborhood on the northwest side of Charleston. Bix thought his team looked like a yuppie street gang when they entered the hall, where they caught the attention of a half dozen old guys sitting at the bar drinking beer. *Not a bad crowd for a Tuesday night.*

Bix briefly introduced himself to a couple of men at the bar, but he could see in an instant that it wasn't the venue he needed—low ceiling, metal posts throughout the room holding it up, limited access. He let them know that Mr. Thigpen would contact them the next day about an event that they may be interested in attending.

Back in the car, Bix read another email from Peem about Max News: "Snds lik smbdy in our cmpgn is tlling thm. Nd to fnd out if they hve a srce in our fckng orgnztion." The next message was from his friend JD Ebsen, subject line: Coming to SC." "Finishing game day today in Columbus, arriving in SC tomorrow morning, in Charleston by 10 a.m."

"Perfect," Bix replied. "Will have a site for you by then hopefully. Travel safely. Thanks."

They arrived at the Red Schoendienst gym at 9:30 p.m. "I'd like to be out of here in a half hour, and we won't have time to go to the Field office in Scepter," Bix said.

"Where the fuck do you have to be?" Thigpen asked.

"Thigpen, you are impressive -- the eloquence of Philip Marlowe and the sartorial splender of Lord Byron."

"You didn't answer the fucking question," Thipen said.

"You didn't ask nicely," Bix said.

The building was an imposing structure in Romanesque-Revival style that resembled a medieval fortress in red sandstone, clearly over a hundred years old. A facility manager, Charlie, also looking over a hundred years old, met the team in the parking lot, which was barely large enough to fit half a motorcade. "I love this building," Bix announced as he shook Charlie's hand. "I bet a lot of people do."

"Yeah, it's kind of a landmark," Charlie said. "We try to take good care of it."

The team introduced themselves then took the tour with Charlie in the lead, turning on the lights as they roamed from room to room. It was beautiful, and it was one of the worst event sites he'd ever seen. Bix's heart sank lower and lower as they walked through the building, divided into many small rooms accessible only by stairs and small elevators. The sole room in the building that remotely matched their needs, the gymnasium itself, was gorgeous, tall ceilinged, heavy beamed, and the complete antithesis of a good event site. It was long but exceptionally narrow, with limited access from the street.

Bix explained his thinking to his team; they could tell he was in a hurry because he usually asked for input. "There is no possibility we could set up this room any way but length-wise. It's too narrow. If we set it up the other way the press riser would be about five feet from the main stage, and we can't orient it on the bias. So, the press riser we need to build would take up the entire width of the room back there," he pointed to a far end of the gym, "which would also block the doorway, and the main stage would have to be set up on the other end on, and there is no option for a cutaway. Charlie, I've got to tell you this is a great space but it blows for our purposes. I'd bet the farm we'd need to bring a generator to power this puppy. Am I right?"

"Yeah, we don't have a lot of electrical capacity."

"Is it available Thursday evening so we can build our Site?"

"We can let you have it as early as you'd need on Thursday."

"On the plus side, there are three offices we can use for holding rooms and access to an alley where can put the generator. And we could fill the place with a hundred bodies. I may not have a choice, but I can't commit to this. Charlie, this is a beautiful building, and my guess is that we will do the event here, but I have to keep looking."

Mike asked, "Are you sure?"

"Ben, you tell me. Did you find any other venues that seemed like they might work?" Bix asked.

"There are a couple other possibilities but these were the best. There's one place I didn't mention because it's in Scepter County and I didn't think you'd want to go there, plus it's on the east side of the county, it's a much longer drive."

"We'll check it out tomorrow early," Bix said. "and I'll email headquarters and ask them to vet this place just in case. I just got an email from JD telling me he'll be here by mid-morning. Thigpen, we will still need a hundred and fifty bodies, and Mike, as you're looking at contractors tell them we need a quote on this site too, just in case. I'll make a decision by mid-morning, and we can plan a walk-through tomorrow early afternoon."

Bix thanked Charlie and headed for the door with his team in tow. It was almost 10 p.m. and he wanted time to go back to his room for a few minutes before meeting Storie.

Maddeningly, Thigpen demanded they find food. "I haven't fucking eaten since fucking breakfast and I'd like to get some food before we get back to the fucking Hotel Chez Got-Rocks."

Bix couldn't argue; he'd forgotten the food thing all day. "How about McDonald's?" They all agreed. He knew they would. He could feel the minutes ticking away as they sat in the drive-through line, and he knew he'd be forced to go to his room no matter how late it was to inspect himself for errant food splatters and tooth debris.

"You seem antsy," Mike said. "Is everything alright?"

"You mean besides this trip?"

"You never get antsy about a trip."

"Nope, we're groovy. Totally."

"Totally? And I totally believe you."

Bix buried himself in his emails once again. To Alecia: "The Red Schoendienst Gym at Madison Jr College may work, barely. I may have no choice. Let's vet it. I'll keep looking."

Shaunesy's assistant wrote to say that her boss would see him in the morning at 9:30, and that Bix was to hold on all Advance preparations until they met.

"Naturally," Bix thought. "I suggested 10 a.m. and O'Shaunesy had to make it different." He wanted to not reply. As Democrats, neither the RFD nor his assistant would find that at all strange, he reasoned, but he was once again compelled to show *common courtesy*, if for no other reason than his one-man crusade to get Democrats to learn some. He'd found at least Republicans returned their phone calls and emails, and Democrats could take the lesson. He replied "Will see him at 9:30 a.m. Thank you. P.S.: Tell Shaunesy to hold his dick until I get there." Then he deleted the last part.

He shuffled through his list of emails and confirmed a meeting with the mayor at 1:30 the next afternoon, and by that time they were back at the hotel. Bix instructed Freeway to let him out in front of the hotel before they parked, and Thigpen chided him again. "Where the fuck are you going?"

"Bladder problems," he said as he jumped out of the van. He tried not to appear as if he was rushing through the lobby to the elevators. He heard the sound of the sports report on his television as he opened the door to his suite and knew without looking at the clock that he had only a few seconds to freshen up.

After a spritz and a toothbrush and a change to his cleanest shirt, he was downstairs at 10:30. He walked into the bar and found Storie already seated at a table talking with Kate and Cornelia. Storie stood and hugged him, then she kept her arms around him as she pulled back to look at him in the eyes, then she smiled and hugged him again.

"How do y'all know one another?" Bix asked Storie and Kate, "or was this a MO-tel bar pick-up?"

"Good accent," Storie said. "You know my penchant for hanging around MO-tel bars. Kate and I worked together at the end of the Clinton administration, and, as destiny would have it, we just ran into one another here in this bar."

"How do you guys know one another?" Kate asked.

"We worked together closer to the beginning of the Clinton admin- istration, and a little before that," Storie said, "before he became jaded."

"He must have been a lot of fun back then," Kate said. "Not so much now."

"That's a bummer," Storie said. "Good thing it's late and we're only having one drink, or, no, wait, excuse me, I'm having only one drink. Bix will drink carbonated water."

"Not me," Bix said. "Can't tolerate the bubbles any more. Too fizzy."

Storie laughed her laugh and took the opportunity to walk around the table to hug Kate and say goodbye. "It's great to see you, and Cornelia, it was wonderful to meet you. I'm going to make Bix watch me drink now." She took his arm and led him to a small table at the farthest end of the lounge.

They sat down and more than ten years of disconnection disappeared in an instant because Storie started with a compliment. "You look fan- tastic! You've really kept yourself well."

"That's kind of you, but I've seen the photos," Bix said.

"No, I'm serious, you look great."

He was predisposed to believe her, or anyone who gave him that kind of compliment. "And you are strikingly beautiful, as always."

"Thank you, but I've seen the photos too. Tell me what you've been up to, other than the campaign." She knew it was a question with no an- swer."Well, let's see. I'm in training for this year's Branson, Missouri, Hot Dog Eating Contest. Almost won it last year but some Korean chick beat me."

Storie was, as ever, the appreciate audience. She laughed heartily. "That had to be tough. It's wonderful to see you. I knew you couldn't resist another campaign. You thrive on this."

"No, I thrive on human blood and the odd Twinkie with a Diet Pepsi chaser. Are you enjoying yourself?"

"Yeah, I'm having a good time. The campaign's been great. I en- joy the people I work with, mostly. It's a little disorganized at the top, you've probably heard, but it's still satisfying. It's a groundbreaking campaign in many ways, just like yours. Are you still having fun? Your reputation certainly continues to grow, probably along with your head."

"I get no respect so you needn't worry there. Speaking of which…"

Mike, Thigpen, Freeway and Ben walked in as the waitress arrived at Bix and Storie's table. Thigpen spotted them first and led the group over.

"So is she your bladder control problem?" he asked.

Bix looked at Storie and nodded toward Thigpan. "Case in point," he said.

The waitress interrupted, "Would you care for drinks?"

Storie ordered a beer.

"And this gentleman here," Bix pointed to Thigpen, "would like Scotch and Quaaludes on the rocks, and you can bring me a sharp implement."

"Yes sir," she said. "Would you like anything to drink along with that?"

"I'll order when you come back with it."

Mike greeted Storie, and she stood up to hug him. Bix hadn't realized that Storie was so well-known and well-loved. "You guys worked together at the end of the Clinton administration, right?" Bix asked.

"Of course," Mike said.

"That's a touching story and I apologize," Bix said, "I haven't introduced everyone. Everyone, this is Storie. Storie, this is everyone. Well, I'd love to ask you guys to stay but then you might do it. Thanks for stopping by."

"Guys," Mike said, "let's take a hint. We want to sit near the television anyway so we can watch the Primary results. It looks like we're losing. Storie, it was great to see you again. Hopefully you'll be around for the next couple of days. We're gonna have a blowout on Friday. You should come. You'd still have time to drive to Columbia for your boss's rally."

"Maybe I will. I haven't seen one of Bix's grand productions in years. Can you get me in?"

"I think maybe we can," Mike said. "If you'd like we can get you a photo with The Candidate too, and have him sign it."

"How much will it cost me?" Storie said.

"A modest donation, small bills, brown paper bag," Bix told her.

The boys left and Storie asked, "So where were we?"

"I was waxing philosophic about how difficult it's been for me to cope with my perfection and was inquiring how you've grown to accept your own so graciously for all these years."

She laughed. "It's been tough, but luckily perfection comes easily for me, so it balances out. You know you really look good."

"You're wearing gin goggles."

"I haven't started drinking yet."

"Maybe I will," he said as the waitress was delivering Storie's drink. "I'll have a glass of red wine. Whatever you have at the bar."

"You're going to have a whole glass of wine? This *is* a momentous occasion. Am I safe, or do I need to sleep with a baseball bat under my pillow?"

"Right. You know what happens to me after one drink. I get talkative and self-entertaining for about a minute then I fall asleep. Then I drool. You're safe unless you get in the way of my head hitting the table."

"I'll see to it you get home safely," she said.

They talked for an hour about everything under the sun—national politics, domestic politics, international politics, state politics, local politics, political figures, the latest political gossip—everything under *their* sun. There was little in their conversation about the previous ten-plus years except political references, and once when she corrected him about the time that had passed since they'd seen one another. "It's been closer to twelve years," she pointed out.

Bix could sense that she, unlike him, enjoyed a warm relationship with her candidate and passion for her political mission, and she sensed that he still cared deeply about the causes that had motivated them when they were young—those issues that fell within the "moral test of government," as Hubert Humphrey said, despite his concerns about creeping cynicism.

"When you're young," she said, "your heart is supposed to be bigger than your head, and you attach your loyalty to people as much as policies."

Such loyalty was often misplaced, they agreed, and in the Democratic Party, at least, it was unrequited most of the time. They had each learned the lesson independently but both had learned it the hard way, beginning with the fight that caused their split, which had come over two Congressional candidates. "Lousy Congressional candidates," Bix thought to himself many times. They'd fought over a couple of lousy Congressional candidates in a lousy primary; a lousy trifecta. Bix's candidate, a man whom Storie didn't like because of his philandering ways, beat Storie's candidate, a woman who had used her official staff from her previous elected position as a city comptroller for personal errands and campaign work. Bix's candidate was whupped in the general election by a tax-cutting Republican who'd been fined for voter fraud.

No two people had ever clashed over a worse cause. It had irritated him ever since; where he had normally been buoyant, he'd taken on a touch of fatalism. Unlike him, she seemed to have kept her joie de vivre, and it spilled over and splashed on him. Given that effect, she couldn't see that he had become at all curmudgeonly.

"Have you kept up your Farsi?" she asked. It wasn't an off-the-wall question. He'd learned Farsi while he was studying for his master's degree in International Relations, and had allowed his skills to deteriorate before they met. She prodded him to keep current and helped him, through love and understanding, to overcome his loathing of homework. Her absence was a handy excuse to quit. It occurred to him for the first time that his Farsi might be useful if ever he found Jamir.

"No, but I hope I can remember enough if the situation ever calls for it. Insha'Allah," he said.

"That's Arabic," she pointed out.

"Then I've got a problem."

She turned the conversation to the present tense. "Tell me, what's the deal with your regional field director, Shaunesy? What a doofus. Why'd you guys hire him? Not that I'm complaining—we see him as a definite asset for our campaign. He's alienating a lot of people down here."

"He's a friend of Larry Drule's."

"Larry Drule." Storie sounded out the two words slowly, contemplatively. "He asked me out four or five times a couple years ago. He wouldn't quit, and I don't find him to be attractive or interesting in any way. I actually began to think he was stalking me. It was creepy. *He's* creepy. The thought of him makes my skin crawl. His face looks like it's been pressed against a screen door."

"Interesting take on our deputy campaign manager," Bix said. "I'm happy to see that he doesn't only have that effect on men."

"He asked me about you several times back then. It was like he was fixated on the fact that you and I used to be a couple, and he never missed a chance to trash you in some way. It made me like you all the more. If he told me the two of you were BFF's I would have assumed something was wrong with you."

"Thank you, Mr. Drule, for your negative endorsement. What's the deal with his friend Shaunesy?"

"Mr. Shaunesy was trying to get on with our campaign three months ago and they wouldn't return his phone calls. Drule gave him my name and told him to contact me, but I didn't return his call either. It's not like Drule was a great reference."

"Why not return his calls?" asked Bix.

"He's a schmuck. His daddy is a big real estate guy in New York and he got him a job in the last administration as like, director of the Office of Vermin in the Small Animals Administration of the Department of Housing and Urban Decay. Even the rats didn't trust him. He's shown up for a couple weeks in Field positions in the last two presidential campaigns just to get his ticket punched, and he's terrible. So, congratulations. He can drive down morale as fast as he can drive down your turnout."

"Now I remember hearing about him. He was a deputy assistant secretary or something like that. Career civil servants were resigning just to get the hell away from him."

"That's the guy. He's making my job easier."

"You're welcome."

"You should thank Drule," she said.

"I already did. Once is enough."

The newest twist in their social interaction was the advent of BlackBerry; both devices were going off continuously in their pockets and neither Bix nor Storie could resist monitoring the in-coming from time to time.

"Hey, wait, you're going to love this. Perfect timing," Bix said. "This is from Shaunesy's assistant Laura Ratchel. The subject line is "'S' pins' and you *know* what's coming."

"She wants to make certain that they have as many 'S' pins as they can lay their hands on because Shaunesy wants total access to The Candidate, right? He's gonna try to roll you."

"We'll see. Yep, it says, 'Mr. Shaunesy and I will need 'S' pins for the events on Friday.' She's so warm."

"Are you going to give them the pins?"

"They are way too important for that. I'm going to create a special VVIP credential for Mr. Shaunesy and Nurse Ratched, and probably Mayor Bacon. We need to ensure they receive VVIP treatment."

"Nice touch," said Storie. "Make sure Mike doesn't give me one of your special VVIP credentials. I don't want to be tackled by a bunch of agents if I get too close to your Candidate, or he comes too close to me."

Bix recognized two people walking past the lounge as members of the Max News crew he'd seen earlier, and he had a minor revelation. "Storie, those two are with Max News, and while I don't see any cameras that doesn't mean they don't have cameras on their cell phones, and the fact that we're sitting together is news. Maybe not front-page news, it's more like page-fifteen, below-the-fold, pack-your-bags-and-don't-let-the-doorknob-hit-you-on-the-ass-as-you're-fired-from-the-campaign news. And I really should get back to work. I've got some stuff."

Storie was unconcerned as always when she wasn't doing anything wrong. "Obviously if we had something to hide, we wouldn't be sitting out here in the middle of God and creation. But you're right, perception is everything, and besides, you've got a major rally in two days, which if you screw up, your Candidate won't win the South Carolina primary. And you've also got some people lurking out there in the shadows who would love nothing more than to use this against you. Maybe we could do a late dinner tomorrow, somewhere else, not in the hotel?"

"I'd love to. I'll do my best. Thanks for the grim reminder on the rally too. What's your room number? I'll leave a message on your hotel phone," Bix said.

"Smart," she said. "Paranoid, but smart. You're finally learning."

They stood and he extended his hand. She laughed that laugh, but louder.

She shook his hand. "Why, thank you, Mr. Bix," she said officiously. "It was so good to meet one of our worthy opponents, and I wish you the best of luck in your endeavors."

"Why, thank *you* Ms. Storie. It was good to meet you too, and I thank you for your solicitous wishes. May your endeavors be equally fruitful."

She shot him a sly smile and a lecherous look, indiscernible to prying eyes or camera lenses unless they happened to be anywhere within a thousand feet.

* * *

Bix walked by the front desk to ask if Missy Ballew had checked-in, and found she was still AWOL. He sent her an email asking if she had arrived and cc'd Alecia at headquarters; by that point, her absence was on the verge of becoming unacceptable.

It was nearly midnight as he began to tie up the day's loose ends, first calling the president of the Scepter College Young Democrats, Jerry Litton, who had emailed his phone number and told Bix "I completely support your candidate. Call as late as you'd like. I'll be up." Young Mr. Litton, true to his word, was awake and effusive about his support, which had the ring of authenticity. Bix arranged to meet him at the Scepter Field office in the mid-afternoon for the purpose of tasking him with a sub rosa crowd-building mission.

He replied to Mike's email about meeting with the Scepter Field office at eight-thirty a.m. and emailed Mike, Thigpen, Ben and Freeway to meet him in the lobby at seven-thirty. Thigpen's reply lacked civility.

He emailed Special Agent Emory to promise that a choice for a second site would be make by ten-thirty hours and CC'd Alecia, then wrote

Sophie to tell her he'd be available to talk at seven thirty-five. He added a little droolie-face Keith Richards emoticon.

Peem continued to send emails asking questions and suggesting different approaches to "the issue," as he referred to it, none of which were helpful. Bix thanked him for each one.

By that time it was clear The Candidate had lost the New Hampshire primary and South Carolina would acquire new significance, if not urgency, a challenge that Bix began to relish now that Storie was there to watch.

Storie-struck and glowing, he continued working throughout The Candidate's televised concession speech feeling more hopeful, meaning slightly less pessimistic, than he had in years. The Candidate needed a big bump in the polls, and Bix felt he was in the right position to pay it forward now that Storie had done the same for him. He was in bed at 1:30 a.m.

He woke-up two hours later in a cold sweat thinking about Jamir and Hani, checked his BlackBerry, found there was no news and didn't sleep well the remainder of the night, torn between worry and delight.

10

Hizzoner Mayor Bacon was on the phone to the Chief of Police at 5:00 a.m. with marching orders about the rally at Scepter College and the Advance team.

"Bud," Bacon bellowed into the phone, "Yoah about t' earn yoah keep. Ah want 'ya t' put th' word out through owah wahd wehkahs an' th' counta police that no one's t' go t' this heah speech unless ah say so. Ah don't want these boahs t' get a crowd foah theh little shindig, got me?"

Chief Fry was all over it. "Ah got it, Mistah Mayah. We'll put the wuhd out."

"Gud, gud, y'all do that now, an keep this thing undah control," Bacon said.

* * *

At 6:00 a.m., Bix peeled himself from bed and did due diligence at the coffee maker. He forced down his morning regimen of vitamins, baby aspirin, and a banana, then gulped down a cup of coffee before heading to the gym. In the day's first act of self-congratulation, he thought how incredibly heroic he was for getting up early and cranking it out despite the grueling pace. Given that he had been doing it for twelve years in anticipation of running into Storie again, and the fact that it was happening for real, he wasn't fooling himself. There was nothing heroic in it. It was completely self-serving.

The morning exercise provided an unexpected benefit. One of the Counter Assault Team team members, Guy Manfred, showed-up in the gym ten minutes after Bix had started on the treadmill, still walking, but by that time walking spritely for a geezer. Manfred, half Bix's age with zero percent body fat, nodded hello. Bix finished off the last ten minutes of his thirty-minute walkfest with a run, really a jog, then hit the floor for his signature "top this!" move—fifty push-ups. Real push-ups, not girl push-ups.

As Bix finished, Manfred looked over from the free weights. "Man, that's impressive."

That was the point. Physical fitness and promptness were potent forces on the Secret Service respect meter, although not in that order.

"I do that every hour," Bix said. "Maybe I can qualify for one of your special long-sleeve CAT Team t-shirts. Aren't those given out for physical fitness?"

Manfred admitted to nothing.. "Yeah, right, I don't think you want one of those."

Bix always rode the CAT Team guys about their "special" long-sleeve CAT Team t-shirts, which they presented as souvenirs to women they slept with on the road. The t-shirts were a secret branding—or bragging— device, or scarlet letter, depending on one's perspective. Any young lady who wore one, especially a member of the staff Advance team who had the misfortune of hooking-up with a CAT agent during an Advance trip and then made the mistake of wearing her T-shirt in public, branded herself in an uncomplimentary manner. Bix had received one as a gift from a young female friend on one of his teams who found out its meaning too late, and she was angry about it. Bix kept it in his suitcase, thinking it might come in handy someday given its significance to some of the most macho specimens among several macho specimens with whom he interacted regularly.

Up in his room at 7:00 a.m., Bix tried tracking down Missy again, and for the first time cc'd Egan, genuinely concerned about her safety. He emailed Kate and asked to talk with her as soon as it was convenient, and after another cup of coffee he met the testosterone squad in the lobby. Mike and Bix drove together in the three-car motorcade to Scepter, with Mike at the wheel and Bix on the phone to Sophie.

She answered her phone cheerfully. "Hi, Bix, thanks. I was hoping you'd be able to call first thing. How is everything in Charleston?"

"Getting more interesting by the hour, and based on that diabolical little smiley face you put on your email last night you're about to make my life even more so. Is everything OK with you?"

"*I'm* fine. I've got a couple of updates that you may not like but you'll want to know. First of all, Larry Drule was in Peem's office last night complaining about you, trying to get you fired, or at least taken off the Charleston Advance. He says you've been stepping outside your lane, messing around in local politics."

"What did Peem say?"

"He said he had his concerns too and that he'd monitor the situation," Sophie said.

"That sounds like less than full-throated support, as they say in DC."

"And it gets better. Drule said he wanted to go down to Charleston and oversee the situation. Peem turned him down on that request."

"That's a step in the right direction."

"Here's another one. Dick O'Malley is requesting an interview with The Candidate on Friday, after your rally in Scepter. The Press Office said it sounded almost like a threat. And here's the really interesting part—Peem actually told me to tell you that if you can get your hands on the Manifesto you should destroy it."

"Assuming, of course, that Jamir doesn't know what a photocopier is. I can picture myself grabbing it out of his hands and trying to swallow the thing. Would you mind if we made a bilateral decision at this point to ignore that bit of advice?" Bix asked.

"I didn't say I agreed with it, so yes."

"How about some good news? Anything?" Bix asked.

"Not so far today, but I'll keep looking. Anything I can do for you?"

"Yes. It occurred to me that we should research Columbia's campus publications for the years Jamir and The Candidate attended. I'd like you to see if they are available digitally through the campus library, and if not, can you find a trustworthy student to search their microfiche? How you would go about identifying a trustworthy student is beyond me at the moment. Maybe our campaign has a student organization there. If it can't be done, don't let it vex you."

"If it can be done, it will be," Sophie said. "Even if it was published, they may have used pseudonyms if they felt it might be controversial some day, way off in the future. I'll look for any article that has the word 'manifesto' in its title, just in case."

"That's brilliant, and I don't mean that in the British context. It's actually brilliant. Thank you," Bix said.

"Watch your backside down there in the Palmetto State. There are wolves nipping at your heels," Sophie said.

At 8:10 a.m. they arrived at the Scepter Field office, located in an old red brick storefront that reminded Bix of the Southside Democratic headquarters in St. Louis where he'd gotten his start in politics at the age of seven. The Scepter Field office was sparse, obviously a temporary lease for the building, while the Southside Democrats' office was an institution that reeked of character. The Southside was already old when the Democrats bought it prior to World War I—with its pressed tin ceiling and dark oak wainscoting and heavy wood furniture, it was redolent of cigar smoke and the memories of hundreds of political campaigns. Bix's mother, a local activist, took him there when he was five years old, and the first thing he saw when he walked in were pictures of President Kennedy and Missouri's favorite son, President Truman. For a long time, he thought it was the place where the President's office was located, as if there was an Oval Office upstairs somewhere.

A few years later when Bix returned to Southside to volunteer, he knew the office and the people who worked there fairly well. They had added a picture of President Johnson to the wall near the entry, as well as a small photo of Bix's mother, who had died only a few months after President Kennedy's assassination. The building itself was a place that was important to his mom, a place where, she said, "You get things done that need to be done." A true volunteer, she did it for the love and the fun of it, because she could have a positive impact on the lives of those around her, and she instilled those beliefs in Bix. Politics offered him an outlet for his energy, a way to fill the void left by his mother's death and to provide a connection to her. And there was an allure for him, a feeling of history in the making and an appreciation for the history that had been made. Ancient black and white photos of old-time St. Louis politicians, former mayors, and aldermen adorned the walls and spoke to him of the honor in politics, the nobility in serving. But he was still only seven years old at the time, and could be forgiven such naïve notions. More than forty years later, some of those notions still lingered, for which he could not forgive himself.

The Scepter Field office brought him back to reality. It was decorated in period political campaign chic—spacious and simple with plenty of fold-out chairs and eight-foot tables lining the walls, on which were about a dozen beige telephones. Near the back, next to the bathroom and the copying machine and the water cooler, were two private offices and a conference room. Only a few handmade campaign posters decorated the walls, alongside calendars, regional maps with post-it notes attached all over them, and large white sheets of paper crammed with lists, grids, dates, precincts, and color-coded volunteer names. More than a dozen people were already hard at work throughout.

A tall young woman with dark hair and an air of self-confidence walked out of one the offices and introduced herself to Bix.

"Hi, I'm Nora Jankowsky." She was professional and pleasant and her eyes made her appear to be delighted to see the team.

"It's good to meet you Nora. I'm Bix, this is Mike, who you've talked with already, and these are Thigpen, Ben and Freeway."

"Great, I can put all of you to work immediately. Would you like to do some phone banking?" she joked.

"Anything we can do to help. You just tell us what do to," Bix said.

"Could I talk with you and Mike in the conference room for a minute?"

Bix already suspected what Nora told him when she closed the door.

"I'm Sophie's friend," she told them.

"Finally some good news," Bix said. "It is very nice to meet you. Sophie's been very discreet. First, how are you, and B, what's Shaunesy's dysfunction in life?"

"I'll put it this way. I'm glad you're here. Shaunesy arrived two weeks ago and he's having a very negative impact on the staff, the volunteers, local supporters, the lot. We had a highly organized phone bank operation with health care workers calling health care workers, veterans calling veterans, fire fighters calling fire fighters, retirees calling retirees—all the way on down the line. Shaunesy threw all of that out the window. He said everyone should be on the streets, going door-to door.

Tell that to a bunch of retirees. 'Time to strap on your walkin' shoes, grandma.'"

"Is the phone bank operational at all?" Bix asked.

"It is, but barely, and we aren't achieving the outreach and voter I.D. we need. And when we don't meet our goals, he tells headquarters it's our fault."

"What's Shaunesy's relationship with the local political leadership?"

"He's got his assistant, Nurse Ratched, calling political leaders and asking them to come to his office rather than him going out to meet them, which makes them peeved. Some haven't bothered to meet with him. He spent his first two days in Charleston organizing his office, or, depending on who you're asking, 'decorating' it. He didn't call or meet with a soul. The few times he *has* ventured out, he's seen driving around in his new Mercedes with New York license plates, which isn't received well either. *That* got around quickly. He doesn't have the sense to park down the block and walk a little farther so it isn't so noticeable. Once our local leaders meet him, it's a completely different story. Then they hate his guts."

Bix laughed.

"I've spoken with the political leadership in my district," Nora said, "and it's universal: no one can believe we hired him. He spends his days in his office talking on the phone to God-knows-who. It certainly isn't anyone around here. And he hates Advance people. He told me flat out not to talk with you."

"OK, he may have been right about that," Mike said.

"We've had one staff meeting since he's been here," she said, "and it was just an hour-long rant about what we are and aren't trying to achieve, and how we'd been doing it all wrong. After that, all of his dictates have been sent to us via email from Nurse Ratched."

"You paint a grim picture," Bix said, taking a moment to rub his eyes.

"Is there anything we can do to help?" Mike asked.

"Your presence will get everyone excited again, which will be great," she said.

"I hear that a lot," Bix said.

She laughed. "Sophie told me I'd like you. How about if you guys stay here for the next two weeks and help me fight back? Other than that, there's not a lot you can do to help my situation. Shaunesy is friends with Larry Drule, the deputy campaign manager. I don't see how we can go over his head."

"We'll try going around him, then," Mike said. "He said we might be able to use some of your space to work from for organizing the rally. Is that OK with you?"

"I love it. You guys can have one of the private offices, and feel free to use the conference room. And as you can see, we've got plenty of space out in the main room."

"Won't Shaunesy allow you to organize at the rally? You can get a lot of email addresses and a lot of volunteers out of a crowd of thirty-thousand people," Mike said.

"Thirty thousand? That's incredible! Where will you get all of those people?"

"We pay them," Mike said. "Five bucks each. We were hoping you would pick up the invoice since we're doing it in your district."

"That's an Advance expense," Nora said, laughing. "I've got five bucks I can throw in. I'll buy you one audience member."

"I'll take it," Bix said. "And we appreciate your generosity, in addition to letting us use your office. If you don't mind, Mike and Thigpen will work out of here. Mike is running the rally and Thigpen does Crowd."

"We'll do anything we can to help," she said. "A lot of our volunteers would love to get involved. I was pretty upset when Shaunesy told me we couldn't be involved in the rally. We can get a lot of benefit out of an event that size, and no one wants to miss out on the fun."

"Technically," Bix said, "if your volunteers are working the rally it qualifies as being 'out on the streets.' Mike can help you organize it, and Thigpen will pass along to you all of the volunteers he develops independently."

"What about Mayor Bacon?" Nora asked. "Shaunesy told me I can't talk to him anymore, either. I think it's because he doesn't want me to hear how much Bacon dislikes him, but Bacon still comes in here from time to time, like yesterday after he left you. He wants you to take *our*

Candidate to *his* senior center, and he said he could cause a lot of trouble if you don't agree."

"This was after we met with him, after he left the college?" Bix asked.

"Yes, he told me he'd just left you and he'd talked President Gilliman into letting you do the rally there."

"Which is pretty much true," Bix said. "I kind of expected him to want payback for his efforts but I was hoping it might take the form of a photo with The Candidate kissing his ring. Did he mention what form of trouble he would cause, by any chance?"

"He said he could get the Board of Regents to cancel your rally, not let you use the college as your speech site."

"Mike, what about the contract?" Bix asked.

"I've got a copy of a contract that has been filled in but not signed," Mike said.

"As long as they filled in the particulars—location, date, time—we've got enough to make a case. Maybe now would be a good time for you to go back to the college and get everyone to sign it. I have to go look at another potential site for something else we might want to do," Bix said.

"Nora, it was nice to meet you," Mike said. "Thank you for everything, I will be back here in a couple of hours."

"One other thing before you leave," Nora said. "There was a television news crew from Max News in here late yesterday. They were asking questions about what we do here and they took video of the main room, but I told them that they would have to talk with our Press Office to answer any questions. They asked me if I knew you, Bix."

"And of course you told them, 'Only his legend,'" Mike said.

"Right," said Nora.

Bix walked into the main room and rousted Thigpen, Ben, and Freeway, who were busily working their BlackBerrys. "Thigpen, this office is now your little oyster. Be kind and try not to frighten anyone. What's your schedule today?"

"By eleven a.m. I'll have twenty volunteers and be able to start putting twenty thousand flyers and a thousand posters out on the streets in

Scepter and the surrounding areas. The number of volunteers will grow as the day goes on. I've got volunteers coming from Charleston to pick up another five thousand flyers and five hundred posters. We'll have them all distributed by tomorrow afternoon. By noon I'll have a phone bank up and running, and we're using the laborers union contacts in Philly that Cornelia followed up on to make phone calls into the area."

Bix was shocked, amazed and befuddled. "You said all of that without a curse word. I'm proud of you, my boy. Really proud."

"Fuck you," Thigpen said.

* * *

Bix and Ben piled into Freeway's van for the last two potential Site visits. After two slow drive-bys it was clear that Bix had no choice. He pulled the trigger on the Schoendienst Gym, emailed all the concerned parties, had Freeway drop him off at his car in Scepter, and beat hasty feet back to Charleston for his 9:30 a.m. meeting with Shaunesy. Bix was on time to the minute and Shaunesy wasn't there.

The campaign's Charleston regional headquarters were located in a half-vacant strip mall, and Bix noticed that there were no staff or volunteers anywhere. He found Shaunesy's office and introduced himself to Laura Ratchel, who didn't smile and didn't move a muscle. She said that Shaunesy would be arriving soon and asked Bix to take a seat.

Bix paced around instead and checked his emails. Missy had finally checked in at the hotel, so he knew she wasn't lying by the side of the road somewhere. He asked her to confirm that she had the RON checklist, and then noticed an email from Bob Baycroft. "Got a call early this morning from a reporter from Max news, asking about you, Jamir, Hani and a manifesto. Told them I was ignorant. Thought you'd want to know."

Never one to be an alarmist, Bix decided for a change of pace. He walked outside of the office to email Peem. "Wht th fk?" was the subject line. He felt it was best to begin in Peem's native tongue. "One of my contacts, former Amb. Baycroft, who suggested I contact Jamir's brother-in-law in Jordan, was contacted by a reporter from Mx Nws this morning asking questions about Jamir, Hani, the manifesto and me. Any idea how Mx Nws knows these things, and now about the ambassador?"

It was a stumper to say the least. To say the most, Bix thought, it could be a felony. Bix scoped out the parking lot as if he sensed an evil presence watching his every move.

Sure enough, at that very moment, exactly 9:55 a.m., Shaunesy arrived and looked surprised to see Bix standing in front of the headquarters. "I thought you said ten a.m.," Shaunesy said.

"I did. But Laura told me to come at nine-thirty instead, which I replied to in the affirmative, and as a result I arrived at nine-twenty-five. It's really no big deal. Don't worry about it."

Shaunesy didn't apologize. "Come on into my office and give me a minute." When they entered he proceeded to open his laptop and begin looking at his emails while Bix sat in the chair in front of his desk and fumed. Bix checked his BlackBerry again and contemplated several violent scenarios against Shaunesy's person as minor entertainments until, at about 10:00, Shaunesy finally spoke.

"Tell me what you're doing in Scepter."

"I'm doing a rally at the college, and you're invited," Bix said.

"Well, I knew that, but what's going on?"

"Don, I'm not sure I understand your question. Are you asking what's going to happen at the rally?"

"Well, I need to know what's happening, and when and where The Candidate will be, and where I will have some time with him and some of our more prominent supporters," he said.

"Absolutely," Bix said. "The Scheduling Office told me they'd already briefed you. We will do a greeting when The Candidate arrives at Scepter College at about 11:30 Friday morning. You will need to be there no later than 10:30 a.m., and you can invite ten local leaders to greet. We will need to have their name check information—full name, date of birth, Social Security number, race, sex, if any—by tomorrow morning so we can get them vetted."

"Well, what do you mean by a 'greet,'" he asked.

"They will greet The Candidate when he arrives. We do it indoors out of respect for the Secret Service's security concerns," Bix explained.

"Well, how long will we have with him?" Shaunesy asked.

Whatever Bix said wouldn't be long enough, and he certainly didn't want to tell Shaunesy that it would last less than five seconds per person. "As long as The Candidate deems appropriate." He wanted to stop there, but he felt compelled to tell the truth. "Usually he shakes hands with everyone and we take a group photo with one of their cameras and ask that person to email it to everyone else. It works out well."

"Well, I've told my people they would have time to talk with The Candidate and ask him some questions," Shaunesy shouted. "Are you telling me that's not going to happen?"

"Probably not," Bix said. "You can put in a request to Headquarters, but at the moment I don't have a Q and A session on my schedule."

"Can I get a copy of that?" Shaunesy said.

"Headquarters sends those out. And Don, I don't mean to be rude, but I had our meeting on my schedule from 9:30 to 10:00 because that's what your assistant scheduled, and it's 10:07 now, so I've got to go. If you have any other concerns or questions call me." Bix got up.

"Well, I'm not done here. I've got other things I need you to clarify for me."

"Happy to. Call me." His quick departure apparently surprised Nurse Ratched, who was munching on a chocolate chip cookie and mumbled something that sounded like "That was fast" as he passed by her. Bix smiled and thanked her for her help as he walked.

He scrolled through his emails quickly on the way to the car. Kate emailed him that she had arranged a meeting with WXDL Radio in Scepter at 12:15 to produce their radio ads promoting the rally, and confirmed she'd be at the college by 10:30 for a pre-walk-through meeting.

Alecia wrote to verify that the Schoendienst Gym was vetted and approved, which he forwarded to Shane, then a phone call with a local number appeared on the screen. He thought it might be Shaunesy again but he answered anyway. It was LuAnn, Mayor Bacon's assistant, who put him through to the mayor.

"Bix, I wont t' talk 'bout this Senia Centa ishuh. Whaeh d' we stand with that?"

"Same place as yesterday, Mr. Mayor. I told Headquarters you wanted us to go there either before or after our rally and that it's a beautiful location, but I haven't heard anything new. Frankly, given the drive time alone, I don't see how they can approve it on this trip. How about you? Did you mention it to the big boys in Chicago?"

"Ah've certainly let ma feelin's be known, but ya see we could have some problems with the Boad a'Regents at the college. Many of them think we oughta go ba the Senia Centa as well, an' that could cause a problem fo' yoa ralleah."

It was a thinly veiled threat. "I understand what you're saying Mr. Mayor. I'll talk with Headquarters again and let you know what I find out when we meet at 1:30. Is that all right with you?"

"It's up t'you whetha ya want ta wait that long. This could have a sevvea impact on yoa rally," Bacon said.

"I understand Mr. Mayor. And you understand that I don't have a dog in this fight, and I'm happy to do whatever I'm told by the people who sign my paychecks. You know I'm just the guy who moves the furniture around."

"Ah undastan' that Bix. An' ya undastan' this ain't pusonal," Bacon said.

"That never makes it any more pleasant, does it Mr. Mayor?"

"Ah s'ppose not, but see what you can do foa me. Ah'm stickin' ma neck out foa ya."

"That's not all you're stickin' me with Mr. Mayor. I'll see you at 1:30." He could hear Bacon laughing as he hung up.

He emailed Alecia and Egan about the mayor's threat, as if there was anything they could do about it, at about the time he found an email from Shane Emory reading "Chief Fry tells me The Candidate will be dropping by the Bacon Senior Center on Friday before going to the college. True? OTR"

Bix replied, "Not unless they kidnap the protectee. I'm guessing it won't come to that."

* * *

He sped back to the College of Scepter for his 10:30 pre-walk-through with Mike, Ben, and Kate. She'd left Cornelia at the hotel to work with Missy on press accommodations for the RON.

"Mike, tell me some good news," Bix said when he saw the group standing in front of the Administration building.

"I've got a guy who can produce our banners by tomorrow night. This being South Carolina, the man had a ready supply of indigo blue canvas," Mike said. "And the best part, only two hundred bucks each. Cheap."

"That's the best news I've heard all day. Thank you, that's huge. OK, now, what have you done for me lately?" Bix said.

"I've got a signed contract, too."

"No, Mike, you've got the holy grail. Thank you. The Mayor's threatening to take away our site if we don't do an event at the Bacon Bits Building—not that a signed contract would prevent him from shooting our rally in the head. It's not like we'd file a lawsuit."

"For what it's worth, I think the steamroller effect is already beginning. It would be difficult to stop this from happening at this point without a lot of grief," Mike said. "And, good news, we can build on the old cistern mound."

"This is all good news," Bix said. Things are turnin' around, I can feel it. It's gonna be good times and a bag of chips. I can *feel* it. Can you both feel it?"

Kate deadpanned "Yes, I can feel it. Oh yeah, that's it. Oh baby, it's happening. It will be all beer and Skittles from now on." Bix hadn't seen such emotionlessness on a person's face since George W. took his first oath of office.

"Kate," Bix said, "I knew I could count on your enthusiasm. Now, let's spot exactly where we want the press to have access, the various perspectives we'd like the TV cameras to shoot. Are we in agreement that The Candidate should stand on a 'pod' stage, maybe twenty-five feet in front of a long set of tall bleachers, maybe sixty feet in length?"

"That works for me," Kate said. "I know you guys have your own distinctive styles."

"Is that a good thing?" Mike asked.

"Very good. For one thing, no one else has any style at all. It's always the same visual—The Candidate standing in front of a tiny little riser full of people and an eight-by-ten-foot message banner hanging above 'em. No sense of place, nothing memorable. The press hate it. They get bored."

"Try telling that to Headquarters," Mike said.

Kate shrugged. "I have. I get no response. They think it costs too much to produce better quality events. I think it's costing the campaign NOT to do it, but what do I know?"

"What will the press think about this event?" Mike asked, trolling for another compliment.

Kate didn't hold back. "I think this rally will blow them out of the water. The size will be unexpected, and I intend to feed them the finest Charleston buffet for lunch. If they don't give us fantastic press coverage I'll be shocked. Shocked. Just don't get your fingers near their mouths as they're eating."

They measured all the distances from the main stage to the press risers, designed the "low" background visual, spotted five different visual angles including a place for the cherry-picker, and chose a Holding Room on the lower level of the Administration Building, far from President Gilliman's and easily secured from unwanted intrusions. Mike had located a gymnasium they could use and a warren of subterranean passageways through which The Candidate could ambulate secretly. Bix was impressed.

They walked the entire route that The Candidate would walk from the motorcade to the greeters, to the Hold, to the catwalk into the rally and to the pod stage, working the rope line, exiting the rally, back to the Hold or the gym, then law enforcement photos before exiting, then departure in the motorcade en route the airport. Simple enough in Bix's mind. With a few minutes left before the walk-through with the Secret Service, Bix took Kate aside to explain Manifestogate, why Max News might be following them around, and why he might get a bit distracted in the next two days.

"I knew something was up with Max News," she said. "I thought you were about to be arrested for corruption or fraud or something," she snortled as she laughed at her own joke.

"For what?" he asked. "Impersonating someone who still gives a rat's patoot?"

"Exactly," she said, "you've been exposed."

"Speaking of a rat's patoot," Bix said, "I'd like to talk to about Thursday night. Have you noticed that we arrive at 8:45 Thursday night, and first real news coverage we get, other than the announcement that he's arrived, isn't until sometime past 11 a.m. the next morning? We're missing the local late night news and the local and national morning news. Nothing until almost noon on Friday. Zip. We're leaving a gaping hole of news vacuum that could be easily filled with some great pictures, and missing an opportunity to promote the rally one last time. It's low risk, and for a few minutes of The Candidate's time we end up with as much coverage as if we'd produced another rally."

"I see your point," Kate looked skeptical, "but what are our options? The airport is a closed arrival and you've promised the Service that we won't be stopping along the way to do an OTR, unless you plan to go back on your word."

"I'm not suggesting we do anything at the airport or stop anywhere along the way from the airport to the RON. However, if there just happened to be a large crowd in the lobby of the Hotel Marianne when we arrived, such a spontaneous demonstration of affection might require The Candidate's attention and draw the attention of the local and traveling press, don't you think?"

"How do you do that without creating a security problem and getting the Service pissed off at us? You can't publicize it."

"I've done this a few times. Service isn't exactly pleased about it, but they don't mind *as* much because there are already a jillion agents and cops in the RON hotel. They don't have to go anywhere to deal with an OTR that's off-site. The hotel's already secured," Bix said.

"How do you get a crowd?" she asked.

"I get the Young Democrats to contact all their friends, quietly, by word of mouth, and organize them to meet at a third location, close enough but not too close to the RON hotel. That way no one knows their ultimate destination. Then we call them at the appointed moment and tell them where to go at the same time we've arranged for one or two of our designated spontaneous supporters to call the local TV stations and tell them what's happening. That way the crowd and the TV cameras arrive at the hotel just a few minutes before the motorcade pulls up. We bring The Candidate up through the bowels of the hotel, and the press is escorted up to the main entrance and allowed to go in and cover whatever happens. Hopefully The Candidate will want to say a few words to his supporters. I may happen to have a bullhorn stashed under the front desk. There's plenty of time for local TV crews to get back to their stations for the 10 o'clock news, which I realize is the 11 o'clock news in this part of the country. Then they'll use it again Friday morning before the rally coverage."

"It has possibilities," said Kate. "I assume Mike and Ben would be at the hotel and you'd need me to escort the travelling press into position?"

"That right. You would want to take special care to get the still photographers off the bus first. We could get an iconic image or two out of this. Mike would secure a place for the press to enter and get the shot, some place they can shoot above the crowd in case the lobby is jam-packed."

She wanted to know the logistics. "You would call me during the motorcade traveling in from the airport and let me know what's going on and alert me to spontaneous crowd, is that correct?"

"That's correct. The conversation would begin with something like 'Imagine my surprise…'"

"I can do that," she said. "The press is going to want to see whatever's happening. I want to make sure we park the press busses as close as we can to the front door."

"Freeway will work it out," Bix said. "This is all hypothetical, you understand. I just want to make sure we're prepared for any eventuality that might spontaneously occur."

"I understand."

"Just to be blunt, I don't want to mention this to Missy. I get the feeling I can't trust her."

"Go with that feeling," she said.

* * *

Bix led his team back to the Quad to meet with Shane and Rudd for the official walk-through. Shane and Rudd were waiting when they arrived. After pleasantries, Mike began to lead off, starting at the motorcade arrival point.Immediately Rudd had a problem.

"Why don't you have the limo pull up in front of the first building we pass, McBride Hall?" he asked. "It's a closer walk from the car to the door. And we could use that building for Hold."

"If we did, then we couldn't get The Candidate from the building to the stage," said Bix. "We would still have to walk around to the Admin building and access the stage from there, and we would have no entrance for the press and no ability to move The Candidate to the small gymnasium that he will probably want to use. And I have no idea where we would put the greeters except outdoors."

Shane agreed. Bix said, "Let's move on."

Mike escorted everyone briskly through most of the remainder of the journey, as if trying to remain ahead of any Rudd concerns, until they stood where the main stage would be. They faced the space where 30,000 people would stand in two days.

"We can't have people behind him when he's on stage," Rudd said. "If there's an emergency situation we're surrounded. That's not going to work."

Mike was apoplectic. "Haven't you seen all of the other events we've been doing for the past year, and all the events that other candidates are doing? That's why we put in a buffer zone around the stage and an eighteen-inch-high catwalk to the stage with four-foot railings and eight-foot wide walking paths." His forehead furrowed. "You can't have different rules for us and everyone else and make up new ones as you go along."

Bix was enjoying the scene. Rudd couldn't win the argument.

Kate spoke up in her matter-of-fact way. "Kurt, this is the way we've been doing it forever. It works—trust us." Only she could have said that.

"It's up to Shane," Rudd said.

"I'm fine with it," Shane responded politely.

"Let's move on," Bix said. He wondered how much of a problem Rudd would be once Shane wasn't around. The man seemed indefatigable.

They discussed placement of the magnetometers through which the crowd would pass. Once again, Rudd was in attack mode.

"We won't be able to get as many as you want. You know your Opponent has a rally in Columbia that day. And it isn't just the equipment—it's the manpower to run them."

"Yes, we know," Bix said. "And we have an agreement with Service that we'll get the assets needed to move our crowd into the Site in a two-hour period. My estimate is based on three hundred to three hundred and fifty people per hour moving through each mag, and you're going to tell me you can move six hundred people per hour through each mag. My opinion is that if everyone was naked and sprinted through the mag's, you'd get six hundred people per hour."

"That's what our uniformed officers tell us," Rudd said. Shane didn't disagree. "But I don't think we can get that many mag's."

"You know, Special Agent Rudd, it shouldn't be this difficult," Bix said.

Mike was seething but stifled it, and Bix was about to continue his commentary in a way he might have regretted later when Kate spoke up. "Let us know what you can do in terms of numbers, and we'll speak to some people on our end and see what we can do," she said. Everyone seemed happy with her telling Kurt that they were about to go over his head again.

Bix concluded the walk-thru with thanks and handshakes and a promise to meet for the next dance rehearsal at 1800 hours at the hotel.

As they walked to their cars, Bix thanked Kate for stepping in at the opportune moment, and moments.

"Somebody had to stop you from lunging at him," she said.

* * *

Mike and Ben stayed behind at the Site to meet with contractors while Kate followed Bix to WXDL Radio.

WXDL was located in a late nineteenth-century, two-story brick building like many of those downtown. With its red and white tile entryway that read '1902 Front Street,' white limestone lintels above the upstairs windows, transom above the door through which Bix and Kate could see a pressed tin ceiling, and Art Deco 1940s-vintage neon WXDL Radio sign that hung in front, the building was a field trip to the past.

Bix glanced at an email from JD Ebsen announcing his arrival, and Bix asked him to go directly to the Schoendienst Gym. He sent the address and contact information, and told JD that once he saw the room he would know exactly what he needed to do. Bix added a little droolie face emoticon, along with, "You can thank me later." He wanted to prepare JD for the unpleasant surprise he was about to receive.

WXDL proved to be a respite from their travails. Radio days, good clean 1940s vintage fun. Kate had never produced a radio ad before and she enjoyed the process as much as Bix enjoyed playing professor. It was a sixty-minute mental vacation as far as he was concerned. Among the pictures of 1940s and 50s country music artists and early rockabilly stars on the walls of the old production studio was a photo of Jimmy Byrnes, South Carolina's distinguished former Governor, Senator, U.S. Secretary of State, and Supreme Court Justice, sitting at a microphone at the very desk where Bix sat. Byrnes was a Democrat and a Truman appointee. Bix examined the photo for a long minute, entranced by the personal nature of this small connection to history. It was a reminder of the timelessness of his profession as well as the fleeting nature of it. He doubted there was more than a handful of the current crop of political professionals and semi-professionals who would know who Jimmy Byrnes was, or cared.

He asked Kate to choose the background music from Mike's campaign CD of pre-approved tunes he had never heard of, and then taught her how to read copy like a used car salesman to provide the voice-over for the script he'd written. She was thrilled. In the ad she sounded like Lauren Bacall selling used cars after smoking a cigarette. It was radio magic.

They downloaded The Candidate's obligatory disclaimer and an hour later walked out with a five-hundred-dollar contract for eighty sixty-second spots to be aired over the next forty-eight hours, plus an agreement from the news director to interview local supporters on their morning and afternoon talk shows. They also carried four CDs containing the ad, three for other radio stations and one for Kate. Bix felt like Sam Phillips after a recording session at Sun Studio.

He feared there would be a karmic price to pay for so much un-adulterated enjoyment. The hour could have been better spent in a gut churning frenzy with one or more of his antagonists or worrying that he had no "Plan B" for anything—site, rain, anti-American manifestos, internal treachery—and no time to create one. He emailed Hani for the fifth time since noon and headed for the next tango with Mayor Bacon.

"Wait," Kate said. She hugged him. "Thanks for a good time. I loved it."

"Me too," he said. "I'm a sucker for living history, things that evoke a different era. It reminded me of the radio stations I saw when I was a kid, my first Congressional campaign in southwest Missourah in towns like Pineville, and Noel and Neosho. Those old stations were nostalgic even then. Now it's *really* nostalgic."

"I'll remember that experience for the rest of my life," she said.

"Bet you can't remember the last time you said that," he said.

"The only other time I said that, I wasn't wearing any clothes. You should be flattered. With that thought, I have to go meet Missy and do the press RON. Cheers."

"I'd blush if there was any blood in my veins," Bix said.

* * *

Mike met Bix at the mayor's office at 1:25 with news that President Gilliman was demanding The Candidate attend a reception with her and a hundred of her closest friends upon arrival at the college. "You knew it was coming," Mike said. "What are we gonna do that won't piss off both Gerta and headquarters?"

"I think we're gonna get a hundred and ten beautifully designed and tastefully laminated VVIP passes," Bix said. "Once we've tagged 'em, we can figure out what we doing with them from there, probably a special VVIP pen near the stage, standing room only, not in the press angle."

"Who are the other ten VVIP passes for?" Mike asked.

"Other than Shaunesy, Nurse Ratched, and the mayor, I'll have seven spares to bestow on those honorable few who deserve our most devoted attention."

"Next time we should mark them by using VVIP gift boxes with exploding dye-packs."

"Not too obvious?" Bix asked.

"Make them red, white and blue. Tell them it's patriotic," Mike said as they re-entered the mayor's lair. This time they were ushered into a conference room on the opposite side of the outer sanctum, where Mayor Bacon, Chief Fry, Fire Chief Sam Friendly, and one of the city's finest boys in blue were already seated around a long mahogany table with an empty water pitcher and eight dusty glasses on a tray in the middle.

"Gentlemen," the mayor said, "come awn in an' have a seat. I wan ta talk about Frahday. Have yah been able ta resolve the schedule to allaoh a visit to ma seniah centa?"

"Mr. Mayor, in all honesty I don't see how it can happen," Bix said. "I haven't spoken with anyone in the last couple of hours but it's not on the most recent schedule I've received, and given The Candidate's schedule on the back side of our event in Scepter, I don't see how they'll agree to it. It would add a half hour in travel time alone whether it's before or after the rally. And that's in addition to you waylaying him in your senior center. That's my honest assessment."

"Ah appreciate yoah honesty, and y'undastand this isn't puhssonel, but yoah Candidate may not be able ta speak at the college if he doesn't stop by an' pay his r'spects to the seniah citizens of Scepter County. They shud'nt be neglected just 'cause they cannot stand in lahn ta go ta yoah rallee. That wud be discrimination," the mayor said.

"Mr. Mayor, we can provide transportation for all of your seniors at the center and give them seats in a special area," Bix said.

"Handicap accessible and everything," Mike said.

"Thaht's vera kind a'you both, but then it wud b'necessara t' uproot all a'those people, an' ah can't ask them ta do thaht. If yuah Candidate visits the centa it wudn't b'necessara t'all."

"I understand, and I will continue to follow-up with Headquarters. If it were up to me we'd go spend an hour there, but I can't unilaterally add another event that will force the entire motorcade a half-hour out its way. They have a tendency to notice things like that. The Secret Service is really in control of the motorcade, truth be told, and unless I have a compelling reason they aren't usually prone to take detours," Bix said.

"Ah could *make* them take a detouah," the mayor said. "Ah've got th' Fiah Chief heah an' Ah could have him tun on all the fiah hydrants along College Road so yu'd haf ta take Hywa nahn past the senia centa. Ah'd drain th'watta towah drah an flood yoa road."

This was the best news Bix had heard in hours. "You mean you'd turn on all the fire hydrants along our motorcade route to flood the street and force us to take highway nine, past your Senior Center, around the far side of town to the college?"Bix looked at Mike and he knew it too. Bacon's threat fell squarely within the definition of a security risk. "If you would like me to, Mr. Mayor, I'll be happy to pass that along."

"No, not'all Bix. You go ahead an' tell yo folks. We don't want'a disrupt the fine rallah youh plannin' on Frahday."

Mike pitched in unexpectedly, "You know, sir, we already have a signed contract with the college to do the event."

Bix winced. It was a snotty thing to say, and it wasn't a good idea to tell the mayor he'd been outmaneuvered in front of his brother-in-law and the fire chief, who was probably also a relative, and the young cop, who probably was, too. Mayor Bacon looked surprised by the news, and just as his face began to register anger Bix steered the conversation back to the subject of Mayor Bacon's immense power.

"I'm certain the mayor is completely aware of our every move," he said quietly, "and I'm just as certain that the mayor knows he can have that contract abrogated for any one of a hundred reasons with just a snap of his fingers. Am I right, your honor?"

"Uh, thaht's right, thaht's right," he said. "Ah wudn't wont t'see it come t'that," he said.

"And we appreciate that, sir. Why don't we go now and I will follow up with your request immediately.".

The mayor gave them their leave, but stopped them before they reached the door. "Excuze meh jess a moment, Bix. Ya know weah gonna half ta send some off-dutah offissas ova ta yuah rallah syat ta provahde prahvit secuahity duran th' ovanaaght owahs, befoah the Secrat Sehviss takes ova. The citah cannot provahd those kinda manpowa resosses."

"Clever," Bix thought. It was a shakedown. The off-duty cops get money and the mayor may even get a part of the action. Bix stepped a few feet back toward Bacon and looked at him with dead eyes. "How many and how much," he said.

"Yuah gonna need abot fahve offissas foah abot eight owahs at twen-ta-fahve dollahs an owar."

"So each officer works an hour and sixteen minutes?" Bix said.

"No, no, no, son. Each an ev'ry one is gonna need ta be theah a full eight owahs."

"Mr. Mayor, you're killing me." Bix wasn't going to lie down without a few counter jabs. "Will these be the same officers who are going to be handing out tickets to our production trucks if they park one foot past a No Parking sign, or calling in tow trucks if their hubcaps aren't shiney enough?"

"Na, those wud be diff'rnt offissas," the mayor said.

"Yeah, well, I want to hire those guys, too," Bix said.

The mayor laughed as Bix and Mike excused themselves, made to the street in record time, and piled into Mike's car. Bix told him to drive to the field office in Scepter and immediately dropped a dime on Mayor Bacon. He called Shane.

"Do you remember Mayor Bacon's desire to have The Candidate go to the Eugene V. Bacon False Teeth Emporium?" Bixed asked.

"Yes. Is he going to get his way?"

"No, it's a half hour out of our way and the building wasn't de-signed with us in mind and there's absolutely *nothing* I can use it for on this trip. However, it seems that the mayor is so intent on seeing his dream come true that he threatened to have his friendly Fire Chief Sam Friendly turn on all the fire hydrants along College Road so the motor-cade is forced to take highway nine past the Bacon Monument. He said he'd drain the water tower."

"He said that?"

"He said that."

"Who else heard him say it?"

"He said it with Chief Fry, Fire Chief Friendly, and a fresh-faced law enforcement officer in the room, in addition to Mike and me."

"I can't believe he'd say that," Shane said.

"He said it. He told me he'd be happy if I said it to others."

"It looks like I'll have to take a couple of my agents and pay a visit to the mayor and the chief and say something to them about security threats."

"I was hoping you'd say that."

"Thanks, Bix. I'm glad you said something."

"I promise not to say anything to anyone if you decide to keep the mayor incommunicado for the next couple of days, behind-bars-wise speaking."

"If we do, we won't say anything."

"Got it. Mum's the word. See you at countdown."

Bix had a rush of euphoria. Mayor Bacon was bound to be chastened by a visit from the men in black—even *he* had to be contrite after that. He emailed Egan to let him know that he had to rat out the mayor for the good of the cause.

Mike asked him, "Am I incorrect about the senior center? Those people don't live there. They show up during the day for activities, right?"

"Exactly. They're ambulatory."

"Our offer was reasonable, then," Mike said.

"Yes, perfectly. Why don't you go ahead find a place at the rally where you could put a couple hundred chairs in the shade in case the mayor decides to take us up on our offer. You might want to put a couple handicapped accessible port-a-potties in there, too."

"I think I hear a plan," said Mike. "Are you going to launch a guerilla action on the Bacon Monument? Will you take hostages? This could rekindle the Civil War, you know. How can you put that over on the mayor? And don't forget Chief Fry."

"I'm not sure yet, but I think it will start with inviting him to accompany us throughout game day and telling him he has to meet us at the Hotel Marianne for departure to the Schoendienst Gym. You know the old saying about keeping your enemies close—this will be one of the rare times I've been able to put that into practice. Usually my enemies are prancing around out there somewhere on their own."

"Free-range enemies?"

"You'd think it'd be healthy, but it's not."

They were having a good time, too good. Pleasant outcomes had occurred in tandem, and a streak like that couldn't be maintained. Bix's Blackberry had been vibrating constantly for the previous half hour, and he smiled at the thought that one of the messages might be from Storie. If so, that would make three good things in a row, and he knew the world would soon collapse around his shoulders.

11

Two dozen emails awaited Bix, along with several voicemails, most of which were from Peem. Nurse Ratched resent the same email entitled "Schedule" three times demanding information. Bix was angry with himself for missing the phone call from Hani, and angrier once he listened to his voicemail.

"Bix my friend, it was so good to hear from you." Hani's voice was distinctive. He spoke excellent English with a slight Jordanian accent and also a slight Southern lilt picked up during three years at the University of Georgia. "I have arrived at Dulles airport and I must tell you, there was what looked like a television camera crew outside of the security gate videotaping people as they exited. I don't know if they were there for me but I turned around and I am waiting in the concourse until they leave. Please call me when you can."

When the team got to the Scepter campaign office Bix stayed in the car and and called Hani, who answered immediately.

"Bix, my friend, is that you?"

"Hani, my old friend, it's good to hear your voice. How have you been?"

"Grand, grand. Are you having escapades on the presidential campaign?" he asked.

"Yes, I am, and now apparently you are, too. Are you all right?"

"Yes, I'm fine. As I said in my message, I don't know if the camera crew was here for me or for another purpose, but they remained there for a long time. After a while I went into the rest room in the concourse and changed clothes. You would have enjoyed my ruse. I put on a Hawaiian shirt that I always bring with me, and a Red Sox cap, and I walked out with a lady pushing a stroller. We looked like a family and the camera crew didn't seem to take notice of me. Was I being overly concerned?"

"Hani, I'd love to be able to tell you that your ruse was all for naught because it would make an hilarious story, but I think they may have been looking for you. Were any of them wearing any identification?" Bix asked.

"Yes, they were wearing baseball caps with the Max News logo and credentials around their necks."

"Hani, I hope you believe in ghost stories, 'cause you're in one."

"Really?"

"Really," Bix said. "Where are you now?"

"I'm in the main part of the airport, and I am considering the possibility of buying a ticket to South Carolina to help you find Jamir. I am beginning to become concerned as well."

"Can you find him once you get here?"

"I believe I can. His cabin is outside of a town that's named after a plant or something like that. Once I see it on a map I'll know it, and I think I can find my way to his cabin once I find my way to the town. I can rent a car in Columbia."

"Hani, that's fairly flimsy. Are you certain?"

"I'm not completely certain, but it's the best I have. Unless you have something better. Would you like to meet me when I get there?"

"I'd love to, but I can't. I'll get someone I trust. And I'll scan a map of the state for plant-like towns. Could it be a flower? Don't worry about it. Let me know about your flight to Columbia—is there a flight today?"

"I think there is. I'll let you know."

"Please stay in touch, hourly if you can. We've got about twenty-four hours to find him before we go from damage prevention to damage control."

They hung up and Bix decided to remain in the car for a call to Peem.

After Bix updated him on the latest news, Peem was appreciative. "How the fuck did Max News know about your friend arriving at Dulles?" He was starting to sound like Thigpen. "How the fuck are they finding out all these things? Who the fuck have you been telling about this?"

Bix was having none of it. "Excuse me, Bob. Are you suggesting I'm the source of your troubles? Would you like to put Drule or his buddy Shaunesy in charge of the Pequod? I'll be happy to give up the tiller."

"No, not at all," Peem said. "It's just that someone's leaking and we can't figure out who it is. The only people who know about your personal contacts are you and Sophie, unless you've told anyone, which I'm not suggesting you did."

"It certainly sounded like you just did. Now I'm thinking about putting out a press release about this completely manufactured crisis." It was the wrong thing to say.

"Manufactured?" Peem shot back. "You think those Max News crews are manufactured? You think those calls from Max News to your friends from the State Department and the White House are manufactured? You think that Max News crew at the airport was manufactured?"

"You want my honest answer?"

"Yeah," Peem trilled again.

"My honest answer is who the hell knows. Regarding this so-called 'manifesto,' if there turns out to be no there there, then yes, it was manufactured. My honest answer is I don't think there's any there there, but only time will tell. So we have to guard against the negative, just in case there's something there. What we know is that Max knows everything. What we don't know is whether they are still finding out everything and the identity of the Quisling in our midst. Does that about cover it?"

"That about covers it. What are you gonna do about it?"

"I'm gonna let Hani find Jamir and hope that he can do it before Friday at noon, and I'm going to need you to send someone down here tomorrow to staff this thing for me. I need a body and I need one I can trust. OK with you? What's happened with Sophie?"

Despite his promise to provide every possible resource, Peem played it coy for some unknown reason. "I don't know, maybe Sophie could come. She has a lot of work here in the office, though. I'll ask her."

"Pardon me, wasn't this something you promised? It's not like I can pick some volunteer and tell *that* person to 'go meet the deputy foreign minister from Jordan and help him find his brother-in-law who holds the key to the possible destruction of the presidential campaign, and by the way don't mention it to anyone.' It would certainly be helpful to have someone we trust, someone who knows everyone who works in the belly of the beast."

"You have a point. I'll ask Sophie if she can go down to meet you. She has a two-year old daughter, so it may not be as easy as me assigning her."

"If she can't, choose someone else quickly."

Peem guaranteed his unwavering support and Bix expressed his appropriate appreciation because it was, after all, politics.

* * *

Things were popping inside the Scepter campaign office. All of the phones and long tables lining the walls were occupied with volunteers making calls, boxes of flyers for the rally were stacked in a corner, and teams of young people were carting away bundles for distribution. Bix stepped out of the way as a group of young men left with posters under their arms, and then watched Nora stand in the middle of the big room seemingly directing traffic. She was beaming. Bix spotted Miranda and a couple of the other college Y.D.'s organizing leaflet distribution. Miranda skipped over to greet him with a hug.

"Are we having fun yet?" Bixed asked.

"You know we are," she said. "This is a blast. We're putting thirty thousand flyers on the streets right now, and we'd love to help at the rally."

"No way," Bix said. "We can't let you have all the fun both before *and* during the rally. We need to split it up to people who are less deserving. While we're at the rally we're going to make you sit here and stuff envelopes, and you'll have to lick each one because we won't give you a wet sponge."

Miranda reacted enthusiastically for a reason Bix couldn't comprehend. She tugged on the sleeve of his sport coat and said, "I know you'll take good care of us. Freeway already told me I could help with the motorcade, and he told me I could watch from backstage during the rally. He said he'd get me a security pin."

"You know he has a wife and five children in Baltimore don't you?" Bix said.

"No, I didn't know that. He seems awfully young to have five children, and he told me he's from Michigan," she said.

"Quintuplets and plastic surgery, and he has a family in Michigan, too. I don't like to judge, but he's reprehensible, and he does have a good plastic surgeon."

Nora wrenched herself free from the madding crowd and greeted Bix with a hug as well. The day was picking up again.

"Bix was just telling me what an old sleezeball Freeway is," Miranda told her. "Luckily, I happen to like dangerous older men." She tugged on his coat sleeve again. "Thanks for getting us involved, and thank you for letting me know about Freeway. I *must* have a conversation with him about that."

"Things have gotten busier since this morning when you were here," Nora said. "Miranda brought in several people to volunteer, and we had some interesting new additions to our volunteer corps."

"Interesting is an interesting word. What do you mean by interesting?"

"See those four young women working the phones over there?" she asked. "When they arrived they told us that Mayor Bacon sent them to help out. They were completely honest and up front. Now, do you see the red-haired young woman sitting next to them at the phones? We're fairly certain that Shaunesy sent her. One of the staff here used to work in the Charleston office and she interned for him. But she hasn't said a word about it, claims to be a first-time volunteer, says she doesn't know anyone in the Charleston office, and I think she gave us a fake name."

Bix had no response, nor the energy to do more than shake his head. "That speaks volumes," he finally said. His back stiffened. "You look like you're doing a magnificent job, however. I hope this is as good for you as it is for us."

"It is. We'll have at least a hundred volunteers working the event. There is life once again in this old District Field Office, and energy.

Thank God. I hope you can get the crowd you want." It wasn't what Bix wanted to hear.

"I hope so, too," he said. "With your help I think we can. Are Michael, Freeway, and Thigpen here?"

"In the back room harassing the volunteers," she said.

"I'll go back and help them then. Thank you again, and keep in mind that if we don't get thirty thousand people we're blaming you, and Shaunesy will probably support us."

"Oh, great," Nora said.

"We love to share the love." His right eyebrow rose involuntarily. "You feeling the love?"

"I'm feeling the love,," she said.

"Now go out there and use that love to get us thirty thousand warm bodies. On the other hand, I don't care if they're warm as long as they're bodies. Find them, bring them, prop them up, and make 'em look happy."

"We'll get 'em, Cap'n." She laughed again.

As Bix walked to the back office he wondered if Nora might have a grandfather complex, which didn't appear likely. More likely, she was smitten with the Big Show that had come to town, and with Mike, who was showing a bit more personality than usual.

Mike and Freeway were hard at work on their cell phones while Thigpen was holding court in the conference room directing phone bank, leaflet, and poster operations. Two of the college Y.D.'s were working in the room, which was strewn with paper coffee cups and Chinese take-out containers. The floor was filled with more boxes of flyers.

Thigpen yelled to Bix to come in. "What do you think of the flyers? I designed them."

Bix picked one up. "You misspelled The Candidate's name," he said.

Thigpen freaked out momentarily as he looked at the one in his hands. "Don't DO that to me dude. Never *ever* do that to me."

"Don't you mean 'don't fucking do that to me, fucking something something'"? Bix asked.

"That's exactly what I mean."

"They look great, and the poster does, too. It's obvious you're moving a lot of paper. Good job. By the way, could you please write down a couple of things on your to-do list?"

Thigpen pulled out a small pad of paper. "Go."

"First, as you are acquiring shuttle buses and the like for your crowd, and putting together a budget, find me four large buses, fifty-passenger or more, that we can task on Friday morning. I'll also need a volunteer on each one, and I'll need them at ten a.m., so you can use buses to shuttle people to the rally up 'til then. I'll let you know on Friday morning where to send them. Does that make sense?"

"Got it."

"And, second, remember to clean this room before you leave. We don't leave blood, we don't leave trash, and we can't leave this place looking like my Crowd Advance guy's apartment. Nora would not be happy with us."

"I was planning on it," Thigpen said. "By the way, just so's you'll know, your good friend the mayor is fucking us. Bacon's ward healers are telling people not to come to our rally unless they get the okay from Bacon, along with some not-so-subtle threats."

"Not surprising," said Bix. "A little unsubtle, but not surprising. We'll work on it. He went into the sparse undecorated office where Mike was intently focused on a phone call while Ben and Freeway labored at their laptops. Mike's conversation was clearly anguished.

"What do you mean you can't do a political event in Scepter without the approval of the mayor's office?" Mike said. "Your business is in Columbia, but you're saying you need the mayor of Scepter's official okey dokey" That's unbelievable. What if the mayor doesn't deign to bless us? You're shitting me...yeah, yeah, yeah, no problem." He hung up and looked at Bix. "We're screwed."

"Give me the least bad news first," Bix said.

"I've talked with three production companies, two in Charleston and this last one in Columbia. They won't work in Scepter County unless Mayor Bacon says it's ok. The first guy I talked to told me it's not worth it—if the mayor doesn't sanction the event, the police hand out tickets like candy. Their trucks are ticketed for unspecified parking violations, they get tickets for tires without enough tread, tickets for excessive noise, tickets for driving a truck on the wrong street. He told me his staging and lighting equipment was impounded for two weeks and he lost several thousand dollars when he did an event for a guy running for Congress who the mayor didn't like. We're running out of time."

"Then go out of state for a contractor," Bix said. "Who's your favorite in Atlanta? Gershon Productions?"

"Yeah. Should I get them? Obviously they don't have time to provide a bid in advance."

"Yes, a no-bid contract. Tell them what you need and have them load up the truck. I'll work it out with Egan. We need to coordinate with JD too. We'll give Gershon both events. Hope they've got everything we need."

"If they don't, they should know where to get it," Mike said. "They may know where we can rent bleachers as well," Mike said.

"Go ahead and rent a cherry picker locally. Make it a big one, and get it before the mayor puts an embargo on industrial equipment. You heard the mayor is actively surpressing our crowd?"

"Yeah, I heard. Ready for another one?" Mike asked.

Bix speculated. "The Candidate's mistress is in town, wants to attend the event and stand on the stage with him?"

"Almost as good," Mike said. "President Gilliman not only wants a greeting for her Board of Regents, she wants to be able to invite what she calls her 'local community partners' and turn the whole thing into a fund raiser. She is literally demanding that our guy spend a half-hour in a reception room doing a fund raiser for the College of Scepter, and she's not sure how many people she wants to invite."

"Can he bring his mistress?" Bix asked.

"I'll check with President Gilliman."

"Anything else?"

"No. Isn't that enough?"

"That's enough for me. Now we get to do something that's both satisfying and worthwhile."

"Is the president of the college Young Dem's coming in?" Mike asked.

"He is, indeed. Ben, Freeway, I'd like you to stay. We're going to teach you how to do a proper OTR that will fill a news vacuum with incredible visuals at no cost, and, by my estimation, little risk."

"We'll either teach you how to do that," added Mike, "or how to piss off everyone on the traveling staff and at Headquarters. Either way it's a learning experience."

"The byword for this kind of operation is 'spontaneous,'" Bix said.

"Spontaneous," Ben repeated.

* * *

Jerry Litton, Scepter College Young Democrats' president, was waiting in the big room as Bix spoke. He was talking with Miranda, who, as Bix found out, was the Y.D.'s treasurer. She helped him find his way back to the temporary Advance office and introduced him to The Testosterones. Bix invited them both to sit down and asked Freeway to close the door behind them.

After they sat, Bix greeted them warmly. "Can I trust you punks?" he said with a straight face.

"You can trust me," said Litton, "but I don't know about her. She's always looked shady to me. Miranda, can we trust you?"

"If I get to meet The Candidate," she said.

"Then I've got leverage," Bix said. "That's good enough for me. We have a secret mission for you. Are you in? Do you think you've got the guts for this?"

Miranda answered quietly, "Oh, yeah."

"First, have either of you ever been to a toga party?"

"No. What's that?" Litton asked.

"That's what I thought—just curious. This has nothing to do with that. We want you to organize a spontaneous demonstration tomorrow night, and we need you to do it on the DL. Do you know what that means?"

"Are you talking about doing it on the down-low, under the radar, on the Q.T., behind the scenes, hush-hush, covertly, secretly, no finger-prints, no footprints?" Litton asked.

"I love this kid," Bix said. "Need anyone doubt that the future of our country will be left in good hands? Miranda, *this* is a wholesome young man, as opposed to…I'm not saying, but you know who."

Miranda laughed and looked at Freeway. Freeway didn't have a clue.

"Here's the deal," Bix explained. "We would like you to organize as many of your friends as possible, quietly, and stage them at a pre-determined location tomorrow night at 8:00 p.m. We are planning to do what we call an OTR, or off-the-record event, as we motorcade into town from the airport. What we would do is call you when we have wheels-down and tell you where to go. Then you call the local TV stations and tell them what's happening, you all jump in your cars and you go to your destination, and we bring The Candidate to you. And fun ensues. Simple. And we only need fixty or sixty people to pull it off, but more is better. Can you do it?"

"*Yeah*, we can do that," said Miranda. "We can easily get you fifty people."

"Definitely," Litton agreed.

"Can you do it by word of mouth alone, no digital trail?" Bix asked.

"I think so. Have you decided where you plan to go?" Litton asked.

"It will be dictated largely by logistics, like where we can pull in a motorcade, press movements, walking routes. We'll just have to let you know when we call you. It will have to be in Charleston, roughly along the motorcade route, so I'll have you stage everyone somewhere near there. We'll pick a location for you to congregate that's relatively close to your final destination."

"This is exciting—will we get to meet him?" Miranda asked.

"I can't guarantee that, but this will be a small group situation and it'll be as good a time as any," Bix said. He could have guaranteed it.

"We'll start organizing immediately," said Litton. "Let us know as soon as you can where you want us to stage everyone."

"Guys, this will be good," said Bix. "We'll fill up some TV time tomorrow night and Friday morning with quality images, and it will help us promote the rally. It's a two-fer."

They talked for another ten minutes about volunteering for the rally, another hot topic, and Bix sent the two off on their secret mission.

"I thought you promised Service we wouldn't do an OTR between the airport arrival and the RON hotel," Freeway said. "You're not going back on your word are you? That wouldn't live up to the code."

"At ease, soldier," said Bix. "When have you ever known me to lie to the Service? When have you ever known me not to live up to the code?"

"What code?" Mike asked.

"Whichever." Bix said. "Freeway, you understood correctly. There will be no stops between the airport and the hotel. This is not to be mentioned outside of this room to anyone. By *anyone* I'm including our RON Advance, Missy. I haven't even met her yet and I don't trust her."

"We understand," Mike said. "You're going to do it at the hotel, aren't you?"

"I didn't say that. I didn't *not* say that either. But now that you mention it, the hotel will be crawling with agents and cops. It would certainly be convenient for them because the place is already secured," Bix said. "I'll give that serious consideration."

"It's going to take more than a fifty people to fill that lobby," Mike said.

"They'll get more than fifty," Bix said.

"What does Kate say?" Mike asked.

"She's down with it," Bix said.

"Does that mean she's up for it?" Mike said.

"Absolutely. If it's happening, she said the traveling press is going to want to see it. She just needs to know where to escort them. Keep in mind it's...what is it?" Bix nodded toward them.

"Spontaneous," Mike, Ben and Freeway said as one.

"Excellent, gentlemen. As soon as I've decided the finer points of my plan I will brief you."

"What about Missy?" Mike asked. "If you're doing this at the hotel, are you sure you shouldn't tell her?"

"Normally I would, but Missy appears to be on her own trajectory. Until I can determine where her loyalties lie, I'd prefer not. She's already late to the party, and she's got enough to say grace over with the RON. I'm going back to meet with her now."

"What do I tell Gerta about her fundraiser?" Mike said.

"Tell her we need approval from Headquarters and that I will let her know tomorrow morning. We need a little more time for the momentum to build. *Then* I can tell her no."

As Bix left he noticed that the number of volunteers in the room had swelled. While most were young, he was surprised at the number of middle-aged and older people who were working the phones, picking up literature, and organizing distribution locations. One tiny senior citizen, a lady decked out in a dark blue running suit with white piping and matching Nike running shoes, her grey hair tastefully coiffed, was happily lugging boxes of flyers out to a Buick sedan parked in front. Bix asked Nora who she was.

"Believe or not, that's Grandma Sadie. She's been volunteering here for a couple of months. She has the strength of an ox."

"Would she sound good if she were interviewed on radio?" Bix asked.

"She'd be great. She's a retired teacher and our biggest cheerleader."

"Good to know," said Bix. "We may want to tap her to do some interviews tomorrow. Has Thigpen mentioned that we will want to do a poster party tomorrow afternoon at about four o'clock, so we get on the five and six o'clock news?"

"Yes, he told me. That will be wonderful. We can get a hundred volunteers in here making posters. This is exciting—thank you so much. I'm glad you're here."

"Now you understand why I do this," said Bix. "How often does one get to hear that in real life? At least in my case, if it weren't for this, the answer would be never." He checked-out the caller-ID on his phone. It was Peem.

* * *

Bix walked outside to answer the call. "Hello, Bob."

"What the fuck is going on in Scepter?" Peem said.

"Just fine, how are you doing?"

"I've got Jimmy Pangborn on my ass about our schedule and he's making not-so-vague threats about endorsing our Opponent if we don't kiss Mayor Bacon's ass. I thought you were going to handle him."

"No, *you* thought I was going to handle him. I thought I was going to get a vacation."

"If Congressman Pangborn endorses her, we're dead. What the fuck is going on?"

"The mayor still has a bug up his butt about us visiting the senior center that bears his name and his likeness. He knows we have a signed contract with the college, which pissed him off, and he's probably pissed off that I outed him to the Service for threatening to create a security risk for the motorcade. So now he's using his clout with Pangborn. But hey, I'm happy to take The Candidate to the Bacon Barn if you want me to."

"How long would it take?"

"Bob, the question isn't simply how long it will take—it's 'what will it cost us?' It will cost us over a half hour in drive time. It will cost whatever time we spend inside the senior center with Bacon as host and master of ceremonies, which could be forever. It will cost us any control over our schedule *and* The Candidate once Bacon lures our boss into his multi-use, multi-room building. And it will cost us the 'event-of-the-day' because IT will be the event-of-the-day. Even if we pool the press, *it* will be the event-of-the-day. The mayor will hijack our news coverage and we will gain no benefit because the mayor supports our Opponent and everyone knows it. At *best* it's an embarrassment, and at worst, the mayor will say something that we regret. I don't intend to provide him that forum. I've offered to provide transportation and VIP seating at our rally for the people who go to his recreation center, but so far Bacon's turned me down."

"Is there anything you can do?" Peem moaned. "I've also got Max News breathing down my throat and I don't need this too."

"You have my sympathy," Bix said. "I've only got Max News, Mayor Bacon, Gerta Dammerung, Chief Buford Justice, a Site agent with a Napoleon complex, a putz of an RFD with a Napoleon face, and bigger putz of a deputy campaign manager with lord-knows-what issues, and you all breathing down my *neck*."

"OK, OK, neck. What's happening with Jamir? Where the hell is your friend Hani? Are you gonna find that fucking manifesto? Max News is calling us every five minutes."

"Hani's on his way. Is Sophie?"

"Sophie's working it out. She may have to bring her daughter."

"Isn't that too much to ask of her?"

"No, it's ok. She wants to help."

Bix shook his head, a worthless gesture on a cell phone but he thought Peem could sense it anyway.

"No, you were right," Peem said. "I need to send someone I trust."

"Absolutely, you should have one of those down here so you'll have, like, one in the area," Bix said. "Here's what I'm going to do. I'm going to stop communicating with you for a while so I can focus on my job. I'm sure you'll be listening on the conference call at five-thirty. Let me know if you want to add an hour and a half to the schedule for the mayor's magical mystery tour."

"Don't fuck this up," Peem said.

"Uh-huh. Tell Egan to approve my budget when I send it in later." Bix was becoming physically tired from the effort of being diplomatic. He was niced out. He hung up the phone and said, "Go fuck yourself." It wasn't cathartic.

* * *

JD at Site 2 was in need of attention before the afternoon ended, as was Missy at the hotel, before the staff meeting and countdown. As Bix drove to the Schoendienst Gym, he couldn't resist the urge to annoy Hani, and Hani was nice enough to answer his phone despite knowing who was on the other end.

"Bix, hello, I am on my way to National Airport to try to get on a flight that leaves tonight." The background noise sounded like a traffic jam on the Dulles toll road.

"You're taking a cab to National?"

"Yes, it isn't a problem," Hani said.

"Were you followed?" The moment he said it he knew that he'd crossed the some line, a point at which he succumbed to groupthink and lost his independent, rational thought. The situation, the issue, the crisis, had its own momentum, its own flow, and Bix had become one of the pumping stations. Everything he did, he realized, added impetus to the perception that an actual crisis was not only approaching but was in fact happening. Bix thought, "I've become one of *them*."

"I don't think so," Hani said. "If I cannot get on the flight tonight I will have a friend pick me up and spend the night at his house."

"Are you still wearing your Red Sox cap and Hawaiian shirt?" Bix asked.

"Yes, I look good."

"Your embassy called and told me they need you to come in right now because they are having a reception you must attend, and you need to have new passport photos taken too," Bix said.

Hani laughed. "That's a smashing idea. I will be happy to do it if you bring the keffiyah I gave you and we get new photos together."

"I look damn good in that thing," Bix said, "I could pass for Florence of Arabia. I know I look authentic because when I go outside in my neighborhood wearing it people throw things at me."

Hani laughed harder. "It is always good to talk with you, Bix. You have serious work but you see the humor in it too, and I know you wouldn't have contacted me if it wasn't serious. Can you tell me what's happening with Jamir? Is there some kind of trouble?"

"You may as well know—everyone else in the world does," Bix said. "Back in the 1980s, it seems Jamir and my boss were terrorist sympathizers, or 'terr symp's as they're known in the trade, and on top of that they were terrorist apologists, or 'terr app's. Their terr symp and terr app beliefs were proclaimed in a well-conceived and thoroughly researched manifesto that must have taken days to write, rewrite, and ultimately perfect. *Then* said proclamation was kept cleverly hidden for years in hopes of having it come to light by nefarious means at some point in the future, thus destroying their careers just when things were taking off."

"Really?" Hani's inflection rose a couple of octaves.

"That's the upshot. Now, because some students at Stearns U where Jamir works are claiming to have seen this manifesto, Dick O'Malley and Max News are on a mission to either find it and destroy the senator's presidential campaign, or find nothing and report the rumor and destroy the senator's presidential campaign. The RNC is probably investigating this as well, and a few other media outlets, and as the rumors grow there will be more."

"Really." Hani's inflection dropped.

"I believe that sums it up."

"This is why your campaign is in jeopardy? This sounds like high school," Hani said.

"You've been exposed to American politics before, haven't you?" Bix said.

"Don't they know Jamir was a Foreign Service diplomat in the U.S. State Department, the one in Washington?"

"Doesn't make a difference," Bix said. "They wrote the manifesto in college, allegedly, but if it comes to light now it's current news. They may as well have written it yesterday. And Jamir is Iranian, he looks Iranian, he sounds British, he's well-educated—ladies and gentlemen of the jury, he's guilty where he stands. And he's disappeared, so he's obviously hiding something. When he shows up he will make for great television, whether it's a manifesto or macaroni with pesto."

"That sounds disgusting. I'm hungry and that sounds disgusting. We will find him and lay this ugly rumor to rest, and hopefully get him on the Martha Stewart show to make his famous macaroni with pesto."

"You are kind to help, despite your sanity. Will you call or email me when you know your flight situation?"

"You can rely on it, and you can count on my vote for king of the senior prom. You deserve it."

Bix roared.

"I knew you would like that," Hani said.

"Yes, but it hurts. You cut too close to the bone," Bix said.

"I know you are doing your job. You must respond whether it is rational or not because either way there might be damage. I understand that, and you must be receiving a lot of pressure from your campaign headquarters, where I'm certain there is much consternation and gnashing of teeth. It is nonetheless silly, and this could create serious problems for me with my superiors, especially if your guy doesn't win."

"I understand, believe me. You can still walk away from this. I wouldn't blame you at all."

"No, I want to help find Jamir and my sister and put this issue to rest."

"If this works out the way I hope, you will end up at my rally," Bix said.

"You're putting on a rally, too?"

"Yes, I guess I forgot to mention it. I apologize. I've been compartmentalizing. I'm doing a rally in Scepter, South Carolina, on Friday at noon. You'd have a good time."

"I would like that a lot. Thank you."

* * *

When Bix arrived at Red's Gym JD was in the parking lot with Special Agent Meyer, his counterpart, attired in a black suit, white blouse, black shoes, squiggly wire, sunglasses, etc. - assessing their options, mapping logistics and assigning places for satellite trucks, generator, motorcade, magnetometer and press equipment.

Jay-Dee exemplified the word "affable." Still in his early thirties, he had an encyclopedic knowledge of American culture and understood every obscure reference Bix ever made, from Myrna Loy and the Jersey Lily to Sacco and Vanzetti. They hadn't worked together for a couple of months. After smiles and man-hugs, JD asked Bix, "What the fuck have you done to me this time? You *know* this is the worst site in the world, don't you?"

"Be nice," Bix said, "it happens to be a favorite of Special Agent Meyer."

"Don't get me wrong. I love the building. It's a fantastic building— it just sucks as a site."

"I don't mind," Agent Meyer said. "I know what you mean, but it will be easy to secure, and there really are no other choices."

"Like she said," Bix said, grinning. "We're stuck. You're stuck. It is a great building, though."

"It is, and that's fun, but it's gonna suck." JD was smiling too, but he made his point.

"You've seen how you will need to build the room," Bix asked, "with the stage at the far end so we can come and go through the hall-way that connects to the Hold?"

"It'll be long and thin," JD said. There is no room for a cutaway shot, and I may have to stack the press riser three tiers high. We'll be packed in there like anchovies."

"Yes, it will, but I trust in your ability to make it look decent," Bix said. "Use the intimacy of the room to your advantage. Maybe Agent Meyer will allow us to shrink the buffer zone since we'll only have a hundred and fifty general public."

"I'd consider that," Agent Meyer said, "because it's a small crowd in a small space, as long as we have good egress."

"We'd appreciate that," Bix said. "And JD, please get an equipment list to Mike as soon as possible. He's getting an out-of-state contractor for both events—Gershon out of Atlanta—and they will have to be our one-stop shop."

"How about a backdrop?"

"The focus should be on The Candidate and his endorser," Bix said, "and if his endorser is who I think it is, we can use veterans for the back-drop and throw up a bunch of American flags behind them, then more American flags at any angle where the cameras may wander. You'll make it look good. We just need a great head-on shot. You can turn lemons into lemonade."

"Yeah, but I can't make a site that sucks suck less," JD said.

* * *

Bix thanked Agent Meyer, bid his farewells, and headed back to the Hotel Marianne to meet Missy. He was already dreading the meet-ing, although not for completely rational reasons. The sound of her name, Missy, had a negative connotation, although the only two people he'd known with that moniker were both completely likeable individuals.

This particular version of "campaign Missy" was causing him distress before he cast his normally avuncular eyes upon her, despite his distaste for prejudging people. He hewed to the gentlemen's creed of an earlier era, the era of Truman, Acheson, Hull and Marshall, who believed that "the way to make a man trustworthy was to trust him." Since there were no women in those gentlemen's professional vicinity in the 1940s to be either trusted or distrusted, Bix averred that they would say the same about women, were they alive today. But Missy's reputation had both preceded her and been recently reinforced, and he didn't have the time to screw around. She would be on a very short leash. She would have to earn her admission into the in-crowd, to know all the things the in-crowd knows and go where the in-crowd goes.

He arrived in the Staff office to find Kate and Cornelia working and waiting for him and Missy. Bix, as usual, was on Republican time, and Missy was late. It was exactly five p.m., a half hour before the staff meeting and an hour before countdown. He emailed her, "Missy, waiting for you in the staff office."

She emailed back quickly, "Be right there."

Bix smiled when he read it. Kate saw his reaction. "What?" she said.

"Missy will be right here," Bix explained.

"I've talked with her about the problems we had last time," Kate said, "including such things as her reliability, remaining focused on those responsibilities that she's been assigned to perform, and I told her to come to me and Cornelia for help or advice if she needed anything. She asked me if I would task Cornelia with the job of pre-registering the traveling staff and I offered advice instead. I told her that was the responsibility of the RON, and she said that task was more 'clerical' in nature."

"Cornelia, were you in the room when she said that?" Bix asked.

"Yes. I thought it might be interesting to jump up and grab her by the throat when she said it, but I assumed you would think it was out of character for me," Cornelia said. "If Thigpen did something like that you wouldn't think it was out of place."

"If Thigpen did something like that I'd take away his Advance man uniform and send him home," Bix said. "If you did something like that I'd assume you had a good reason."

Bix was startled by Missy's entrance into the office, and it wasn't by the sound of the hotel room door closing with a thud. He had set expectations, as hard as he tried not to, and he was surprised at the magnitude of his wrongness. Whereas he'd anticipated a sweet young thing in her early twenties with curly tresses, a button nose, lace collar, a pampered air and an indifferent pose—something akin to a Bostonian Southern belle—in walked NASCAR Missy, a wiry little coppery redhead in her late thirties with the look of experience about her. She struck Bix as a woman who had recently spent time in the pits, judging by the drag race graphic on her t-shirt, her tight, tattered jeans and not sensible high-heeled boots.

She was very nice. "Bix, it's so good to finally meet you. I've heard a lot of good things about you."

"It's nice to finally meet you as well." Bix smiled but raised an eyebrow just in case she hadn't understood the double entendre. She got the point.

"Yes, I'm so sorry about that. I missed my flight."

"How is everything going today? Are you making good progress?" Bix asked.

"What do you mean?" Missy said.

"With the RON," Bix said. This time his eyebrow elevated involuntarily. "Are you working with your Secret Service counterpart? Have you met with hotel management? Have you pre-registered and assigned the travelling staff to specific rooms on the secured floor? Have you been working with Kate to make sure the press accommodations and logistics are arranged? Do you know where the motorcade is arriving and the route up to The Candidate's suite? Have you identified a room for luggage call? You know, that type of thing."

"Oh yes," Missy said. "I've met with Sam Cole, the RON agent, and with the hotel managers, and I saw The Candidate's suite. We're still getting down to the rest of the specifics."

Bix contained his concern. "Missy, we need you to pin all of those things down tonight after countdown. Depending on Kate's needs, you may want to identify a press room too in case we need to do a 'press avail' at the last minute."

"That would be good," Kate said. "We'll go with you after count-down—we can block the press sleeping rooms, too. Bix, where do you want us to hand out room keys?"

"Given the problems we encounter when we do press check-in in the hotel lobby, I'd prefer you hand out the room keys on the bus in the motorcade."

"I haven't seen the manifest yet, but what if we end up with two bus-loads of press?" Kate asked.

"Pre-assign them to bus number one or bus number two on the air-plane, and divide the room keys accordingly," Bix said. "It's only for the twenty-minute ride from the airport to the hotel, so you just need a couple of volunteers. Has Thigpen gotten you a few good volunteers?"

"Yes," Cornelia said, "We met with them today, and they will be in tomorrow morning at eight o'clock. They will be with us for the next two days."

"So you guys are gonna handle the press rooms and give them their keys?" Missy asked. "I don't have to worry about that?"

"We'll take care of the press," Kate said. "You can focus on The Candidate and the traveling staff, and make sure the staff office is fully equipped. We will need another hard-line internet connection, copy pa-per, toner just in case, power strips."

"Can I get a volunteer from Thigpen, too?" Missy asked.

"Yes, or we'll give you one of ours," Kate said.

"What about the hotel management and staff?" Missy said. "The ho-tel manager Mr. Ahren said he would like to have The Candidate greet his hotel staff when he arrives tomorrow night and again when he de-parts on Friday morning, because they're two different shifts. He says that's how they do it. It's only about thirty people per shift, he said."

"Missy, Headquarters would never approve that," Bix said. "The last thing in the world we want to ask of The Candidate is to do a receiv-ing line when he arrives at the hotel after a long day." Bix realized his hypocrisy as it spilled from his lips. "Please ask Mr. Mondi if he would like to greet The Candidate on arrival, and we will arrange a place where he can meet ten or twelve of the hotel's staff on Friday morning. Mr. Mondi can choose who they are, but we will need their name check information tomorrow morning."

"That's *it*? Ten or twelve staff?" Missy asked. "They are doing a lot for us. They go out of their way. I already got their name check information. That's what took me a lot of the afternoon." She handed the list to Bix. She had made the mistake of numbering the names. Bix noted there were seventy-seven.

"Granted," Kate said, "and we fill up about two hundred room nights in their hotel at the government rate. They're charging us for conference rooms, meeting rooms and two suites, and they make a killing every time we eat in the hotel."

"Which is never," Bix said.

"True, but the press will eat here, and they will make liberal use of the bar, even the conservative reporters," Kate said. "Especially the conservative ones. The hotel's profit from those guys alone is considerable, although they don't tip for shit."

"Well, it's always been my motto to take care of the hotel staff because they take care of you," Missy said.

"Always, as in for the past three weeks since you've been doing hotel Advance?" Bix asked.

Kate stepped in once again to contain a possible Bix attack. "Missy dear, it is a lovely sentiment to take care of hotel people, but we also have to take care of the people we work for, and the press, of course. The Candidate sometimes shakes hands with the hotel staff he comes in contact with on a normal basis, but we can't add two receiving lines to his work day..." she smiled slightly and looked at Bix, "unless there is some media benefit."

"Well stated," Bix said. "No receiving line on arrival tomorrow night, and you and I will identify a place tomorrow morning where he can shake hands with ten employees on departure."

"I don't agree," Missy said.

Bix felt as if the top of his head might blow off. He sat back in his chair, entwined the fingers of his hands and rested them on his head, physically attempting to keep the lid on. Only then did he begin to search for the right words, attempting to edit his immediate reaction—a profanity-laced diatribe—before he spoke.

Kate mediated once again, concerned that his editing process may not have been complete before he shared his observations. "Be that as it may," she said, "but we can't make commitments of this type without Headquarters' approval, and we already know they don't, so you might want to, sort of, give it up."

Missy looked as though she was winding up for another endearing aphorism when the remainder of the Advance team filed-in for the 5:15 conference call. Mike, JD, Thigpen, Ben, and Freeway arrived as a pod and took seats at the tables around the room.

"Let's get Headquarters on the phone," Kate said. It was clear to her and Bix that Missy was going to pursue the course of action she decided was correct regardless of their opinions. Bix appreciated Kate's segue.

* * *

Kate dialed the landline on the table next to her, hit the "speaker" button, punched in the PIN, set the phone on "mute" and heard the assembled masses at headquarters as they talked to the Advance team in Minnesota. Team Charleston/Scepter listened quietly for a few minutes while H.Q. wrapped up the discussion of "4-H sheep barn vs. Minot Motel ballroom" as potential Sites for a town hall meeting, then Alecia took over as moderator for her part of the call.

"Team Charleston/Scepter, are you there?" she asked.

Kate un-muted the phone.

"We're all here," Bix said as he settled into the chair next to Kate's.

"Good. Let's go through the schedule," Alecia said, as she began to read through minute by minute, asking for comments or questions at each crucial step.

"We have wheels-down in Charleston at eight-thirty p.m., no greeters, load and go with arrival at the RON at nine-fifteen p.m., go down for the night. Any questions?" she asked.

"Has the hotel agreed to keep the restaurant open late?" asked one young Press office staffer.

"What room will serve as luggage drop-off for the press?" asked another.

"Missy has been here working today with the hotel management," Bix said, "but we haven't had a chance to talk, so Missy, would you like to address those questions?"

"We haven't talked about those things yet," Missy said, "but I will find out."

"There is such a short turnaround time on this Advance," Bix interjected, "we will all pitch in to help on the RON."

"Missy," the controlled cadence of Alecia's voice came through the speaker, "this is why we sent you there. If you have any questions ask Bix or Kate, but we need you to lock down the arrangements for the travelling staff and press. You have the RON checklist. These are questions we need answers to tonight."

"I have some questions about the hotel staff greeting on arrival and departure," Missy said.

"Ask your Lead," Alecia said quickly.

Snap, Bix thought.

She continued, "Bix and Kate, I know you're running as fast as you can to produce the rally and our second event, but if you could take a few minutes to go through the checklist with Missy I'd appreciate it. This is the first RON she's done alone."

Double snap, Bix thought. "We will," he said.

Alecia walked through the remainder of the schedule and ended with two questions: "Will you be able to produce this rally at Scepter College, and will you get a crowd?

"We *will* have the rally at the college," Bix said. "Have we resolved all of the issues? No, but they will be resolved one way or the other."

"Is it the president of the college who's giving you trouble?" Alecia asked.

"It's not just her, it's this Byzantine maze of disconnected special interests and personalities converging on the visit," Bix said, "a mash-up of *Cat on A Hot Tin Roof* and *Animal Crackers*."

"No one understands those references, Bix," Alecia said.

"OK, then it's a really an interesting anthropological study," he said, "if you want to look at it that way, or a Charlie Foxtrot if you want to look at it *that* way. Either way, we'll handle it."

"What's a Charlie Foxtrot?" Alecia asked.

"It's code for a mess caused by a lot of people," Bix said.

"It stands for '*cluster fuck*,'" Thigpen yelled.

The Advance team could hear Headquarters staff over speakerphone laughing in the background.

Alecia was still laughing when she asked, "Can I use that one?"

"It's all yours," Bix said.

"How's the crowd building out there going?" It was Peem's voice.

Thigpen yelled from his seat at another table, "It's going freaking great, just like always."

Bix assumed Thigpen didn't know or care whose voice it was. "Bob, you heard it from the source."

"Are you gonna get your crowd?" Peem asked.

Bix spoke quietly, once again channeling Gregory Peck. "I believe Mr. Thigpen will produce the crowd."

"Bix, this is Eric in Political. I know you're aware of our situation with Congressman Pangborn. I don't have any suggestions, but we need you to diffuse that as soon as possible. You're there on the ground—do you know what you're going to do?"

At least the kid was being honest, Bix thought. "Eric, it would be useful if Headquarters would give me the approval to promise Mayor Bacon that we will come back to Scepter and go to his senior center before the primary, although he might ask me to 'put that in wrattin.'"

"We can't promise him that," Alecia said. "It's possible we'll go back to Scepter, but we can't say so it at this point. We certainly won't be there in the next week, which leaves us less than a week before the primary."

"In that case I don't have an answer for you yet, and if I did you wouldn't want to hear it."

"How's your relationship with the mayor?" Eric asked.

"He loves Bix," Kate interjected. "Bix isn't intimidated."

"It is absolutely true," Bix said. "He loves me. And do you know what that means? It means he will kiss me on the lips as he's screwing me. It means that *he* knows that *I* already know what he is trying to do to me, and he's going to do it anyway. All I can say is that I will have to fix this thing on the fly, because I have to keep moving to stay ahead of his grasp, at which point it could get ugly."

"Bix, this is Larry Drule. I want to make sure you're not taking resources away from the Field office in Scepter, or interfering with their work. I've had some complaints."

The Advance team looked at each other, chagrined in the extreme. Bix thought about his response for a moment and clenched his teeth. Kate looked at him, shook her head "no" and mouthed the words, "Don't say it."

Bix moderated his response both in tone and substance. "This is the same drill as anywhere, Larry. We asked permission." He sounded exasperated. "And we're producing volunteers, not stealing them." Then snarky reappeared. "And I, along with all the rational people on this part of the planet, are under the impression that gathering thirty thousand supporters and potential supporters in one place at one time just down the block from our campaign office would be considered a boon for Field. What's the nature of the complaints, that we're making it too easy for them?"

"There's some concern that you are taking over the Field office and using their volunteers and their resources," Drule said. "I'm also concerned that you're getting involved in the political side and interfering with some established relationships we have with the mayor."

The guy was inching a stake toward Bix's heart.

Kate shook her head "no" again.

"Larry, you are one hundred percent correct," Bix said, "our local RFD—"

Kate cringed.

"—has indeed forged a relationship with the mayor in the week and a half he's been here. The problem is that our Opponent's deputy national Field director has forged a better one. She has been here a lot longer, she has spent a lot of quality time with the mayor, he likes her, and he thinks she's good at her job."

Kate relaxed a bit.

He continued, however. "Shaunesy's accomplished all but four of those things, and he's done it in record time."

Kate stiffened again and looked at Bix. Once again she mouthed, "Don't say it."

"This guy would strike out in a bordello with hundred dollar bills sticking out of his pockets. No one can toler—"

Kate broke in. "Larry, look, we realize the guy has some issues, but we're not doing anything here that we wouldn't do anywhere else under these circumstances. It's a short Advance and we have to be able to function without interference." She held up her index finger to Bix. He didn't speak. The phone line fell silent for a few seconds.

"Guys, this is Bob. We can't let this devolve into personalities. Larry, you need to tell the RFD to back off, and Bix if you could, just keep him as informed as you can. We know you've got a short turnaround time."

"We'll do that, Bob," Bix said. He looked at Mike and mouthed, "You do it."

Mike pointed back at Bix and mouthed silently, "You're the Lead."

Alecia resumed control of the call. "Let's wrap this up. I know you have a countdown meeting soon, and everyone wants to know. Bix, we've been hearing rumors and we've all looked at the Scepter college website. What's the grand visual going to be?"

"Alecia, I'm draping a forty-foot square backdrop over the building with a picture of your face on it," he said. "Underneath it says, Vote For My Boss. We all thought that would be the most effective way of getting votes."

"That's sweet, Bix, and probably true, but I bet that wasn't your final choice," Alecia said.

Mike spoke up, "Alecia, it's going to look awesome. Picture forty-foot tall palmetto trees, in white against an indigo background. Then picture four of them hung between the columns of of the Admin building."

"Sounds dramatic," Alecia said.

"Yep," Mike continued. "The fifth forty-foot banner, on the far left as you look at the building, will be a simple white crescent moon in the upper quarter of the banner, just like on the state flag, also incorporating the word 'Liberty' within the crescent, which is from what's known as the Moultrie flag. It will be very dramatic. It's South Carolina on steroids."

Egan spoke for the first time. "Doesn't that look a little triumphant, like we think we've already won?

"Egan, I was wondering if you'd gone to Maui for a little getaway," Bix said. "Triumphant, how? Because it's a large visual? You asked for a major event to kick off the last two weeks of the campaign, a shot in the arm because the polls are stagnant. I read that as a call for something distinctive, not only high energy but also instantly recognizable to all South Carolinians when they see it on TV. I read that as a call to create a buzz, a sensation that the local *and* national press will talk about if only for a day, but preferably longer—like two weeks. All I'm suggesting is a respectful adaptation of the state flag. It screams South Carolina, but tastefully. It's highly graphic and an incredibly rare opportunity to use symbolism—how many state flags are instantly recognizable to their citizens?"

"Not many, I suppose," Egan said.

"Plus, the college will let us put 'em up 'cause they don't say anything. Those banners, strung across the entire front of the admin building, will *force* the press to take the wide shot, and when they take the wide shot you will see more of the crowd. It's a basic. Would you prefer I use the basic, run-of-the-mill message pabulum on an eight by twelve banner, something optimistic and upbeat like 'South Carolina: It Isn't Just for *White* People Anymore?'"

He was surprised to hear Egan laugh. It didn't happen often.

"No, that might not be appropriate," Egan said. "But how many tens of thousands of dollars will this cost?"

"They were less than you spend on Starbucks in a week."

"How much?" he asked again.

"A grand," Mike said.

"That'd be about right," Bix said.

"That's all? A thousand bucks?" Egan said.

"That's all," Mike said.

"Good job."

"Excuse me?" Bix asked.

"Good job," Egan repeated.

"Pardon me, Egan, I have to address my team for a moment," Bix said. He looked at his team scattered around the staff office. "Everyone, please note the date and time of that compliment, then take the piece of paper you wrote it on, have it framed and put it above your desk."

"I take it back then," Egan said.

"Tear up your sheets of paper, team, and take it as another lesson in the ephemeral nature of appreciation in Washington," Bix said. "Egan, are we good then?"

"We're good."

Alecia's voice came back on. "I hate to ask, but I have to. Can you send a site diagram? I'll understand if you say no."

"I understand you have to ask, Alecia, but Mike would get stuck with that task, so I leave it up to him on this trip," Bix said.

"I will as soon as I can, Alecia," said Mike. "We have a lot of ground to cover in the next twenty-four hours."

"If not, we can let it slide on this trip," Alecia said.

"Thank you, Alecia," said Bix. "Is there anything else we can't do for you?"

"Just the press piece," she said. "Kate, do you have any concerns?"

"No, not really," she said. "Both the national and local press will love the rally. They won't expect it. Afterward we'll feed them this fantastic South Carolina buffet while they file their stories. My only concern is the Max News crews hanging around the hotel and bothering everybody."

"What's that?" Alecia sounded as if she was asking what a news crew was.

Peem jumped in. "That's just the O'Malley thing, Alecia. We're aware of it. We've got it covered."

"Allll *right* then," Alecia took a moment to process what she just heard and realize she should drop the subject. "Let's wrap up. Bix, do you think you need a conference call tomorrow evening before wheels-down?"

"Nope." It popped out his mouth as if he'd inadvertently spit a lozenge.

After a pause, headquarters was heard laughing over the speaker.

"Gee, are you sure, Bix?" Alecia said.

"As much as I enjoy talking with all of you, I think I'm sure."

"In that case, have a good trip. Call me if you need me."

Team Charleston/Scepter signed-off and began a quickie staff meeting before countdown.

"JD, how's the gym site going? Any problems?" Bix asked.

"Nothing you're not aware of," JD said.

"Mike, has Gershon said they can't handle any of our requests?"

"They haven't said anything yet, but they haven't started loading their trucks. They'll have to load tonight and drive here tomorrow. So far they haven't indicated any problems."

"What about your site?" Bix said.

"The site's fine," said Mike, "but Agent 'Rude' continued his harangue after you left. He has tried to undermine every decision we've made, and he still hasn't said whether Service will be able to get anywhere near the number of mag's we need. And he's demanding twenty-foot buffer zones around everything, not just the main stage but also the press risers."

"Around the press risers?" Bix asked. "Is he afraid the crowd will rush the media to get to the buffet table? Tell Rude we won't bring out the food until the mob leaves."

"No, he says that the press and all of their equipment could hurt people in the crowd."

"And he wants our Candidate to be standing in the middle of a big nothing?"

"Essentially."

"These are good things to know. Anything else?"

"No. Isn't that enough?" Mike said.

"Plenty. I bet it will be a fun countdown. Thigpen, how about crowd—how are we doing?"

"Seriously, dude, I don't see how we get to thirty thousand," he said.

"Our media—our paid spots and the interviews Kate is arranging—hasn't really started yet. And we will get considerable press from your poster-making party tomorrow afternoon. I'll come to the Field office tomorrow at noon for an update and decide where we go from there."

Bix then asked Freeway if there were any motorcade or transportation issues.

"No, but the motorpool is gonna rival Patton's march through Europe," Freeway said. "We've got enough shuttle busses and volunteer cars to move the crowd from remote parking, assuming your publicity works and people know about the shuttle system."

"Have you spotted parking and pick-up locations and given that to Kate?"

"Yes, we've got a city map with parking and pick-up locations and created a schedule," Freeway said.

"And we're releasing it to the press tonight," Kate said.

"You've got art?"

"We've got art."

"Then my work here is done. Kate, I already know how Press is going unless you have any other issues to discuss."

"No."

"Cornelia, Ben, Missy, if there's nothing more, we should head downstairs." Bix excused himself to beat the crowd. He had an errand to run up to his room, where he retrieved the long-sleeved CAT Team t-shirt, folded it neatly, and stuck it in his computer bag along with his notebook. He checked the room phone for messages and was happy to hear what he hoped for—Storie's voice with the name and address of a restaurant a few blocks from the hotel. She asked him if he could make it before 10 p.m. He left a message on Storie's room phone that he would try to be at the restaurant by 9:30, then grabbed his bag and took it with him to countdown. He arrived at the Jackson Room at 5:57, seven minutes past Secret Service time but still three minutes earlier than Republican time.

* * *

Once again Bix was struck with the difference between the greeting he received from most of the agents and the non-greeting from Agent Rudd. Shane Emory seemed as content as ever, no sign of stress, no look of confrontation. Bix asked to talk with him outside the conference room.

"What's up?" Emory asked pleasantly when they reached the hall.

"Shane, you've got to get Rudd to stop busting our chops. The guy is making ridiculous demands for buffer zones and he continues to maintain that he can't get magnetometers."

"Rudd has some discretion regarding the Site and what he believes he needs to secure it," Shane said.

"He's demanding a buffer zone around the press area because the general public might get hurt by press equipment. What is that? Is he a traveling OSHE review board? I thought he was there to protect The Candidate. The only reason we separate the press from the public is because we don't want the public to get in their way. Never once have I heard of safety hazards attached to the members of the media—or their cameras. It's staggeringly stupid."

"It's not the best idea I've heard," Emory said.

"And he wants another twenty-foot buffer around the main stage, which would leave us with enough room for about fifty people between The Candidate's stage and the press riser. He's just making this stuff up as he goes along."

"I'll talk with him again. Let's discuss it after countdown."

"I won't bring it up during the meeting, and I'll talk to Mike. It's a site issue, we should discuss it in the small group, but I'd like to resolve it so it doesn't continue to mushroom," Bix said.

Shane agreed.

"And have you met with Mayor Bacon?"

"Yes, I dropped in on him late this afternoon with a couple of my Intel agents, and we told him what we thought of the idea of opening the fire hydrants along our motorcade route," Shane said.

"Did he appear contrite, intimidated, nonplussed?" Bix asked.

"No, he was totally plussed, at least he acted like he wasn't intimidated. He actually got a little belligerent, but I think we got his attention. He said he was just yankin' your chain."

"Did you tell him that you're like airport security—you take all comments seriously?"

"Exactly. We recommended that he should't joke about security issues and left it at that. We made it clear that our badges are bigger than his."

"Thanks, Shane. Sorry to drag you into this." It was another lie. He wasn't sorry.

"Not at all, it was completely appropriate. When you hear nonsense like that you have to tell us. Somebody like Bacon might just do it."

Bix appreciated the reinforcement, and reinforcements.

As he walked back in to begin Countdown he spoke with Mike to wave him off any intended remarks about his differences with Rudd or about changing the rules in the middle of the game. At the same time, Shane stopped and spoke briefly with his abrasive site agent, who was sitting in the front row of chairs, prepared to share his joylessness up close.

Bix, aware that Missy was not in the room, opened the meeting at exactly 18 hundred hours with the usual self-introductions and waited to watch the veins in Rudd's forehead bulge preternaturally when it was his turn. Merely the act of speaking his own name caused Rudd some form of anxiety that was beyond Bix's ability to comprehend. The man then fidgeted from the waist down, his legs and feet moving constantly, looking for all the world like a drug addict waiting for his next fix. Bix assumed Rudd had leg thrombosis. He sat looking at Bix and Shane intensely from ten feet away, enhancing the drug addict effect. Rudd's normally pallid complexion actually benefitted from the extra rush of blood to his face.

After a fleeting thought about Rudd's armed and mental state, Bix began his run-through of the schedule. A half-sentence later Missy arrived, late, with two uninvited guests—the hotel manager and sales manager. Bix was stopped dead in his tracks on the rare occasion of being taken by complete surprise, and the entire room was stilled like a scene in an old West saloon when "the stranger" comes through the swinging bar room doors lookin' for trouble. It couldn't have been more dramatic if the sounds of whiskey glasses clinking and Hoagy Carmichael playing an upright piano in the corner had suddenly ceased. It was a uniquely stupid blunder.

The eyes of sixteen agents and five staff Advance fell upon Bix. Bringing outsiders to a countdown meeting was taboo for what should have been obvious reasons. It was *his* RON Advance who had compromised OpSec, Operational Security, as well as the concept that staff Advance were professionals. The uninvited guests had to be asked to leave, but, like a bunch of high school kids confronted with a faux pas they don't quite know how to handle, no one wanted to create an embarrassing situation. The hotel executives were well liked and faultless in the mistake, and it appeared to Bix that everyone was concerned about making them feel badly.

Bix re-started the conversation the moment Missy and her guests sat, telling Missy that the everyone in the room had already introduced themselves and identified their roles, and he asked he her to do the same and introduce her guests. Upon completing the formalities, Bix redirected the agenda.

"Because Mr. Mondi and Ms. Mackowicz have been gracious enough to take their time to come here I don't want to waste it, so let's discuss our hotel issues at the top so we don't have to make them sit through the entire meeting," Bix said.

Shane nodded his approval and several of the veteran agents looked impressed.

"I'll throw it out for all of you." Bix continued, "Do any of you have any issues you'd like to discuss regarding the hotel, or do you, Mr. Mondi or Ms. Mackowicz, have any questions for us?"

Two of the agents, to Bix's relief, asked questions, as did both hotel executives, with inquiries about closing the gym to public access while The Candidate would be using it, his food preparation, and overnight parking for motorcade vehicles. Bix reassured them there wasn't a need to close the gym while The Candidate was in there sweatin' to the oldies.

It was a substantive few minutes of Q & A, useful for both Advance teams and hotel management, but still an embarrassment for staff Advance. Such an affront to common sense called into question the campaign's ability to hire people who could, like, think.

Everyone seemed happy with the exchange as Bix summoned his inner family court judge and excused his guests with thanks and appreciation for all of their hard work and apologies for the short lead-time they'd been given before The Candidate's arrival. Once they were out the door, Bix had won the approbation, some of it grudging, of his

Secret Service counterparts. He was aware that it was little things like that, and being on time and wearing a tie every once in while, that impressed those guys.

Shane leaned over. "That was nimble," he whispered. "Now I can see why they gave you a job in the State Department."

"You haven't seen anything yet," Bix whispered back. "Missy," he looked to her, "it occurs to me that you may need this time to continue working with your hotel counterparts as well. You were a little late getting started because of your flight situation," he was stretching his diplomacy skills, "and I'm sure you've got a lot of stuff to deal with before arrival in about twenty-four hours, and none of the rest of this pertains to the RON. You should take this opportunity to ditch the rest of our countdown and continue working on your checklist. I'll touch base with you later this evening." She was out the door in another forty-five seconds as she collected her possibles, slowly, and happily tottered out on her high-heeled boots looking as if her guests may have treated her to a complimentary happy hour in the five minutes she had between the staff meeting and countdown, and expected more of the same.

Nothing more needed to be said. The entire diverse roomful of people from all walks of life and all religious beliefs and political persuasions and both major sexes were thinking the exact same thing. "Why the hell did they hire her? Oh yeah, because her daddy's a money guy." Even those agents who had no idea that her father was a fundraiser assumed it to be the reason she was hired, or that she was sleeping with the campaign manager.

"So let's continue on the schedule," Bix began again. Tension mounted in the room as the tick-tock grew ever closer to 11:45 a.m. Friday, the witching hour, "Arrival" at the College of Scepter. The rally site, or, as Rudd viewed it, *his* site. Bix, Mike, Kate, JD, the team, the presidential campaign, everyone who cared about liberty and democracy, didn't share his view. Bix felt he had most of the agents on his side as well, and obviously a few who believed that Rudd was Bix's problem to deal with.

"At eleven hundred and fifteen hours we depart the Red Schoendienst Gym en route the College of Scepter," Bix said. "Any issues with the motorcade?" he asked Freeway and his counterpart.

"Any OTRs along the way?" Agent Burnett smiled as he asked, just as he had the night before. His question broke the tension in the room momentarily. It was the running joke. All the agents believed Bix was going to do something somewhere, they just didn't know where. When they asked specifically, they knew Bix wouldn't lie, but they also knew he wouldn't volunteer the information willingly.

This time Bix was able to answer simply, "Nope, none," as he grinned suggestively. He wanted to keep them on their toes. "At eleven forty-five we arrive at the College, do a 'greet' with about ten local supporters and ten college VIPs inside the north entrance of the Admin building, then go to Hold. Any questions so far?"

After a moment of silence, Mike said, "No."

"We need to have the name check information on your greeters by tomorrow by five p.m.," Shane said.

"We'll get it."

Rudd said nothing.

"Good," said Bix. "So, we remain in Hold while the traveling press set up," Bix continued, "depart Hold at noon, walk through the building's west corridor to the spot where The Candidate will wait for the off-stage announce, then exit through the northwest door into the rally site, on to a sixty-foot-long cat walk to the pod stage."

"I'm still not sure I can get you all the mag's for this event," Rudd interjected. "And I'll have to shut them down at eleven hundred hours so we can take them to Columbus for the other rally."

Bix's reaction was instantaneous—his head recoiled—then he was condescending. "You're telling me you are going to shut down the mag's into our rally an hour before it begins so you can take them to Columbus for our Opponent's rally?"

"Yes."

"Does that mean that we'll open-up the site after eleven a.m. and let everyone in who hasn't been mag'd yet?" There wasn't a shadow of a doubt in his mind how Rudd would respond.

"No, we'll have to shut down public access after that point," Rudd said.

"An hour before The Candidate arrives?"

"Yes," Rudd answered.

"You're telling me that you're going to limit the size of our crowd?"

"Well no, you just need to get everyone in before then," Rudd said.

This is such crap. Mike and Kate knew it was crap, and Bix assumed most of the agents *had* to know it was crap, too. He couldn't let it pass unchallenged, but didn't so much *decide* to call out Rudd in front of the entire assemblage as much he was compelled by his sense of the absurd.

He smiled at Rudd. "I'll bet you a hundred dollars that's not going to happen." Then he continued to stare at him and grin, mimicking a kinder version Mayor Bacon's intimidation act, attempting to turn Rudd's proximity against him.

"I can't bet," was Rudd's witty retort.

"Ya got me there. In that case I bet you a nickel," Bix said.

"I can't bet," was the next witty retort.

"Then let me put it this way," Bix said quietly, with unmistakable conviction, the smile melting from his face. "Within five minutes of the end of this meeting, Shane is going to get a phone call from someone to whom he cannot say 'no' telling him that that's not going to happen. Then Shane will tell you that that's not going to happen. Or we can cut out the middleman and decide right now that that's not going to happen. Either way, it's not going to happen." He said it with such self-confidence that even he almost believed it.

Kate whispered to Mike, "Do you notice how his nostrils flare and his jaw tightens when he's angry?"

"Adorable, huh?" Mike said."He's pissed, and he's got Rude by the balls."

Rudd remained silent, uncharacteristically.

Announcing it to the room left no doubt in anyone's mind that Bix had embarked on a teaching moment, a "place-putting" exercise, and that he'd reached the end of his rope, and Bix was known by one and all for the length of his rope.

Shane spoke up. "Let's get together after countdown to flesh this thing out."

"Good idea," Bix said. "Right after I make a phone call."

Shane M.C.'d the next few key points on the schedule, shepherding the meeting through the rally to ensure there would be no further comments from his site guy. When he reached 1 p.m., the point where The Candidate finished working the rope line and returned to Hold, he deftly returned the chair to Bix with a question. "Do you foresee The Candidate remaining in Hold to eat lunch while the press eat lunch and file their stories, or do you expect he will go to the gym building and shoot baskets?"

"He'll shoot hoops no doubt, and he'll probably have Peaches bring his food to eat on the plane. It's a long trip to L.A on airplane food alone."

The remainder being pro forma logistics—"down" time and return by motorcade to the Charleston airport—Bix wrapped up the meeting as quickly as he could. No one objected. An instant later he looked at Shane. "I'll meet you guys back in here in a few minutes after the crowd disperses."

He walked out without making eye contact with anyone on either side of the aisle, found an empty conference room, and after four minutes and two phone calls returned to the Stonewall Jackson hoping his "five-minute" prediction would be proven accurate.

He gathered his team and waited for the last few non-essential personnel to finish their conversations and exit. Shane, Rudd and their Site 2 agent, whose name Bix couldn't remember, waited and talked on the other side of the room.

"Who'd you call?" Mike asked him.

"First I called Egan, to cover my rear end, then I called a friend in Washington," Bix said. It would remain a mystery.

He tried to procrastinate after that, talking with the team about prospects for the upcoming baseball season, drawing out the time, anxious to see if Shane received a phone call before they began the latest round of Spy vs. Spy. It was an audacious comment that Bix had made, really a threat, and he'd never, ever, said such a thing to an agent in public. It was a direct challenge to the site agent's credibility and to his manhood as far as Bix was concerned. He was surprised the room didn't gasp when he uttered it. But he put his own credibility on the line as well and was uncharacteristically nervous about whether his mouth had written a check that his clout couldn't cover.

Shane soon led Rudd and his Site 2, an ungainly fellow in a dark suit, white shirt, dark tie, black shoes, etc., who looked as if he shaved on a weekly basis with a flint knife, over the great divide to Bix and his team, where he suggested everyone sit. Rudd and his Site 2 took seats next to the center aisle but remained on the Secret Service side of the room. Bix decided to double down on the adolescent Alpha male thing: he walked over and took a chair next to Rudd's, then grinned at him pleasantly as he sat, as if was taking his seat in a theater next to a stranger. Rudd appeared uneasy. He moved his chair ever so slightly away from Bix's with an almost imperceptible sideways butt thrust. Bix moved his chair a few more nanometers toward Rudd's with a similar move, then grinned at him again. He wasn't sure how long he could keep the Marx Brothers routine, especially if his trumpeted "phone call" to Shane didn't materialize. Kate, Mike, JD, and Freeway were obviously enjoying the scene.

Not unexpectedly, Shane assumed the role of "good cop," which was his nature. It seemed to Bix that it was the least Shane could do, considering the circumstances. Nothing that Bix or his team had said or done, that he could think of, broached the level of irritation that Rudd's confrontational attitude was causing. It was the Service Lead's responsibility to control his team.

And it was with absolute confidence in the rightness of his cause and absolutely no confidence in his timing that Bix entered into the discussion. As a result, he was shocked to hear the words that came out of Shane's mouth.

"You know, Kurt has a point about the magnetometers. We don't have that many to go around. It looks like he is going to have to let them go to Columbia to supplement that event."

"That's not our agreement," Bix answered calmly. "It's never been our agreement. Since the invention of magnetometers it's never been the understanding between Advance and Service. I'll agree to let you shut down the mags only when the event begins, which is when The Candidate is announced to the stage."

Rudd jumped into the fray. "Well, we're going to have shut them down at eleven hundred hours this time. We didn't know you were going to do this big of an event. You should'a asked us first," Rudd said.

Bix was becoming increasingly animated. Once again he grinned broadly. "Ask you what exactly? Where we are allowed to hold our event or how many people we're allowed to invite? You're joking, aren't you?"

"No, of course he didn't mean that," Shane said.

"Do you think we've got the space to allow the press to come in and see it, too, or do you think we should make them sit in the bus and wait outside?" Bix asked.

Neanderthal Site 2 decided to add his unique perspective. "That wouldn't be so bad as far as I'm concerned."

Bix winced, as did Kate, Mike, and J.D in tandem.

"All right," Bix said. "Here's the way I understand it. *We* put on the events, and Service acquires the assets to move our crowds into our events within two hours. That means for a noon event, we open the gates at the latest by ten a.m. and leave them open at least 'til noon. You'll have to forgive me if I've been getting that wrong for the past three decades."

It may have been an exaggeration. He couldn't remember when magnetometers first reared their ugly portals, but he wanted to make the point.

Rudd began to speak again, in a lower voice, an apparent attempt to sound like the final word on the subject. He went from tenor to a tenor profundo. "Well I don't know what we can do about that now. We've already made the arrangements."

"Then I can say with total certainty that The Candidate will tell his Detail Leader to instruct you to open the gates and allow all of the people into the rally who have been kept out for the previous hour," Bix said.

"That's your decision," Rudd countered, "but once we shut down the mag's and tell them that no more people will be allowed in, they'll go home."

"Not if I have volunteers circulating through the crowd promising them that they will get in once The Candidate arrives. I'll send out someone with a bullhorn," Bix said. "I've done this before." His right eyebrow rose involuntarily as he glowered at Rudd.

Providence once again cast its benevolent gaze upon Bix. He heard a magic bell ringing in the distance. It sounded like a cell phone far away, or in someone's pocket. He raised his hand a little, then his index finger a little more, and turned his head to the music and smiled. It was coming from the inside pocket in Shane's dark suit coat. "Shane, I think that may be for you," he said with a twinkle. He was pushing his luck.

Shane pulled the phone from his pocket and looked at the caller I.D. He stood up, and as he walked away said, "This is Shane," and then, "Yes sir."

Bix looked at the group. "We'll finish this conversation when he comes back." It might have been a call from Shane's wife for all Bix knew, but he looked at his team sitting across the aisle and smiled again. It was his best defense against his growing aggravation and any subsequent uncontrollable invective.

Shane reentered the Jackson Room after less than a minute, replacing the cell phone in his coat pocket as he ambled back to his chair. When he sat down he looked at Rudd and said simply, "They get to keep the magnetometers until The Candidate arrives."

If *that* didn't send a message nothing would, Bix thought. On the inside he was screaming, "Eat *that* punk! Don't *ever* mess with the big dog. Stick *that* in your pipe and smoke it. Please, stick *something* in your pipe and smoke it. You need to chill." On the outside he was magnanimous. His only comment was a quiet "Good, let's move on, then."

It was becoming clear that Rudd was not an individual with whom Bix could reason, and he was certain the episode would have no impact on Rudd's heavy-handed concept of protection. Harsher disciplinary methods against Rudd would soon be called for, but it wasn't the time yet.

"Shane, one last thing, buffer zones," Bix said. He wanted it resolved before he left the room and he felt he had the momentum. "We do ten-foot buffer zones around The Candidate, and we create our own space for the media, which *is* a buffer zone if you want to look at it that way. None of this twenty-foot stuff."

"Agreed," Shane said. Rudd scowled. Bix smiled and said, "Thank you."

The Advance team had work to do and miles to go before they rested for the night. Bix ran through a few minor outstanding details regarding Press access and buffer zones at various points along The Candidate's path, and wrapped up the meeting with a curt, "I think we've exhausted this topic to everyone's complete satisfaction for the moment, and I'm sure you gentlemen need to go back to work as well, so Shane, let's you and I talk later tonight." He shook hands with Shane and thanked him but didn't bother to reach out to Rudd or the Neanderthal.

Upstairs in the Staff Office with his team five minutes later, Mike was triumphant.

"Rude will think twice about screwing with us now," he said.

"No he won't," Bix answered.

Kate agreed. "Bix is right. Rude won't change. We're the enemy, and he clearly had a bad childhood. On the other hand, I think the other guy is just going along with Rude because he's the Site 2, but I think I can make nice with him. He'll be ok."

"The Neanderthal?" Bix asked.

"Mike and I decided to call him Knuckles," Kate said.

"Knuckles is better. Less pejorative. I'll go with that."

* * *

Twenty more emails and voicemails awaited on Bix's BlackBerry, and he was frightened to look at it. He suggested to the team that they go out and find dinner for themselves while he remained at the hotel to deal with other pressing aspects of his trip that were, like his libido, slowly heating up, but unlike his libido, could not be ignored. He began to worry that he might not have time for dinner with Storie.

12

Bix began to sort through his emails on the way up to the Staff Office. Messages from Peem, Sophie, Hani, and Egan showed-up prominently on his BlackBerry, as did one from John Garianni, his friend from Max News, with the subject line "Call me at home." Bix didn't bother to open it. He called Garianni immediately. When no one answered he left a message.

Sophie wrote to tell him she was booked on a flight out of Chicago that arrived in Columbia airport at 10:30 a.m. the next morning, with her daughter Chelsea in tow. She added the contact information for two Stearns University students who were friends of Jamir's and leaders in the university's Young Democrats.

Bix trusted Y.D.'s. The process of Advance, by its nature, forced him to judge people quickly, and he believed it was unlikely that a Republican college "rat fucker" a la Donald Segretti or Dwight Chapin would spend months or years burrowing in with a Young Dem's organization for the purpose of finding out their secrets or sabotaging a political campaign. But he never put it past guys like that. All it took was one aspiring young Dick Cheney infiltrating the Y.D.'s disguised in a backwards-facing baseball cap to confirm people's worst impressions of all political types—the Young Republicans for doing something so despicable, and the Young Democrats for being such doofusses.

Bix immediately emailed the two Stearns U students, expressing his interest in engaging their help, in vague terms, and asking them to call or email him.

Hani had written to tell Bix he didn't arrive at Washington National in time to catch the flight to South Carolina, but had purchased a ticket for a flight that would arrive the next morning at 9:20 a.m.

"Just an hour earlier than Sophie's arrival," Bix thought. They could pose as a family. He emailed Hani with the news, subject line: "You've got a beard." With a cc to Sophie, he wrote, "Hani, Sophie from our office is also on this email. She is arriving in Columbia at 10:30 a.m. You'll recognize her. She is traveling with her nine-month old daughter Chelsea. I think you should meet and travel together to find Jamir. Sophie, I suggest you rent a car in your name. Hani is hot right now."

When he finished writing, he saw another email from Garianni with an emphatic subject line, "Call me from a landline!"

Bix decided it might be wise to read his email before calling. Garianni wrote, "I saw your cell phone number on my caller I.D. You didn't read my last email. Call me from a landline!"

If ever a single exclamation point carried any more foreboding, Bix couldn't remember when. "There is no way on God's green earth that this is going to be good," he thought as he moved to a chair next to a real telephone. He made the call and found himself slumped over with his forehead propped up by his hand—the body language of resignation.

When Garianni answered, Bix was hesitant to ask, "Is everything all right?"

"No. I lost my job. At the end of the day the news director called me in and fired me."

"Jesus, John, that's wasn't a coincidence, was it?"

"I don't think so. He said they were downsizing, and that was it. I think they know that I talked with you, and I think they might be hacking your email or voicemail or listening in on your cell phone conversations."

"And you lost your job over it? Are you all right? What are you going to do?"

"I'll be fine. The thing is they still have to pay me for the remainder of my contract, which is another six months, but they wanted me gone today. I'm not worried about finding another job. The question is what are *you* going to do?"

It was a great question. If Garianni's accusations were true, Bix had been the leak. He'd been giving them the keys to the kingdom all along. He felt violated by his own naiveté. He took it for granted that he was being bugged when he was doing overseas trips for the White House, but never took the threat seriously in the good ol' U.S. of A.

"Please let me know if there is anything I can do for you," Bix said. "You're the one who's out of a job."

"If I get really desperate, I'll see if your campaign will hire me. That will be the point you'll know I've reached my nadir," Garianni said with a laugh. "But *you've* got a problem on your hands. You have to assume they know everything you've said or done up to now, and all of your contacts' email addresses and phone numbers."

"Must I?"

"You'd better. I don't know and don't care how much there is to know about what's happening inside your campaign, but the producers with O'Malley's program seem to know everything. "

"Is there any chance they were monitoring *your* phone or email?" Bix asked.

"I used my personal phone, my iPhone, and email account. It's more likely it's you."

"Looks like I'm going to be living la vida paranoia until I get another form of communication," Bix said. "I'm so sorry to hear your news, and knowing that our friendship caused it is very difficult. This changes things, without a doubt, but I don't know exactly how at this moment."

"Don't beat yourself up," Garianni said. "It was Max News that caused it. You've got enough to blame yourself for in life. Don't add this to the list."

"You are too kind. And if you and your family need a place to stay you can come live with me on the Island of the Damned. Coincidentally, my next door neighbor is Dick O'Malley."

* * *

After they hung up Bix sat back in his uncomfortable chair and mulled his options on that warm winter evening in the seventh-floor Staff Office in the tastefully appointed Hotel Marianne in the historic environs of old Charleston. He noticed his heart was beating a little faster and he didn't enjoy it. None of the options presenting themselves allowed him to continue wiling away the hours as he would have preferred—attending to all the previously identified crises with which he had to contend. The first idea that came closest, the option that would get matters back to almost normal, was acquiring a new cell phone, or four, that night before the stores closed. First, however, he wanted to share his glad tidings with Peem and Egan at their offices, then Hani and Sophie on their cells, from the Staff Office phone. He took the chance of calling Sophie and Hani to prevent them sending more emails with information Max News could use.

Peem's and Egan's voicemail answered their office phones, to his relief. His messages to them were brief: "I think I'm being hacked. Don't call or email me until I get a new phone. I'll call you with the new number." He left a similar message for Hani on his voicemail, but Sophie answered her cell.

"This is Sophie."

For an unknown reason Bix felt comforted that she answered. "Sophie, Bix. Did I get you at a bad moment?"

"Not at all, I assumed it was you by the area code. This is a good time. I'm home on the computer still doing office work, and I just put Chelsea to bed."

"Good. I wanted to tell you never to call or email again," Bix said.

"That's rather harsh. Are you running away from the campaign?"

"No, but apparently I'm the mole who's been giving Max News all of our secrets. A reliable source has suggested that Max News might be hacking me."

"No shit? That's federal."

"I know, which makes it difficult to believe. Who would take that chance?"

"People who have something to gain and think they can get away with it."

"If it's true, they may be tapping into all of my contacts, including you, so they may be listening now. If that's true, Max News can stick Dick O'Malley up its ethically challenged rosy-red rectum."

"No shit," she said. "So we should keep this brief. What do you want to do?"

"I'll get new phones tonight and have Ben Oliver deliver one to you at the airport when you arrive, since you'll recognize one another. When you and Hani hook up, you can both use it."

"Good idea. What about email?"

"Don't chance it. It's just as easy, or easier, to hack emails, and they may have access to the entire campaign email system."

"In that case I'll see Ben tomorrow at the Columbia airport and I'll call you as soon as I get my new phone and your new phone number," Sophie said.

At the risk, in his mind, of seeming alarmist, Bix called Special Agent Emory, who reassured him he did the right thing once again. "You have an authoritative source, so we have to take it seriously," he said. "This could compromise OpSec. As a practical matter, there isn't a lot that can be done about it before wheels-down tomorrow night. If Max News was really doing this, and they're smart, they will have stopped and packed up their equipment the moment they knew you and your friend spoke. The best advice I have is to do what you're planning to do—go into lockdown until you have new cell phones, and stay off the campaign email system."

Bix moved faster than he had in months to find a store that sold cell phones, and deemed it a glass half full situation when his first choice, a Radio Shack in north Charleston, was open and ready to fix him up with four dime-a-minute phones, which he loaded with ten hours of talk time despite his assumption they'd each be left with five hours by wheels-up on Friday.

Weak from lack of food and wracked with stress from his incredibly stressful life, Bix then deemed it essential to the success of the entire Advance trip that he fulfill his commitment to Storie. "Solid reasoning," he thought. "For the good of the mission, I must meet Storie. And eat food."

She had left a message on his room phone to meet her at Hernando's Slideaway Burger Bistro, a basement café five blocks from the hotel, with the promise that it offered fast service and much more than burgers.

She added, "It's my favorite place in Charleston and one of its best kept secrets. We won't be interrupted there."

He was ten minutes late arriving, still too early to be on Democrat time, and far too early for Storie to be irritated. After checking his teeth in the rear view, he jumped out of the car and located the narrow set of stairs down to the eatery, where he was greeted by a smiling Storie, and a smiling Kate, Mike, JD, Thigpen, Cornelia, Freeway, Ben, and Nora, all seated at the same long table. Nora was seated next to Mike. Bix sensed that some chemistry had occurred since they met the day before.

"Is this wonderful or what?" Bix asked. "All of my favorite people together at one time."

"We knew you'd like us to join you," Kate said.

"Pray tell, how did you know that?"

"Because you're so inclusive and generous," Mike said.

"Does that mean you've concluded I'd like to pay for this, too?"

"You don't have to do that," Kate said. "We simply want to share the bounty of your friendship, and Storie's, but especially Storie's."

Storie sat looking bemused. "It's a complete coincidence. What was I gonna do?" She turned her palms skyward and lifted her hands.

"Where's Missy?" he asked the team.

"We invited her, but she said she wanted to keep working. I think the hotel executives were treating her to dinner," Kate said.

"By the way, *we* aren't the only ones hanging out here," Mike said. "Look over there." He nodded to a far corner of the dark room. "It's Shane and a couple agents."

"Them I don't mind," Bix said, "unless Rudd's with them."

"No, no Rudd," Mike said.

"Well, hell, let's invite 'em over. The more the scarier. They look like they've had their dinner," Bix suggested. Then he did it.

Shane and Sam, the RON agent, and the head of the CAT team, Bix's morning workout partner, Guy Manfred, were pleased with the invitation. After a few seconds of jockeying they squeezed into a space at one end of the large table, next to Bix and Storie, and ordered beers. Bix ordered a burger and a diet caffeinated soft drink, stoking for his post-dinner late night workload, as did Storie.

"Good to see you again, Storie," Shane said.

"You know one another?" Bix asked.

"Of course, Storie's been on several trips we've done with her boss. You know we're not exclusive to you. We protect other people, too," Shane said.

"Now I feel so cheap," Bix said. "I thought you only loved us."

"No, we're protection sluts. We'll protect anyone the Treasury Department tells us to," he said.

The exchange set off an hour of spirited conversation, war stories, editorial comments, and subdued raucous behavior. Being the only forum where war stories from previous Advance trips found an appreciative audience—an audience of other Advance people—everyone in attendance over the age of thirty held forth with their own legends of looming disasters averted through brilliance and audacity, and world-class screw-ups from which the American public had been shielded, thank goodness.

"Mr. Howell told me that you once almost killed the Vice President in a motorcade in Saudi Arabia on the way to a meeting with the king," Shane said to Bix.

"It's almost true," Bix said, "however, it *was* Saudi Arabia, which belongs to the Saudis, and I didn't have much influence over their driving protocols. I was in the lead car in the motorcade, and they *were* going over ninety miles an hour, and our driver, who I think was a prince and wasn't chosen because of his driving skills, *did* almost drive into a bridge abutment, which caused the Veep's limo to swerve and almost crash into another bridge abutment, but other than that I'm relatively blameless. I asked them to slow down, and then I asked them not to kill us. The Staff van came closest to crashing. It was three-freaking o'clock in the blessed a.m."

"Why were you going to a meeting with the king at three a.m.?" Mike asked.

"The king liked to have his meetings in the middle of the night. It's only a hundred twenty degrees out then," Bix said.

"I've heard that when you meet the king," Kate said, "everyone just waits around all night until the he summons you, then everyone jumps in the motorcade and heads over to the palace."

"It's true. It's like an audience with Michael Jackson, but less gaudy, and with less security," Bix said.

"Did you say something to the Saudi government about the motorcade?" Mike asked.

"Oh, yeah," Bix said. "The Secret Service and I had a 'come-to-Jesus' meeting with the Saudis the next morning, with all fifty-two of their top princes. I think it was the first time they'd ever attended a 'come-to-Jesus' meeting. I impressed on them how much bad press they would get if they killed the vice president."

"What'd they say?" Mike asked.

"They said that when his majesty calls they must arrive as quickly as possible. I think it had as much to do with his majesty's limited ability to remain coherent. He'd had a stroke or two by that point. Our interpreter told me later that the king rambled on—mostly mumbled on—about why we had 'this woman' as secretary of state, and how strange it was and how he wasn't happy about it. But that's not what the Saudi interpreter, who was the prince in charge, told the vice president. His interpretation was 'we look forward to working with your new Secretary of State.' Whatever the prince said the king said is what the king said," Bix explained.

Manfred, the CAT team guy, asked Bix a "bragging rights" question. "Was that your strangest OCONUS trip?"

Nora asked, "What's OCONUS?"

"Outside the continental United States," Bix said. "I'd have to say that was among the strangest. Any time you're dealing with an absolute ruler, especially one who represents religious, tribal, and ethnic symbolism, and *especially* one who has billions of dollars to dole out to thousands of princes and retainers and pet projects, it gets interesting. The Advance team stayed in the guest palace in Jeddah, a converted Intercontinental Hotel, and we ate the same buffet for breakfast, lunch, and dinner every day for two weeks. The buffet was the size of half a football field; it had everything, but it still got repetitive. But we ate there because it was free and the White House only gave us a ten-dollar per diem, because everything was supposedly free. Jerks."

"What was the best international trip you've done?" Storie asked.

"Jordan, by far. It's the holy land without the b.s.—at least it was then, in the mid-nineties. Jordanian royalty are very western, another example of foreigners speaking English better than most Americans, and their queen was American. *And*, my favorite, their archaeological sites are among the best on earth and there are *thousands* of them. I flew by helicopter from Amman to Petra and back again four times during the pre-Advance, the Advance, and during the President's visit, and the landscape offered up visions from a thousand to four thousand years old, from ancient civilizations to Crusader castles, and there were hundreds of tells, these large mounds that are the layered remains of ancient cities built up for millennia, with thousands of holes dug into them by people searching for artifacts. It was quite dramatic, swooping over the land of Edom at fifteen hundred feet in skyborne motorcades, over the ancient city of Philadelphia, the Dead Sea, Jericho, Wadi Musa and Madaba, with side excursions over Wadi Rum and Aqabah, which were made famous by Lawrence of Arabia. It was exceedingly cool to have Jordanian Royal Air Force helicopters at my beck and call. The first time we flew to Petra they circled several times very slowly over Aaron's Tomb, that'd be Aaron, the brother of Moses, on the highest mountain overlooking Petra, Jabal Harun. It would have taken us three hours to hike up there. It was surprising how often you would look down and see, out in the middle of a vast expanse, a lone Bedoin tent and a herd of goats nearby grazing the sparse desert growth." He looked at Storie. "Very biblical. You would have enjoyed it."

"Yes, I would have," she said. "You should have been an archaeologist."

"Yes, I should have," he said.

Bix, Storie, and Shane, the three oldest, regaled their younger compatriots with tales from the dark ages, twenty years prior, before the Internet, when the only method of communicating in real time was with a telephone, on a desk. The fetuses sat in astonishment and utter confusion as to how Advance could be accomplished without cell phones or smart phones or laptops or GPS. Storie diplomatically avoided telling war stories that involved Bix, and vice versa, but it still left each of them with a rich trove of classics. She had heard of some of his exploits through mutual friends, and seemed delighted to hear them from the horse's mouth. Bix, like Theodore Roosevelt, had to be the bride at every wedding and the corpse at every funeral. She was, as ever, an engaged audience.

Upon wolfing down a scrumptious burger and an hour and ten minutes of stimulating conversation, Bix's pocket was about to catch fire. More emails and voicemails were burning up the campaign BlackBerry despite his warnings, and he was feeling guilty for taking time to eat. None of Bix's Advance dinosaur friends would have given it a second thought. "Guilt" was a wasted emotion in their eyes.

He excused himself from his compatriots with reluctance…one more reluctantly than the rest. He laid down a couple of crumbled twenty-dollar bills and asked Shane, Kate, Mike, and Ben to accompany him outside for a minute. He told Storie he'd come back before leaving. It was all very clandestine.

Once outside he handed Kate and Mike their new cell phones, and handed Shane a business card. "I've written our new cell numbers on the back of this. Distribute them as you see fit. By the way, guys, the campaign has bought you new phones to use for the remainder of the trip, and try to use your email as little as possible. Max News may be listening, or hacking. Ben, I need you to deliver this phone to Sophie Mackenzie from our office. She's flying in to Columbia tomorrow morning. I'll give you the flight details and some thoughts about what you might encounter there."

"Got it," Ben said.

"We shouldn't be surprised," Kate said, "but I suppose that's why we're Democrats. We're always surprised at shit like this. Do you have the goods on 'em?"

"Maybe, possibly, suspectedly. We have enough reasons to use extra caution. Treat this trip as you would if you were in the Soviet Union, or the Nixon era, or Chicago," Bix advised.

"That bad?" she said.

"That bad."

After a few profanity-laden summations from all concerned, Bix went back into Hernando's basement bistro to say goodnight and found

Storie in the process of leaving. She had timed it to coincide with Bix's re-entry. "Walk me to my car," she said as she turned him around back toward the door, and as they walked out together they met Shane and the team coming in.

Kate and Mike said goodnight to Storie and went back to their table, while Bix kept Shane for an extra moment. "Shane," he asked, "can we get an 'S' pin for Storie without going through another background check so she can move around freely? Haven't you run her name several times now? Aren't you planning to give her one later in the day when they have their rally in Columbia?"

"Sure, I can do that. I'll give it to you tomorrow evening before we leave for wheels-down, and you can give it to Storie when you see her." He turned to Storie. "Are you coming to the rally in Scepter?"

"I wouldn't miss it," she said. "It's oppo research, first hand. The Candidate's message, how they produce their rally, things like that. Maybe Bix has some new tricks up his sleeve that I've never seen." She smiled.

"Old dogs don't have sleeves," Bix said. "Thank you, Shane. If the press notice she's at the rally, can I tell them you invited her?"

"I'd prefer not," Shane said. "My bosses and my wife might think that's a little squirrely."

"You're not being a team player, Shane. Remember, you're there to take the bullet," Bix reminded him.

"Which would be a lot easier than taking the wrath of my wife. She already thinks I took this job to get away from her."

"Didn't you?"

"Yeah, but how she found out is what I want to know," Shane said.

"I don't believe a word of it," Storie said. "You reek of 'clean-cut.' I've met his wife—she's gorgeous."

"You've met his wife? At one of your events?" Bix asked.

"Yes," Shane said, "I brought her to a town hall meeting they had in Columbia, where we live."

"Are you bringing her to *our* rally? I'll be hurt if you don't," Bix said.

"I was thinking about it. She would enjoy it."

"Bring her, and if you have any kids, bring them too," Bix said. "You obviously don't need my help getting them in, but if they would like to watch the rally out front, feel free to put them in the VIP section. They'll have easier access backstage from there. We'll introduce them to the senator."

"Thanks, Bix," Shane said. "That'll be great."

Storie and Bix walked back out onto Market Street and meandered slowly down to the Meeting. Charleston upheld its end of the ambiance bargain. The air was sultry and moist. Just as Bix was remembering how much he hated moist—it made his hair frizzy—Storie redirected the conversation.

"Don't tell me you don't love this," she said.

"I hate it," he said. "It makes my hair frizzy."

"Don't be a wise guy, you know what I'm talking about."

"Oh, that 'this.' If by 'this' you're referring to campaign Advance and not politics writ large, then yes, I suppose so. It's the most challenging experience there is short of a war zone, foreign or domestic. All of your antennae are out, it requires skill sets you never even knew you had, and it constantly tests the ones you think you have. Not only are no two days ever the same, no two *hours* are ever the same. And if I concentrate really hard, then tilt my head and squint my eyes just so, I can create the illusory effect that I'm accomplishing something meaningful. It's gotta be meaningful, right? I meet with important people, I'm involved in matters that could affect the future of our country, as cosmetic and vapid as those matters may be, and I'm nothing if not peripatetic. It has all the earmarks of worthwhile activity, therefore it must be, and worthy my complete commitment. Right?"

"You're acting cynical, but when I see your guy on television and there's something memorable about the visual, not just another talking head shot, something in the environment that tells me about the message he's trying to convey, I assume you did it. Or if it's just a really massive, huge, ginormous rally, then I assume it's you, too. You give the press better material to work with and you make it easy for them to do their jobs, and they know it, and so does your campaign. It's reflected in your media coverage."

"Once again, you're being gracious, but this isn't an act. It feels like I'm working in the Grand Hotel—the faces constantly change but everything remains the same. Media coverage has become an onslaught, and we've become merely part of the din," he said.

"Our campaign thinks you're kicking our butts, you personally."

"We're Democrats—we get more respect from our opponents, but it's usually Republicans."

"True, but it's also true that our media shop keeps telling our Advance people to produce events that look more like yours," she said.

"Does that mean if I produce a really lousy rally your Advance people will emulate it?"

"You can try."

"The birth of a new political strategy, and you can say you were there at its conception," Bix said.

"You still love this, and your campaign respects your skills. You've trained most of their Advance staff—hell, you've trained most of ours. And they tolerate your eccentricities. They basically let you do your thing."

"You're projecting your own experience in politics on to mine, and yours has been very different. First of all, everyone loves you, especially your bosses, and they let you do your thing because you're the best at what you do and *everyone loves you.* You've mastered your craft. It makes no difference who wins the nomination, you will be in high demand. As the official poster boy for little people I'd like to ask you not to forget us when you're running the country."

"Now who's being hyperbolic?"

"Not in the least. You've got the gift, you've always had it, and you read everything and remember everything you read. *You* should run for office. That would be one campaign I'd like to be in on."

"Not interested. But I wouldn't mind doing an Advance trip or two from time to time, just to keep in my hand in. In what other profession does one have complete license to run over self-important blowhards, yet still show them compassion once they're aware they've been steamrolled?"

"Are you talking about anyone in particular?" Bix asked.

"Not unless you are," she said.

"I'm not, unless you have someone in mind."

"No, but for some reason I believe you are about to have a hankerin' for some Bacon, jes' about Friday morning," Storie said. "Also, if I'm not mistaken, you may be planning an unscheduled event when your Candidate arrives tomorrow night."

"You're good. How do you perceive all of that with the limited information you have at your disposal?"

"Mike told me to be in the lobby by 9:15, and knowing you, it didn't take much to surmise you were doing another Bix special spontaneous impromptu media event. Will you have several adorable children on hand to play Suzuki violins, for the obligatory adorable children shot?"

"That one was unique to Milwaukee. This OTR will be a 'one shot' for both TV and print. Just The Candidate talking to the crowd, as he is overwhelmed and humbled by their spontaneous outpouring of affection."

"Shane won't mind?"

"No, there'll be a hard barrier between The Candidate and the crowd. I'll bring him up from the loading dock through the bowels of the hotel and pop him out behind the front desk. The hotel's already teeming with cops, and we'll know the crowd, by-and-large. Service won't mind too much—it will be spontaneous, what could I do?"

"What exactly? And what are you going to do to Bacon?"

"Nothing. Certainly nothing spontaneous. To the extent possible I am going to give Mayor Bacon everything he wants."

"To the extent possible?"

"Yes," Bix said.

"Which means he won't get bupkis. You're going to give him one of your dancing lessons with no music."

"That's something entirely different, but yes, it's all in the choreography."

"Keep in mind that he takes heart medication and he's fifty pounds overweight. Don't stress him too much."

"The Mayor? Me stress *him*? He drives around town at ninety miles an hour. He thinks he's a freaking super hero. There is nothing I could possibly do that would in any way stress him. I might cause him some slow, brooding anxiety, but no stress."

"Good," Storie said. "I'm getting to like the guy. I have a thing for geezers." With that she walked over to Bix and kissed him on the lips.

He kept his wits about him. There was no muscle memory left in his mouth, but he maintained some memory memory, and he remembered to kiss her back.

After a long kiss, then an interlude, then another kiss, then his amazed realization that he hadn't drooled even once, he addressed the situation head on.

"I want to be clear about this. You did not ask my permission."

She kissed him again. "If I had, what would you have said?"

"It would have given me the opportunity to inquire about your oral hygiene." He kissed her. "Luckily for you it seems ok." He kissed her again. "Refreshing, like kissing a rain forest."

"I had a mango margarita before you arrived," she said.

"Can you drive? Your judgment is obviously impaired."

"I only had one. You go back to work. I can hear your BlackBerry vibrating constantly — the world is looking for you and the darn thing might cause you to become overly stimulated."

"This from the woman who just planted her lips on my lips in a provocative manner, then you blame my BlackBerry? Unfair."

She kissed him once more before climbing into her car. "This isn't over," she said. "My lips aren't done with your lips yet. Be forewarned."

"Your threats don't scare me none. You punks think you can scare us geezers, but I won't be scared off by you or anybody. I don't scare easy."

"You're scared all right. I can see it in your eyes," she said. "No, wait a second, they're just bloodshot. Don't stay up too late."

He was wearing the dictionary illustration of a silly grin as she drove away. The wolves nipping at his heels had a taste for silly grins and the people who wore them, but they couldn't eat this one off his face. He was impervious, armored for the remainder of the trip. At least that was his fantasy, or part of it.

An avalanche of digitized photon particles bombarded his BlackBerry screen as he logged on. He held it away from his body, aware of the ineffectiveness of a silly-grin shield against radiation poisoning. All of the local and national actors in Bix's little Advance melodrama were represented in the spontaneous outpouring of "you'd better" and "I want." Bix remembered Jim Kane's observation about the predatory instincts of people who claim the right of prima nocta for The Candidate's visit. "They all come out at night hoping to hump you one last time in the darkness at the end of the day, when they know you're tired and they hope you're vulnerable. At night the demands get weirder and the threats to get crazier," he told Bix. "Be prepared for it."

If Max News was in fact hacking his email, they were handed an archive of useful material that night. Despite Bix's admonitions to headquarters staff, they continued to utilize his email, phone, and voicemail as if they hadn't heard the news.

Among the incoming phone calls in his Caller ID were four listed as "anonymous" over the space of the previous hour, but with no corresponding voicemails. He assumed it might be someone from the campaign exhibiting appropriate caution.

He returned to the Hotel Marianne slowly, the long way, along the waterfront on East Bay to the Battery, then on Murray Boulevard and north on Ashley. Charleston's stately antebellum homes were a gift to succeeding generations, beautiful to behold, and as a living history they bore testament to the folly of conflict and the ethereal nature of anger, once felt so vehemently, that eventually passes quietly away.

* * *

At the hotel he parked in his "special" space around back, vaulted up the inside fire escape to the seventh floor and took up residence in a corner of the Staff Office for Workday 2.0. In protocol order, he planned to respond by phone to Peem, then email Bacon, Bacon's assistant LuAnn, President Gilliman, Gilliman's assistant, Egan, Shaunesy, Nurse Ratched, Mike (another problem with Rudd), Philpot, and a Max News producer who had left a message on his voicemail asking for an interview.

Once again he went retro, using the landline telephone attached to a cord. Peem greeted Bix's call with his usual indefatigable good cheer.

"Where the fuck have you been? You can't disappear like that. You can't pull that Advance bullshit on me."

Bix hung up. He thought he'd give Peem a chance to rethink his opening.

The phone rang and he assumed it was Peem. "Hello."

"Don't you ever fucking hang up on m..." Bix hung up on him again.

The phone rang again. Bix answered it "Hellooo."

"Don't hang up," Peem said.

"Don't yell. You know I can't stand yelling, particularly when it's aimed in my direction. What the fuck are you yelling about, anyway?"

"Where the fuck have you been?"

"Would you care to rephrase that?"

"Where have you been?"

"Exactly where I said I would be. I left you a voicemail over two hours ago telling you what, when, why, and not to fucking, ah, excuse me, not to email or call me because I believe I'm being hacked, or bugged, by people other than you," Bix said.

"I didn't get that," Peem said.

"I left it."

"I'll check."

"You do that."

"So what have you been doing? Who's hacking you?"

"Max News is listening in on one or more of my digital connections with the world. I went to Radio Shack and got new cell phones for Sophie, Kate, Mike, and myself and I will give you the numbers over the phone, no email. I'd prefer you wrote them down there."

"No shit?"

"No shit."

"Did you report it to the Secret Service?"

"Of course."

"So what now, other than using new cell phones?"

"As few emails as possible, which means less communication with headquarters, which I'm heartbroken about. Beyond that, I'll keep moving right along as I planned."

"Yeah, well, that's the thing. Our senior foreign policy advisor is concerned about you bringing the deputy foreign minister of Jordan into this without talking to him. Oz thinks it adds an international component that could prove embarrassing."

"Mister G. Fitzswald Smith thinks it could prove embarrassing, and I should have discussed it with him?"

"Let me conference him in. He wants to talk with you. Could you hold a minute?"

"You have the most delightful ideas," Bix said.

After an eternity, Peem and Oz appeared on the line. "Bix, Oz here. I've got some serious concerns."

"So do I. You go first."

"I understand your friend Hani is the deputy assistant foreign minister in Jordan," G. Fitzswald said. "Doesn't that appear a little extreme to you? Don't you think you should have discussed this with me first?"

"Only this afternoon, as Bob was accusing me of being indiscreet about our little top-secret operation, did he tell me that only a few people at headquarters were aware of our little *issue,* and he didn't mention you, Oz. Bob, at what point did you tell me that you were briefing Oz? And Oz, at what point did he mention to you that he sent me here to diffuse a potentially embarrassing situation because—and I'm quoting here—'you have international connections and you know Jamir personally?'"

"He told me you worked at the State Department," Oz said.

"Which you didn't know. Do you know Jamir or Hani Al-Saleem? Is your area of expertise the Middle East or the Persian Gulf? Have you ever been in a situation where you had to keep the media from screwing you? Do you think Hani and I are completely insensate? Do you think I rode in on a load of lumber this morning?"

"No, I didn't say that," Oz said.

"Yes, you did. You spoke volumes. It may be true. I may be as thick as a brick. If so, then you're screwed because I'm here and you're there and the time is eleven fifty-nine p.m., both literally and metaphorically."

"No, you're right," Peem said. "This whole thing is going to be resolved in the next day and a half, one way or the other."

"Bob, when you sent me here to find Jamir and told me to use my international connections, did that mean I was supposed to turn around and call Oz and ask him if he knew how to find him? Which, I guess, as long as I have you on the phone I should ask, Oz, do you know how to find Jamir, and do you have any advice as to how we should deal with the media?"

"No, but I'm worried about the implications of involving a deputy assistant foreign minister from a Middle Eastern country," Oz said. "Don't you think we should talk to him?"

"*We* have talked to him," Bix said. "You mean you."

"Yes."

"It was suggested to me that the implications of not squashing this rumor by Friday afternoon could be catastrophic," said Bix. "While I disagree, this was the urgency with which I was tasked, and getting caught with a senior Jordanian official who speaks better English than most Americans and looks better than most of 'em too, didn't seem like the worse of two fates. Were you aware that he played tennis for the University of Georgia for three years or that he can speak English just like a bootlegger if he wants? To that end, Hani is being a very good sport about this." At that moment it occurred to Bix that if he mentioned Hani's cloak and dagger episode at Dulles Airport it could undermine his case that he had "everything under control." He decided to move on to other talking points. "He *is* Jamir's brother-in-law and the best hope we have of finding him. Should I send him home?"

"I don't think we need to do that yet," Peem said.

"You guys didn't really think this thing through, did you?" Bix asked.

Silence.

Bix continued, "Assuming we're not stupid, and assuming we didn't simply blunder into this without weighing the risks…." Bix was certain he'd weighed the risks somewhere along the path, but he couldn't remember exactly when, or what they were, "…and knowing I have less than twenty-two hours before wheels-down, at which point my options become even more limited, unless you have something helpful to offer, wouldn't it be wise to allow me to do my job, gentlemen?"

"We don't want you to think we're trying to interfere with your job," Peem said.

"Yes, I know you don't want me to *think* it, but it's true nonetheless."

"Bix, just be careful is all we're saying," Oz said.

"I wouldn't have thought of that. Thanks, Oz. Now, unless you tell me that one or both of you are coming to Charleston and take the responsibility for this Advance trip, I'm going to move on to my next order of business with another one of the colorful individuals who is spreading sunshine in my life, one Mayor Bacon. Bob, just so's you'll know, I'm going to give His Honor everything he asks for. If he wants The Candidate to stick around for a dinner of rocky mountain oysters at the local trucker restaurant, I'm sayin' yes. Is that OK?"

"Whatever you think is appropriate, Bix," Peem said. "The Candidate will even use ketchup if you want him to."

"That's the spirit. Now Bob, write down these phone numbers, and Oz, you can ignore them." Bix read-off the new phone numbers and their owners.

"Bob, call me on that phone *only* if you really need me. I'll try to pick up, but you should be able to leave a secure voicemail if I don't. No more emails, just in case. If you must send an email, write Mike and Kate and ask them to tell me verbally. And please, for the sake of basic courtesy, check your own voicemails from time to time so we don't have to go through this tribal ritual again."

It was a remarkable performance, a tour de force of calm dismissiveness, and he was impressed. Soaring to heights of moral certitude, beyond the petty turf wars and crisis mindset, carried aloft on the wings righteousness, he'd left both Peem and Oz stunned. The silly grin shield worked.

Once again, just after the knick of time, another of Jim Kane's sage observations occurred to him. "In politics, 'being right' is sometimes the worst thing you can be." Bix knew instantaneously he'd won the battle, not the war, and it would come at a price. They would feel compelled to make him pay. The moment he hung up they began affixing blame and molding rationale—Bix had a terrible attitude, he wasn't a team player, he was arrogant and needed to be knocked-down or knocked-off—and he knew they'd come back with a touch of vengeance. He knew that they thought they would ultimately win whatever conflict they were concocting in their crisis narrative. How they would define "winning" was still very much a moving target.

There was nothing he could do about it—if they wanted to throw Bix under the bus it would be easy, and he had no defense other than achieving perfection: making all the positive things happen and all the negative things not happen. "Mental note," he thought, "Scarlett O'Hara." Easy to remember, "Scarlett O'Hara," shorthand for "I can't think about that right now. If I do I'll go crazy. I'll think about that tomorrow." Wiser words were never spoken. It wasn't as if he didn't try to achieve perfection on every Advance trip he'd ever done.

This time, however, he'd set the barre kind of high. He'd raised expectations, and no one in the Democratic Party ever endangered his or her career by aspiring too modestly.

Mayor Bacon's latest email, cleaned-up and forwarded by LuAnn, was lucid and forthright, and verged on the menacing. Under the subject line "Final approval pending," a dead giveaway that LuAnn had a hand in crafting it, he wrote, "People have been advising me to have your rally permit revoked until we come to an agreement on outstanding issues. President Gilliman remains unsatisfied with arrangements for a proper reception by the Board of Regents, and we must resolve your visit to the senior citizens center. Please call me first thing in the morning to avoid any further disruption in your activities. Mayor Eugene Bacon."

That was clear enough. It was time to throw the Hail Mary, promise him direct access to The Candidate and a little private quality time, knowing he would use that time to cajole, browbeat, harass, and intimidate The Candidate into a side trip to Bacon's Wrinkle Factory.

Bix replied to the mayor and cc'd LuAnn. "I have a solution you will like. I'll call on you at your office first thing tomorrow morning. Bix." Easy peasy. He hit Send, committing himself to another full flown conspiracy, requiring another set of dominoes to fall in precise order and another couple hundred people to act by remote control in precisely the way that he, the Bob Fosse of political operatives, hoped they would. No problem—he was invincible, and he decided to enjoy the feeling while it lasted, which he assumed wouldn't be long.

Mike, JD, Ben, Thigpen, and Freeway wandered into the staff office as their last stop before bed after a nightcap in the hotel bar. Bix still wore the silly grin.

"What's going on?" Mike asked. "You're grinning like a Cheshire Cat."

"There are a variety of reasons, not the least of which is I've just committed The Candidate to sharing his limo with Mayor Bacon on Friday morning, and I've committed us to kidnapping a couple hundred senior citizens from the Bacon Center at exactly the moment when Mayor Bacon gets in the car en route to the Schoendienst Gym. Freeway, I'll need you to coordinate the buses, and Ben, I'll need you to work your magic on the old folks. Can you make old people sprint?"

"I can do that," Ben said.

"Excellent. I'll need those buses to arrive at the Bacon Senior Center the exact minute our motorcade departs the hotel. Ben, you should have approximately an hour and fifteen minutes to get the people loaded, over to Scepter College, through security and into our special VVIP area. Thigpen, we'll need to move them into the site quickly and we'll need enough chairs for everyone. Get a couple of wheelchairs, too. I already asked Mike to get two handicap accessible port-o-lets...make it four handicap-accessible port-o-lets. Four stools, no waiting."

"How do you expect us to kidnap two hundred old people and get away with it?" Freeway asked. "Someone is going to be upset. You know how old people are, no offense intended."

"No offense taken," Bix said, "I also know how short-sighted neophytes can be, no offense intended."

"No offense taken."

"However, you make a valid point," Bix said. "Somebody or bodies in this large group of ancient hostages is going to get wise and start complaining. Freeway, since you thought of it, make sure there's food! Hot dogs and soft drinks will work, with condiments. Old people love free food. And Mike, make sure that one of our EMT trucks is stationed close to them. I'm assuming we'll have two EMTs for a crowd this size."

"We'll have the EMT trucks," Thigpen said, "but I still can't guarantee your crowd. We're busting our asses and I'm not feeling thirty thousand people yet. People are afraid of Bacon. He controls everything, including county services. Nobody wants to fuck with him."

"Give me an update at noon tomorrow when I come by the Field office," Bix said. "By then we may begin to notice the effects of our media. Remember, they just announced this thing to the press a few hours ago. Between the news coverage, radio ads, phone banking, and all of the paper you're putting on the street, you'll begin see more movement."

"What about Gilliman and her fundraising reception?" Mike asked. "Have you decided how we're going to handle her and Bacon? He's also saying he'll shut us down if Gilliman doesn't get her reception for the Board of Regents."

"I'm betting Bacon will be willing to throw Gilliman overboard if he believes he'll get his way on the senior center. Don't you think?" Bix said.

"That makes sense, but remember Gilliman could cause us problems without Bacon's help."

"We have to take care of the College Board in some manner," Bix said. "Start by finding a room where they can congregate on-Site, preferably far away from The Candidate's arrival point and preferably with close access to their special outdoor seating, and an escort to show them the way. And make sure we have enough VVIP credentials on lanyards. VVIP's love credentials. Be sure to put 'All Access Pass' on it."

"Which really means 'no access anywhere except the VVIP area,'" Ben said.

"Only if your glass is half empty. It means total access within the VVIP area, which has the best amenities in the house."

"And if they leave the VVIP area, what happens?" Ben said.

"They're free to go into the public area, if they can find their way back into it through the maze of bike racks. Most will give up. If they try to get near The Candidate, Service has a 'tase on sight' order."

"From whom?" Ben asked.

"Me," said Bix.

"Too bad they don't take orders from you," Ben said.

"Yes, too bad, but the good part is they always entertain my constructive suggestions. Are you set for tomorrow morning, driving to Columbia to meet Sophie?"

"Yes, I've got all the information."

"You've seen Max News crews skulking in the shadows around here and you may run into one at the Columbia airport, and yes, they are stalking us, as well as Sophie and another friend who you may meet named Hani. Try to avoid the cameras. If you're ambushed just smile sweetly and say 'we're getting ready for a big rally in Scepter.' Might as well get some publicity for us if you they stick a camera in your face."

"Got it," said Ben. He was wise enough not to ask too many questions. How he learned the concept of plausible deniability at such a young age was an amazement to Bix.

"Mike and Thigpen," Bix continued, "ask our firefighter friends in if they have a half dozen healthy men who would like to volunteer at Scepter College. We'll pay their expenses if they come from out-of-state. You may have to get them from Georgia."

"We just came in to check our emails and say goodnight," Mike said. "Now we've got a dozen new tasks and we're involved in the greatest kidnapping conspiracy since Cruella de Vil, and we all know how that turned out."

"Not really. I assume not well," Bix said.

"Not well at all."

"By the time we're done with them, the Bacon Brigade will be thanking us for the best time they ever had," Bix said. "As a matter of fact, we need to make a couple of signs for the buses with the words BACON BRIGADE in big bold capital letters and get some attractive young college YD's to serve as hosts on each bus. I bet none of the Baconers will press charges."

"What do you bet?" Ben asked.

"Your freedom of course, but if you're arrested we'll get you the best lawyer in our price range," Bix promised.

"That's what I feared," Ben said. "Is this some sort of hazing ritual? I'm driving to meet Sophie in Columbia, then I'm helping coordinate an event that no one knows about, then I'm supposed to shanghai the entire remaining population of Scepter's greatest generation. What's next, vote fixing?"

"The kid's starting to catch on," Mike said. "We don't ask new Advance people to commit out-and-out felonies on their first Advance trip—that won't happen for another two or three trips, but it comes with an increase in your day rate, so it's all good."

"By the way, have you found a place to get your first Advance trip tattoo?" Bix asked.

"Tattoo?" Ben said.

"Of course, it's a tradition for all real Advance men, and women. We all get a tattoo marking the date and city of our first Advance. All of us got one, didn't we, Freeway?"

"Sure, I got a tattoo with a little capitol dome on it because my first Advance was in Des Moines, in front of the state capitol building, October 3, 2004."

"My first Advance was in Bismarck, North Dakota," Bix said, "so I got the battleship Bismarck tattooed across my chest. You should get a tattoo of the administration building at the college with our banners up. Or The Candidate's face."

"Uh-huh," Ben said. "Let's see your battleship."

"That's personal, and one of the ladies might come in here at any moment and it could cause her to swoon, totally inappropriate. You need a tattoo if you want to be a *real* Advance man, one of the cool guys."

"We'll take him out tomorrow," Thigpen said. "I saw a tattoo parlor a few blocks from here on Market."

"I think I'll pass on being a real Advance man," Ben said. "I'll be a faux Advance man for a while."

"You're lettin' down the entire team, dude," Thigpen said.

"I'll try to live with the guilt.."

"Mike," Bix said, "one more task. Get a few extra feet of bike rack if you can. We're going to want to have a hard barricade between The Candidate and the rest of the motorcade when we pull up to Administration building."

"I already have extra for these unforeseen circumstances. As long as I was ordering a mile of bike rack, an extra few hundred feet didn't seem like a lot."

"You are a good man," said Bix. "All of you are good men or someday will be, I have no doubt. Obviously I have confidence in you or I wouldn't be expecting so much."

"Obviously we're all you fucking have to work with," Thigpen said, "or you wouldn't be expecting so much."

"Remember, I chose each one of you for this team," Bix said, "although you're right, Thigpen, I had a fairly limited universe of people from whom I could choose. The question is, are you the elite, or are you just the guys who had good enough connections to get your foot in the campaign's door but too were too stupid to avoid Advance? Were you so naïve as to be sucked in by the glitz and glamour and girls, blithely ignoring the possibility that someday you might be asked to put in a little hard work, risk a possible prison sentence, be branded for the rest of your life as a convicted felon, be marked for the rest of your life with a tattoo of The Candidate's face, stuff like that?"

"Oh, definitely the elite," Mike said, "as well as the glitz, glamour and girls. We're totally with you Bix, except for the prison sentence."

"And the tattoo," Ben said.

"Before I go, how do you want me to handle Rudd?" Mike said. "Now he's telling me that we can't build the catwalk."

"Can't?" said Bix. "Where the fuck does this guy get off? How the *fuck* is that a security risk?"

The room gasped.

"Bix said fuck," JD said. "You said fuck. I've never heard you use that word in anger."

"Rudd finally pushed you over the edge," Freeway said. "He went a bridge too far."

"No, it was Rudd and Drule and Peem and Shaunesy and Bacon and Max News and to some extent Gilliman," Bix said. "There I said it, fuck fuck fuckety fuck. So how the fuck is that a security risk?"

"So don't fuck with Bix," Mike pointed out. "Rudd had a dozen scenarios whereby The Candidate is either grabbed by someone or falls."

"And of course you explained to him how we construct catwalks with railings and chicken wire to guard against grabs or falls," Bix said, "and you explained that we count on that shot of The Candidate's entrance for the front page of the morning newspapers, and how we've done it many times before in rallies just as large as this one, and he's trying to fuck with our media and our politics?"

"Yes. He wasn't moved."

"We're building the catwalk whether Rude's moved or not," Bix said. That shot is money in the bank…a guaranteed, above-the-fold, full-color, tells-the-whole-story morning news photo. Now I'm riled. He can't possibly continue to believe he has veto power over our visuals."

"You can guarantee that shot will be used in the morning newspapers?" Ben asked.

"Absolutely, they can't resist it. We build the catwalk so it faces the cutaway riser on the other side of the stage at exactly eighteen inches off the ground. The 'stills' get a great shot of The Candidate reaching down over the railing—which is lined in red, white, and blue bunting—reaching down as the crowd is reaching up to him to shake hands, looking up with faces that are literally glowing with happiness, and with thousand-watt HMI's pointed straight at them. It's a great photo, literally irresistible to the still photographers. But the catwalk has to be exactly eighteen inches high. If it's twenty-four inches, the picture you get is a sea of disembodied hands reaching up from an unseen abyss as if grasping for help, no faces at all. It looks like a scene from Dante's Inferno. We made that mistake only once."

"That was my fault," Mike said. "As for Rude, he just doesn't like us. It's the only explanation."

"That would be justifiable if he had gotten to know us first," said Bix. "I'll email Shane—again—and discuss it rationally, if that's still possible. SO. To summarize," Bix pointed at each one of the responsible individuals as he recapped the midnight suprastaff meeting, "buses, bus signs, escorts—Freeway, tell your friend Miranda she can ride in the motorcade in the VIP van, she will escort the Mayor—bike rack, union guys, VVIP area, port-o-potties, hot dogs and soda, Board of Regents, Sophie's cell phone, no tattoo, and I need Mike and Ben to be certain of the walking route from the motorcade to behind the front desk for our non-OTR. Everyone remember the operative word for the hotel arrival tomorrow night?" Bix asked.

"Spontaneous," they said in unison.

"Brilliant," Bix said. "And not in the British sense of the word."

Guarding against further bouts of Bix's late night inspirations, the Testosterones departed quickly. The next morning was soon enough to find out if more indignities were to be heaped upon them, and there was a good chance that Bix might forget any new inspirations by then even if he wrote them down. Emails from Nurse Ratched and Egan awaited perusal.

Ratched's email, on behalf of Shaunesy, was a masterpiece of diplomacy matching anything produced by the Bilderberg Conference. "Mr. Shaunesy," she wrote, "requests 25 security passes for his reception committee at Scepter College, and awaits confirmation of staff pins for himself and me. We may be unable to provide all the names and their security check information until the event. He would like to know when he will have time to meet privately with the Senator. He expects to hear from you by 9:00 a.m."

"One delusional political poseur at a time," Bix thought. Providing name check information for people who were to meet The Candidate was basic, unquestioned. Headquarters had to vet the names politically and Service had to run them for a criminal history. He concluded that Shaunesy was trying to pull a fast one, to sneak someone in under the radar.

Bix replied with equal diplomacy. "Headquarters has told me the RFD can have 10-12 guests to meet The Candidate. They have discussed this matter with Don. He will have to choose whom he wants and provide their name check information by 5:00 p.m. tomorrow. Additional guests are welcome to watch from the VIP area. I have no private time on the schedule for Don with The Candidate. He will have to arrange that through Headquarters. I'll touch base with him tomorrow as soon as I can." *They'll love getting that one.*

Egan's latest email missive, a three-paragraph consternation celebration regarding the Bacon-Pangborne threat, the Max News hunt for Jamir and the manifesto, and the deputy assistant foreign minister of Jordan's involvement and the budget ended with an amusing anecdote regarding The Candidate's "concerns" in that nebulous, Washington-speak, I'm-suggesting-something-but-I'm-not-really-saying-it kind of way that Bix found so appealing. Egan wrote, "We briefed the boss about the situation in SC and he has expressed some concerns about outcomes, whether we will get a bad bounce from any of this, and the wisdom of involving your friend from Jordan."

Bix wrote his reply and hit Send before giving it a second thought, purposely. "Tell the senator I share his concerns."

Only then did he contemplate the wisdom of his terse response. He reopened Egan's email and wrote a codicil: "and approve my budget, get Drule/Shaunesy off my back…"

His BlackBerry rang mid-diatribe. It was the unattributed Washington phone number that had shown up twice before so he thought nothing of answering it. "This is Bix."

"I'm Dick O'Malley and you're the punk who tried to stop me from getting close to your candidate the other day in New Hampshire."

"Punk? Have you seen me? Point of fact, I did stop you, but only after you'd climbed past one barrier and stampeded through a secured area. Who is this really?"

"It's punks like you who give politics a bad name," O'Malley said.

"I thought it was politicians who gave politics a bad name, and phony journalists working for propaganda machines disguised as news organizations that give the media a bad name, or did I get that wrong?" Bix's mind raced with names of so-called colleagues who may have time to make a crank call in the midst of a campaign. "Who *is* this?" he asked again.

"I'm just a working man trying to do my fucking job, and you're a punk flack trying to protect his overlords," O'Malley said.

"Ouch. A punk flack? That's tough, hard hitting. This *must* be O'Malley. How's this? Quoting a veteran journalist from a *respected* news organization, 'Dick O'Malley is an oozing human-shaped pustule.' Hopefully you're taping this conversation."

"Fuck you, punk."

"Dick, did you call me for some purpose other than harassment?"

"I want you to know I've got you on my radar. I know you and your boss are dirty and I'm going to take you down." For the first time Bix began to believe it might be O'Malley. He sounded like O'Malley and he sounded like he'd been drinking.

"So, harassment. Dick, why would you tell me this? Wouldn't it be classier to just do it and keep your mouth shut about it? You're a big star, *Dick*. You've let your anger run away with you."

"You can be as glib as you want, but I got the goods on you guys. Whether we can find that manifesto or not, it's gonna get ugly for you and your campaign in about thirty-six hours from now."

"It was ugly the moment you showed your face. Let me ask you this—would a professional journalist call someone he's investigating for the sole purpose of terrorizing that person? Can you imagine Murrow, Cronkite, Brokaw, Sawyer, or Couric doing that? OK, maybe Couric. Look, *Dick*, if you had the goods on anyone you wouldn't be calling me out of frustration. By the way, I used to date your wife, so I understand you may have other concerns causing some of your frustration. I heard even the Viagra isn't working for you anymore. Try taping that limp thing between a couple tongue depressors. Give Yvonne my best and don't worry, she married you for your money, anyway."

"Well you can stick—" O'Malley started.

Bix hung up. "I'm gonna be very disappointed if I find out that wasn't O'Malley," he thought.

He finished his email to Egan, sent another to Philpot reporting the possible O'Malley intrusion—"Just got a call from D. O'Malley. He threatened me"—then closed up shop and walked down the fire escape one floor to the safe harbor of his room for another glorious four and a half hours of sleep. Awaiting him was a voicemail on his room phone, a woman's voice he assumed was Storie, saying only "Thanks for a great dinner."

"That woman is the soul of discretion," he thought, and his grin returned.

It was well past midnight, not the time for introspection, and Bix was exhausted. Despite that, he shocked himself with a set of questions that could have been a revelation. Did he need Storie's approval for self-validation? Did he feel like less of a person, or less of a man, without her, or more of a man with her? *What a horrible thought. Yeah, probably, but not so that anyone else would notice, except for the stupid grin.* He did his ablutions and went to bed.

13

Another brutal wake-up call, another grizzled image in the bathroom mirror coupled with another resolution to hydrate better, another slow walk down to the basement health center, and another slow start on the treadmill for another twenty minutes before Bix began to feel normal. He finished off with twenty minutes of jogging and his fifty push-up routine and a brief morning conversation with Agent Manfred, who once again praised his physical prowess. Bix's morning was brightened by the sound of Sophie's voice calling on his brand new temporary cell phone as he walked back up the stairs to his opulent mini-suite on the sixth floor.

"Bix, good morning. I'm at the airport waiting for my flight to Columbia and thought I'd share some more good news," she said.

"Thanks again for doing this. Is Chelsea with you?"

"Yes, she's right here, being an angel."

"What's the good news?"

"Peem's letting Drule come down to Charleston tomorrow, in time for your first event."

"Pourquoi?"

"Peem said it's not to get in your way, but it seems inevitable."

"You're very wise. This is payback for last night. I dissed 'em."

"Think about it, Bix," Sophie said. "Oz never worked in the State Department or the White House, he's a Capitol Hill guy. So is Peem. Neither of those guys can call up a bunch of ambassadors and put out an international manhunt for Jamir. That's a world they don't know. This is a turf thing and a power thing now. They want to control it, but haven't a clue how."

"So they're sending Drule? Tell me how he fits in."

"Drule just kept asking and Peem finally said yes. I think it's all he could think of," Sophie said. "He knows it will irritate you. You're taking this *very* well."

"Totally self-serving. You might have a poor impression of me if I started bouncing off the walls. And I'm still in a public space in a hotel stairwell. You wouldn't want to be around once I get to my room and close the door. Is there any good news?"

"My flight will be on time, and I've connected via email with your friend Hani. We'll meet up in the secured section of the airport before we exit. He told me he's wearing a funky tourist get-up—Hawaiian shirt and Red Sox cap—so I bought a disguise, a fanny pack."

Bix laughed, "What a wonderful image, you and Hani and Chelsea disguised as tourists. Did you reserve a mini-van?"

"I did! I did!" Sophie laughed. "I was thinking about painting a mustache on Chelsea but I thought it might be too much."

"Not in the least, considering the circumstances. Make it a Groucho mustache."

"And I'll stick a toy cigar in her mouth. We'll blend in with the crowd."

"In all seriousness, play it safe. I got a disturbing call last night from someone claiming to be Dick O'Malley, railing about his vendetta to destroy The Candidate and our campaign and me personally. He sounded drunk and he sounded desperate. Max News has dedicated a lot of resources to this, so he may be feeling the pressure to make something happen. And I told him I used to date his wife, which may have added fuel to the fire, but I couldn't help myself."

"Date as in date? Or date as in schtup?" she asked.

"Such an indelicate question coming from such a delicate lady. A gentleman doesn't schtup and tell. Look, this is uncharted territory. You're in South Carolina now, so *you* be careful. You could just as easily become a target."

"I will try my best, but Chelsea lives for thrills, so I'll call you when I arrive and meet up with Hani. I'll let you know where we're headed."

"Safe travels. I'll tell Ben Oliver to meet you at the car rental counter with your new cell phone for the trip. Thanks for the heads-up on the Druler."

"Don't let the Druler drool on you," she said.

* * *

At 8:00 a.m. the Staff Office on the seventh floor rattled with activity similar to Nora Jankowsky's Field Office with volunteers already seated at their tables, printing press credentials, answering two landline telephones, stringing credentials on lanyards, hand printing directional signs reading "Press This Way," "To Main Press Riser," and "National Traveling Press Only," the latter to be placed at the entrance to the food tent where lunch would be served.

Kate and Cornelia were hard at work drafting a media advisory and answering calls from members of the media who wanted to know where to park their satellite trucks or dump their displeasure over The Candidate's lack of media availability during the trip. And deftly, quietly, surreptitiously, they were placing Grandma Sadie on the local radio and TV talk shows to publicize the rally. Grandma Sadie was a true believer, natural promoter, and entertaining as hell. "A gift from heaven," Kate said, and Bix agreed. They named her the rally's local official spokesperson, and she played her part to the hilt, beginning the evening before when she spoke with a local news crew that arrived unexpectedly at the Scepter Field office.

Bix asked Kate if she'd had success arranging more interviews for Sadie. "We've gotten her on three local radio talk shows and one noontime TV news program," she said. "You saw the TV interview she did last night on the local CBS affiliate. She knocked it out of the park. She was spry and feisty and as cute as a button. They showed it on the six o'clock and eleven o'clock news."

"No, I didn't see it but I heard about it," said Bix. "It gives us the perfect alibi for Sadie's overnight media stardom. Once she did that first interview she became a hot commodity, now everyone is clamoring for her. She's a self-perpetuating phenomenon."

"Exactly. I hadn't thought of it like that," Kate said. "It's another spontaneous occurrence. Sadie gained celebrity status locally, her Q factor skyrocketed, now all the local media want to interview her. It's the ultimate in leaving no fingerprints."

"Who's making the media calls?"

"A volunteer, and she's calling from home and not using her own name. I told her to use yours."

"Perfect, a real fake false name. You're a natural at this."

"Now everyone in the Charleston-Scepter media thinks that you're a soprano," Kate said.

"I will be by the time Peem and Drule, and Drule's house elf, Shaunesy, are done with me. Have you seen Kate yet?"

"No, she hasn't been in. We're taking care of press RON manifests, room assignments, check-in, information packets, and drink vouchers for the hotel bar. I'm assuming this trip will be a replay of our last trip. We won't count on Missy at all."

"I'll email her and set up a meeting later this morning," Bix said, "along with Cole and Freeway. He's at a place in his motorcade and transportation arrangements where he can help Missy for a few hours today. We've got lots of time. It's not like arrival is tonight or anything."

Kate walked with Bix into the hallway. "How's your spontaneous demonstration coming?"

"There's no question in my mind we'll get a crowd, although I have no evidence to back it up. Mike will tell our Scepter Y.D.'s today where they should marshal their troops. We've chosen a restaurant-slash-bar with a large parking lot about a mile from our hotel where they can congregate. Other than that, be ready for my astonished phone call soon after we depart the airport en route the RON."

"We will react with aplomb. Get us the crowd and The Candidate and we'll get you the press. Good luck with Mayor Bacon."

* * *

Bix and Mike met once again outside Scepter City Hall to confer before re-entering Boss Bacon's gilded palace of power. The morning was clear and bright and fresh, reflecting Bix's new dawn of optimism. The early sun glared low down Main Street in a scene that could have easily been set in the early 1940s. He loved it.

"What are you going to do if Bacon doesn't accept your offer of a limo ride in lieu of a commitment to visit his senior center?" Mike asked.

"At that point it's what I call a 'St. Louis stand-off': two sides, one selfless and mission-driven—me—the other self-serving and ego-driven—him—in pitched but fleeting conflict over who gets the last barbecued pork steak. At the end of the day, it'll be me wiping the sauce from my lips."

"So you're taking this seriously, then?"

"Let's look in his eyes when we discuss it. Ultimately we have the weight of thousands of people, local voters, who will be arriving at Scepter College tomorrow expecting a rally. Is he going to want the blame for cancelling it?"

"I have a feeling he won't give a shit," Mike said. "These people down here don't even like barbecue sauce. They're a bunch of vinegar perverts."

They both took a deep breath before entering city hall, a building suffused with an atmosphere that hadn't changed since the Great Depression, oppressive and wonderful at the same time.

LuAnn stood up at her desk and greeted them warmly when they entered the sanctum, then scurried back to the mayor's private office to tell him they'd arrived.

"It finally hit me," Bix said, "I've been searching for an apt description of this. If Boss Tweed hired Liberace to decorate Tammany Hall…"

LuAnn came out to wave them into Polyphemus's lair, flashing a sly smile and knowing wink. "Good luck," she said.

Bix glanced back at Mike as he walked through the entrance.

The cave's occupant had the appearance of a man who only a moment before had been picking his teeth with the rib bone of a sheep he'd just eaten whole, under a big freaking chandelier. All he needed was a tunic made of hide. Once again, he didn't stand to greet his guests despite the close relationship they'd forged.

"What? You're not delighted to see us?" Bix said. "You remember Mike." Neither one bothered to wait for an invitation to sit.

Bacon leaned forward and touched the button to an intercom on his desk.

"Yes, Mr. Mayor," LuAnn could be heard through the speaker.

"Get Bud in heah," he told her.

"Right away," she said cheerfully.

"Are we under arrest?" Bix said.

"Na, na, na, nuthin' lak that. I jus' thaut that Bud shud heah all th' deetails with his own eahs. Altho I shud lock you boays up jus fo givin' me such a hahd taim. Ah've gone out onna limb for you boays."

"Which we appreciate, we really do," Bix said. "And the campaign appreciates it. I told them what you did to help us get the site."

"Yeah, and ya told th' Secret Sehvice that Ah was a secuahty threat t' yoah Candadate. They didn't appeah t'beh *happay* 'bout that."

"That's not true, your honor," Bix said. "I told them that you threatened to turn on the fire hydrants along College Avenue, and *they* said it was a security threat. If you recall, I asked your permission to pass it along, and if *I* recall correctly, you said 'Fahn, fahn, tell whoevah you wanna tell' or words to that affect, which I took to mean 'Fine, fine, tell whomever you want to tell,' unless I misunderstood."

"Noa, y' didn't misundahstand. I probably shouldn't have used that pahticulah tuhn of a phrase."

Chief Fry slowly opened the mayor's door and lugged his girth into the closest chair, panting as if he'd sprinted all the way from his office twenty feet down the hall. He wore his full rig—holster, pistol, ammo, hand cuffs—attached to a wide shiny black leather belt slung low beneath his ample belly, along with his "Chief" cap. Bix and Mike stood and shook his hand, which he offered reluctantly, surprised by the gesture.

"Bud," Bacon said, "Bix heah has a pr'posal to make 'bout gettin' his Candidate to our senia centa. Do ya' have a solution to your dilemma?"

"I believe my proposal is the best chance we have of making it happen, or planting the seed to make it happen next time he comes anywhere near here," Bix said. "The only way it can be accomplished on this trip is if you ask The Candidate directly, and the best opportunity you will have to do that is if I put you in this limo with him when we depart the hotel, before we arrive at our first site."

"Ya' mean you've got anotha place to go that mornin' befoa you git t' Scepter?" Bacon asked.

"Yes your honor, I've been tasked with producing another event tomorrow morning, and we'll be going there first."

"Ya' tellin' me you coulda made th' decision t' go t' ma senia centa all along an' ya' decided to go some whea else instead? Yua not makin' this ana easia on y'self, Bix."

"No, this was planned from the beginning," said Bix. "It just hasn't been announced. It's a secret, and you're invited."

"Unless that thea secret event is a visit to my centa, Ah' don't see how it does me much good, an' Ah don't see how that does ya'll much good eitha."

"You'd have an opportunity to pitch the idea to the senator directly, and he will find it difficult to say 'no' to a man as important as you. I've been honest with you from the beginning. I don't believe it will happen on this trip, but I'd bet dollars to donuts you'll get a visit on his next trip."

"That thah is a two-step PROcess," the mayor said, "and I never believe in a two-step PROcess when Ah've got to pay up front. Then if it don't happen I'm just a clod y'all wapped-off y'all's boots on the way through ma town."

"We'd never wipe you off our boots, Mr. Mayor. What have you got to lose? It won't cost you money, and this ain't Japan. You won't lose face."

"Unless you go around telling people you got screwed," Mike said. "The only thing we're gonna say is how gracious you've been to give us a fair shake."

"Or, if you'd prefer, what a tough son-of-a-bitch you were to negotiate with, whichever you'd like," Bix said.

Chief Fry jumped in to defend the mayor's honor. "Boa, you kain't taulk t' th' maya lak thet."

Mayor Bacon laughed. "Nah, nah, Ah undastan what Bix hea is sayin', an' it's ok."

"Thanks, Mr. Mayor. The chief obviously doesn't understand the finer points of politics," Bix said. He was confident the mayor wouldn't mind the backhanded smack-down to his brother-in-law.

"Nah, nah, nah, Ah undastan what ya'll gettin' at. But ya gotta undastan my position. This hea will look lak Ah've got no control ova ma own countay, an' Ah'll have anakky on ma hands."

"Anarchy? After all the ass-kissing we've been doing?" Mike said. "There were defendants in front of the Inquisition who had it easier than us."

Bix laughed in case the mayor didn't understand it was a joke, sort of. "That might be a little hyperbolic, but you're certainly no pushover, Mr. Mayor."

Chief Fry felt the need to interject once again. "Y'ain't seen nothin' yet if ya think ya'll can mess with us an' get away with it. We can make things hahd, reeel hahd."

Bix smiled. "I'm sure you can, but why would you want to?"

The question seemed to stump Chief Fry.

"Especially when it can trigger a federal investigation," Bix continued. The chief appeared to blink nervously at the suggestion, but Bix allowed for the possibility that he may have been reading more into Fry's reaction than was warranted. "Mr. Mayor, if you allow our event to move forward unimpeded, you can invite The Candidate to your senior center personally without all the rigmarole of dealing with Scheduling staff. What do you say? Several thousand people are showing up here in about twenty-four hours expecting to hear a speech. Why disappoint them?"

"Y'all go on ahead with y'plannin' on y'event tomorra an we'll see what happens," Bacon said. There was nothing telling in his voice as he said it, but his eyes seemed to go dead.

"Thank you, Mr. Mayor," said Bix. "We'll see you tomorrow morning at the Hotel Marianne at eight a.m., and bring your family. I'll introduce all of you to the senator, take a few photos, and then head to our first event." He looked at the Chief and glowered. "Chief Fry, does that sound like a plan to you?"

"Whateva the maya says is what Ah do," Fry said.

"Thanks, sir." Bix smiled. "And I promise NOT to give an interview to the Scepter Daily News thanking you both for all of your efforts to help our Candidate and praising you as a true liberal. I know how well that would go over down here."

"Yua inventive, Ah gotta say that," Bacon said. His eyes remained lifeless. Bix stifled a smile.

"Thank you, Mr. Mayor. I try my best."

After appropriate courtesies and a thank you to LuAnn as they exited, Mike turned to Bix.

"That was too easy. I don't like the way he said 'an' we'll see what *happens.*'"

"They've got another trick up their sleeves," said Bix. "I'd bet the farm on it. Have your rapid response team ready to go tomorrow morning early, no later than eight a.m., before people start showing up to get in. Make that seven a.m."

"How about finding a lawyer in Charleston who can be part of the team?" Mike asked.

"Good idea. I'll contact headquarters and ask them to find one; it will give them something to do that will be helpful."Back upstairs, Mayor Bacon had another directive for his chief of police. "Bud, weah gonna need a secuhity pahrimatah around th'college. Ah'd say about a mahle radius ought ta' about do it. We need t'guard against cah bombs so we gotta enshuh theah no cahs anawhah close t'th'place.

"Thaz a gud idea theh Mistah Mayah. Ah'll get pahkin' control on it immediately."

* * *

Out of the den of Beowulf, back to the environs of the reluctant Republican, Bix and Mike motorcaded to Scepter College and their nemesis of the hour, President Gilliman. Bix was certain that Gilliman, given the intervening time and opportunity to reflect rationally on the events that were unfolding before her, would be fairly keyed up. He was being kind.

Ushered into Gilliman's office, asked to sit and wait while she stood outside her door issuing secret instructions to Charlene for an eternity, Mike began to show his irritation. He paced the room, stopping to appreciate her wall décor of framed photos and making harrumphing sounds as his eyes moved from Republican to Republican. It was only after she re-entered and took her seat behind her large dark desk that Mike once again sat.

"It doesn't look like you get many Democrats around here," he said, catching her off-guard.

"No, ahh, we don't get many of those around here, but I look forward to having more."

"You gotta invite 'em to get 'em," he said, unsmiling.

Bix didn't mind Mike's mild upbraiding of the president. It set her back on her heels momentarily, and clearly most of the photos pre-dated her tenure as president. They were evidence of choice, not serendipity.

Bix's cell phone went off for the tenth time in ten minutes, and he felt no compunction about checking the caller ID.

"I apologize, I have to take this call," he said as he walked out of the office. It was Hani.

"Hi Bix, I wanted to tell you we've arrived at the Columbia airport and there's another Max News crew waiting at the security gate."

"Are you still in the secured area of the airport?"

"Yes. Sophie is going to go ahead and get the rental car, and I will go out and meet her at the street outside of baggage claim."

"Do you have an idea where you're headed?"

"I believe it's Florence, so we're going there."

"Thank you, good luck, and don't trust anyone except your GPS. I'll call you back soon."

Gilliman roared back into true fighting form when Bix returned. Her opening salvo started abruptly. "I can still have this whole thing cancelled. We need to come to some agreements here."

Bix forced another smile. "It's good to see you again too, President

Gilliman. We're fine. Everything seems to going well. We're having a lovely experience on your campus. And how are you feeling about things?"

"Well, I'm a little *concerned*," she emphasized, "that we're getting ahead of ourselves and I want to make sure the college is well represented."

"I don't know what you mean," Bix said. "The college will look great on television, The Candidate certainly won't say anything that will embarrass the school, and the Secret Service will go ballistic if you cancel at this point because we'll still have to do it somewhere else and the only thing the college will get out of it will be bad press." He couldn't help mentioning the Service again. It was a cheap tactic, but it was his best leverage. "Tell me how I can help you and I'll tell you what I can do."

"You can assure me that the senator will come to our reception, and I would like to meet with him in my office before he gives his speech," she said. "We have opened our college to you and expect you to honor our traditions."

"You have traditions surrounding the visits of presidential candidates, something you told me you've never seen since you've been here?"

She wasn't deterred.

"I'm talking about our traditions of hospitality and courtesy," she said.

"What part of Scepter College's tradition of hospitality includes blackmail?" he asked.

"You're very clever. Be careful you aren't too clever."

Bix grinned, genuinely amused. "No one's ever accused me of that."

The door to Gilliman's office opened and in walked the campus director of Security, with whom Mike had met the day before, and the administrative director who had signed their contract for use of the site. Both seemed friendly.

"I was just discussing our options with Bix and Mike, and we appear to be at an impasse," she said.

"And President Gilliman was just telling me about Scepter College hospitality," Bix said.

Agent Rudd walked in and stood next to the wall on Bix's far right.

"Agent Rudd was in my office so I invited him to come with us," the director said.

"Good to see you again Agent Rudd," Gilliman said. "As I was saying, we seem to be at an impasse. We have invited the senator to join us for a brief reception prior to his speech, and we would like to hold it up here in the reception area. Agent Rudd has agreed to have the senator attend and I have asked Bix to confirm the senator's participation. If it proves to be necessary, we can shut down the campus to everyone except the students, faculty, and staff of the college to ensure a higher level of security."

Mike was ready to start a fistfight. Bix was, too, but he was wearing his cleanest shirt.

"Happily, despite Special Agent Rudd's gracious acceptance of your kind invitation, he has nothing to do with The Candidate's schedule, and the problem is two-fold. Under these circumstances I could not agree to let The Candidate attend a fundraiser as the guest of honor. To use a word the Special Agent Rudd should know well, it is simply 'inappropriate' to try to use him in that manner."

Agent Rudd butted in. "I was just talking about his attendance from a logistical standpoint."

"Point taken," Bix said, "but President Gilliman took it to mean that you were consenting to his attendance. Second, there is no time on the schedule. None."

He began to pause, then wound up again. "And there's a third reason. If we bring The Candidate, we also have to bring the press. He doesn't go unless the press goes, too, that's the agreement."

It was, sort of.

Mike couldn't contain himself. "And then we have to move the press and provide space in the room for them. You don't want television cameras in the faces of your guests, at least not at a distance of three inches."

"We could go to another building where there's more space," the admin guy suggested.

"Thanks, sir," said Bix, "but we still don't have time on the schedule and it would require even more time and effort to move to another building. Here's what I will do to take care of your special guests, which we have been planning all along. We will have front-row access and chairs for them in our *very* special VIP area with its very own port-o-potties, and the senator will shake their hands as he is working the rope lines, hopefully not after they have used the port-o-potties. If you would like to invite him back in the future to attend a fundraiser or participate in any other campus activity I will endorse your invitation because you've been so gracious to allow us to come here. That's what I can do on this trip."

"I don't know," Gilliman said. "I don't think that's going to be good enough."

"Fine, cancel it," Bix said. "I can see the headline now in fifty point type. 'PRESIDENT GILLIMAN CANCELS SPEECH BECAUSE CANDIDATE WON'T COME TO HER PARTY.'"

Gilliman squirmed slightly.

He stood up from his chair. "We've already prepared a backup plan to move the event to downtown Scepter, to the town square," he lied. "Conveniently, we have a representative of the Secret Service attending this meeting, so they can start planning immediately. I'll call my Headquarters and Kurt can contact Shane and tell him the news. Kurt never wanted to do the event here anyway, isn't that right?"

"It was for security reasons," Kurt explained to Gilliman. "I didn't want to hold the event outdoors, that's all."

"And the college's history of violence concerned you," Bix said.

"What violence?" Gilliman asked accusingly, forgetting she was the first one to broach the subject of potential violence the day before.

"I apparently got some bad information on that," Rudd said.

Mike knew Bix well enough to play along with his bluff. "I counted," he said to Kurt. "There are twenty-three businesses around the square, and another dozen or so within a half-block on each side. Good luck securing that."

The first reasonable utterance to escape Agent Rudd's mouth suddenly spilled out. "Mike makes a good point. Moving the site at this point will create some problems for us. It would be better if you could work this out."

"I agree," Bix said.

Gilliman was outflanked. Her natural affinity for conservative law enforcement types compelled her to retreat.

"I see your point, Kurt," she said. "We don't want to make this more difficult for you than it needs to be."

"Thank you, President Gilliman," Bix said. "We will do everything in our power to make this a convenient and enjoyable experience for your VIPs. They'll have special parking set aside, a special VIP entrance so they don't have to go through the long lines, and the best seats in the house. If any of your VIPs hate the accommodations, you can blame us—that's what we're here for. Isn't that right, Kurt?"

Agent Rudd grunted. It sounded as if he agreed.

"Mike will remain here to continue preparing, and I will be available in case any other problems arise, which I assume at this point they won't." Another lie. He assumed the opposite. "Mike, I'll see you at the Scepter headquarters in an hour. President Gilliman, gentlemen, thank you again for your gracious hospitality."

It was impossible to overuse the word "gracious" in his estimation.

14

On the phone to Sophie the moment he left Scepter College, Bix found her at the wheel of a rented minivan on a highway somewhere in South Carolina in a state of near panic. She put her phone on speaker.

"I see that Ben connected with you at the airport," he said, referring to the new cell phone.

"Yes, he found me, and so did everyone else," she shouted. "We weren't able to get out of the airport unnoticed. Now there's a Max News van following us and I don't know what to do. I've got Chelsea with me. I don't want to speed up and try to ditch them, and they're practically on my tail."

"Can you spend an hour driving back and forth on the same high-way? That would at least cause some frustration for them *and* for you. And try calling me on my BlackBerry number and leave a fake message about your destination. Email me too. Tell me you're heading toward Timbuktu to find Jamir. It's worth a try. They may still be listening."

"We'll try it," Hani said.

* * *

Peem had left three more messages on Bix's new cell phone. In one, he made a passing reference to Hani's transit to the US from Jordan and Ambassador Baycroft's email suggestion about finding him. The only problem with Peem's comment was that Bix hadn't told anyone the specifics of his interactions with Baycroft. It was a reference to an email and a voicemail that Bix had received from Baycroft two days before, and even Sophie hadn't been told the details.

There were only three possible explanations. Either Max News was hacking Bix's BlackBerry and they had told Peem, or the campaign was hacking directly, or Bix had mentioned it and simply forgotten the comment. The latter seemed unlikely, and neither of the other two possible explanations fell within his comfort zone of comprehension.

Bix decided to confront Peem on the subject. He hoped there was another, less malignant, explanation.

Peem answered his cell phone with his usual condescending commentary. "Well, it's about time you returned my calls. Are things continuing to fall apart in South Carolina?"

"Bob, you can stow the negativity," Bix said. "It's not helpful. Remember, it was you who sent me. What does it say about your judgment, and lack of support, and the quality of your Regional Director, if things are falling apart here?"

Peem was temporarily speechless.

Bix decided to go on the offensive. "You mentioned my friend Ambassador Baycroft's comments. What were your concerns?" He wanted to hear the extent of Peem's knowledge on the subject before asking him the ultimate question.

"I'm concerned about this escalating beyond our ability to control it. Both Ambassador Baycroft and your friend Hani are fairly high ranking officials."

"How did you hear about Baycroft's comments? I hadn't mentioned them to anyone."

"You told me."

"No, I don't believe I did."

The question had caught Peem off guard. Without a reasonable cover story, Peem stammered, "Well, maybe Drule told me."

"And would Drule know? I certainly didn't mention it to him."

"I'm not sure. Maybe you told him or our Regional Director."

Drule's involvement took a sinister turn. He ran the computer operation at headquarters that analyzed voter targeting data, the band of nerds ensconced in a secured office space away from the rest of headquarters operations who spent their days hunched over computer screens raking volumes of behavioral information gleaned from unspecified sources too classified to reveal outside their own enclave.

"Uh huh," Bix said. "And is Drule authorized by you to monitor staff emails and voice messages? Is that what falls under the category of technical support from HQ?"

"Not possible," Peem said. "He's analyzing voter databases and marketing data. That's not your concern. Don't even think about that."

"Are you telling me what I can and cannot think? Isn't that a bit Orwellian, or at least ironic?"

"Not in the least," said Peem. "I'm suggesting you keep your focus on the trip."

"Uh huh. I also have some suggestions but I'll hold those in abeyance until the trip is completed. Do you have anything helpful to tell me or are you just calling to annoy me?"

"I wanted an update on the current situation with Jamir."

"If I knew anything more than I did last night I would have informed you, or Drule would have. Call him. I'm certain he'll be happy to update you. And unless you have something constructive to tell me, I am going to desperately try to concoct a scenario whereby you guys *aren't* hacking my messages, and then I will re-focus on the trip on which I am supposed to be focused before you focus me to death." He didn't wait for a reply. After he hung up he decided it would be advisable to buy another temporary cell phone on his own dime and dial "star 67" to anonymize it before every call, to anyone, and never use his email except for the most mundane of housekeeping messages.

The incident left him shaken. Knowing who to trust in politics was always a tricky path to navigate. The concept of loyalty in the Democratic Party was as dead as the dodo bird, and he'd accepted the fact that political relationships were transactional at best. But he felt foolish to have believed that simple, situational respect might still exist among his colleagues on the same campaign. His fellow dinosaurs' constant admonition, "They only respect you after you've fucked 'em," seemed inarguably true.

* * *

True to form, Missy didn't answer her phone when Bix called during his drive back to Charleston to confirm her attendance at the RON walk-thru meeting he'd called for 11:00 a.m. Freeway immediately answered his phone, also true to form, and told Bix he'd been trying to find Missy for the previous forty-five minutes with no success. Bix asked him to keep looking, and emailed Agent Cole to let him know he was on his way back to the hotel.

Upon arrival at the Hotel Marianne he started his walk-thru solo, sans Missy and Secret Service, to view the alternate route he expected to take that evening. The motorcade arrival point would remain the same as planned, as would The Candidate's entrance door next to the loading dock, but Bix's secret OTR plan took him through a different maze of corridors, past the service elevators that would eventually take him to the secured suite on the seventh floor, under the executive offices, and up to the lobby level behind the hotel's front desk. If the lobby was packed that evening with spontaneous revelers, as expected, The Candidate could address his supporters from that vantage point and maintain a semi-secure separation from the crowd.

As Bix climbed the dark set of stairs that would take him to a little-used corridor under the executive offices he noticed a dark form standing just beyond the top of the staircase. It quickly became apparent it was two forms, standing so closely together they seemed as one, and almost as quickly he recognized the frizzy hair of his RON, Missy, in the clutches of a man who had his left hand inside the front of her blue jeans. Then he noticed that she had her hand inside his unzipped trousers.

Obviously startled, they separated. The man, whom Bix recognized as the hotel's assistant general manager, withdrew his hand from Missy's pants with lightning speed while he attempted to maintain his composure. Missy, withdrawing her hand with what appeared to be calm deliberation, immediately regained her nonchalance, as if Bix had walked into a sitting room and found them sipping tea, discussing the weather.

It infuriated Bix, and he was surprised by his own reaction. He was certainly no Puritan—it was none of his business if Missy felt the need to grope a new acquaintance in a tacky hotel service hallway. It was her lack of concern that she was acting in a manner that might be viewed by others as inappropriate or compromised her ability to function. This was a person who felt no fear of being held responsible for her actions, and Bix assumed it was her sense of privilege, an expectation that her father's influence would protect her from repercussions. She could have at least shown *some* concern, even slight embarrassment would have worked.

It occurred to him that he shouldn't hold her to a standard that he himself hadn't upheld due to his interaction with Storie. Despite the fact that he was continuing to do his job and Missy had yet to show any commitment to doing hers, and despite the fact that all of his interactions with Storie had been "G-rated," he trod lightly and said nothing.

"Hi Bix," she said almost with indifference. "I'll be up in the staff office for our meeting in a few minutes."

He couldn't help himself. "Once you two remove yourselves from each other's genitals I'd like to talk with you privately, Missy. I'll see you in the staff office in five minutes. That'll give you time to wash your hands." He felt a genetic predisposition to react like his eighty-five-year-old father might have, but stifled it.

Rather than issue her a private reprimand, Bix called Kate and asked her to participate in the conversation he was about to have with Missy. The idea was born of pure paranoia. He worried that Missy might accuse him of sexual harassment or worse if the conversation wasn't to her liking, and he wanted another person in the room, preferably female. At any rate, if Missy could show she was accomplishing the tasks she'd been assigned as the RON, he didn't want to castigate her.

Kate was already working in the Staff Office with Cornelia and their two volunteers when Bix arrived. He asked her to step outside into the hallway and he described the scene he'd observed. Kate was incensed. "That's in poor taste," she said. "If nothing else, it's classless. It undermines her ability to work with the hotel staff, which is her one and only job here."

"Yes, but is it a double standard for me to chastise her for her behavior when I've been talking with Storie for the past two days?" Bix asked.

"Have you been feeling her up in the service hallway?" she said.

"Feeling her up?" Bix inquired with mock astonishment. "In the hallway? Not lately. We usually go to a flophouse that charges by the hour. Or in my case, by the minute."

"I didn't think so. There's a quantifiable difference between socializing out in public with an old friend who is well known and respected by all of us, and crotch-diving in the shadows of the service corridor with the assistant general manager of the hotel where The Candidate, the traveling staff, and the entire press corps will be staying tonight. Her tryst may have been videotaped on a security camera. You'd be within your rights to send her home immediately and tell Headquarters the reason."

"Then we wouldn't have a RON Advance," Bix said.

"We don't have one now," Kate countered.

"Let's see what she's accomplished when she gets here. If she has the staff room assignments completed and she's met with her Secret Service counterpart, she's off the hook. If not, I'll blow her up. Who knows, maybe it's true love and she's gonna marry the guy."

"Yeah, and maybe she has no discretion and no business representing a presidential campaign, unless maybe it's Kinky Friedman's."

Ten minutes later Missy could be heard in her room adjoining the staff office. When she finally opened the door and sauntered in, she was holding a legal pad with her notes regarding room assignments.

Bix asked her to accompany him back into her room and invited Kate to join them.

"That was one of the more unexpected exhibitions I've stumbled upon in a while," Bix began. "In retrospect, do you think it might be ill-advised to place yourself in a compromising position with the hotel staff, given the circumstances of our work here?"

"We were just fooling around. It was innocent. What d'ya expect?"

Kate spoke up. "We expect, and I expect the campaign would too, that you'd comport yourself with a little class when you're out here representing a man who could be the next President of the United States. It's not too much to ask, is it?"

"Hey look, no harm was done," Missy said. "And besides, we're dating. He's a nice guy."

"Dating? Since when? Yesterday?" Bix asked. "Forget it. It's none of my business. We'll come to your wedding. What I want to know is whether you're prepared for arrival tonight. Do you have the staff manifest and room assignments? Have you met with your RON agent?"

"Yes, and I have the staff room assignments and billing information entered into the hotel's computer system," Missy said.

"Good. And you've arranged for the general manager, and *only* the general manager, to greet the senator when he arrives?"

"Yes."

"I don't want to see your new BFF on arrival. You can place him tomorrow morning for the exit handshakes with hotel staff, along with no more than nine other people, *max*," Bix said. "If there are eleven people in the room as we're leaving, I'll pass you by."

"I understand." Missy didn't look sincere when she said it. She may have assumed it was an empty threat, which it was. The Candidate wouldn't walk past without a greeting.

"Now, let's go meet Agent Cole for our walk-thru and you can show me where you've chosen to do the hotel handshakes on departure," Bix said.

Kate went back to the staff office to continue her press arrangements and was replaced by Freeway, who, along with Bix, Missy, and Agent Cole, walked through both arrival and departure scenarios. Bix found a location in a separate meeting room where Mayor Bacon and his family could greet The Candidate before they left for the Schoendienst Gymnasium, and informed Agent Cole of his plans to allow Bacon to ride in the limo en route.

* * *

Bix called Sophie and Hani within seconds of pulling out of his parking space headed for Scepter. Sophie answered the cell phone after too many rings for his comfort and he once again sensed the worst. Once again, he was wrong.

"We ditched 'em," she said." We pulled off the interstate and drove into the sticks, and after about a half hour of two-lane roads I found a grove of trees next to a rest stop and pulled up behind them. They drove right past. It was fantastic. We're doubling back now, headed toward Florence in a roundabout way. I'm going to give you to Hani."

"Sophie was a regular double-o-seven," Hani said. "I don't think they'll find us again. The scenery here is beautiful. Is there anything you want us to do?"

Bix was philosophical. "Thank you, Hani. You're on your own compass now. The mission remains the same. Come back with Jamir or on him."

"I thought that only worked for shields," Hani said.

"You're right. I get confused when I attempt to give a pep talk. However it works, find Jamir so we can shoot down this nonsense. In flames, preferably. The flamier the better." He'd convinced himself, by his own infallible logic, that there was no there there, and, being Bix, decided that an equally dramatic display of the facts was called for. Fact One, Jamir looked like an Iranian Omar Sharif, with a Midwest accent, and he would look good on television. Bix was set on putting him there.

* * *

A half hour later, Bix and Freeway were at the Scepter Field office for a welcome meeting with Nora, Mike, Ben, Thigpen, and JD. The place was a beehive—bouncing happy faces scurried throughout the office working the phones and carrying stacks of flyers and posters for distribution. It may have been Bix's imagination, but the mood of anticipation seemed electric. Many of the volunteers greeted him as they would an old friend, another part of Advance that Bix loved.

Nora was happiest. She hugged Bix and Freeway as if she'd known them for years and looked at Mike as if she'd known him in the biblical sense, which Bix thought may have been the case. The Candidate's visit was like an injection of adrenalin, reenergizing the group of Field organizers and local volunteers who had been demoralized by Napoleon Shaunesy and Nurse Ratched.

"You guys can see we're kicking butt," Nora said. "We've signed up at least fifty new volunteers in the last day alone, and they're out there promoting the rally. Everyone is completely jazzed. Do you think we'll get our crowd?"

"Thigpen's the guy to ask about that," Bix said. "Thigpen, what d'ya think? Will we get thirty thousand bodies?"

"I still don't see thirty thousand yet," he said. "Right now I'm seeing less than twenty thousand from the response to our phone banking and the calls that are coming into the Field Office. The mayor is fucking us to death."

"Our paid media only started less than fourteen hours ago," Mike said, "and Grandma Sadie's been on a couple of radio shows promoting it. That'll make some difference, don't you think?"

"They help, but I think we're gonna need some fucking help from God to get thirty thousand people," Thigpen said.

It gave Bix an idea. "Excuse me." He took his cell phone from his pocket. "Shit, it's Headquarters. I have to take this. Calls like this are never good." He walked out of the small meeting room quickly and dramatically and into the hallway nearer the main room where the volunteers could hear him but still close enough for his compatriots to hear as well.

"This is Bix," he said as he stood closer to the volunteers who were working the phones. "Yeah, yeah…no *shit*! You're joking. *Oprah*?" he asked in a strident whisper. He then turned around and walked back through the hallway, past the meeting room, nearer the bathrooms at the rear of the office. "Yes, of course, we can send a driver and an SUV. What time?" He paused momentarily. "No *shit*! That's great news— when can we announce it?" Another long pause. "No sooner than that?" Another pause. "Yeah, I understand. Let me know. This will help, a *lot*."

Several of the volunteers, including the ones who had been sent by Mayor Bacon and the mole from Shaunesy, overheard. He'd never whispered so loudly in his life.

He walked back in to the meeting room and closed the door behind him. The Levolors that could be closed to block the view into the big room were wide open. "We'll see if that does anything," he told his team. "Now I want us all to high-five and smile a lot." He leaned over the table and raised his right hand and everyone in turn stood up and high-fived him.

"You're a scamp," Mike said.

"Thigpen asked for help from God," Bix said, "Oprah was the closest I could get. Don't say anything to anyone." He looked at Nora. "If anyone asks, you can't confirm or deny. Mum's the word."

"My lips are sealed," Nora said. "This will spread like wildfire. Nothing leaks faster than a rumor that we can't talk about. I guarantee that Mayor Bacon and Shaunesy are hearing about it this very second."

"That was my hope. Are we set for the poster-making party this afternoon?"

"Fucking straight, dude," Thigpen said. "We'll have at least forty people here at four o'clock and Kate has alerted the press. We'll have some great shots on the news at six o'clock and headquarters is sending out blast emails today."

"Then I'm confident we're doing everything possible to promote this thing," Bix said. "Let's get back to the gritty details. Freeway, is Miranda prepped to meet us at the hotel and accompany Bacon from the time we arrive at the Schoendienst Gym until we arrive at Scepter College?"

"She's ready. And I've got the right person to pick up Larry Drule at the airport in Columbia. He'll do whatever we ask," Freeway reported.

Bix changed the subject quickly. "Are you and Ben set with your buses for our Bacon Senior Center run?"

"We're ready to go when you give me the word," said Ben. "They'll be standing by as you depart the hotel en route the Schoendienst Gym."

"J.D., what's the latest on the build at the Schoendienst Gym?"

"It's still the worst site I've ever seen, but we'll start the build tonight at ten p.m. when Mike's contractor arrives."

"Mike, when do we start the build at Scepter College?"

"They'll start unloading at midnight and we'll be finished by six or seven a.m. Are you going to come?"

"You know I will. Have I ever missed one? Have you invited Nora to drop by the hotel tonight to see our candidate when he arrives?"

"Yes," said Mike. "She will be helping Ben and me, just in case anything spontaneous occurs," Mike said.

Nora smiled.

15

Adam Strayberg called from his room at the Hotel Marianne to inform Dick O'Malley, who was still in his office in New York, that the trail had gone cold. O'Malley took the news with his usual geniality.

"What the fuck! What you're telling me is that you fucked up! We're gonna look like a bunch of fucking *clowwwns*," he stretched out the word, "because you can't find one measly little person and you can't keep track of one of those campaign assholes. How didn't I pick the wrong senior producer?" O'Malley was poor at trying to insult his staff without insulting them.

Strayberg nearly snapped. He'd had enough of O'Malley's…everything, and more than enough of providing his boss with plausible deniability, but then he couldn't quite say the words. "They think we're hacking them, and we practically are, so we've had to be more and more careful. They've got different phones and don't use their emails. Their Headquarters hasn't been as careful so we're still picking up useful information from time to time, but Bix and his buddies have gone cold." Hoping the information he had just imparted may have come as a shock to O'Malley, he asked, "Should I go on?"

O'Malley acted as if it was all part of a normal conversation. "No, that's OK, I get it. I understood that you had a news crew following a relative of Parviz's. Isn't that producing any results?"

Strayberg was surprised that O'Malley was aware of the "tail" that Max News had put on Hani, although he'd briefed O'Malley three times. "The guy's name is Hani Al-Saleem and he's a brother-in-law of Parviz's. Our crew started following him and one of their campaign staffers, who has her child with her, at the Columbia airport when they picked up a rental car, but then they lost them as they traveled east toward the coast then started driving in different directions. Our crew is still out there looking."

"You see to it that you find him. I'm traveling all the way down there tomorrow to do a live remote in some hell-hole small town so you better have more for me than a bullshit rally. I've seen enough bullshit rallies. I'm spending a shitload of money on this story and this is your ass on the line, too."

Strayberg wasn't frightened of O'Malley, only the feds. "Good thing it isn't your money."

"I watch every penny this unit spends!" O'Malley screamed. "I am held *accountable* for every penny this unit spends! I have given you shitpots of money to track down these *corrupters*, and I expect the goods. Track them. Follow them. I don't care what you've got to do. I don't care who you have to kill."

"Corrupters?" Strayberg thought as he waited to hear O'Malley walk-back the last statement, but O'Malley never did. Finally he spoke as bluntly as his courage to admit legal culpability allowed. "We're already coming dangerously close to the edge to find your alleged manifesto and your alleged dirty politicians, but so far there has been more alleging and less evidence. Murder, at this point, might be considered bad taste." He knew they were long past "dangerously close," and well into "going over" the edge.

O'Malley wasn't amused. "Alleged! Alleged? There's fucking dirt there, I told you so. I can fucking smell it, so you find that Parviz guy and his fucking manifesto. And I got another dirtbag for you to investigate— that Advance guy Bix what's-his-name. I want you to nail his ass to a tall fucking tree. I want you to get that punk and bury him. You got it? You're the senior producer on the most important program on television, and I assume you want to keep it." He slurred the last sentence badly.

"Put down the fucking booze, Dick, and stop making threats or I'll shut down this operation completely. I may decide to do it anyway. I don't know how I let myself get sucked into this, but I promise, if *I'm* off the most important program on television then *so are you*. If I don't find Parviz and I don't find his manifesto, it means there was nothing to find, and I'm going to come home and come into work the next day and we're both going to rack it up to experience. Isn't that right, Dick?"

O'Malley was quiet for for a moment. Strayberg waited for an answer. "I suppose that would be the wisest course of action," O'Malley finally muttered, "but find that son of a bitch."

* * *

Bob Peem saw the caller ID on the secured landline phone on his desk and answered immediately. "Yeah, boss. What's up?"

It was The Candidate, calling from his Holding Room, normally the facility manager's office next to the community center gym, at an "Economic Roundtable" in Las Vegas. "Bob, how much of the situation in South Carolina is truly a problem and how much of it do I have to worry about?"

Peem was confused. "Ah, I don't know. You're going to have to be more specific than that. Are you talking about Bix, Parviz, the manifesto thing, or the right-wing news media?"

The Candidate was tired. "No, Pangborne keeps calling me about my events in Scepter and that local mayor. Why does he care so much about that guy? It's gotten to the point where he's threatening to 're-consider his neutrality,' as he puts it. These guys always have to push their weight around. Are they just hunting for excuses to endorse our opponent?"

"That could be," Peem said, "but Mayor Bacon delivers a lot of votes to Pangborne so he's beholden. That's my best guess. Bacon's going to deliver a lot of votes to our opponent too."

"How do my numbers look in that district?"

"It's winnable. At the moment you're within the margin of error."

"And the mayor there wants me to do what, exactly?"

"It boils down to his Eugene V. Bacon Senior Center, which will cost us at least an hour on our schedule, and that's conservative, so we can't do that and the rally too. We obviously can't cancel Senator Curley's endorsement event tomorrow morning, and Bix has overpromised on the rally, so he's into it up to his ass."

"What's he promised?"

"We told him that we consider this our kick-off rally for the last two-week push, so naturally he's gone crazy. He's promising a crowd of thirty thousand, and he's got forty-foot banners."

"What do they say?"

"They don't say anything, thankfully. He's got five banners, four palm trees and one crescent moon that says 'Liberty' in the middle. It's supposed to represent the state flag."

The Candidate's troubled caution kicked in like an involuntary muscle movement. "Isn't that going to look a little triumphant? What if he doesn't get thirty thousand people to come—how does that look? It sounds like Bix is pissing off the local mayor and playing fast and loose with the outcome of this primary, and my wife is going to think I'm an idiot for letting this all happen. Does that sum it up?"

"You could look at it that way," Peem said. "Bix might be distracted. I found out that his old girlfriend, who is our Opponent's deputy national Field director, is down in Charleston now too, and they've been seen together."

"Their national Field director—isn't that Storie Toller? How did Bix ever get her? She's hot."

"I don't have the answer to that question. And yes, she's quite beautiful, and she's smart. We need to keep her in mind when we win the nomination. She's been doing a very good job of organizing the southeast states. If they beat us in the South Carolina primary it will be because of her organization." Then he added emphasis. "Bix shouldn't be talking to her now, just for appearances if nothing else."

"Is Bix going to find Parviz?"

Peem noted that he used his last name. Up until then, he'd been saying Jamir, and it sounded friendly and familiar when he said it. Peem wondered if his boss was beginning to separate himself from the appearance of a relationship. "He's not sure, but he thinks Parviz's brother-in-law is the best lead he has." For no thoughtful reason other than another involuntary political muscle reaction, Peem took the opportunity to add more negative perspective. "All of Bix's eggs are in that basket. If this isn't resolved by tomorrow morning we stand to take a lot of damage. The blogosphere is heating up to a point where it can be reported by the right-wing media." He didn't know what that meant, but one of the computer geeks had said it to him an hour earlier.

"And all of our eggs are in Bix's basket. Right?"

"I'm sending Larry Drule down there to help out."

"When?"

"Tomorrow."

"Not tonight?"

"No, but Sophie is still down there. She's keeping an eye on the search for Jamir. You'll see Bix tonight. Ask him how it's going. Ask him about the mayor."

"I don't want to get into a conversation about it. There's no point to that. He'll just give me that Advance b.s., then he'll do exactly what he wants to do, anyway."

"Your decision. Is there anything you want me to tell him to do?" Peem offered.

"Tell him to get me out of this thing with the mayor and resolve this thing with Parviz."

"I'll tell him."

"And tell him to tone down the rally. I don't want it to look like we think we've already won this thing. We need to show a little humility."

"I'll tell him."

The appearance of humility was, to this Candidate and his senior staff, what Judge Wapner was to Rain Man, eliciting similar repetitious verbal behaviors as well.

Bix needed to know that his OTR, scheduled to spontaneously erupt in less than eight hours, was likely to do so as planned. He told Mike he wanted to talk with Jerry Litton, the YD's president, and the two walked out of the Scepter Field office on to the street. Mike called on his new disposable phone as they climbed into Bix's rental car.

"Jerry, it's Mike and Bix. I have you on speakerphone. Can you talk?"

"Wow, both of you. That's cool. Are you calling about our project?" He was a very smart young man.

"Yes we are," Mike said. "What's your crowd estimate at this point?"

"I'd say we're over a hundred. We're doing it as you wanted, by word of mouth. It's tough to get a good count.

"Is everyone clear about where you're supposed to meet?" Mike asked.

"Yes. We're putting out the word to meet in the parking lot of the Piggly Wiggly on Meeting Street by eight p.m.," Litton said.

"Who chose that place?" Bix asked. "Was that you, Mike, or you, Jerry?"

"That was Jerry's idea," Mike said.

"That's genius, Jerry. You're a natural Advance man." Bix said. "I think I know the answer to this, but are you set with phone calls and emails to local television stations?"

"Yes, Bix. We're pre-programmed. I've got eight people. Four are calling one each of the newsrooms in the four TV stations in town, and four are emailing them."

"Good man," Bix said. "There's an ambassadorship in this for you. Just call Mike when you graduate and he'll set you up."

"Everyone's very excited," Litton said. "We appreciate you letting us do this. If there's anything else you want us to do, we're happy to do it."

Bix cautioned. "Just the one thing, Jerry. Try your absolute best to keep this thing off those Internets. You know, those tubes and things. If this goes digital there will be some very unhappy federal law enforcement officials who will be very happy to take it out on me, and I'll be forced to name you as Mr. Big and blame you for everything. That's how Democrats thank their own—you'll be wearing a bus on your back."

"I understand, Bix. We're keeping it off the grid."

"Good man. As soon as we have wheels-down I will call Mike, and then Mike will call you and tell you your final destination and any other instructions. Then you rock and roll with your spontaneous crowd and the news media. And try to look wholesome and unthreatening when you flood the place. OK? Are we cool?"

"Yessir. We're cool." Litton was anything but cool.

* * *

"Shane, my friend, perfect timing," Bix said into his little flip phone as Mike left the car to go back inside the Field office. Bix covered the tiny mouthpiece. "You have fun in there," he said to Mike. Mike smiled and gave him a thumbs-up. "It seems like we haven't talked in a long while. How are things going on your end?"

"We're doing great."

It couldn't have been the entire truth or he wouldn't have been calling.

"Things are doing relatively great on this end, too." Bix also didn't speak the entire truth, but his troubles didn't really affect the Secret Service. "So we're good? Should we talk later at the airport?" He couldn't help but be a wise ass.

"No. Actually, I need to meet with you sooner than that. Could you do a mini-countdown meeting at the hotel before we leave for the airport?"

Bix didn't speak immediately. He took off his small round tortoise-shell glasses and rubbed his eyes. "Of course, Shane. If you want to, I'm there. Just let me know when and where. I'm not sure my entire team can be there, but we'll try. Anyone in particular you would like to see?"

"Mike would be good, and your transportation guy, Henry, and Kate. We just want to go over timing and logistics for tonight and tomorrow."

It sounded unthreatening, almost rote.

"Do I need to bring a jar of Vaseline?" Bix asked.

"No, no, not at all. If it was anything serious, I'd suggest we meet immediately."

"I'll bring the Vaseline, just in case," Bix said.

16

Larry Drule called his hand-picked Regional Field Director for southern South Carolina three times that day. The first time Drule called to celebrate his success in being sent to Charleston to, in his words, "oversee everything," the second time to gloat about it, and the third time, at 3:30 in the afternoon, to reassure Shaunesy that "they can do whatever they want at the rally." Drule assessed the situation with the insight and eloquence that only a keen mind could conceive. "I've got a fucking hard pin. I can do what ever I fucking want, and if I want to bring a thousand fucking people to the Holding Room, that's my call." He spoke in low tones but spat the words nonetheless.

Shaunesy was elated, which he showed by smiling with his upper lip. "That's all I needed to hear. We'll go to town on Bix's ass." He had, for reasons unknown by rational man, managed to make it personal. He wanted to punish Bix for the sheer enjoyment of punishing.

Drule finally found his way to an actionable thought. "Go ahead and invite our people, and I'll find a private room where they can talk to our guy," he said, referring to The Candidate. "Tell them to meet you at our Scepter Field office no later than ten-thirty, and I'll walk them over to the rally."

"Laura and I will start calling them immediately," Shaunesy said."

"What time will *you* get there?"

"I'll be there around ten-thirty. I want to be at the college with our people before the motorcade arrives. You'll enjoy this: I told Bix to send a driver to pick me up at the Columbia airport." Then he laughed a laugh that was subdued into a chuckle, to keep it humble.

"Good one," Shaunesy said as he smiled once again with his upper lip, which made his nose squinch, which pushed his wire rim glasses up on his face, which made him look even more like Napoleon Dynamite.

* * *

"Bix," Mike said, sounding a little agitated. "I'm still at the Field office and I just received Shaunesy's greeters list. There are only five names on it. What's up with that?"

"The little son-of-a-bitch is going to try to roll us," Bix said, "and that's an insult to the bitch. He has a list of people, but he just doesn't want to tell us and he's holding down the number so he can add more of the ones he's not telling us about."

Mike agreed and felt a desire to reiterate. "That little son-of-a-bitch. And now Drule will be there to cover for him. What are they up to? Why would they do that?"

"Who knows?" Bix waxed poetic in his Will Rogers manner. "Men do all sorts of things for all sorts of reasons, but it usually boils down to greed, lust or power. Sometimes all three. Both Drule and Shaunesy are most certainly tormented by unrequited lust, and they have to confront the evidence in the mirror every morning. It must be traumatizing for them, which makes them mean. So you would have to add 'anger at the world' as another causal factor. My guess is it's all four with those guys."

"So what you're saying is that you finally met a man you didn't like?"

"Two. I got lucky."

"What are we going to do about it?"

"We're not going to give Shaunesy an 'S' pin and we will endeavor to deflect Mr. Drule and his hard pin."

"And if that doesn't work?"

Bix answered in monotone. "We're just honest men trying to do our jobs, so I'd say tase 'em, bro. Tase the bastards. Tase 'em all."

Mike's mood lightened considerably. "We can do that, but then we lose the moral high ground."

Bix laughed. "That's a good one."

* * *

Mike promised to be back at the Hotel Marianne for their last minute mini-countdown meeting no later than 5:00 p.m. Bix emailed Kate and Freeway about the meeting, but didn't alert the remainder of his team, who were off doing their tasks. At as afterthought, however, he decided to request Missy's presence. He then emailed Kate and Thigpen to tell them he wouldn't be stopping by the Field office during their poster-making party, that he expected to see a ton of great TV coverage on the local news at 6:00 p.m., and that he still expected to see them back at the hotel by 5-ish, depending on how the poster party progressed.

Once back in his hotel room, he felt compelled to lie down on the couch with his legs resting up on its armrest, reasoning that it pushed blood back to his brain. He set the alarm on his BlackBerry for twenty minutes and took the pause that refreshed. It was going to be a long night under the best of circumstances. He was, as ever, the eternal optimist when he wasn't worrying, and he always expected the best, except during those parts of the day when he was awake.

At the appointed minute he was jolted from a too-deep slumber, feeling more regurgitated than refreshed. He shuffled into his kitchenette and grabbed the Diet Pepsi he had stashed in the refrigerator for such emergencies, and then began to doubt the efficacy of his nap tactic.

That trusty old BlackBerry was lit-up with reams of useful if not desirable information and all of it had to be addressed. He saved the less desirable-looking emails until the caffeine began to take effect.

Emory emailed Bix asking for a 17:30 meeting time, once again in the Stonewall Jackson room, and promised to be finished by 18:00 when he planned to depart for the airport.

Bix confirmed with Shane and sent the information to his staff. By 5:00 p.m. it was clear that the Kate Hillhouse, Nora Jankowsky, Thigpen poster party media event collaboration had been successful.

Kate emailed with the news that five camera crews, including the Max News national news crew, had covered the event.

"Max News was there, but they only took video," Kate said. "They didn't try to talk with us. Strange."

Thigpen emailed with his own event update. "We got at least 80 fucking people making rally posters, and TV camera crews out the ass."

"Coming from you, I understand these to be good things." Bix took one last non-hard-pinned walk up the stairwell to the seventh floor before it was secured by agents prior to The Candidate's arrival. In the Staff Office he found Cornelia, Ben, and Freeway working diligently alongside their three young volunteers who were threading string through press credentials to be distributed to local press at the rally site. Bix noticed that the credentials looked nice. They were well-designed, three-color, and laminated, an extravagance by campaign standards. He was certain that Kate had taken advantage of the non-union nature of South Carolina's labor force to get a one-color price, and he liked them. He was certain that Headquarters would think they were too celebratory, too expensive-looking, not humble enough, and he knew Kate had thought about Headquarters' reaction, too, and come to the same conclusion.

Seeing all the fetuses hard at work warmed his heart. Seeing "Ol' Uncle Bix" warmed their hearts, he imagined. They greeted him enthusiastically, eager to share their entire day's activities. It was enlightening. They were confident and competent and Bix was impressed at how well they were nailing down the details of their rally, the like of which none of them had ever witnessed, much less produced. There wasn't an ounce of fear or a hint of self-doubt in the group.

Bix made his feelings known. "I hate you punks. When I was your age I was still wearing loafers because I couldn't figure out how to tie my shoes. You guys look like you've done a thousand of these. You're boppin' right along."

"That's because you're a good Lead," Cornelia said.

"There is that," Bix said. "All right, I like you punks again."

Kate, Mike, and JD walked in as their Press 2 and Site 2 were reporting and they listened as well. Kate once again beemed like a proud aunt. "They've got their act together," she declared.

Mike complimented Ben and tweaked Bix. "Ben's been doing a great job, especially considering all the extra work you laid on him with this senior center bus movement."

At that moment, exact 5:10 p.m., Missy walked into the Staff Office.

Bix nixed the bus chat. "Ixnay on the us-bay."

Missy didn't seem to notice.

Ben restarted the conversation. "It's OK, I've got the time because Mike is such a great Site 1, and he's really doing most of the hard work on the rally." He said it straight-faced but couldn't help but break a smile at the end.

"These kids are good," Bix observed. "They show more respect for their elders than their elders show their elders."

Kate pointed to the error of his reasoning. "That's because we know you, Bix. We, on the other hand, maintain a distant, dispassionate relationship with our subordinants, and therefore they fear us."

Cornelia added, "And she beats me regularly. That's pretty effective, too."

"I told you that was our little secret," Kate said. "Now you don't get lunch."

Good cheer and gallows humor permeated the Staff Office, which was Bix's preferred Advance environment. It was his ten-cent psychological attempt to develop comradeship and egalitarianism in the team, to some extent born of cynical optimism, the certainty that everything would eventually turn out just fine and it *will* be a giant pain in the patoot getting there—but mostly to open the avenues of his team's creativity, particularly the younger set's ability and willingness to step in and solve problems. He wanted them unimtimidated, to think and act on their feet.

Missy sat at an eight-foot table nearest Bix. "Sorry I'm late. I had an issue with hotel management."

Bix grinned the grin of a man who, if he were watching as an outside observer, would have thought the situation was comedy gold. "Pray, tell," he said.

She hesitated a moment. Bix assumed she was thinking up something. It was NASCAR Missy at her best, Southie mixed with South Carolina. "Well, the Secret Service needs the suite directly below the senator's suite, and the people who are in that suite say they can't leave until seven o'clock, which doesn't leave the Service with any time to sweep it, since their bomb sniffer dogs will be at the airport at that time."

She *had* just thought that up, and everyone in the room knew it. Bix really didn't want to pursue the point, but, as Lead, he felt compelled by the expectations of his team. "That's a Service issue. How did it become yours?"

"I was there to help," she said. "I thought it was our job to help the Secret Service."

Time stopped. The Staff Office stood still for an eternity. The team looked to Bix. He looked to them. Then he said nothing. The volunteers continued to string press credentials, unaware, and Bix opted to let the issue die with no further comment, except for "Not really." He quizzed his team on a few of the details of their preparations then led his senior staff and Missy down the stairwell to their rendezvous with the agents, who were waiting in the Stonewall Jackson.

* * *

"Bix, thanks for doing this," Shane said. "I promise to keep it brief. I know we all need to get to the airport."

"How can we help you, Shane?" Bix said as he and his team pulled chairs out of their theater-style configuration and sat informally among the agents. Agent Rudd and his Site 2, Knuckles, were in attendance, as was Special Agent Guy Manfred from the CAT team, RON Agent Cole, and Transportation Agent George Faustich, Freeway's counterpart.

"Let's just run through the schedule," Shane said. "We still have wheels-down tonight at twenty-thirty hours from what I'm told by the Detail Leader. I want to confirm one last time that you have no plans for an OTR. We're hearing rumblings about a drop-by."

"Shane, and George, since I know you're especially interested in this subject, you have my word that I have no plans to go anywhere but straight to the hotel, and I will make no plans. It's the end of long day for the senator, and I doubt that he or anyone on the plane would want to add to it. *They* want to go straight to the hotel, and I promise I won't suggest any diversion. If the senator has a hankerin' for some exotic Charleston cuisine, I'll send someone to get it."

"Your word is good enough for me," Shane said.

Bix's nearly fatal flaw was that unuseful emotion: guilt. He hadn't lied, but he shaded the truth, and he felt guilty. It was his 1970s sensitivity, part of the American culture during his formative years. He couldn't help it, but he could live with it. The other dinosaurs, who were much older than Bix, were formed in the early 60s, the Mad Men years, and the concept of guilt occurred to them only when Bix brought up the subject, which they continued to find precious.

He reminded himself that without *that* media coverage of an adoring crowd greeting The Candidate on arrival in the lovely but understated confines of the Hotel Marianne, that he, and the campaign, and The Candidate, would have no press for thirteen long hours. It was dead time, during the most critical time for statewide publicity and, not inconsequentally, crowd building. He could live with the guilt.

Shane continued with his agenda. "Very quickly, I can't be there at your rally site tonight during your build. Agent Rudd will be there, and he still has concerns about your site plan, and I won't be able to get there until about oh-five-hundred hours. I'm asking that you don't finalize all of your construction until I get there to see it."

Agent Rudd's leash had just been tightened a little.

Mike spoke up. "Shane, that might not be completely possible. We'll do everything we can to be flexible, but we've already agreed to the size of the buffer zones and our secured walking routes, and we won't deviate from those tolerances because Kurt will be walking around with a tape measure."

"You bet I will," Rudd sneered. Knuckles laughed menacingly.

"Which I appreciate," Shane said, "and I expected he would. I'm asking that you do what you can to be able to adjust things at the last minute. I know it's tight."

"I will do everything I can to accommodate Agent Rudd and be flexible," Mike said. "Right now my schedule calls for completion of staging and lighting by five a.m., which includes the press risers, because we have to start laying electrical at that time. I'll do what I can do."

"I appreciate it. Those are the main points. Bix, when will I see you at the airport?"

"I'll be there an hour before wheels-down. If I know my candidate, he'll be early. Let's plan to meet with our motorcade drivers at nineteen-thirty hours. We have no greeters and no press. It'll be easy."

Kate turned to Bix as team Charleston/Scepter walked out of the Stonewall Jackson Room.

"Don't you feel guilty, taking advantage of such a nice guy?" she asked.

"Terribly," he said.

* * *

Freeway left immediately for the airport, as did Shane and the other agents who needed to be there two hours before wheels-down. Agents Rudd and Knuckles along with Mike Pitcher remained at the hotel, sharing an elevator to the seventh floor where, like pugilists in a ring, they went to their own corners—Rudd and Knuckles to their Command Post and Mike to the Staff Office. None of them spoke during the journey.

Bix, Kate, and her volunteer Valerie, a junior at the College of Charleston, car-pooled an hour later to the cargo distribution center on the back side of Charleston International Airport, away from the public, where Secret Service protectees normally arrived and departed and where the Service could secure the plane and where the motorcade had "ingress and egress." The forces of good were already massed. Gaggles of mostly men and a few women in dark suits, white shirts, understated ties, and squiggly wires in the ears clustered and moved around the scene among other gaggles, paramilitary types in full combat gear, state highway patrol officers, local law enforcement officers, and the local federal prosecutor, who was always invited by the Secret Service as a part of their on-going outreach to people who matter to them.

Kate parked at the end of the line of various motorcade vehicles—limos, SUV/war wagon, staff and EMS vans and other support cars—immediately in front of the two press busses. Her rented van was designated Staff 3/VIP, and it would be used to transport one person that evening, a relative of Senator Hollings's who was a lawyer in D.C. and a supporter of The Candidate.

Freeway ran over and promptly scotch-taped the appropriate motorcade signs in the front and back windows. "The drivers are over there," he said, pointing nearby. "Shane and George are already there talking to them, of course."

The scene, like a picture of the family vacation in the family photo album, was strikeningly familiar. The foreground remained the same, same bodies, same poses, but the background had changed. Different geography, flora, and fauna. One lone news van from the local NBC affiliate stood in the parking lot with its stinger raised high into the air.

"Game time," Kate said. "As soon as we have wheels-down I'm going to go tell that local news crew that they should go to the hotel," she said as she walked away to complete her press tasks and coordinate with Volunteer Valerie, who was "staffing" the Press 2 bus. Press 2, the less prestigious and usually the rowdiest of the Press vehicles, was where Valerie was expected to hand out room keys to the journalists on her manifest, and potentially be ritually sacrificed so they could drink her blood.

Freeway's drivers were huddled next to the chain link fence that separated the parking lot from the tarmac, a spot where they usually migrated, as if it was in the DNA of people who volunteered to drive in motorcades. Unlike three days earlier, Bix couldn't see anyone's breath.

Bix moved quickly to join the motorcade gaggle before Shane and George frightened their drivers, and then he went into his routine to create the right atmosphere, make sure everyone was chillin'. The script changed to suit the occasion, but some parts of his patter were classics.

"I think this is the best looking group of motorcade drivers we've ever had," Bix said to the group, and it went on from there—introductions, charging a fee to take photos, making extra money to go on vacation, take the motorcade drivers with him on vacation, Secret Service will shoot you down in the street like a dog—these were timeless.

Once again, the volunteer drivers were fascinated and awed by the magnitude of the undertaking. Once again Bix had to admit to himself that, for sheer entertainment value, the Secret Service and SWAT team and CAT team and state and local police presence really made the pregame show. George provided a lively Secret Service briefing and handed out the small tin security pins—the capital "A" in white, this time over a horrible lime green background.

Time flew as Bix and George listened to the sound of their own voices, and all too quickly the assembled mass of vehicles and bodies were called to move out to the runway and await wheels-down. At 8:20 p.m., ten minutes early, the campaign plane touched down in Charleston. Bix called Mike at the hotel, Mike called Jerry Litton in the parking lot on Meeting Street, and Jerry mobilized his forces to descend upon the Hotel Marianne. Media calls and emails flooded the ether within a minute, and the spontaneous eruption of enthusiasm moved inexorably to converge with the next President of the United States in the lobby of the Hotel Marianne.

The plane pulled up, stairs were moved into place at the front and back exits, the motorcade pulled-up next to the plane, and Bix waited on the tarmac near the Lead Marked Car. No one, least of all The Candidate, wanted a briefing at that point after a long day, and Bix didn't want to answer any questions that might come his way. If his smiling countenance had been desired on the plane, it would have been requested, and as a "load and go" it was a simple matter: Get off the plane and get into your car.

Once The Candidate, staff, and press were loaded, Freeway flashed Bix the "thumbs up" from his position outside Staff 3/VIP, and Bix and Shane took their places in the Lead Marked Car in the back and front seats. Bix shared the back seat with Shane's boss, Special Agent in Charge of the Charleston region Rob Farrow. Shane asked the driver, State Trooper Captain Contarini, to begin moving slowly, and as they drove through the security gate Bix called Mike once again to tell him they had departed the airport en route to the Hotel.

By Bix's calculation the entire process of taxiing in and unloading took about twelve minutes, more than enough time to give his spontaneous revelers a head start inflicting themselves on the hotel. Mike reported no activity, so Bix hung up and engaged in the usual pleasant chit-chat with his compatriots and waited for his cell phone to ring. And Shane's. They would both receive the news about the same time.

Shane's rang first. He checked the caller ID briefly then answered, "Yeah, Sam." Bix knew it was the RON agent. Then Mike called.

Bix answered indifferently. "Yeah, Mike."

"Bix, this is the call where I tell you that we're starting to get a crowd in the lobby of the hotel, and there must be at least a hundred people here, and you tell me you'll call me back for an update in a few minutes, and then you call back and tell me to find an alternate route from our arrival point to the hotel lobby, just in case The Candidate wants to address his loving subjects."

"Really?" Bix said. "How many people?"

"This is where I tell you that the crowd seems to be building," Mike said.

"Well, monitor the situation and I'll call you back in a few minutes to get an update," Bix said.

"I think my update will be something like 'the lobby is packed with people' and we should inform The Candidate."

"Got it, let me call you back."

Shane hung up at the same time, and Bix leaned forward. "Shane, was that Sam telling you there's a crowd brewing in the hotel lobby?"

"Yeah, he says it's a large number."

"What's his estimate?" Bix asked.

"Over a hundred at this point and it's getting bigger."

"Will you ask Al to tell the senator?" Bix said, referring to Detail Leader Caputo.

"I was just about to call Mr. Caputo now," Shane said. He lifted his right arm and spoke into his sleeve: "Please inform Renegade there is a large crowd of people in the lobby."

"I'll call Merle." Bix called the Trip Director and informed him of the situation at the hotel, and Merle asked him a simple but unobvious question. Bix was impressed.

"Are they there for us?" Merle asked.

"Great question," Bix said. "It could very well be that the Partridge Family is doing a concert in town and these are David Cassidy groupies, but apparently they are our supporters."

"That's kind of a dated reference, but you understand. I don't want us to go rushing into the lobby and find out that everyone's there to see Britney Spears."

"I'll tell Mike to make sure they're there for us, but I'm pretty sure." Bix hung up and began a casual discussion about "options" with Shane while he killed a little time before calling Mike again.

His phone rang and he assumed it was Mike with another update. It was Missy, and Missy was exceedingly agitated. Management had been serving her free espressos from the hotel bar.

"Bix, have you heard about the crowd in the lobby of the hotel?"

"Service told me," Bix said, "and I was just about to call you for an update on the situation."

"It's going *nuts* here," she almost screamed. "We need to get these people out of here. We won't be able to get into the hotel with this big of a crowd."

"How many people do you estimate are there?"

"Hundreds," she said. "It's nuts. The hotel management is very upset, and Sam isn't very happy about it, either. Should I tell the police to move them out of the lobby?"

"No Missy, please don't ask them to do that," Bix said in his calmest voice. These people are apparently our supporters. We don't want to treat them rudely." He decided to jump ahead a step and give her a task that would focus her energies away from tear-gassing a bunch of Young Democrats. "Just in case the senator wants to go see them personally, why don't you and Sam find a secured walking route from our arrival point, through the back hallways and up to the lobby? You should know the hotel fairly well by now. Isn't there a way to do it?"

"I'll talk to Sam. I don't know if he's going to go for that," she said.

"Missy, if The Candidate decides he's going to address the crowd, he's going to address the crowd. I'll call Mike and tell him to find you and give you a hand. He's done this sort of thing before. You need to find the walking route up to the lobby."

Bix was amazed at her lack of understanding. It occurred to him that he hadn't witnessed such ham-handed political instincts since Al Gore.

Shane heard the exchange. "Is he going to address the crowd?" he asked.

"Dunno yet, but I'd say it's a definite possibility."

Shane called his RON agent to tell him.

Bix called Mike. "How many people are there now?"

"At least two hundred," he reported.

"Be prepared for The Candidate to do a drop-by, and go find Missy and help her. She's about to call out the attack dogs, and we don't want this to turn into blood bath." Then he called Kate, riding in Press 1.

"Kate, apparently a spontaneous crowd of supporters has gathered in the hotel lobby. I thought you might want to know in case the senator wants to go talk with them. The press will want to cover it, and they won't be able to get to their hotel rooms until the crowd disperses, anyway."

Kate responded as a professional reacting to unexpected circumstances. "Thanks for the heads-up. Do you think we should plan to drop off the press close to the front entrance?"

"That's a great idea. Why don't you call Freeway and coordinate with him, and you can escort the press to the lobby. Maybe there's somewhere you can set 'em up so they can see what's going on."

"Mr. Caputo has informed the senator about our crowd," Shane said, "but he's skeptical."

"*Our* crowd?" Bix thought. "Good sign—we have joint ownership." He sensed that Shane might be getting suspicious about a set up.

"The senator wants to see what the situation is there before he makes a decision," Shane continued. "It doesn't sound like the senator is all that up for shaking hands."

Bix could understand. It had been a long day on the campaign trail. He called Mike and got the word he'd been waiting to hear.

"The lobby is packed," Mike said, "and three local TV stations are here. I can't imagine how they heard about this. It's completely unexpected. Sam and I found a way to walk from the loading dock, under the executive offices, and up behind the front desk. As long as we have that hard barrier between The Candidate and the crowd, Sam's okay with it."

Bix assumed that Mike was in the company of his friendly neighborhood Secret Service agent who could hear his end of the conversation. "Thanks, Mike. I'll inform the powers that be and get back to you. Tell Missy and Sam to be prepared, and keep Missy out of our way."

Shane confirmed the same information through Sam, and it once again went back up both flagpoles, Staff and Secret Service. The size of the crowd, the optics of a packed lobby, and the presence of TV cameras sealed the deal. The Candidate reluctantly agreed to listen to Bix and Mike make their case for a stop-by after they arrived at the hotel.

Bix thought, "Can't the man just say yes and get it over with? No one twisted his arm to run for the presidency." It was one of the things he liked about Sen. Curley four years earlier. Curley may have been a distant sort of fellow, but he trusted his Lead Advance and never said no to an opportunity Bix presented to him.

Bix called Mike and then Missy with "Bravo," code for five minutes away, and Missy once again protested. "This isn't gonna work. The hotel management is very upset because their regular guests can't use the lobby or check in."

"Tell the hotel management that this will all be over in ten minutes, just as quickly as it started," Bix said. "After we arrive I want you to wait for us at the service elevator. We'll bring him back to you to go up to his suite. Do you understand?"

"I'm the hotel *Lead*," she protested.

"There is no such thing. You're the RON, and it's your first RON, and if you don't listen to *your* Lead, it will be your last." He said it with no hint of vitriol, and didn't mention that he intended to make it his life's mission to make it her last Advance trip, anyway. In four hundred years of doing Advance, he'd only blown up one Advance person, a man whose faults were so egregious and attitude so vile that it could not be ignored. Missy was neither egregious nor vile in Bix's opinion, but she sucked so badly at her job it couldn't be ignored. "You take him up to his suite. I'll take him to his campaign events."

On arrival, Missy did not forget to position the hotel manager, "Mr. Ahren," as she referred to him, for his obligatory greeting, and twenty seconds of personal attention from The Candidate appeared to calm his nerves about the traffic jam in his lobby. Bix promised him it would be over shortly, and then escorted The Candidate to another hallway past the loading dock entrance, into the Operations Manager's empty office, where they huddled with Merle and Mike.

The Candidate spoke first. "I really don't feel like shaking a bunch of hands. It'll take half an hour."

Bix countered with what had been obvious to him from the beginning. "You don't have to shake any hands. You go up and talk to them, thank them for being there and for their support, you 'high-five' a dozen people who are smashed up against the other side of the front desk, then you leave. It will take less than five minutes, and we'll make the news tonight and tomorrow morning."

The Candidate's decision was not made instantaneously. Long seconds ticked by. "Looks like I'm going up to the lobby."

Bix asked Mike to tell Missy to wait at the service elevator. "Remind her we will bring him back to her there when we're finished upstairs."

He called Kate to inquire as to the whereabouts of the traveling press corps and she requested two more minutes to move them into place where Ben had spontaneously secured several chairs and a few upholstered benches for the press to stand on. "Spontaneous press risers," he called them, "SPRs."

"We're going to need to hold here for two minutes while Kate moves the press," Bix told his boss, not waiting for a response. "I want to see what's going on up there. I'll be right back."

In twenty seconds he and Mike, along with Shane and Sam, were standing behind the front desk looking out on a scene of happy madness. Dozens of young people were pressed against the public side of the front desk, pushed by a thick crowd packed belly-to-back all the way to the far walls of the expansive beaux arts lobby. Bix noticed a double spotlight attached to the mezzanine balcony railing above, washing the crowd with a dramatic glow and lighting the sea of faces. "Where did that come from?" Bix asked.

Mike knew he'd scored a coup. "I asked the hotel concierge to call their audio-visual people, and I asked them if they had a spotlight we could use. They happened to have *that*. Do you like it?"

"If some photographer wins a Pulitzer for this he or she will have you to thank," Bix said. "Go around and tell Kate to escort Scooter back behind here. She'll love it."

"Who's Scooter?"

"Scooter Kailian. He's an independent shooter embedded with our campaign. This is the kind of thing he loves. By the way, do you notice anything else?" Bix asked, ever mindful that Shane and Sam were still there.

"Yeah, we need something for the senator to stand on so he can be seen." Mike said.

"Do you happen to have something?" Bix asked, wide-eyed.

"Not yet, but by the time you bring him up I will." Mike thought he might have seen a step stool somewhere nearby, possibly under the sales manager's desk down the hallway, where he'd stashed it earlier in the day.

"See you back here in a minute," Bix said.

Shane and Sam remained quiet. They looked like they were feeling put-upon but had no recourse, no alternate plan of action other than telling all available agents and local P.D. to converge on the lobby. Both agents remained passive, acquiescing to the inevitable with constraint, as if they were tourists being robbed at gunpoint.

Bix spotted the national press corps arriving at the back of the crowd next to the local TV crews, called Kate to confirm they were in place, walked back through the dank underbelly of the hotel to retrieve The Candidate, and then led him back up to the lobby, not mentioning the local visitor attractions such as Missy's groping location along the path. He did plan to regale Merle with the lurid tale of Missy's hallway porn scene at some point.

The Candidate did not stop once he reached the step stool, which would have raised him a respectable two feet off the floor. Instead, he stepped on it and jumped up to the front desk itself, then stepped onto the counter and stood directly over the heads of the groundlings just inches from his feet. The crowd roared its approval.

Bix thought, *"That's* not gonna go over well with the boys."

Shane, Sam, and Al confirmed his feelings in a nanosecond. If looks could execute, Bix would have been dead where he stood.

Bix went wide-eyed once again, then watched as Shane and Sam leaned over the desk clutter and each grabbed one of the Candidate's ankles, while Detail Leader Caputo moved between them and attempted to reach up and hold on to the back of The Candidate's belt. Then they all looked over their shoulders at Bix once again, unsmiling.

The decibel level rose, the hotel trembled, and Bix worried that plaster might fall from its ornately molded ceiling.

Once again he felt pangs of guilt, but this was great television. The Candidate stirred the adoring horde with a rouser of a stump speech, all the time pinned in place by three Secret Service Agents holding his lower extremities. Kate showed up behind the desk with Scooter, who stood on a chair behind and to the left of The Candidate taking over-the-shoulder shots and then ran up the stairs to the mezzanine for some overheads.

It was over and done in less than four minutes, faster than Bix promised. The assembled masses were happy, The Candidate was happy, the national press corps was happy, the local press was very happy, and the Secret Service wanted to kill Bix. They didn't have the goods on him, no concrete evidence that he had planned it, only their gut, but they trusted their guts. Their problem was two-fold—they couldn't act on gut alone, and what could they do about it, anyway?

The Candidate high-fived a dozen college kids squished against the counter, including an exhuberant Y.D. president Jerry Litton and a few of his hand-picked crew. He then stood on the step stool and gave everyone a last wave, heard the thunderous roar one last time, and sprinted back down the hallway that led to the service elevator.

Once in the elevator with Missy and his gaggle of agents, The Candidate remained silent, as did everyone else, until Missy asked the question, "So, how was it?"

"Yeah," Bix thought, "how *was* it?" Direct feedback was not a feature of The Candidate's personality.

"It was good," he said.

* * *

Upon reaching the seventh floor Bix parted company with the entourage. Missy was more than capable of directing The Candidate down a hallway with the help of four agents.

Before he walked away, Bix told Merle he'd be in the Staff Office or his room until 11 o'clock, when he planned to visit JD's Site build at the Schoendienst Gym and then drive to Scepter for the overnight build.

Merle thanked him. "If I'm still up at three a.m. listening to our agents bitch about how you rolled them with that crowd in the lobby, I'll know where to find you," he said.

"That was spontaneous, dude," Bix said. "I will take no credit, nor would I be given any."

Mike arrived as they were talking, his smile reaching almost to his ear lobes. "The press ate that up. They said they were the best visuals they've seen in months. Scooter was going crazy."

"It was a good hit," Merle said.

"And the Sistine Chapel has a good ceiling," Bix said as he walked away, taking Mike with him.

They couldn't avoid walking past the Secret Service command post a few doors down from The Candidate's suite and tried unsuccessfully to blend in with the lovely red-and-pink-flocked wallpaper lining the hallway.

Agent Faustich called out from inside the room, which was lined with electronic gear on tables and another half dozen agents, half of whom sat on chairs where the bed had been removed. "Bix, good event! How long did it take you to organize that?" The other agents looked up from their work. They had already heard about the mob downstairs and none believed that Bix was innocent until proven guilty. He looked guilty. He was guilty. However, he'd stopped feeling guilty.

He stuck his head inside the doorway of the converted hotel room and grinned. "That was spontaneous. Ask anyone."

Agent Faustich was good-natured but made his point. "Spontaneous, my ass."

"I wish I was that good," Bix said. As he turned to leave, Shane appeared, having just left The Candidate alone in his suite.

"I can't prove it, but I know you did it," Shane said. "And I have to admit, you didn't lie. I didn't ask the right question. You didn't try to go somewhere else for an OTR. You brought the OTR to us."

"That was pretty spontaneous, Shane. You know I haven't had time to build another crowd that size. At least it was someplace you already have secured, where there were plenty of agents and cops. That has to help."

"Without a doubt, it makes it a lot easier," Shane said. "And next time I'll know to ask the right question."

Mike couldn't help himself. "You have to admit that it was incredibly dramatic."

"I'm just glad it didn't become more dramatic," Shane said. "I'm sure they took some great pictures. I saw that Kate brought around that spikey-haired, kind of freekie photographer. He was climbing over stuff like a mountain goat."

"Yep, Scooter," said Bix. "I suppose that's why they call him Scooter. Thank you for rolling with the circumstances, and I know the boss appreciates it too. He knows this isn't easy."

"In the crush of activity tonight, I forgot to give you Storie's 'S' pin. Tell her to keep it for her boss's rally later in the day." Shane handed Bix the tin pin and he looked at it briefly before stashing it in his sport coat pocket. It was a simple rectangle with a white capital "S" on a red background. Bix would check his large bag of spare day pins from his previous trips for matches, duplicates, just in case. It was always good to be able to pin people at a moment's notice.

Bix and Mike both noted Shane's gentlemanliness, his lack of a grudge. "Thank you, sir," Bix said. "I'll give it to her tonight. She said she'd drop by our build at the college after midnight. We'll see you there after oh-five-hundred hours."

"You will eventually," he said, sounding accusatory, as if he had said, "I've been nice enough to treat this experience as a teaching moment, but I'm not a fucking fool," summarized in only three clean words.

Bix shook his hand. "See you in the a.m."

* * *

Bix checked in briefly at the Staff Office, where his minions were gathering or already clattering away on their laptops before setting off for their sites. The room was scattered with the detritus of two days at full speed—reams of copier paper, copier trash, office supplies, empty fast food containers, odds and ends of clothing and personal possessions—and Bix could feel productivity surging through the air.

Bix found JD seated at one of the long tables, its white tablecloth not as pristine as two days before, hunched over his laptop. "How's your site prep going?" Bix asked.

"Sucks," he said.

"That's great!" He profferred an upbeat response, as if he hadn't heard what JD said. "How about the rest of you? Doing OK?"

"My ass is draggin'," Ben said.

"That's great," said Bix. "You're doing a good job. You're all working very hard and you don't need me, but I'm headed down to my room in case you do. But don't. Please tell Kate and Freeway when they arrive. I will see most of you at your sites in a couple of hours."

He was down the stairs and into his suite, his sumptuous refuge, in less than a minute. It was nearly 10 p.m. but he went straight to the refrigerator and pulled out a Diet Pepsi. It was no time, as far as he was concerned, to live cautiously. He needed it. He wanted it. He would dance with the devil—one twelve-ounce can would sentence him to sleeplessness, and he might still have to imbibe another before the night was through. He drank it with abandon, and shortly he could feel the caffeine surge through his system. "That means I've had two surges in less than ten minutes," he thought. "Dangerous territory."

Many messages awaited, several of which couldn't be ignored. Given a few moments to gather his thoughts, they appeared more like a gathering of storm clouds. It was late in the day to have so many uncontrollable moving pieces swirling in three dimensions. Jamir, Hani, Shaunesy, Drule, Bacon, Fry, O'Malley, and Gilliman were potential wild cards, capable of distracting or derailing a perfectly good day's worth of history-making media events. Together, the sum of still-unresolved issues, self-interested parties, and simple shinanagans could sink the entire primary election, or worse, a thought with which Bix tried not to concern himself. He threw back another shot of Diet Pepsi.

His emails and voicemails self-selected into two categories: Emails from people who wanted something and voicemails from people who really, really wanted something.

Nurse Ratched wrote, "Mr. Shaunesy and I need our "S" pins asap. Pls let us know where to get them." LuAnn wrote to ask where she "should drop off Mayor Bacon and his family at the hotel, and where to wait for them at the Senior Center as Mayor Bacon has directed." Charlene, in President Gilliman's office, wrote to tell him that the college VIP's would congregate in Colonel Marion meeting room on the first floor, as Gilliman directed, for The Candidate's drop-by. Peem wrote, "ND UPDAT IMMDTLY."

Peem also left a voicemail, which sounded as if he was calling from the ledge outside his office window. "I heard about that fucking *stunt* you pulled tonight at the hotel. You're lucky I don't *blow you up*. Your ass should be out on the street looking for Parviz. If you bring any shit like that with you tomorrow I will *have you disintegrated*. Call me immediately."

"Ouch," he thought. Sophie and Hani were first on his call list. He found them comfortably, if not happily, ensconced in a Motel Six, in separate rooms, outside of Florence.

Hani was distraught. He was talking with Sophie in her room after she had tucked in Chelsea for the night. "We have accomplished a total of nothing today," Hani said. "This has been the most frustrating day of my life. I thought I knew where to find Jamir and Abia, but I was too optimistic."

Sophie took the phone. "We're just tired because we spent a lot of time dodging the Max News van and not looking for Jamir's cabin. We plan to be up and out by six a.m."

"How is Chelsea holding up?" Bix said.

"She's fine. We let her get out and run around a couple of times today, and she loves eating out, so she's in heaven."

Pessimism, not one of Bix's favorite -isms, crept in for the first time and found comfortable lodging next to his cheery outlook. It was dawning him that they wouldn't find Jamir, or at least not in time. He was out of ideas and saddled with creating the next day's lead story for every meaningful national and local news outlet. He began to understand how the Secret Service had felt a half hour before when they had to suck it up and take it whether they liked it or not.

"In that case," Bix said, "get a good night's sleep, eat a hearty breakfast on the campaign's nickel, and I'll talk with you after six a.m."

* * *

Peem was unhinged when Bix called. "What the fuck have you—?"
Bix hung up.

Peem called back. "Don't you fucking hang up on—"

Bix hung up.

Peem called back. "Don't hang up."

"Haven't we been through this before?"

"Don't hang up. You letting things get away from you down there?"

"Bob, just tell me what your problem is. Other than all the great press that we just got from a total investment of five minutes of The Candidate's time, on a zero budget, why are you scraping your fingernails on the blackboard?" It was his simplistic attempt to affect Peem psychologically.

It worked. Peem flinched. "Don't say that. It gives me the creeps. While you're off organizing OTRs you should be finding Parviz and his so-called manifesto. Where the fuck is that going?"

"As of five minutes ago," Bix said, "it's going to bed in a Motel Six on Highway Ninety-Five outside Florence, South Carolina. And the campaign is paying for two rooms. All of which I'm sure you already know from Sophie."

"Which means you don't have zip," Peem said.

"No, *you* don't have zip," Bix pointed out, "and it's because of helpful suggestions like I 'should be out on the streets looking for Parviz' instead of spending thirty seconds of my time saying, 'Hey, let's get a crowd so we can get some good press during the fourteen hours that we could be promoting the rally, not to mention our boss's candidacy, instead of complete media silence.' Tell me, have you had any *more* luck finding Jamir or that manifesto?"

"We were counting on you. You're supposed to have all of these international connections, not just a connection with our opponent's Deputy Field Director. What's happened to all those?"

"They all stopped giving a shit about this presidential campaign the same time I did, which was about two seconds ago." It was also time to shove Peem back over the line he'd crossed. "Bob, you can have my resignation now or tomorrow afternoon. Those are your choices."

"That's not a choice, it's a threat, and that's not why I called."

"That wasn't one of your choices."

"Fuck you, neither. I don't want your resignation." He seemed nearly ingenuous.

"Why have you chosen to become such an incredible dick? Was it something I said? Something I didn't say? My personal hygiene? Or lack of it?"

The question caused Peem to think outside his ego walls for an instant. "Everyone's on edge here about the manifesto issue and the O'Malley factor. We don't know where it's going to go or what that rancid son of a bitch will do, and it's not clear that you have a handle on things."

"Now there's a rational concept, Bob. It's not at all clear to me that I'm handling anything correctly either, including my career choices, but in our favor, there is an irrefutable law of physics that says you can't take pictures of nothing. No pictures, no permanent damage. No manifesto, no story. It then becomes just another episode of right wingnut blogger porn they will use in a giant circle jerk to satisfy each other's lust for indignation. For anyone functioning at fifth-grade level, it's too patently ridiculous to be true, and you don't lose any votes because you never had the stupid or venal demographic in the first place."

"Does that mean you've given up hope of finding Jamir for the foreseeable future?"

"Bob, I've abandoned *all* hope of anything, so you would have to include that. It doesn't mean I'll stop trying, unless you keep talking."

"Do what you can to make this go away, and don't go rogue again. We can't have you fucking freelancing around creating media events without telling us."

The correct response would have required too many obscenities than Bix could remember conveniently, so he opted to use his well-rehearsed line, hoping that might still irritate Peem. "That was spontaneous, dude."

* * *

The room phone rang as Bix was searching his emails for more good news, and his reaction was Pavlovian. Storie. He smiled, his heart pumped faster and he jumped to answer it.

It was Shaunesy, calling from the lobby. "Well, hey buddy, I was just in the neighborhood," he said without a hint of fake friendliness. "I'm down here in the bar with Merle and some of the traveling staff. They said you'd be in your room. I thought I could pick up our security pins."

Shaunesy was downstairs clutching the most important people of the moment who were accessible, and he thought that proximity gave him super powers.

"Don, we still don't have them yet, but Mike will have yours when you arrive at the rally tomorrow with your greeters. I thought I'd mentioned that already."

Shaunesy ignored the comment. "Well, the people I'm escorting are crucial to our success in the primary. I'm concerned that we'll get tied up with the crowd and not be able to get in."

"Not if you follow the instructions that we gave to Laura."

"Well, what happens if we *do* get hung up?"

Bix, having not honed his skills at self-censorship in the previous twenty-four hours, spoke honestly. "Don, I have a concern as well. My concern is the small list of greeters you've given us to name check, only five. My concern is that you are either not doing your job very well, or you're going to roll me and try to bring in a much larger group of people who haven't been vetted. It makes me reluctant to give you an 'S' pin. At any rate, whatever I decide to give you, you'll have to get from Mike when you arrive tomorrow morning with your group. You can tell Merle exactly what I said." He knew Merle would agree, and it felt good to say it.

Shaunesy's physical proximity to the traveling staff wasn't having its desired effect, and at that moment it was a liability. "Well, Larry is arriving tomorrow morning and he'll resolve this," he said before hanging up.

Bix emailed Merle. "No 'S' pin for Shaunesy."

Merle replied from his perch in the bar. "He's frnds wth Drule."

Bix replied, "I dnt care if he's bth Mthr and Fthr Teresa. Bad juju. No pn."

Merle responded appropriately. "Its yr call."

"Fkng strate," Bix replied.

* * *

The room phone rang again almost immediately, and this time he cringed. All it took was the one previous call to make him jumpy about answering the phone again. It was Storie.

"Hey, that was a great entrance, truly epic," she said. "Did you tell him to jump up on the desk?"

He returned to fighting trim instantaneously. "Yes, absolutely. That was completely my idea."

"Bullshit," she said. "But the place was on fire and he couldn't help himself. You did *that*, and it was great. Talk about iconic images. You're going to get some great pictures out of that OTR, and it took less than five freaking minutes."

"Why don't you hire me?" Bix said. "Not your campaign, just you."

"I would if I could afford you, and at the moment it looks like I can't afford you. I just received a call from my boss railing about being seen talking to you. She was pissed."

"What are you going to do?" Bix said.

"Do? There's only one thing to do—not be seen talking with you. We'll talk in private. Screw her. She'll be the first one on the phone to your campaign if we lose. She's probably talking with you guys now."

"Best be cautious. Do you think you shouldn't come to our build tonight?"

"Hell, yes, I'm coming. Who's going to be around at one a.m. to see me? I want to see what your rally site looks like, and I want my 'S' pin so I can wander around freely."

"Et tu, Storie?"

"Sure, why not," she said, "if I can get an 'S' pin, it's golden in the middle of a rally."

"And you know I'm going to give it to you, don't you?"

"Darn right you will, because everyone likes me."

"*Everyone* don't count. Only one person's opinion counts and that person's still not convinced."

"How long do you have before you have to leave for JD's site?"

"Ten minutes."

"Then why don't I come up and convince you now?"

"Why don't you?" Bix said.

"I will."

She did. He was convinced, and his lips were numb from the convincing. The process took a little longer than ten minutes. Once he acquiesced, she said she would see him in Scepter at 1 a.m. and made a rapid exit with her "S" pin.

17

JD was outside Schoendienst Gym directing the load-in when Bix arrived at 11:45 p.m., and it appeared that much of the equipment was still in the trucks or scattered around the parking lot. Special Agent Meyer was standing, smiling, at the top of the metal staircase outside the gym's fire exit door, looking down on the scene from above. Bix waved to her as he pulled up.

He stopped the car next to JD. "I hesitate to ask, but how's it going?"

"Bix, good to see you. It sucks. Where the hell have you been?" JD said.

"Is there anything I can do to help?"

"No, I'm just giving you some of the grief that this site has given me. It's taking us longer than I expected to move our equipment inside the gym. The place wasn't built for a twenty-first century presidential campaign event."

Bix shouted to Agent Meyer and shook his fist in the air. "This was your suggestion."

She smiled and shouted back, "Yeah, but you picked it. I'd like to get some sleep tonight, too."

He couldn't argue with her logic. "Should I stick around?" he asked JD. "I'm the one who said you couldn't use volunteers because it's supposed to be clandestine."

"Yeah, but you also told me to hire extra production crew, which was a good idea. I've got plenty of bodies. Why don't you come back in a couple of hours? We'll have made some progress by then."

"You sure? I've got my work gloves. I can tote stuff."

"Go ahead to Scepter," JD said. "I'll call you if we have an emergency only the Lead can fix." He laughed.

"Don't rub it in." Bix slapped him a high-five as he drove away.

* * *

It was a brand-new day when Bix arrived at the Site build in Scepter, exactly 12:30 a.m., where the immense job of unloading trusses, staging, lights, speakers, scaffolding, bike rack, generators, cable, bleachers, and a sizeable cherry picker of brontosauran dimensions was moving along better than he expected. Spotlights strategically placed around the site lit the landscape and the workers and the equipment in an otherworldly glow, isolating it from the night like a scene from science fiction novel set in a penal colony on the moon. Light rock music played above the construction racket and a couple dozen beat-up coolers stocked with sandwiches and soft drinks were scattered among jackets and hard hats.

Mike was driving a fork lift hauling bike rack in front of the cistern, near where they would soon build the main stage, and Ben was standing on the forks holding the bike rack in place with his own body as Mike maneuvered. Both were thoroughly entertained, especially Mike motoring about in his new playtoy.

"You love boppin' around in heavy industrial equipment, don't you?" Bix said.

"This is why I do these events," he said. "Guess what? We're ahead of schedule. You got here just in time. We're about to put up the banners first, before we build the main stage and bleachers. They were just delivered and they're still drying. We've got them laid out on the ground over there." Mike pointed to the far side of the Site, away from construction. "Go look. They are seriously spectacular."

Mike and Ben jumped off the forklift and walked with Bix, who examined his prize banners intently for several seconds and didn't speak. It was a lot to take in.

"Are they what you expected?" Ben asked.

"That's a big visual," Bix said.

"That's a big visual," Mike said.

"Maybe they *are* too triumphant," Bix said.

"Ya think?"

"Yep, I'd have to say they're too triumphant, just like I was hoping. They're perfect."

Mike was laughing. "Damn right, they're triumphant. Headquarters can live with it, or eat it."

Bix high-fived, then low-fived him as they laughed, a celebration seasoned with hints of smug.

"Are you piloting the cherrypicker to put them up?" Bix asked him.

"No, it's a tall one, a little too high off the ground for me. I'll leave it to the professionals. A few college maintenance guys told me they'd do it."

In a fit of self-satisfaction, Bix strapped-on his work gloves and helped the volunteers unload and move bike rack along the site perimeter for a half hour while Mike's stevedores man-handled their equipment into place, positioned the freshly-minted banners, and then started the process of raising Bix's VSV (Very Special Visual). He walked over to supervise the installation of his creation.

He and Mike stood on the cistern, directing two workers high above in the cherry picker as they pulled, then yanked, on the ropes that were threaded through grommets at the top, middle, and bottom of each banner. Straining to mount the heavy banners perfectly between the columns, the workers found Mike's and Bix's direction invaluable as they shouted "a little lower on that side" and "that one needs to be centered" and pointed a lot.

"Now I know how Christo feels," Bix said.

At 1:15 a.m., Democrat time, Storie arrived, proudly wearing her "S" pin on the front of her blouse despite the fact that she didn't really need it for another nine hours. Bix noticed his lips were still numb and applied some ChapStick.

She climbed on to the cistern and stood next to them as they admired their VSV, two-fifths of which were in place, with a third quickly rising. "That is going to look absolutely amazing. It's brilliant. By the way, I saw a couple of our Advance guys over there checking out your site," she said. "They're the same ones who are doing our rally in Columbia later."

"It's still a semi-free country," Bix said, "assuming one of our employers wins the next election it should remain so for a while longer."

"They're going to steal our ideas," Mike said.

"They can steal your methods," Storie said, "but they can't steal the soul of your creativity."

"Truer words were never spoken," Bix said, "although I have no idea what it means."

"It means that our Advance office will keep telling our Advance teams to produce the same crappy little events over and over again, and they will," Storie said.

"Yeah, we've noticed.' Mike said.

Grateful as he was for Storie's presence and the middle-of-the-night respite from the world, Bix was compelled to look when his BlackBerry unexpectedly registered a phone message, surprised that he hadn't heard it ring, and then listened to it, unaware and unconcerned about its contents or the chain of events it would produce.

It was a voicemail from Janet Townsend, back in New Hampshire, and Bix knew immediately that he would get no sleep at all before The Candidate's speech. He growled audibly.

"That's not good," Storie said.

"As much as I would love to stick around..." Bix started.

"That would prevent you from leaving," Storie said.

"Mike, see you back here in about three hours, maybe four, and Storie, Mike will show you where you can hang out and not be seen in McBride Hall over there, which is where we will bring the mayor. I'd give ya a hug, but people might be watching."

Storie responded, "That's OK, I'll hug you later."

"I was talking to Mike," he said.

"I would strike you," she said, "but people might be watching," then laughed that hearty, infectious laugh.

* * *

Janet's voicemail, pleasant and extremely helpful under normal circumstances, became ominous when Bix realized that everyone and their geek operatives were probably listening in or watching or both. She said simply, "Bix, hi, it's Janet Townsend. It's almost midnight. I hope it's not too late. Bob Baycroft told me you were looking for Jamir, and Jim and I were just visiting him and Abia in South Carolina. We know where they are. They're vacationing near Orangeburg. Our mutual friends the Denbos let them use their cottage off of Wild Hearts Hollow Road way back in the woods. I'll send you an email with directions." She didn't leave her phone number and it was blocked from registering on caller ID.

He could not find her number in his new-fangled BlackBerry address book fast enough. After fumbling for a couple of agonizing minutes he found it and called her in a futile attempt to intercept the email before she sent it. "Orangeburg?" he thought. "Hani wasn't too far off. An orange is a plant."

She had left her message and sent her email an hour earlier and they had taken that long to reach Bix in South Carolina, apparently some kind of digital mix-up at the border. He left a voicemail for her and hung up to find her email, with complete directions to Jamir's cabin, in his in-box, and he wondered if Max News's hackers or Drule's spy geeks were sleeping. Assuming that the ones with zealotry and profit motive were probably awake, it was a race to see if he or Max News would get to Hani's cabin in Orangeburg first.

* * *

Max News producer Adam Strayberg was awake in his hotel room in the Marianne when he received a text and a phone call simultaneously from his Internet monitoring contractor, his computer geeks, who, as it turned-out, were on the job twenty-four hours a day.

One of their managers, Danny, called to tell Strayberg the timely news. "We got a hit on Parviz. Sir, we know right where he is."

"Great," Strayberg said. "Where is he?"

"He's in Orangeburg, less than an hour and a half from Charleston."

"Can you email the directions?"

"I'll give them to you over the phone," Danny said, "no emails on this one."

Strayberg dutifully wrote the directions on an index card, asked if there was anything else he needed to know, thanked Danny, and got to work assembling his team. By 1:30 a.m. he was waiting in the lobby for his camera man, sound man, assistant producer, and driver, and while he waited he concluded that Dick O'Malley needed to be informed, briefed, kept in the loop because O'Malley would be disappointed not to have found out in real time. Despite the late hour, Strayberg felt obliged.

O'Malley was, as predicted, happy to hear the good news at that early hour. "You woke me the fuck up to me up to tell me this shit?" he inquired of Strayberg. "What the fuck is wrong with you? I have to catch a flight down there at seven fucking a.m."

"I thought you would want to know that we I.D.'d Parviz's location and we're on our way to find him right now, as we speak."

"I expect you to do your fucking job like a fucking professional and have it ready when I get there. You go do that and let me get back to fucking sleep," O'Malley said.

Strayberg hung up, pleased to have done his duty so well. His sole concern was that O'Malley might not remember the conversation when he awoke, so he planned to remind him, just in case.

By 1:45 a.m. the Max News crew was moving along smartly up Highway 26 in their oversized white GMC van, stuffed as it was with the latest technology to track down and transmit the finest in news coverage from anywhere in the world.

* * *

Bix hated driving through the middle of the night more than he hated not being asleep in the middle of the night. An hour and fifteen minutes after his trek began, after finding Five Chop Road, the turn-off onto Wild Hearts Hollow Road, the left onto County Road Z, and the second gravel road on the right after passing two lakes and climbing a long steep hill, he was slapping himself across the face, hard, to remain awake. Avoiding wildlife that suddenly appeared in his headlights gave it the feel of a spookily surreal video game he was playing while sedated.

After one more turn, a left turn on a dirt road next to a mailbox in the shape of a golf bag with clubs with the name 'DENBO' painted on it, Bix rolled-up to a quaint little cedar shake Colonial cottage nestled among tall pine trees. It was the picture postcard image of a safe refuge. Once again the guilt snuck in. "I'm just about to destroy their idyll," he thought. He tried to remember the old saying that comedians use: "Potential career-shattering inconvenience plus time equals humor," or something like that. *Maybe someday we will all find this amusing, and we'll laugh.* Either way, he had to knock. He tapped his car horn lightly before he got out, made no effort to muffle the sound of the door closing, and slowly walked to the cottage in the dark quiet. If the guy inside had been an American, he would have feared being shot. The three wooden stairs up to the porch creaked ominously.

He knocked and waited. No lights came on and he heard no sound. "Maybe they skeedadled," he thought. Suddenly he heard a voice behind the door.

"Who is it?"

Bix thought he heard an Iranian/English/Midwest accent in the three words.

"It's Bix. Is that you, Jamir?"

"Bix?" Jamir said as he opened the door. "You always make the most dramatic entrances."

Bix was nearly thrown back off the porch by what he saw emerging from the dark house. Jamir had been on sabbatical, writing a book in the woods, cut off from civilization by choice. It took a moment for Bix to compose himself. Jamir could have been cast as the "mullah in a bath robe" in the next Kathryn Bigelow movie.

Jamir shook Bix's hand and embraced him. "What are you doing here?"

"I've come to tell you you're going to have to shave off your beard," Bix said.

"In the middle of the night?" Jamir asked.

"I tried calling first."

"We don't have cell service here. Why do you want me to shave my beard?"

"Because you will look better on national television tomorrow."

Jamir's pained expression was evident even under his heavy beard. His eyes said it all, then his mouth said more. "What the hell are you talking about and why *on earth* would I want to do that?"

"It's about *your* old friend and my boss, the next President of the United States, and your embrace of radical Islamic philosophy as expressed in a manifesto you wrote together calling for jihad against America, and apparently motherhood, puppies, and light jazz."

"A *manifesto*? What the hell are you talking about?"

"Something you wrote in college." Bix could see the lightbulb go on over Jamir's head, then realized it was Abia turning on a hall light before she walked down the stairs, dressed in jeans and a heavy sweater.

"Bix, is that you?" she said.

"Hello, Abia. How lovely to see you again. What are you doing here?"

She laughed and kissed him on the cheek, "I was about to ask you that same question."

"I've come to kidnap your husband, and you, more than likely."

"Let me hear what you've got in mind before I make a decision. Would I have to shave my legs? And would you like some coffee?"

Jamir's expression widened. "Please, forgive my manners. Come in. Let's sit in the kitchen and talk."

"Coffee, yes, legs optional. You can wear slacks."

Jamir seemed animated. "I know exactly what you're talking about. We wrote it in college. It wasn't published in the school newspaper. I think somebody may have printed it, but we printed a few copies of our own and gave them to friends. One of them was a friend who works with me now at Stearns. He told me a year ago he still had it, but I never thought of it again."

"What does it say? Are you calling for death to America?"

"Not that I recall. It was about American-Iranian relations, and we used the word 'manifesto' in the title, but it wasn't all that provocative.

We concluded that Americans don't understand Iran and have mishandled relations with them for a long time, but I'm sure we pointed out Iranians' positive view of Americans and the good relations we had historically."

"So, no big deal?" Bix asked.

"No big deal."

"Can you get a copy?" Bix said.

"I might have to get it from my friend at Stearns. We can go back tomorrow if you'd like."

"This is where the kidnapping comes in," Bix said to Abia as she handed him a cup of instant coffee. "Would it be too much of an imposition to ask you to do it now, and then bring it to Scepter? We're racing the clock a bit on this one, old man." It was a familiar reference from their striped-pants days at the State Department, their inside joke.

"What's in Scepter? I'm not asking too many questions am I?"

"We're putting on a lovely rally that you would enjoy, and we also have Dick O'Malley and an army of Max News apparatchiks trying to sink our campaign with the rumors of your manifesto. Apparently some students at Stearns have seen it, and naturally the non-Democrats amongst them characterized it in an unflattering manner and have been blogging about it. O'Malley is going to report it live from Scepter after our rally tomorrow."

"I'd really prefer to stay here," Abia said. "I'm writing my dissertation and I don't want to shave my legs."

"The other part of this," Bix tried to remain upbeat, "is that we believe Max News has been hacking my BlackBerry, which is not a euphemism. Janet Townsend sent me the directions to your cottage via email and I have to assume they are on their way here now."

"Is this where I strangle you?" Abia asked.

"Not yet. You should wait until they arrive so they can get it on video."

Abia wasn't pleased. "This means we have to pack up immediately and head back home? I was so enjoying it here."

"If all goes well, you'll be back here tomorrow night and this will all be an amusing footnote in your lives," Bix said.

"What if all doesn't go well?" she asked.

"In that event, your husband's college buddy doesn't get to be president, they are skewered by the press, all of you get to be a joke on late night TV for a while, and Republicans ride it for as long as they can until it dies."

"I'll pack up, but I don't want to go to Scepter," Abia said. "I'll stay at home while you go."

"I can get your brother Hani to come pick you up."

"Hani's here in South Carolina," she said excitedly, "looking for us?"

"Didn't I mention that? I decided that bothering you and Jamir wasn't enough, so I got Hani to fly in. At the moment he's shacked-up in a skeezy motel outside Florence, with a woman and her baby."

"Hani? In a skeezy motel?" Jamir said. "With a woman and her baby? Bix, are we being punked? Is this a reality show prank? Tell me this isn't a sick, perverse stunt."

"It *is* a sick, perverse stunt—it's called American politics. How fast can you guys be out of here?"

"We can leave in a half hour," Abia said.

"I'll shave the beard when I get home. It's a little labor intensive," Jamir said.

"Which I appreciate more than you know," Bix said. "Is there somewhere you could get a fast haircut too? We need the 'State Department Jamir' and not the 'sabbatical intellectual Jamir' for our TV audience."

"I can guarantee the beard and I'll see what I can do about a haircut."

"I'm grateful for that, at least," Abia said to Bix. "I hate his beard."

"Abia, by tomorrow evening you will be back here in Shangri-La, lounging in your pajamas, sipping Sambuca by the camp fire, and your remuneration for this inconvenience will be a fresh-faced Persian Omar Sharif," Bix said. "Insha'Allah."

"You realize, don't you, that you mixed about five or six completely different cultural references in one promise?" she said.

"That's how I got the job at State. Be sure to turn your phones on when you leave. I hope they are charged. If not, plug 'em in. Here's my cell number." Bix handed him his card with the BlackBerry cell number scratched out and the new number written-in, as well as Sophie's/Hani's cell phone. "Whatever you do, don't email me." He took the card out of Jamir's hand and scratched out his email address then handed it back. "I think they're hacking that, too, and when I say 'they' I have no idea how many 'theys' there are. I will start trying to call Hani and Sophie about five-thirty, and I'll ask them to come get you and escort you to Scepter."

"As soon as I can find that article we'll have a road trip," Jamir said. "This will be fun. I will contact my colleague at Stearns as early as my conscience allows."

Bix lifted his hands and looked skyward. "The man still has a conscience," he said with exasperation as he walked over to Abia for a good-bye hug. "I suppose that's why you married him."

"I married him because he resembled a Persian Omar Sharif," she said.

It looked like Jamir may have been smiling under his beard.

"Please start trying to contact your colleague an hour sooner than your conscience allows, Jamir. You're the Lone Ranger and the cavalry here, kind of a Clayton Moore Army of One. If you could arrive in Scepter some time before the nick of time, I'd appreciate it."

"As soon as I can. When do you need me, my friend?"

"The nick is noon, Jamir."

* * *

Fewer than fifteen minutes back down the dirt road driving at practically zero miles per hour over the rocky and pot-holed terrain, Bix saw headlights through the trees in the distance. In farm country, it wasn't unnatural to see people moving around at 3:30 a.m., but Bix was always biased against the wee small hours. Long ago he realized that the percentage of bad things increases in the middle of the night, and at the moment the thought of Max News vans skulking on remote country roads in the middle of freaking nowhere increased that percentage exponentially. He pulled over and turned off the engine and lights, after which he realized how silly he looked.

Another minute and a half passed as he waited for the mystery vehicle, long enough to believe it may have turned onto another unseen dirt road as it wound through the hills, and long enough to consider his options: starting the car and driving past them as fast as possible, which wasn't very fast, which would have given them an opportunity to see his face, or turning around and driving back to Jamir's cabin and attempting to block the road with his car, which didn't include an exit plan, or remaining where he was, rather obviously pulled-off to the side of the road in a dark car, where he could lie down on the seat and try not being seen until they pulled up next to him.

All were ludicrous. It was a prime moment to find humor, but he only found stupid. It was Spy vs. Spy time again, so he decided to double-down. A diversion was called for, a mad dash at breakneck speed to draw them away from Jamir.

He started the car, kept the lights off, and waited. Crouching low in the seat, he hoped he might be able to catch a glimpse of his adversary before he took evasive action on the chance that it was Farmer Brown or a cat burglar and not a Max News crew. As it reached a point where he could see that it was a white van, he turned on the headlights, sat up, threw the gearshift into drive, and gunned the engine, flying onto the road just beyond the van as it passed, kicking up rocks in his wake.

As he bounced down the one lane road at a reckless twenty-five miles per hour feeling like Bonnie and Clod, he glanced into his rear view mirror and waited to see if he was being followed. He realized it could also have been a county cop out of whom he had just scared the shit, and as a result, when he saw that the van had turned around and began to follow him he wasn't relieved. So he doubled-down again. He stepped on the gas until the car almost hit thirty and waited for the red lights to appear behind him, assuming that any cops in that area of the country were probably fans of Max News and wouldn't find his story amusing.

The white van was clearly losing ground behind him as he roared on to County Road Z, paved but still only a lane-and-a-half wide, and he punched the accerator briefly. Worried that he might lose his tail, he backed off the gas until he could see their headlights once again, trying to draw them away far enough to give Jamir and Abia time to escape their hideaway. A few seconds of video of Jamir in his beard would be worth a million bucks to O'Malley and Max News.

Another five minutes into the cat-and-mouse game, the cat quit. On a long straight section of Wild Hearts Hollow Road, Bix could see the van in his rear view mirror stop and turn around, presumably headed back to the cottage. If Jamir and Abia really left within a half hour of Bix's departure, the Max News van would experience déjà vu all over again as they passed in the night. Bix could only hope, because he couldn't call Jamir until he was once again within cell phone range of the twenty-first century.

* * *

Abia's cup of instant coffee had had little impact on Bix. The drive back to Charleston and Scepter was another autoneurotic slapfest, another fix of caffeinated beverage and another kidney ordeal. Bypassing his planned Red Gym drop-by in order to be on time for his zero-five-hundred meeting with Mike and the rally team, he arrived at Scepter College to find his Site 1 alternately angry as hell and pleased as punch, which is what Mike wanted to do to Agent Rudd.

"Top of the mornin' t'ye, Mr. Pitcher. How are things in Scepter?" Bix said.

"Not all tickety-boo, I reckon. Do you want to the good news or the bad news?" Mike said.

"Relieve yourself of the bad news first."

"That son-of-a-bitch is screwing with us again! You aren't going to believe it this time." Mike was on the verge of open hostility, his diplomatic veneer pealed away.

Bix was shaken from his torpor. "Rude?"

"Who else? The son-of-a-bitch says he won't give the Advance team 'S' pins, because he says *we* don't need to be in the secured areas unescorted. He said that since you have a hard pin, if *we* need to go into the secured areas *you* can escort us." Mike's face was contorted by the time he finished speaking.

"The Advance staff gets no 'S' pins?" It took Bix a moment to process. "And I have to escort my team into secured areas? Where is that son-of-a-bitch?"

"Agent Rude is near the stage with some agents waiting for Shane."

"Let's go have a frank conversation."

They passed Kate, Cornelia, Ben, and Thigpen innocently meandering to the zero-dark-hundred walk-through. Bix asked them to wait for him where they were, outside of the blast zone, where Bix intended to have it out with his self-appointed nemisis.

Mike turned to Bix as they walked. "There's one other matter. I'm certain that Rude will bring it up."

"What is it?"

"You'll see. You're gonna love it. It should be the last nail in Rude's coffin, and he's going to serve it up to you on a silver platter."

"I'm intrigued, and I hope you're right. I thought we'd already buried him a couple of times. His problem is that he doesn't realize he's dead, like that guy in *The Sixth Sense.*"

They found Rudd, Knuckles, and four of their colleagues already attired in dark suits, white shirts, subdued ties, squiggly wires, etc. at 4:55 in the a.m. in the middle of a construction site, looking somber and mulling the stage.

Bix greeted each one with a handshake and a smile until he got to Rudd, at which point his smile faded. After holding out his hand and forcing Rudd into the terribly uncomfortable poise of acting civil, Bix confronted him. "I understand you're withholding staff pins from the staff and tasking me with escort duty. What is wrong with you?"

Rudd stiffened and even the little hairs in his freshly cut butch hairdo seemed to bristle. "You're entire staff doesn't need access to the protectee," he said, the vein in his forehead bulging.

"Excuse me, now you're controlling access to The Candidate?"

"When we need to. And I don't have that many 'S' pins, anyway. We're short."

Bix let the "short" comment slide, choosing not to make his attack personal. "Special Agent Rudd, do you really want to go down this road again? Does anyone here really think he's going to win this argument?" Bix looked at Rudd's backup as he said it.

The cluster of agents demurred, their loyalty, at least publicly, going first to their organization. Bix took their silence as validation.

It was an impasse. Certainly Rudd would never back down and Bix's blood was up. The combination of caffeine, sleeplessness, and modicum of self-righteous indignation was lethal. Bix was hoping it would be lethal for Rudd and not himself. He'd found out the hard way that diatribes could be suicidal if not handled deftly.

Shane arrived to see an expression on Bix's face that he had not seen in the previous two days. "What's wrong?" he asked.

Bix took the lead. "Kurt, would you like to explain the situation, and your decision, to Shane?"

"Mr. Emory," Rudd began, "we are low on 'S' pins and the protectee's holding areas are tight, so I thought it would be a good idea to restrict the number of pins we handed out."

"He's saying that he doesn't want to give staff pins to the staff," Bix said. "Does that about sum it up?" He stared at Rudd.

"They all don't need to be in our secured areas," Rudd countered.

"So *you're* controlling access to The Candidate?" Bix was doing his best to exude incredulousness. "What if I want to task one of my site staff to get a briefcase from the motorcade and deliver it to the Staff Hold?"

"Then you can escort that person in since you have a hard pin," Rudd said.

"So now you're tasking me?" Bix's anger reach full flower. He stood closer to Rudd and looked down on him. "You don't seem to understand the dynamic. *I* say who has access to The Candidate and *you* guys make sure they don't kill him. In over thirty years of doing Advance for people who had Secret Service protection I've never *once* worked with an agent who made even the remotest suggestion that the staff shouldn't have staff pins, and I've never *once* had an agent try to task me or my staff." It occurred to him that it wasn't a completely true statement. Service regularly tried to suggest what staff Advance should be doing, and sometimes they made good suggestions.

Mike stood nearby looking too tough to *need* a gun.

Bix paused for a second and affected a contemplative pose. "Which reminds me, how old are you Agent Rudd, about twenty-eight or twenty-nine?"

Rudd remained silent, as did Shane and the other agents.

"Which means I've been doing this longer than you've been alive." He said it as if it was a recent discovery, a "eureka" moment. "You cannot unilaterally change the rules that have been in place for decades. This beggars the imagination." He looked at Shane again. "Shane, where do you want me to go on this?" It was a veiled suggestion that he would make a call to Washington if necessary.

"Give me a minute," Shane said, and then looked at Rudd. "Let's talk." The two walked to the the other side of the mostly completed stage, where they couldn't be seen. Bix, Mike, and the other agents waited.

Shortly Shane and Rudd returned. Rudd wouldn't look at Bix or Mike.

"Kurt will give you the 'S' pins, but he has another issue to talk about," Shane said.

Bix looked at Mike, who was standing and smiling where he couldn't be seen by Rudd or Shane.

"I'd like them now," Bix said.

"They're in my car," Rudd said.

"Fine, you can get them after this. What's your other issue?" Bix didn't change his aggressive posture.

"Your stage is too close to the crowd on this side and it needs to be moved over at least two feet for our team to function. If you don't move it, we will."

"Another threat?" Bix stood back a few feet an assessed the situation. "You mean where the rope line and chairs are set up on this side is too close to the stage? It looks like ten feet to me, and knowing my site man, I'd bet he's measured it, although I know you don't bet."

"Yeah, but we got an obstruction with the wall of the cistern. I've got enough guys to move this thing if you won't do it," Rudd said. Shane was once more silent on the subject.

Bix could not comprehend what he was hearing on any rational level, and he thought at that moment that he and Mike must be the only reasonable people in the meeting. The cause of Mike's unusual schizoid/irate/pleased/furious/tickled disorder immediately became apparent. "Are you *freaking* kidding me? Is this a *freaking* joke?" he said to Rudd, accentuating the pseudo curse words. "You're just pimping me now. Tell me you're just pimping me."

"I'm dead serious," Rudd said, "and I'm dead serious that we will move this stage in five minutes unless you instruct your crew to do it."

"Shane, come with me." Bix said, resolute in his righteousness. "The rest of you stay here." He made the hand sign of "stay" at Rudd that he would have used on a dog. Rudd didn't move.

Mike moved to where Rudd and the other agents could see him, smiling, and it confused them.

Bix escorted Shane to the rear of the long catwalk where The Candidate would enter, then up the stairs and back down the catwalk to the six-foot high stage, then over to the edge where they could look down on the buffer zone, the space separating stage from rope line, as well as on their colleagues, who could hear Bix's every word.

Bix spoke directly to Shane. "Put yourself in my shoes for a moment. It's five a.m., you're wrapping up a major 'build' and you have your sightlines meticulously mapped and measured. If you were me, and you agreed to expand that buffer zone just to show what a team player you were, would you prefer to move this two-ton stage, which is already loaded with equipment and hooked up to thousands of feet of electrical cable, which would take twenty guys and an hour or more, or would you prefer to move that line of fourteen-ounce plastic folding chairs and a few pieces of bike rack back a few feet? Which seems like the more reasonable choice to you?"

Rudd's consuming desire for a confrontation, his seach for an excuse to throw his weight around, had blinded him to the most obvious solution to the mini-crisis he had manufactured, and neither he nor any of his team of agents had noticed the idiocy of his threat.

Bix was finished with subtlety. "The lack of common sense here is so immense it can be seen from outer space, like the freaking Great Wall of China."

All the agents except Rudd appeared embarrassed in front of their boss, who was clearly embarrassed.

"I see your point," Shane said.

"Agent Rudd," Bix shouted down to him. "Which would you rather do? Move this two-ton stage or move a few chairs and some bike rack?"

Rudd said nothing. The other agents remained quiet as well.

Divine inspiration struck in that instant. Bix pulled out the CAT team long-sleeve t-shirt from his shoulder bag, the item he'd been carrying for more than twenty-four hours in case of such an occasion. He stood up and held it open. Every agent knew what it was and what it meant.

"Kurt," Bix said, "I want to give you this as a token of our time together. It's been both satisfying and fulfilling for me, and I hope for you, too." He threw it down to Kurt, who caught it briefly then threw it on the grass and began to walk away as Mike, Shane, and the other agents exploded in laughter. Mike retrieved the t-shirt and held it up to his chest.

"Kurt," Bix yelled, "please don't be angry just because I didn't have an opportunity to kiss you on the lips first." Then he shouted louder. "Kurt, aren't you gonna stay and help move the stage?" The finale was all Groucho: "Don't leave in a huff. You could take a minute and a huff."

Shane seemed relieved. "I guess we solved that issue."

"Whad'ya mean 'we,' kemosabe?" Bix said.

Shane laughed again.

Bix stayed on message, "I want to get those 'S' pins right away. I'm certain Kurt is completely trustworthy, but—"

"I understand," Shane said. "I'll get them for you now. Does that resolve all of our outstanding issues as far as you're concerned?"

"I thought all of our outstanding issues were resolved at our last countdown meeting, so I'm not a credible source on that topic."

"Let's assume we're good to go."

Mike met Bix and Shane at the catwalk as they came back down to ground level. In his mind he was doing a victory dance, though he maintained a façade of dignity. "Shane, thank you for your help. You can imagine that this has been a difficult situation for us, unique, really." He kept his comments vague and non-accusatory.

Shane was only a little less unspecific. "You have my word that we will do a de-briefing on this Advance. Agents must always be cognizant of their people skills. In Rudd's case, I think he's just nervous because it's the first time he's been in charge of a site."

"*That's* his problem," Bix said. "He thinks he's in charge of the site. Tell him to look up the word collaboration and brush up on civil liberties."

Mike could hardly wait long enough to express his joy. After he and Bix walked away, after double-checking to see that he wasn't being watched by the agents, he threw up his hands, danced a James Brown jig, then shook Bix's hand. "I had completely forgotten about that CAT team t-shirt. It's the perfect metaphor. You made him your bitch. If I had video I'd put it on the WWF website, under 'He Made Him His Bitch.'"

"Why didn't you tell me about Rude's demand to move the stage? I might have missed the absurdity," Bix said.

"I knew you'd see it."

"Don't assume. We might still be out there arguing about that freaking stage."

"I would have mentioned it eventually, but I reckoned you'd see it."

* * *

A minute later, standing on the far side of the Admin building, Mike regaled Kate, Ben, and Cornelia with a theatrical presentation of the Rudd smackdown, punctuated with a demonstration of Rudd's reaction.

"If that doesn't shut him up, nothing will," Kate said.

Bix was less optimistic. "I predict that nothing will, but I suspect that Shane continues to grow more skeptical of his Site guy. That can't be good for the Rudester."

Ben briefed Bix on the buses, Kate counseled Cornelia concerning common press corps complaints, Mike mused on Rude's moves, and Bix thanked Cornelia and Ben for their excellent work and asked them to leave so he could conduct a double secret meeting with Kate and Mike.

Mike's spirits remained high despite a lack of sleep. "Double secret? So what's up, Otter?"

"I found Jamir Parviz. I've been to his cabin in the woods outside Orangeburg."

Kate registered surprise. "You did? You've been to see him? What happened?"

"He had a gun. I didn't have a choice."

Kate was incensed, "Stop that," she yelled in a whisper as she became physically abusive on Bix's left arm and shoulder. "What the freaking hell happened? You spoke with him?"

"We spoke, they spoke—Jamir and his wife, Abia. They were a lot nicer than you guys would have been if I'd come knocking at the door of *your* remote cabin at two a.m."

"Don't even think about it," Mike said. "I don't care who's losing what election."

Kate had no time for it. "I will drop a dime on your ass if you don't tell me exactly what happened with Jamir, in detail, leaving out no pertinent fact."

"Jamir will come here. He first needs to go to his home outside St. George to find a copy of the manifesto, which he tells me is nothing, and to shave, which I told him was something, and in a few minutes I need to call Sophie and Hani and ask them to pick him up at his home and bring him to the College of Scepter and get here before the rally starts. That's the facts, ma'am."

"Jamir is coming here? Is that a good idea?" she said.

"I expect to be hearing that several times before the day is done. The Candidate himself told me they were still good friends, and I know him personally. This wasn't a huge leap of faith."

"So if the manifesto is nothing, what is it?" she said.

"I didn't ask."

"You didn't ask?"

"I didn't need to. He said it was nothing. Nothing was good enough for me."

"What about his wife?"

"She didn't need to shave."

"Is she coming to Scepter, do they have a small child, preferably a baby?"

"Abia will remain at their home while Jamir comes adventuring with us."

"How's he look?" Kate asked.

Bix knew what she meant: how will he "read" on the boob tube? "He looks good, like a young Persian Omar Sharif, once he shaves. At the moment he looks like your worst nightmare."

"Whaddya mean?" she said.

"Talk about 'consorting with known terrorists," he said. "If they got video of Jamir looking like he did when I saw him, it would be worse than that. It would be 'consorting with people who *look* like known terrorists.' By the way, I forgot to mention that I had a run in and a chase scene with a Max News van at three in the morning on the back roads of Orangeburg County as I left Jamir's cabin in the woods. Since you're the Press person, you should probably know about it. Eventually they stopped chasing me and turned around, I assume to check out the cabin. Hopefully it gave Jamir and Abia enough time to leave and get on the road back to their home."

"You've had an eventful night," Kate said. "How much caffeine have you drunk?"

"Too much, yet not enough. At this point I'm willing to spring for one of those seven-dollar shots of espresso from the latte bar in the hotel, which I will do when I arrive there in exactly an hour and ten minutes."

"You *are* in bad shape," she said. "What's the upshot of all of this? What happens next?"

"I'd like you to plan an informal media avail for Jamir when he arrives, after they've filed their stories on the rally," Bix said.

"I'll plan on it. Are you alright to drive?"

"Not just to drive, but to drive and talk on the phone. I have to call Sophie and Hani. Hopefully they're up, and hopefully they can leave quickly to retrieve Jamir. And I still have to hit the Schoendienst Gym on the way back, and hopefully JD won't hit me when I get there. Mike, I will see you when we arrive with the motorcade. I'm sure we'll talk a couple dozen times before then. And Kate, I'll see you back at the hotel sometime before departure. Break a leg."

* * *

"Good morning, Bix," Sophie said quietly when she answered her new secret cell phone.

"Did you and Chelsea get a good night's sleep?" Bix said.

"Well, it was a long night, but we finally settled in. If Hani slept well I'll let him drive today. Maybe we'll have better luck. Anything new on your end, other than Storie?"

If Bix had been drinking a beverage while he was driving and talking on his cell he would have done spit take right on the dashboard. "I assure you, Storie hasn't been on my end in quite some time. Many years in fact."

"I am so sorry. I didn't mean it like that. I meant it in a positive way."

"Like, it's nice to see it when old people get together?"

"Exactly, as long as they're not exhibitionists about it. No PDAs. Nobody wants to see that."

"We'll keep that in mind. By the way, I thought you might like to know that I found Jamir."

"You have *got* to be kidding me. Overnight?"

"No, I knew about it yesterday but I forgot to mention it because I'm so old, and it amused me to see you driving around the state aimlessly and needlessly."

"Touché," she said. "No more 'old' comments. By the way, how old are you?"

"Fifty-two."

"Really? You don't look fifty-two, whatever that looks like."

"It looks a lot worse than it used to."

"Nora said you and Mike look handsome."

"Nora may be thinking more Mike than me."

"Oh, really? I'll have to ask her. So tell me, where is Jamir? Hani will be excited to see him."

"If you can leave soon, I'd like you to pick him up at his home near St. George. Hani has the address. It's right down Highway 95 from where you are now. Then bring him to our rally in Scepter. Can you do that?"

"We can definitely do that, but is it a good idea? All the press will be there."

Bix defended himself. "Yes, I think it's a good idea. We can explode this myth today and allow the campaign to move on to other petty crap that has no bearing on whether or not our Candidate can govern."

"Does he know?"

"I'll tell him when I see him, before we depart for the first site."

"Does Peem know?"

"I'll call him in a while. It's only six a.m. and remember, I'm not sending emails from my BlackBerry."

"I'll tell him if you'd like. I need to call him anyway, if only to let him know where I'm going."

"That works for me. I'm sure I'll be hearing from him after that."

He gave her both Jamir and Abia's cell phone numbers and told her they should reachable soon if not immediately. "Call me, Mike, or Ben as you are getting close to Scepter," he told her. "We'll have a place for you to park and an escort to the Staff Hold at Scepter College."

18

Dick O'Malley's leadership skills, the very traits that had served him in his climb to icon status in the world of yellow journalism, were evident when Strayberg called at 6:00 a.m. to inform him that their quarry, Jamir, had not been captured. Unlike his reportage, O'Malley's indignation was genuine, as was his predilection for negative reinforcement with subordinates. "What the fuck do mean, 'you think he slipped past you?' Either he fucking did or he fucking didn't."

The senior producer expected no less. He'd witnessed O'Malley sprint to the Hotel Marianne bar within a minute of arriving the evening before, hoping to find one or more star-chasers to share some revelry. By 10:00 p.m. O'Malley was slurring his words and draping himself on a couple of right-wing bimbos who were more than happy with the attention. Strayberg explained, "It was the middle of the fucking night, Dick. We were on country roads. They drove by so quickly, we couldn't get a shot through their windows."

"Whaddya mean 'they'? How many were there? I ask you to find one guy, now you've got a fucking party of thouzans." It sounded to Strayberg that O'Malley was still slurring.

"Two fucking cars drove past us, that's all. Tell me what the hell I was supposed to do."

"You're supposed to know what to fucking do. Why do I pay you and that fucking research company all that fucking money if you can't figure it out and get the job done? I've got a fucking show to do in a few hours and you haven't done shit to find this story. How fucking difficult could it be?"

"More difficult than you finding blow-dried hussies with inch-thick make-up to buy drinks all night."

"Thaz none of your fucking biznesh. What IS your fucking biznesh is where the fuck are you and how come you aren't fucking back here yet? This oughta be the most important broadcast in a generashun, and you can't find your own dick. What the fuck is going on?"

"What the fuck is going on is we're going to Jamir's home to see if he's gone there. You gotta problem with that? You want to do this show without me? Go ahead."

Once again O'Malley was forced into retreat. "Adam, Adam, Adam, you know that's not what I mean. You have a job to do. We have a job to do. We have to show these assholes up before they get power and we have to do it today, right now. We have to find this guy Parviz before anyone else gets to him. I'm counting on you. We're all counting on you."

"Don't hand me that 'your country needs you' shit. You ain't Uncle Sam, Uncle Sam doesn't give a shit about ratings, and you aren't helping yourself by sounding like an advertisement for the Betty Ford Center. If anyone got a picture of you and your newfound friends last night your wife would throw you out on your ass. If you can't spend your valuable time working on this story, maybe you should spend a little time worrying about that."

"My wife doesn't give a shit about that and it's none of your fucking biznesh anyway. You do your job and don't worry about my by goddamn personal life. Just you find that slimy Parviz son of a bitch. This isn't rocket surgery."

"Yes, Dr. Von Braun, you're absolutely right for a change," Strayberg said.

Strayberg hung up and told his colleagues in the van, "You didn't hear any of that."

* * *

J.D. had, for the sake of his sanity, placed himself into a state of resignation regarding his site, the Schoendienst Gym, by the time Bix arrived at 6:15 in the painful a.m. for a final walk through. Bix surveyed the massive amount of equipment they had stuffed into the tiny, scrawny space. All of the room in the space was overhead, with the gym's thirty-five foot gabled ceiling soaring above, but the room's footprint was little more than the size of the basketball court. It looked smaller with staging, press risers, sets of stairs, lighting trees, miles of wires, and twenty stevedores filling up floor space. The back hallway was a spaghetti dish of cables running to every available electrical source, from wall outlets in the two back offices, from the basement and from the portable generator they had set up in the alley next to the dumpster.

Bix could see the light had gone out of JD's eyes, and he accepted responsibility. "My god, JD! Look what I've done to you. I've stripped you of your dignity and saddled you with a burden that is too great for anyone to bayaah. That's 'bear' in South Carolinian."

"This sucks," JD said.

"*There's* that old JD we all know and love," Bix said. "It will look pretty on television. It's just one shot, and that's all we care about—one shot and one sound byte. Senator Curley and the boss standing next to one another. You've done a great job, this is actually perfect."

"Perfectly sucky."

"One heads-up," Bix said. "That little gallery upstairs." Bix looked up to the the second level of the gym, set back from a railing, where three rows of bench seats twenty feet long overlooked the court. "I'm planning to put Mayor Bacon up there with Miranda as his minder. He'll be in the motorcade from the hotel."

"Are you putting him in the limo?" JD said.

"That's the plan."

"Has The Candidate agreed to that?"

"Not yet, but he will when Mayor Bacon is stepping into the limo with him and I ask, 'Is it OK if Mayor Bacon gets in the limo with you?'"

"It's for his own good," JD said.

"Yes it is, but I may mention it to him beforehand," Bix said.

"That might be wise."

"Do I have anything to worry about with the site?" Bix asked.

"Nope," JD said.

"In that case, give Special Agent Meyer my regards and I will see you in a few hours."

* * *

The Hotel Marianne was astir in its entirety when Bix arrived a little before 7 a.m. Pods of people, many of whom were in uniform or in dark suits, white shirts, and sensible ties, moved about purposely or clustered in small groups talking about nothing in particular, waiting for game day and the cavalcade to begin.

His first stop was the Staff Office, where he found Missy asleep on a couch that she had obviously asked hotel management to provide at the last minute, and he was certain she had said "charge it to the campaign account." He left her there undisturbed, thinking that she was at least sleeping at her duty station and not in her bedroom and might really be achieving her highest and best performance at that moment. Soon enough she would be awakened by traveling staff or Advance team members for whom Game Day had begun at the hotel, and soon enough she would be forced to confront her tragic reality—being expected to act responsibly for another five or six hours before the agony ended.

In the hallway on his way to the Secret Service command post Bix happened to pass the big cheese himself, The Candidate, headed for the gym with two agents. Bix knew the drill. The boss wouldn't break stride as he walked past people along his path, which was fair. The man wouldn't make it to the gym at all if he stopped along the way to talk to everyone who wanted his ear, and Bix didn't expect it. Nor did Bix expect to break his own stride as they passed, as he was not above acting hissy from time to time.

"Bix, my man," The Candidate's voice boomed as they whooshed by one another so quickly the sound of his voice created a doplar effect.

Bix continued to walk, focused straight ahead. "I've got news about Jamir," he said loudly, "You'll want to know."

The Candidate did at least look backwards as he responded, "We'll talk after this."

"I know," Bix said without turning around. For once he and his boss were on the same page, not-wanting-to-deal-with-someone-wise speaking. Bix's briefing about Jamir, the manifesto, the Mayor, and Dick O'Malley could wait until just before they departed for their first site.

19

Freeway, in the process of organizing his motorcade in front of the hotel, called Bix at 7:05 a.m. with the news that the young man who was tasked with picking-up Larry Drule—Manny, a trusted malcontent from the college Y.D.'s—had arrived at the airport in Columbia and was waiting for Drule's flight to arrive from Chicago.

"Is he carrying a sign that says "Mr. Drule" on it?" Bix asked.

"He's got the sign," Freeway said.

"Has he been briefed fully on the questions he should ask Drule?"

"He understands completely, sir," Freeway said.

"He understands that the less he talks, the better?"

"He understands completely, sir."

"He knows not to give Drule his real name?"

"He knows."

"You are a great American, young sir. I will see you soon in the Staff Office. If Missy isn't awake yet, you have my permission to wake her, gently, if possible."

"Ja, wohl, mein Herr."

* * *

Shane was drinking coffee in the Secret Service C.P., staring intently at the screen of his laptop, clattering away on the keyboard, doubtless composing a document of an official nature. His immediate reaction upon seeing Bix was, to Bix's tired eyes, remarkably positive, considering what Bix had perpetrated the night before, which made Bix a "perp." Depending on the company Bix was keeping at any given moment, being a "perp" was either horribly shameful or great street cred.

Shane stood to greet Bix with a smile, which quickly turned neutral when he asked, "You're not planning any more spontaneous demonstrations today are you? No OTR's along the motorcade, no crowds showing up in unexpected places where we might reasonably anticipate seeing open space? Anything at all under any possible scenario?"

Bix was chastened. "No, nothing under any scenario. I'm putting Mayor Bacon in the limo during the first leg of the motorcade, and Bacon will attempt to strong-arm the senator into agreeing to visit his senior center, but it won't happen. You have my word."

Shane's smile returned. "Perfect."

"To that end," Bix said, "we're going to need Mayor Bacon to turn off his cell phone when he gets into the limo. Might you want to remind him of that? It would seem more official coming from an actual official."

"Why don't you want the good mayor to receive any phone calls while he's with you?" Shane asked.

"A very perceptive question. But maybe I don't want him making any phone calls."

"All he'd have to do then would be to turn on his phone," Shane said. "You don't want him getting any calls while you've got him. What's up?"

Bix spoke quietly, in machine gun staccato. "Oh, well. In that case, the answer is either 'you don't want to know' or 'it's none of your business,' but either way, you don't want to be involved in my attempt to pull off the largest kidnapping of senior citizens in history. Do you?"

"No, I don't suppose I do," Shane said discreetly. "But I don't want to be an accessory to a crime, either."

"It's either be an accessory or the motorcade makes a giant detour to the Bacon Senior Center on West Freakin' Ishkabibble Avenue on the outskirts of hell-and-gone-from-here, and another 'spontaneous demonstration' not of my making erupts when all the local cops find out about it and call all of their friends and families and tell them to go there to play *Meet The Candidate.* It's your choice."

"I'll remind him to turn off his cell phone before he enters the limo," Shane said.

"And we will do everything in our power to ensure our events today remain uneventful."

"That's all I can ask," Shane said.

* * *

Once again in the sacred personal space of his suite, Bix decided he would spend one more night enjoying the Hotel Marianne's hospitality whether or not anyone said he could. He could count in minutes the amount of time he'd been there while awake, and only minutes more while asleep. After wheels-up, he wasn't checking out—he was staycationing.

However, it was Game Day. He was sponged and pressed in fifteen minutes and back up the fire escape stairs to the seventh floor and the Staff Office in eighteen. Missy was up. Freeway, Kate, Cornelia were hard at work on their laptops, except for Freeway, who, Bix could see as he walked closer, was playing a video game. No one had made coffee, which Bix proceeded to do. While the coffee pot wasn't particularly hygienic, he was grateful for the clean stryofoam cups that Cornelia stocked when she requisitioned the in-room amenities.

"Freeway, when is Miranda arriving?" Bix asked.

"She'll be in the lobby at oh-eight-hundred hours," Freeway said, and he wasn't kidding. He had begun the military talk within a week of being assigned to his first Advance trip and his first Motorcade.

"Great, I will meet the two of you down there at eight," Bix said.

"Have you seen the news coverage this morning?" Kate was smiling.

"I completely forgot," Bix said. "It seems like that was a week ago. Did we get anything good?"

"Look at this," Cornelia said as she handed him the *Charleston Daily Post and Courier*.

On the front page above the fold was a half-page color photo of The Candidate standing on the hotel's front desk amid a sea of supporters, dramatically lit under the spotlights Mike had acquired, with the headline in fifty-point bold lettering, "NOW IT'S A RACE."

"That couldn't be more perfect," Cornelia said.

"I couldn't agree more," Bix said, "but I always wonder if they're making a lame double entendre when they use the word 'race' in any way."

Kate was positive. "Did you see the local TV news coverage? *Great* coverage, great visuals. It led the news last night at eleven and this morning at six on all three local affiliates. And all of them talked about the rally at Scepter College. It was a very, very good hit."

"Thank goodness," Bix said.

"Thank *you*," Cornelia said.

Bix brightened. "I like this woman. Kate, did I mention that I like this woman?"

Kate laughed, "Cornelia, knock it off. You're going to lead him to believe he's competent. When he starts thinking that he's insufferable."

"Of course Bix knows he has lots of good people around him," Cornelia said.

"Don't believe it for an instant," Bix said. "Without me, these people are nothing, *nothing*. And do you know who I am?"

"Who?" Cornelia said.

"I'm the Lead. Which makes me the Lead of nothing, *nothing*. It's very depressing."

Kate continued laughing. "It serves you right for getting us involved in this Charlie Foxtrot."

Cornelia, ever diplomatic, pointed to the positive. "You put on one *heck* of a spontaneous demonstration," she said. "The senator and his traveling staff woke up to that news coverage this morning. That's a lot of good press for very little effort. That has to make them happy."

"If they haven't noticed, we will point it out to them," Kate said. "However, we have many miles to go and many rivers to cross before we sleep, metaphorically speaking. It will be a long freaking day, un-metaphorically speaking."

"And one gourmet Southern buffet lunch for our long-suffering traveling press corps," Bix said. "We could do everything right and see our coverage blown because the caterer blew lunch, so to speak."

"We'll get 'em the food, it'll be good, and they'll be happy," Kate said. "They'll give us the coverage we're looking for. It will be a spectacle."

"Damn, we're competent," Bix said.

"Don't go crazy," Kate said.

* * *

Manny West, the young Democrat with a nonconformist's flair for political intrigue who had been asked to chauffeur Larry Drule, was having
second thoughts by the time he located Drule at luggage pick-up. His
taste for subterfuge waned as he considered the potential ramifications
of taking the deputy campaign manager for a wrong-way ride through
South Carolina. Manny seemed perfect for the job—he was the kid who
would have been the barracks scrounger in an Army unit in a World
War II movie—but despite his pledge that he was prepared for whatever
abuse Drule might hurl, including, if necessary, physical assault, he had
begun to have cold feet. Freeway assured him that any kind of criminal
complaint or jail time was unlikely at best, if he just played dumb, and
Manny said he was up to the challenge.

Somehow he missed Drule at the exit gate, giving him more time to
worry. By the time he found Drule at the baggage carousel he was ready
to play it straight. He didn't have to admit to a conspiracy to commit
devious acts, he simply had to say nothing and deliver Drule directly to
Charleston in time for the first event, at which point the guy would be
Bix's problem.

Drule spotted Manny with his sign just as the carousel delivered an
oversize black suitcase into Drule's outstretched hand, nearly pulling
him into the conveyor belt. After wrestling it over the lip and on to the
floor, he made his first mistake.

"Hey you, kid," Drule yelped, "get my bag."

Manny walked to him. "Are you Mr. Drule?"

"No, I'm Mr. freaking Rogers. You're late. Where's the car?"

"No, I wasn't late. I was at the gate." He was thinking, "Oh, I could
SO take your ass for a ride," but said, "The car's in the parking garage.
Would you like me to get it?"

Drule didn't bother to look at him. "Get my bag. You can leave it at the
curb with me while you get the car. Go-go-go—I'm in a hurry."

Manny's trepidation disappeared. He hadn't even needed to introduce himself using his fake name, Bill Smith, which he was prepared to give if Drule asked. Drule wasn't going to ask, at least not on the first part of their journey. Manny retrieved the rental car the Advance team had given him, picked up Drule and his oversized bag curbside, and drove straight to Interstate 77 with Drule in the back seat thumbing intently on his BlackBerry. As Manny pulled on to the highway, Drule looked up long enough to ask, "Do you know where you're going?"

Manny improvised one of the responses Freeway had suggested, "To where they're holding the rally?"

"Yeah," Drule snarled, and returned to his thumbing.

Drule was making it easy for Manny to understand why the Advance team wanted him out of their way, in Freeway's words, "for as long as possible." His only concern was about the laws he might be breaking, and he had asked Freeway directly, "What if he tries to have me arrested?"

In a two-minute treatise, Freeway schooled Manny on the historic and illustrious career of political prankster Dick Tuck, and Manny, the in-house anti-establishment young Democrat, was a ready disciple. Freeway, worried that he might be creating a monster, cautioned Manny to "keep it classy, be creative, and make sure no one gets hurt." He added, "and not breaking the law helps. And play dumb."

Drule and Manny were hurtling North on Highway 77, within the speed limit, in the opposite direction of Charleston, Scepter, the Advance team, Mayor Bacon, and Drule's co-conspirator Shaunesy, and Manny's mind was at ease.

Manny, aka "Bill Smith" if Drule ever asked, was taking Drule to Rock Hill in the northern end of the state, where there the campaign happened to be sponsoring a rally for college-age volunteers at Winthrop University later that evening. "It was all a misunderstanding," Manny would explain when they arrived, as soon as Drule decided to go postal. "I thought you were one of the speakers for our rally tonight." He practiced the lines in his head a few times for inflection, and settled in to enjoy the ride when he heard Drule call Shaunesy to let him know when to expect their arrival. He feared for a moment he'd be confronted with the name of an actual destination.

Drule leaned forward, with his BlackBerry still planted on his cheek, and tapped Manny on his shoulder. "When do we arrive?"

He was making it too easy. "We should be there in another hour or so." Manny said.

Drule didn't thank him. "Shaunesy, did you hear that?" he squawked into his cell phone. After a pause, he said "I will see you and your people at the campaign headquarters by ten, we'll walk to the college together and be there for his arrival. As long as I'm escorting them, it doesn't matter what pins they do or don't have. I can take anybody wherever I want. Be at your headquarters by the time I arrive."

Drule stuck his nose back in to his BlackBerry while Manny continued driving North on Highway 77.

* * *

Miranda and Freeway waited in the lobby for Bix, seated appropriately in a love seat that had served as a press riser the night before. They were sitting and talking very closely when Bix arrived to choreograph the next steps in his unpleasant distraction avoidance ballet.

"I'd like to commend you both for keeping your hands to yourselves in public. We've had some difficulties in that regard recently, and I suggest you Purell one another's backs after you get up, but do it in private." Bix was impressed with Miranda's transformation from Goth Material Girl to young professional. She was turned out as if it were a job interview to the point of removing her nose ring, and he was pleased to see she had shown so much effort to be situationally appropriate. "Miranda, thank you for being here. Doesn't Freeway look spiffy? Very official."

"This is the first time I've seen in him a suit in all the three days I've known him," Miranda said. "For all I know, he dresses like this most of the time."

"Valid point. How would you know? It feels like we've known you forever. You're like family, like a daughter to me and, I'm certain, like a sister to our Henry here. Am I right, Henry?"

"You're right, Bix." Freeway was having no luck stifling his silly grin, even sillier than the one Bix had been wearing a couple of nights before.

"OK, family," Bix said, "let's get down to cases. Miranda, you will be escorting Mayor Bacon. We will introduce you to him when he arrives. Your actual 'escort' duties won't officially begin until we arrive at the Red Schoendienst Gym, which is our first site."

Freeway spoke up. "You're going to go with us in the motorcade from here to the gym; we'll be in a van marked with a "VIP" sign in the window, with me, and the mayor will ride in the limo with our boss. After we arrive and the mayor gets out of the limo, that's when we will pick him up, and he is never to be allowed anywhere close to our boss again."

"Henry, Henry, that's a little blunt," Bix tried to soften the tone. "Miranda, it is true that the mayor will need to be escorted to a place where he can watch our first event at a distance, to a VIP viewing area, and then he will not get back into the limo with the senator when we depart for the College of Scepter. We will need you to escort him to the VIP van as soon as we're done with the first event."

Freeway jumped in again. "Yes, but there's more. We need you to keep him busy, distracted, and keep him from receiving or making any phone calls."

"How do I do that?" she said.

"Today's operative phrase," Bix said, "is 'please turn off your cell phones,' or better yet, 'the Secret Service asked us to turn off our cell phones.' We will have that message reinforced along the way by real or imagined Secret Service agents, so all you have to do is watch him and bust him if he tries to turn on his phone."

"Yes, but there's more to this strategy," Freeway offered, again without being asked. "We need you to keep him distracted. Once we pick him up at the Schoendienst Gym, don't stop talking to him. Whatever you do, don't let him have an instant of peace."

Miranda was worried. "He'll think I'm an idiot."

Bix offered solace. "Not if you have an intelligent conversation. Ask him about himself, he'll think it was an intelligent conversation, as most men would. He'll be flattered, as most men would be."

"Tell him he's legendary," Freeway said. "He'll think you're a genius."

"I can do that," Miranda said. "It worked on Henry.

"It worked on Bix, too." Storie had walked up behind Bix and eavesdropped on the last sentence.

"Which is crap," Bix said. "It was I who told you that I was legendary, and you believed me for a while."

"Until I saw that picture of you at the age of, like, twelve, briefing Jimmy Carter, and Carter's looking at you like 'who is this pre-pubescent punk?'" Storie said.

"I saved a lot of money on razor blades back then, and what the President was saying to me, at that very moment, was 'you are one legendary and handsome son-of-a-gun, and I can tell you're jes' gonna keep gettin' better lookin' as time goes on.' That's what I recall him saying."

"Good recalling," Storie said.

Miranda opined, apparently genuinely, "You're such a cute couple. You're perfect together."

Bix stood stunned, speechless. He tried to think of something to say that was amusing but not insincere. Storie appeared, to Bix, to be more comfortable in her own speechless skin, happy to let silence reign. Bix felt fidgety but dared not move a muscle, including the ones controlling his mouth.

Storie was Princess Grace and Madeleine Albright rolled into one. "We are, Miranda. We are. And individually, too."

Storie was also smart enough to perceive Miranda's role in the ensuing drama. She looked at Bix. "Is she your sacrificial virgin on this trip? Are you going to allow her to be abused by Mayor Bacon when he finds out he's not getting his trip to the senior center?"

"No, that part will be played by Freeway, and yours truly. We will be fully accountable. We simply want Miranda to distract him for a while, just talk to him, and we're the only ones who are still virgins so no one else gets sacrificed," Bix said.

Storie laughed, "Another fanciful fiction," then looked at Miranda. "I'll help you when you get to the college. I can escort you and the mayor to the VIP section. It will give me an excuse to be there. I can say the mayor invited me. He likes me, you know."

"It's true, Miranda," Bix said. "She's the main reason he won't support us, and I'm counting on you to make him like you, too. To be blunt, your job is to keep him off his phone, with his phone *off*, for as long as possible, beginning when he arrives at the gym, throughout that event and during the motorcade to Scepter College. Freeway will show you where to go at the gym, and you already know Scepter College, so it will be a cakewalk. Someone official will ask him to turn off his phone when he enters the limo, and other official looking dudes will mention it from time to time. By the time you arrive at the college, you can ease off. It will either be too late, or okay for him to place or receive calls by then. Can you do it?"

"I can do it. I'll write an outline of subjects I can discuss."

"Thank you for this, Miranda," Bix said. "There's an internship in this for you."

"You offered me an ambassadorship yesterday. What happened?"

"Seeing you today, we'll do the ambassadorship first, then the internship. You'll be sick of wearing suits after the ambassador thing is over."

"Hey, I rock this suit," she said.

"You rock it and a half," Freeway said.

"What he said," Bix said.

"Storie, what's your sign?" Miranda asked.

Bix was clueless for an instant.

"Pisces," Storie answered instinctively.

"Bix, what's your sign?"

"Feces," he said.

"What?" Miranda said.

Storie explained. "When fish swim in it, they die."

He excused himself, as did Storie, and when they rounded the corner back toward the latte bar Storie rounded Bix and planted a kiss on his lips. It was another sneak attack.

"If I did that to you," Bix said, "you could reasonably call it harassment."

"And it would be, becaues you're bigger than I am. But you could swat me away like a bug, and you haven't," she said. "So it's not."

"There is no hope. I must endure it. Can I buy you an espresso?"

"You'll spring for the seven dollar shots? You must not be feeling too harassed."

"Intoxicated by your kiss is more like it. It will go away as soon I stop feeling used."

They drank their espressos quickly, realizing belatedly that they were committing the unnatural act of talking in public once again. Storie wished him luck and said she would be in McBride Hall, away from the press, when the motorcade arrived. They shook hands, Storie shot him the glance, and they went their separate ways.

20

Another half hour passed in the car on the highway to Rock Hill before Drule happened to look up from his device to see a road sign indicating that they were almost to North Carolina, and even he was smart enough to realize that Charleston and Scepter were in the southern end of South Carolina.

"Hey, where the fuck are we going?" he asked Manny. "That sign said we're almost all the fucking way to North Carolina." The volume rose. "Where the fuck are you taking me?"

Manny knew the jig was up. Phase two began. "Rock Hill sir, where we're holding the rally."

"What fucking rally in Rock Hill? I'm supposed to go to the senator's events in Charleston and Scepter. What the fuck is this?" He was yelling by that point.

"Aren't you speaking tonight at our college rally in Rock Hill? At the event at Winthrop?" Manny wore the dumbest expression he could conjure.

"Bix told you to do this, didn't he? He told you to fuck me and drive me to Rock Hill, didn't he?"

"Sir, I've never spoken to anyone named Bix, and I thought you were one of the speakers for tonight's rally. I just offered to help the campaign, and our volunteer coordinator told me to take you wherever you wanted to go. *You* said you wanted to go where we're having the rally tonight."

Drule leaned up and stuck his face as close to Manny's ear as he could reach. "You turn this goddamn car around and get me down to Charleston before I have your ass on a stick. What's your fucking name?"

Manny was thinking, "My fucking name? My 'fucking' name is usually Oh God Yes, Oh Please Yes, Oh God," but he tried to affect a fearful pose. "It's Bill Smith, sir, and really, I apologize, this has been a big misunderstanding. Can you give me an address where you need to go? I'm not as familiar with Charleston."

Drule pulled a copy of The Candidate's schedule and threw it up to the front seat. "The address for the places he will be at every minute of the day is written in that. Look it up, asshole."

Manny was very close to making another rash decision as he turned on to the next exit ramp and entered back on Highway 77 headed South, but admirably stifled his true feelings once again. Drule's hit parade kept on playing. He called Shaunesy to inform him of the mix-up. "This motherfucker fucking kidnapped me halfway to fucking Canada before I called him out. I have no fucking idea how long it will take to get there, and I sure as hell can't ask this motherfucker."

It was becoming too consistently personal for Manny's taste. A really senseless gesture was called for, and he drove past a few exits before he found the right venue. Drule continued his diatribe to Shaunesy, then to his secretary at headquarters, then the state Field Director, before Manny exited at Highway 34. Drule was still on the phone with the state Field Director when he leaned up once more to show a personal interest in Manny's thought processes. "Where the fuck are you going now?"

"I've got to find a bathroom."

"This punk's fucking me with me," Drule said into the phone. "He's fucking with me."

Manny had pulled up to a gas station with a restaurant attached and a local county sheriff's car parked in front, went inside and sat down a couple of booths away from two deputies who were enjoying a few minutes' break over cups and donuts. He ordered coffee and waited for Drule to grasp the situation.

Within a few minutes Drule walked in, steam rising from his limp ears, ready to lash out again, but the presence of sheriff's deputies and a family of four with children seated in a booth just beyond them forced Drule to affect an appearance of civility. He sat down across from Manny, locked his eyes on the abused youth and spoke very quietly. "What the hell are you doing now?"

"Mr. Drule," Manny said confidently, not quietly, "it's like this. It's a simple matter of respect. You wouldn't like it if someone treated you like dirt, so why do you think it's right to do it to me?" He thought it may have been loud enough catch the ears of South Carolina's ever-vigilant law enforcement officials.

"Look, Bill," Drule feigned normalcy, "why don't we talk about this while we're driving to Charleston? The senator expects to see me this morning. I've committed to him that I would be there. This is important for the campaign."

"No, you don't seem to get it." Manny spoke louder. "I expect an apology and a promise that you'll knock off any more abusive language. I'm a volunteer. This kind of verbal assault is completely unacceptable. Do you treat your paid staff that way?" He looked over at the sheriff's deputies to see if he had witnesses.

Drule saw the look and he repositioned his body in the booth so he could address the officers as well as Manny. "I see what you're trying to do here," he said. Then he turned to the officers. "This guy practically kidnapped me and now he's made me late for two very important events that are occurring this morning, and he's mad at me for being angry about it."

"I'm sorry, deputies," Manny said, "but this gentleman has been rude to me since I picked him up at the airport. I'm just a volunteer, *his campaign staff* asked me to pick him up." Manny knew his audience—two South Carolina county sheriff's deputies. He was relatively certain that Drule's association with that particular presidential campaign wouldn't stand him in good stead among at least a third of the local population. "He keeps telling me what a bigshot he is and he's called me every name in the book, like mother eff, a-hole punk." Manny was also aware of the family nearby and the deputies' sensitivity to their sensitivities. They had both turned in their booth to face Drule and Manny, their equipment-bristled belts making it hard to twist between table and seats.

Drule was unapologetic and overly excited for his audience. "He kidnapped me to the other freaking end of the state."

Manny explained, "It was a mix-up. He said he wanted to go to the campaign rally in Rock Hill, and then he said he wanted to go to Charleston. It was his mistake." Manny couldn't have acted the part of the "innocent abused" more convincingly if he'd had good make-up and lighting.

One of the deputies, a middle-age man in surprisingly good shape and a sincere demeanor, extricated himself from his booth and walked over to Drule. "Would you like to press charges, sir?" he said in a South Carolina accent, not surprising for a South Carolina deputy sheriff, and he was wearing a name badge that said "Acuff."

"No, officer, that won't be necessary," Drule said.

"You're working for one of the candidates in the upcoming primary?"

"Yes, officer." Drule didn't explain further.

The deputy sheriff didn't ask which one. Any Democrat was bad. "I suggest you gentlemen work out your differences." He looked at Drule. "If you would prefer to call a cab rather than rely on this young man, you may do so." He looked at Manny. "You are under no obligation to transport a person who you do not want in your car."

Manny showed compassion. "I know this gentleman is under a lot of pressure. I just don't want him taking it out on me. He just met me. He doesn't know me, and I was asked by his campaign to volunteer. Now I see why they're in trouble."

Drule jumped like a chihuahua that had stepped on a June bug. "I *don't* know this punk. I think it was a set-up, and I think he was told to drive me in the opposite direction from where I need to be."

Deputy Sheriff Acuff may have had Grand Ole Opry DNA. Drule's comment sounded like a straight line, and a wry wit found its mark. "Why would someone from your own campaign try to sabotage you like that? I would think you'd be very popular among your colleagues," he said in a drawl.

Drule sat looking at Manny. Manny didn't move a muscle. Drule knew he was outnumbered.

The deputy sheriff felt the need to ask, "Do you have any proof of the allegations you're making against this young man?"

Drule was brief. "No, officer."

"Then I suggest you work out your differences soon. We don't need any disturbances, particularly caused by people who are enjoying the hospitality of our state and asking for our votes."

"Yes, officer," Drule said.

"Thank you, Deputy Sheriff Acuff," Manny said. "Say, I'm originally from Tennessee. Are you related to Roy Acuff at all?"

"Distant relatives. Our folks are all from around here," the deputy said.

"Well, he's one of my favorites, and you kinda favor him," Manny said, drawling a bit.

"I take that as a compliment," the deputy said. "He's one of my family's favorites, too."

Drule remained silent, leaning over the table on his arms and elbows.

Deputy Sheriff Acuff walked back to his table, sat down and continued drinking his coffee, which was cold. "Velma, could you freshen this up?"

Manny looked back at Drule. "Sir, the ball is in your court. Either you climb off my back or you can take a cab to Charleston. What can you do to me—have me fired from my volunteer position? It's your call."

"Look, we got off on the wrong foot. I apologize for calling you names. Let's just get going to Charleston. I can't be any later than I already am. We will probably not make it to the first event now, anyway."

"Do you promise to knock it off?" Manny said.

"Yes, I promise."

"I've got to use the restroom before we go." Manny took the time to wash his hands extra thoroughly.

They drove the remainder of their trip in silence except for Drule's constant clattering on his Blackberry.

* * *

"Mr. Mayor," Bix said, "thank you for being here." It was the first time Bix had seen him away his home turf and the mayor looked slightly out of place, even a little awkward, in the ornate but tasteful hotel lobby in downtown Charleston. Bix noticed a woman walking toward the mayor at a distance, followed by an entourage of either family members or an odd assortment of random children and women security guards. The women and children looked like an average lot of nicely dressed people, but the woman leading them was a bombshell. She reeked understated elegance, a sixty-something, silver-haired picture out of *Vogue* magazine in a St. John knit dress.

Bix literally stopped and waited to see what happened, sensing the outcome. For no apparent reason under heaven that Bix could conceive, she walked up to Mayor Bacon and stood next to him, without hesitation, as if they were married.

"Bix, this is ma wawff, Mrs. Paula Christine Bacon."

For the tenth time that morning Bix was stupefied and he was beginning to enjoy the ride.

Mrs. Bacon spoke first, extending her hand, "Bix, it's so nice to meet you." There was a hint of Charleston accent in her voice. His insides turned to liquid. "Ah've heard so much about you from Eugene. I believe he regauds you highly."

Bix's feet became clay; the incongruity of it was off-putting. "Mrs. Bacon, I didn't know..." he began, then stuttered. He didn't know "what" exactly? That the mayor was married? That he was bringing his wife? No, Bix knew or would have assumed both. He stuttered on, "I didn't know..." He couldn't figure out a particularly good ending for his sentence. "I don't know what I didn't know, but I am so glad you're here. Thank you for coming. Is this your family?"

She laughed, aware that Bix was flummoxed. "Please call me Paula. Yes, these are our daauughtas and our granchildren."

It was an unexpected onslaught. Bix loved it. The Mayor was showing his "regular person" side, the side that wanted to get the entire family's picture taken with The Candidate who could be President. His wife was a revelation, and Bix was certain they were both aware of it.

Ever one to ask himself "how can I use this for my advantage," he sensed an opportunity. He invited her to be his buffer between The Mayor, her husband, and The Candidate—the man who would be President but doesn't like being stuck riding in the same car with pol's he doesn't know or doesn't want to know. "Paula, would you like to ride in the limo with your husband when we go to our first event?"

The mayor, who didn't anticipate or want company, any company, on his private limo ride with The Candidate, couldn't appear ungracious to his own wife. He said nothing.

"Why Bix, that's vera kind of you. I would love to. Just poent me in the right direction."

Mayor Bacon stood there, snarled a little, and moved on to the next subject. "Well thaa's settled then. Bix, wha don't y'all show us whea you would lak us ta go."

Bacon knew he'd been had. Bix felt badly for him a little, and an equivalent amount of that old-fashioned guilt set in, but not enough to make him change his trajectory. "Yes, sir, Mr. Mayor, we have an intimate meeting room around the corner where we have some refreshments for you and your family."

They made small talk as Bix led the way. Mrs. Bacon even did *that* enchantingly, so much so that Bix realized only as they were entering the Jeb Stuart Room that he hadn't checked to see if Missy ordered refreshments. Assuming the worst, he was pleased to be wrong. Coffee, tea, and a small array of pastries awaited, along with several comfortable chairs. As he reminded himself to thank Missy for her conscientiousness, he remembered he had placed the order with the general manager the previous evening.

"Mr. Mayor, Mrs. Bacon, I will come back with the senator in a few minutes," he said reluctantly, due solely to the presence of Paula Bacon. One thought replayed in Bix's mind—"What the...?" He decided to take the stairs up to the seventh floor to work his tired muscles.

Kate, Cornelia, and Missy were in the Staff Office when Bix re-entered. "Ladies," he said, "I just met the mayor's wife," then he sat down, looking star struck. "It's simply remarkable."

"Remarkable good or remarkable bad?" Kate asked.

"Remarkable incredibly good, which is incredibly weird. She is intelligent and attractive, really exquisite," Bix said. "I don't get it, and I don't admit that very often."

"It sounds like you're in love," Kate said. "Don't you risk pissing off the mayor?"

"You could certainly say I'm smitten. You will be too when you meet her. She has that kind of beauty. You'll want to look like her when you're her age. *I* want to look like her when I'm her age. I don't get it."

"Isn't she a lot younger than the mayor?" Cornelia asked.

"No, she is definitely age appropriate. They had to have been married for a long time, since he was young and good looking. I can think of no other reason other than maybe he threatened to wipe out her entire family if she said 'no.' If I had met her when I was in my twenties and she was in her thirties, and she wasn't married, I would have made a nuisance of myself, and I would have respected her good taste if she'd had nothing to do with me."

"Whenever you met any attractive woman when you were in your twenties, I'm sure you made a nuisance of yourself," Kate said.

"Unkind, and untrue," he said. "I would never have been a nuisance if the woman in question was already attached to someone bigger than me. Go introduce yourselves to Mrs. Bacon and tell me if you don't agree."

"We'll go downstairs to meet her before we load the press," Kate promised.

Bix was compelled to check his multiple emails and voicemails, all of which were pressing business. He had been watching the "incoming" closely to make sure he didn't miss any calls from his team, or Sophie and Hani, or Jamir, but one voicemail from Thigpen rated special attention. It was strange for two reasons, the first of which was that Thigpen's number hadn't appeared in his caller I.D.

Thigpen was supposed to be preparing the last minute touches of his crowd management plan—barracades, rope lines, volunteers, liaising with Secret Service Uniformed Division magnetometer teams. Instead he was out crowd building, or trying to make sure that the crowd that showed up had the ability to park within a five-mile radius.

"Hey dude," his message said, "I'm in jail. OK, not really in jail, but I'm at the Scepter Police Station and I think I'm under arrest. I'm pretty sure of it. They took my cell phone so you have to call me back on this number. Could you get me out of here?"

It was an attention grabber. A man with a heavy-set Southern accent answered the phone when Bix called back. "Sceptah Police Station."

"Do you have a Mr. Thigpen in your facility?" he said.

"Yes sir, he is in our holding cell with the others. Who is calling?"

"My name is Bix Stevenson, and I am representing him." The police officer on the other could construe what he wanted to construe. It sounded official enough.

"Yes, sir, I'll get him."

Bix was relieved. At least he'd been arrested with others. The chances diminished that he'd been busted for holding up a Seven-Eleven or boring a group of volunteers to their deaths.

Thigpen was soon on the line. "Dude, you gotta get us outta here."

"It depends. What did you do?"

"The cops have been out since six a.m. putting up 'No Parking' signs, not only on every street around campus, but on every fucking, er, excuse me, freaking street in town. We were out taking a few of them down, you know, so our volunteers had somewhere to park, and the cops busted us."

Bix was proud of him up to the part where he was arrested. The wise old Lead would have cautioned against that, as he had consistently throughout his career, oft' repeating "and please don't get arrested" to his teams. Being very wise, he assumed that national staff being arrested might create bad press. Being paranoid, he assumed he was being recorded at that moment, even though it was only Scepter.

"I am *so* disappointed in you. You *know* you should have asked permission from the police and Secret Service, both of whom would have been completely understanding." The mouthpiece on his little cell phone dripped with sarcasm. "I will get an attorney down there as soon as possible, and I'll call Shane to see what he can do."

"Thanks, Bix. I know now I should have gone to Chief Fry and asked him first." Thigpen's saw Bix's sarcasm and raised him two disdains for authority. "I'm sorry to let you down."

"Not just me, you let your nation down today. Live with that son," Bix said. "Live with that."

"It will be difficult, sir." There was no question in Thigpen's mind what Bix meant. "I know I must rebuild your trust in me."

Bix planned to bitch slap him later for getting arrested, but he admired Thigpen's initiative. "I know you will, son. Take the next few minutes in detention to consider the consequences of your actions, and let me know how you plan to improve. I have to go."

He sat back in his chair to view game day's unfolding from the thirty-thousand foot level, and took the moment to chat with himself. The Scepter Police were putting up No Parking signs all over town, not at the behest of the Secret Service. Service never asks for such extreme crap and Shane can't do crap about it. This is Mayor Bacon showing us who's boss. It could work. *Bacon could pork my crowd. Ha! Damn, that's lame.*

He used a landline in the Staff Office to phone Mike and tell him to send the attorney they had recruited down to the jail and to assign a few 'take-down' teams to follow the cops as they posted No Parking signs. Bix ended the call with one request: "Tell the attorney to stay at the Police Station, just in case anyone else shows up."

Bix went to Merle's room and filled him him. "Thigpen's been arrested for taking down No Parking signs that the Scepter Police are putting up all over town to supress our crowd. We've got a local attorney who can deal with it, and I'm going downstairs to reason with the mayor, who is obviously pulling those strings. I'd appreciate it if you would tell Philpot and I'll brief the boss when I come back upstairs for departure. Did you get all that?"

"Did you sleep at all last night?" Merle asked.

"No, not a wink. This is all artificial. And I found Jamir Parviz. I've got Sophie bringing him here."

"What?" The word shot out of his mouth and his eyeballs.

"Yep. Seemed like the thing to do."

"Is that a good idea?"

"Everyone keeps asking me that question. The answer is, 'we'll find out.' Gotta go."

He disco'd down the seven floors of stairs, passing the Secret Service post-standers for the third time, and found Paula Bacon in the Jeb Stuart Room talking with one of her daughters. The rest of the Bacon brood was milling about the refreshment table while Mayor Bacon stood in the corner talking on his cell phone. Settling on an impromptu strategy, Bix walked straight to Paula and her daughter, that feeling like the most convivial way of drawing Mayor Bacon away from the phone and into a conversation.

"We need a few more minutes upstairs," Bix told her.

Paula was understanding, as expected. "Weah in no rush, Bix. You take all the time you need. I know you must have a thousand details to attend in such a highly complex environment." It was pure Scarlett O'Hara after graduation from Bryn Mawr and qualifying for AARP.

"None more important than seeing to it that you and your family enjoy the utmost in hospitality that our humble circumstances can afford." Bix was channeling Jeb Stuart himself, knight cavalier of the Confederate cause. If he'd been riding a horse at that moment, it would have reared. Mayor Bacon appeared to be trying to wrap up his call and join his attractive wife and Bix quickly.

"Whah that's the fastest I've seen him move in yeahs," she said serenely. "You must take that as a compliment, Bix."

"Thank you for saying so, Paula," he said.

"Eugene, my deah," she said when he arrived showing the stress of his thirty-foot sprint, "please do not feel you have to hurry. You are un-used to it, and we do not need any untowahd events casting dahk shadows ova ahwa joyous occasion." She said it so kindly he could only agree.

"Mrs. Bacon is absolutely right about that, your honor," Bix said. "This is supposed to be one of the fun days, one of the good days we'll remember. It helps not to take any of it too seriously. I try my best not to." Bix was setting up his "let my people go" from jail argument that he planned to have with the good mayor as soon as he could button-hole him, when the mayor interrupted Bix's improvisation.

"Ah undastan' wha y'all would see things at a'way," Bacon said, "with one of yoah boys unda arrest for intafearin' with a police offica's official dutas. Ah jus received a call from ma brotha-in-law tellin' me he's got a few of yoah campaign people in his facility."

Mrs. Bacon directed her next observation to Bix. "The chief is not my brotheh, Bix, he's Eugene's sisteh's husband. I want to keep the blood lines cleah in this situuation," she said.

"I understand what you're saying, Mrs. Bacon. I've met the distinguished Chief Fry, and I wouldn't have guessed that you share any DNA," Bix said. "Yes, Mr. Mayor, I just heard about that. It seems your city's finest were putting up No Parking signs where we had told our volunteers to park, as well as everywhere else within a day's ride from Scepter College, but the volunteer parking locations had been cleared with the Secret Service. Thigpen thought he had the approval to open those locations for the people who had been name-checked."

"Now, Bix, son, it kinda sounds to me as if yoah Mr. Thigpen had gone fahhh beyond a few parkin' spaces and was removin' our parkin' control sahns willy-nilly, hitha and yon. Now we jus can't have that in owah town."

"A question is begging to be asked here, Mr. Mayor. Why would your police force be restricting parking everywhere, willy-nilly, hither and yon, within a five-mile radius of our rally? Doesn't that appear extreme, biased, unobjective? Are you trying to suppress the size of our crowd?"

"Eugene," Mrs. Bacon said, "Ah you doin' that to Bix and his candidet for prezident?" She didn't wait for an answer. She knew her husband. "You tell yoah boys to let those people park in youh town, and let Bix's campaign folks out of yoah nasty jail. *You* don't lak bein' in theah, I cannot imagine that you would make anyone othah than real criminals r'main in theah."

"Now Paula, deah, those pahkin' arrangements are a security matta. The Secret Sehvice have asked that we provide a secuhity perimeta' and we want nuthin' untwawd happenin',' as you would say." Mayor Bacon was doing the Scepter Two-Step and she knew it. "And it was foah secuhita reasons that those folks wuh placed unda arrest. They pose a risk ta the community."

Bix kept his mouth shut. The Bacon extended family stood milling at a distance, except for one daughter, who stood close by.

"Let his people go," Paula said sternly, with no hint of humor. "And allow them to have theah rally. That man's goin' to be elected president and he will rememba this."

Bix's day was getting brighter and brighter, affecting his sunny commentary. "That's the second time I've wanted to kiss a member of the Bacon family, Mr. Mayor. The first time was you in President Gilliman's office the other day."

Bacon had no idea how to interpret Bix's remark, whether to laugh, or have someone beat him up. His expression was that of a Rottweiler deciding friend or foe.

Paula put the situation into perspective for her husband. "Eugene is a vera good kissa, Bix. You may wish to try him first."

"I will do that, Mrs. Bacon. Thank you for your insight. Mr. Mayor, will you let my people go, or do I have to kiss you? Be apprised that my oral hygiene this morning is not good."

Paula squealed with laughter. She reminded Bix of Storie, not in appearance but in manner, intellect, and appreciation of smart humor.

Bacon couldn't help chuckling, but resisted Bix's entreaties. "That is outsahd my area of jurisdicshun."

"Nonsense, Eugene," she said.

Bix stopped smiling. "Mr. Mayor, my only recourse will be to send out dozens of volunteers to take down your signs, and while you're brother-in-law is arresting them, I'll send out more. I'll fill up your jail. Better yet, I'll send out only African-American volunteers. Your jail will be filled with dozens of young African-Americans. Given your history, your legacy, that could wipe out all the good you've done for all these years. And I'll make sure the press get a picture of it. It will be the lunch counter demonstrations all over again, only this time, *you're* 'the Man.'"

"He's got ya theah, Eugene." She continued to laugh.

Bacon winced, his eyes glancing around the room. "The police will allow your friends to leave, but the No Pahkin' sahns that've been posted alreada remain up, is that cleah?"

"I can't promise that, Mr. Mayor. We must have places for our crowd to park, and you're peeing all over my parade." He looked at Paula. "Pardon my language, ma'am."

"Not at all, Bix."

"Frankly, Mr. Mayor, this is *not impartial* nor is it *fair.*' Bix hit him with the unvarnished truth, enunciated. The old 'fair and impartial' argument always worked with politicians—or not.

It was a blow to Bacon's integrity, thanks only to his wife's presence. The good mayor had no idea when he brought her along that day, expecting to play the big dog, that his "vera own waff" would kneecap him.

"I will tahlk with Chief Fry about our situashun and woek things out."

"Thank you, dear. That's kahnd," Paula said. Years of experience at the controls had given her an instinctive reach to the right buttons.

Bix, proving he could function intellectually on at least the level of a bonobo, mirrored her behavior. "Thank you, Mr. Mayor. That's very kind of you."

"Let's don't push owah luck," he grumbled.

* * *

There was no Paula Bacon upstairs in The Candidate's suite to buffer any of the negative reactions Bix was anticipating in his next briefing. He called Ben on the way, checking the status of the senior citizen movers. His young Site 2 sounded confident. "I have three over-the-road, fifty-eight passenger buses with signs in the windows that say "Mayor Bacon Bus Brigade" waiting at a location less than a mile from the Bacon Senior Center. As soon as you call me I'll give them the word and I'll drive ahead with my bullhorn to organize the seniors. As soon as we fill one bus we'll send it, then the next. If we need to run a shuttle we can do it."

"Did you remember your cattle prod?"

"I have it right here, set to 'stun' just like you said. And I've got a guy with a boom box and a CD of John Philip Sousa music. *That* will get them moving."

"I'm impressed. You've made me a believer. Seriously, it sounds like you have everything well organized. Have fun with this."

"We will," Ben said. "Drop by the VIP area at the rally. We have other surprises in store."

"Are you producing a carnivale?" Bix said.

"Very close. You'll have to come by and see."

"Please don't be getting the geezers drunk," Bix said. "If someone falls down and breaks a leg, or worse yet, dies, the press might get a picture of it."

"I'll have a large tarp waiting nearby to cover any bodies," Ben said.

"Good Advance," Bix said.

* * *

The Candidate was standing in the living room of his suite looking at his BlackBerry when Bix entered, at which point he began walking around as if maintaining movement would make him an elusive target. After exchanging the mandatory "good mornings," The Candidate kept moving and Bix sat down, uncharacteristically, thinking that a stationary, immobilized position might alleviate some of The Candidate's yips about being cornered into human interaction.

The Candidate didn't get directly to the heart of the day's matters. Rather, he told Bix "Let's wait for Merle and Philpot to get here" and resumed his fascination with his phone.

Bix took a seat and dug in his bag for a black notebook stuffed with maps, receipts, business cards, and miscellaneous papers on one side and a yellow legal pad on the other. He opened it to the page on which he'd written, "Friday briefing," subtitled "sh*! I'd sooner not discuss," placed the notebook on his lap and fought the urge to look at his own BlackBerry.

Another two minutes passed before Philpot walked in, cheerful, enigmatically upbeat. "Hey, Bix, I hear you found Jamir. Or he found you—which was it?"

"I definitely found him," Bix said, never certain whether Philpot was making good-natured small talk or making a point that only he and The Candidate understood. "I knocked on his door in the middle of the night, as a matter of fact."

"Was he alone?" Philpot asked.

"Was he alone?" Bix said. "No, the place was full of hookers."

"I meant, 'was he there with other people who might look like they were involved in questionable activities,' that's all."

"Who might those people look like?" Bix asked.

"Like suspicious-looking Middle Eastern terrorists," Philpot said. "Of course."

Too much coffee and too little sleep were powerful combatants in his inner duel between satire and civility, always allied on the side of satire. "That narrows it down," he said, taking the road too-often traveled. "In that case I would have to say yes. He was there with a woman. She looked Middle Eastern but spoke fluent English, which I found suspicious. She was very gracious too, which was suspicious, because I woke them up at two a.m., and she offered me coffee but I was reluctant to drink it because, who knows, maybe she put something in it, and she told me her name was Abia, which sounded like an alias when I heard it in 1997, when she was first introduced to me as Jamir's wife, by Jamir no less, but it may still be a ruse. She's kept her face fully exposed the entire time I've known her, which is suspicious for a Middle Eastern-appearing female, and I personally witnessed her attending several parties in Washington where U.S. diplomats were in attendance, and she was always suspiciously engaging during the many conversations I've had with her."

Philpot either brushed it off or didn't notice. "Is she coming here with him?" he asked.

That woke up the Candidate. "*With* him. What does *that* mean?"

"If I tell you, a full-fledged briefing could erupt, and Merle isn't here yet. Do you want to wait?" Bix was having a good time even if no one else was.

"Tell me," he sniped.

"The short answer is 'no, she's not coming with him,' Do you want the long answer?"

"Yes."

"Jamir is on his way here with Sophie and a mutual friend slash brother-in-law whose name is Hani Al-Saleem. If it sounds Middle Eastern that would be appropriate, Jordanian actually."

"Is that a good idea?" the senator said, with hints of acid.

Philpot entered the fray, "I was just gonna ask that."

"The short answer is 'yes,' Bix said. "You want to get this behind you as quickly as possible, and we want to dump it, er, ah, give it, to the press after our rally in Scepter after we've knocked their socks off with the best visuals of the campaign, and one of the better speeches, I'm certain, as well as a fine feast of Charleston cuisine. You know that Dick O'Malley is planning to do his hit job on you and Jamir *live* on Max at that time, which sort of forces our hand, collectively speaking."

"What about the manifesto? Did you ask him about it?" Philpot said.

Bix assumed his answer would provoke a negative reaction, and he *so* wished he'd been more aggressive in pumping Jamir for excruciating details of an article written thirty years before, otherwise known as wearing out your welcome at three a.m. "Yes, I asked. He said it was nothing. He and his alleged wife are going home first and he will try to find a copy."

"That's all?" Philpot said. "It's nothing? What kind of nothing is it? Has anyone vetted this thing?"

"Dunno," Bix said. "'Nothin' was good enough for me."

"We're handing this to the press on a silver platter," Philpot said.

The Candidate was leaning in the direction of conservativism on the issue by way of avoidance. "That's what I was thinking. If it's possible to misconstrue something, they'll do it. And what happens when he gets here? Does he do a press conference? Do you expect me to entertain him? Have you thought this through?"

"No to the press conference, yes to light media mingling, no to the entertainment, and never to the 'thinking this through' thing," Bix said. "I thought you and Jamir were friends. I thought you might be happy to see him, to know that this manifesto dust-up is b.s., and put it all behind you."

The Candidate wasn't convinced. "If it turns out like that."

"This could either be a good thing," Philpot opined, "or a disaster of epic proportions."

"I disagree," Bix said. "It could also be a screw up of small or medium proportions, landing anywhere along the spectrum of potential debacles. We should do an office pool."

"What do we want to do here?" The Candidate asked Philpot. "Do we want to see Parviz…"

There it was again, referring to Jamir by his last name.

"…or do we want to resolve this issue in another way? I really don't need to see the guy."

Bix was astonished. "Jamir" had been reduced to "Parviz," then the "old friend" had been demoted to "the guy." *With old friends like him I wouldn't need casual acquaintances.*

"If you don't want to see him, you don't have to," Philpot told his boss. "It's your call."

Being a team player, Bix embraced the logic of choices. "Overlooking the fact that he has driven all night to come here and help you, and that his privacy is about to be invaded by Dick O'Malley whether he likes it or not, and that he should *at minimum* be allowed to defend his name before it becomes a joke on late night talk shows, you could totally blow him off if you feel like it. When he shows up, I'll leave him standing at the outer security perimeter."

"I won't blow him off. That's not what I'm talking about."

"It sounded like it," Bix said, "and it sounded like Philpot thought it sounded like it."

"No. Of course I'll see him."
"But you don't trust him?" Bix asked.

"It's been a long time since I've seen him or spoken with him," the man-who-would-be-president protested, as if it were reason enough, and then stepped away to nowhere in particular.

Bix took it to mean that the conversation had been called to a halt, but he wasn't finished. "My plan is to escort Jamir to a separate Holding Room. We can sequester him there for the entirety of the rally and the down time afterward if you prefer. He will understand completely. I won't say *what* he will understand completely, but he'll understand."

"He'll understand that he was screwed," Philpot said.

"Yes," Bix said.

"Philpot will deal with it," The Candidate said. And that was all he had to say about that.

* * *

Game Day lay ahead, along with a passel of surprises that Bix couldn't wait to share with the boss. Merle arrived at the opportune moment to discuss the day's travel plans, motorcade-wise, a subject destined to evoke all of The Candidate's most basic political instincts: his keen understanding that all politics is local, his sheer joy of the game and the people he encountered every time he spent time with Democratic political leaders around the country. Merle, as Trip Director, knew that better than anyone. Bix needed him as a buffer.

"Senator, we need to let Mayor Bacon ride in the limo with you just from here to our first site, about twenty-five minutes."

It was another Candidate attention-grabbing bombshell, setting off the loudest Candidate explosion Bix had witnessed, and Bix was the intended target. First came *The Candidate's Gaze*, followed by a stinger of a question so intimidating it was known to melt the spines of much stronger men and women.

The Candidate stopped migrating around the room long enough to perform *The Gaze* and express, with a simple query, his contempt for the idea of having the mayor inflicted upon him.

"Why?" he said.

In that one word he could convey nuanced derision. There was no rising inflection at the end, the line delivered in deadpan, a practiced recital, perfected through years of controlled disdain, part of the condescension-management regimen he had adopted in his youth when he realized he was smarter than everyone else.

"I thought you'd never ask," Bix replied, also in deadpan, practiced through years of watching Marx Brothers movies and seeing in them metaphors for Washington, DC, guides through the farce of national politics. "There are several reasons why. Do you really want to hear them?"

"Not really, but it may be important. I hope it's relevant."

Merle spoke up in Bix's defense. "Bix wouldn't have made the commitment if the reasons weren't relevant."

"Thank you, Merle. As with anything in this line of work," Bix began, "what's relevant is open to interpretation. What is inarguably pertinent is that Mayor Bacon was in a position to make life miserable for me, and by extension, you, anywhere we wanted to function in Scepter County, if he didn't get something on this trip. I assume you have heard from Congressman Pangborne about him, and I assumed you wanted Pangborne off your back. Well," Bix averred, "this is what the mayor gets. He gets the opportunity to lobby you personally to visit his name-sake senior center, and do so on this visit, which we can't do because you've got to be wheels-up by two p.m., and we get the ability to produce our rally in the best location in the entire county."

Unimpressed, The Candidate's disaffection for the "share-a-ride" concept continued. "So, I have to play the bad guy and tell him no."

"Not at all. In fact, you should tell him what a bully idea it is and how much you would love to go see his senior center today. As soon as we arrive at the first site, you tell me you'd like to go to the Bacon Center, to which I will respond conscientiously, 'Sir, I must tell you we don't have time to go there and still be on-time for wheels-up;' to which you should reply, 'Make time,' after which I will respond 'Yes, sir.' Does that make sense?"

"Not really." The Candidate was corralling his scorn well. "How do we get from there to not having to go?"

Merle moved to the side of skepticism. "Yeah, how do we not go to the senior center as we've committed to go?"

"We won't have to go, I promise, I think," Bix said. "And you won't have to be alone in the car with him. You will be joined by his lovely wife, Paula, who you will thoroughly enjoy, I promise. The trick is to grant the mayor his wish, and I will make the rest not happen."

"How?" The Candidate found it was beneficial to keep his hostility brief, making it less difficult to pedal back to a position of friendly co-operation if the situation warranted.

"Advance tricks," Bix said. "How about if I tell Merle, and he can decide whether you really want to know? Deal?"

"Deal."

Of course it was a deal. "End of conversation," Bix thought, "the perfect resolution." Bix could deal with Merle and Merle could deal with The Candidate. Kismet.

21

In the elegant confines of the Jeb Stuart Room, after introductions to the Bacon clan, The Candidate acted as his own master of ceremonies, hustling the entire Bacon family through a fast photo op. Then, quicker than The Candidate could say "I understand you both are riding with me today," and "Let's do this thing," he hustled himself, Paula, and the mayor away from their brood and out to the waiting motorcade, parked in the alley behind the Hotel Marianne, near the dumpsters, exactly where they had arrived the night before but aimed in the opposite direction.

Bix walked in the lead with Shane, whispering as they went, "Don't forget about the cell phones."

Shane was ahead of him. "As soon as they hit the limo," he said.

The entourage, now including the mayor and Mrs. Bacon in its ranks, walked out to the loading dock and down the cement stairs to the waiting cars. Press busses, staff vans, and law enforcement vehicles both large and small were full of their officially designated riders.

As The Candidate climbed into his regular slot in the back seat, opposite the driver, Shane escorted the Bacons around to the other side. "I need you to turn off your cell phones at this point," he told them. "Please turn them off completely. Our electronic countermeasures will mess them up and they send false signals."

The duo dutifully complied before they got in. Bix could see the quizzical look on The Candidate's face when he heard it, but the Bacons weren't in a position to witness his reaction. He turned and looked out the window at Bix with same questioning appearance and received a grin and a knowing nod in reply as Bix pivoted, then walked with Shane at his side to take their places in the Lead Marked car.

Bix acknowledged his counterpart's effort as they walked. "Thank you, sir. That was masterful." Once they took their seats Shane signaled the driver, Captain Contarini of the highway patrol, to move out slowly. Bix called JD to tell him they had departed en route his location, and then he called Ben. "Send in the clowns," he said.

"They're on their way."

He then called Mike for an update on the rally and found him uncharacteristically agitated.

"There is freaking no one here. No one!" Mike told him. "There were only a few hundred waiting at the mag's when we opened them. It was freaky. It's never been like this. We're fucked. We're just fucked."

"How long have the mag's been open?"

"Just a few minutes, maybe ten," Mike said.

"Is there a steady stream?"

"You might call it a steady trickle."

"Get Thigpen to send his No Parking sign removers to start knocking on doors. Get them our bullhorn and tell them to drive up and down streets like a sound truck. Tell them to tell people there's free food, Oprah, David Cassidy, anything, I don't care," Bix said.

"How about free money?" Mike asked.

"Tell 'em we got that, too."

Bix hung up and settled back to chat with Shane, SAIC Farrow, and Captain Contarini, and then take a leisurely scroll through the emails on his neglected BlackBerry. He was not surprised to find some scorcher Subject lines on recent emails from Peem, whose vitriol so ranneth over that he forgot that someone, Max News among others, were probably hacking Bix's campaign account. "Call me immediately!" was the kindest of the stream. "What the FFFF are you FFFF'ing doing!!!" may have been the most accusatory, but there was a lot of competition in that regard.

* * *

Two minutes later Ben arrived at the Bacon Senior Center to rustle up the old folks. A minute after that, the Bacon Brigade buses pulled up to the front door, along with the young man with the boom box and the Sousa CD, and three lovely young Y.D.s from the college who had volunteered to act as bus hostesses. Ben asked boombox boy to wait for his cue, took a deep breath, put himself in the mindset of a Presidential Advanceman, and transformed into the persona he had chosen for his mission—that of a guileless volunteer.

He walked excitedly to the front desk, where his broad smile and brief cover story—"I'm here to pick up people for the VIP section at the rally at Scepter College"—did not win the dowager receptionist's heart or mind.

Instead he was greeted, unsurprisingly, with "Ah haven't heard anythin' about Mayah Bacon's bus cahavan t'tha College."

In an instant he transmuted to "caring huckster," Mother Teresa by way of Ed McMahon. "No disrespect intended, ma'am, but is there someone you could call? I've been told that the people here are supposed to be the *special* guests of Mayor Bacon, and I would hate for them to miss it. From what I saw, they went to a lot of trouble to make a nice VIP section at the rally and provide these beautiful buses to chauffeur them there and back."

"Ah undastand. Let me call mah boss."

A flustered young man who looked as if he could be another relative of the mayor's, with his potato nose and square-set torso, walked out of an office behind the receptionist's desk. "What ken ah do fah yah, suh?" he asked, then listened attentively as Ben pitched his story. Apparently confused, young Mr. Something Bacon scratched his head. "Ah'm gonna half ta talk wid th' mayah 'bout this. He nevva menshunned nuthin' 'bout a bus toah ova ta tha college."

Ben encouraged him to do so and crossed his fingers, preserving his innocent eagerness for the heavily talcum-powdered crowd that was beginning to gather around him in the Center's glass-enclosed atrium. As the flustered facility manager began dialing his cell phone, Ben began to organize, striking up conversations with the seniors who were milling closely. With assuredness befitting a brass-balled professional political operative and the eager face of a Mouseketeer, he was was a natural leader for the active aged. He instructed them to get their friends for Mayor Bacon's Bus Brigade and be ready to leave immediately.

Young Something Bacon stopped dialing long enough to point out what was becoming apparent to Ben. The Senior Center had been put on alert to expect a visit from the mayor and The Candidate, swelling the crowd and its expectations of having the big show come to them, not the other way around.

"Mayah Bacon tole me," said Something Bacon, "that he was bringin' th'senatah heah t'daay."

That certainly made the job of highjacking everyone in the establishment a bit more challenging. How much more challenging, Ben could not predict.

When young Something Bacon stopped once again, the news was both good and bad. "Ah cain't seem ta get 'hold the mayah, and I cain't 'prove nuthin' thet the mayah hasn't 'proved. Ya'll gonna hafta wait 'til I ken git 'hold a him."

Ben wondered if young Something Bacon was an alum of Scepter College, shook it off, and decided he had only one choice if there was any chance of salvaging the mission. At some point in the next hour, maybe in the next five minutes, Mayor Bacon could turn on his phone and Ben would be facing federal charges. But he had remembered to wear his Super Advanceman underwear, emboldened by Bix's tales of old Advance superheros of yore who saved the day through quick thinking and fancy footwork. He doubled-down on his story, his mission, and his desire to avoid federal prison.

"*Not for a moment*," he proclaimed. "I've been told that Mayor Bacon is going directly to the rally at Scepter College and is hosting all of the Senior Center members in the VIP section." Then he played his ace in the hole, "AND, MAYOR BACON IS PROVIDING FREE FROZEN MARGARITAS AND FRUIT SMOOTHIES, YOUR OWN PRIVATE BATHROOMS, CHAIRS FOR EVERYONE *RIGHT* UP FRONT, AND THE BUSES WILL BRING YOU *RIGHT* BACK HERE WHEN IT'S OVER. WHO'S UP FOR THAT?!"

Ben's "Ed McMahon" side burst forth. He could have sold dozens of sets of steak knives in the back of the produce section at the local Piggly Wiggly that day.

The crowd roared "Yeah!" with gnarled fists thrust high into the air.

"THEN LET'S MOVE OUT!" Ben yelled.

He walked out the front door of the Eugene V. Bacon Senior Center, spotted his boombox boy leaning against a bus talking with one of the female Y.D.s, and cued him to start the music. John Philip Sousa began his patriotic march, the Y.D. hostesses scampered up into their buses, and Ben commenced ushering the closest of his enthralled captives to their destiny with VIP status.

Young Something Bacon stood behind the front desk watching the scene, punching numbers into his cell phone, holding it to his ear, putting it down, pushing "End," and repeating the action over and over. The obsessive compulsive nature of it pushed Ben to move ever more quickly, rounding-up seniors from the far ends of the Center and pushing them to the front door in wheel chairs to speed the process when necessary. He recruited boombox boy and the hostesses whose buses hadn't been filled yet to help cajole, manhandle, muscle, or otherwise convince their prey to join in the fun.

In a back room of the Center, Bacon Multifunction Room G, to be precise, Ben found a group of about twenty people hiding as if they feared an attack by hostiles. They were family members of some of the Senior Center regulars, brought by their grannies to shake hands with the mayor and his very own captive, the presidential candidate himself. After a few calculations, Ben told them to get on the bus with their geriatric family members and suggested they stand if there were no more seats available.

Young Mr. Something Bacon continued to redial his cell phone while a stream of Bacon Center patrons marched out to the busses, where they were given special VIP credentials bearing Mayor Bacon's name, the Official Seal of the City of Scepter, and a tasteful graphic of the Senior Center.

Ben squeezed as many as he could into the first bus, sent it on its way, and the senior citizens kept coming, all wearing comfortable athletic-style footwear. He found it propitious that his kidnapping victims were already appropriately shod for the exodus, and remembered he was stealing them from an activity center, not an old folks' home. Nonetheless, he was glad that Mike had placed the rally site's EMS unit next to the VIP area.

* * *

Five minutes away from the Schoendienst Gym, Bix called JD with "Bravo," setting in motion arrival protocols that the two had established earlier to ensure a smooth transition from outside to inside.

JD and his counterpart, Special Agent Meyer, met the motorcade curbside. Rather than greet The Candidate and lead him to his Holding Room as he would normally, JD was tasked by Bix to wear a suit and tie, which he would not have normally, along with his "serve kit," the ear piece and squiggly wire that connect to walkie-talkies, or "hand-held units" as the agents referred to them, despite the fact that the Advance team wasn't using walkie-talkies, and to grab Mayor and Mrs. Bacon and deliver them and Miranda to a separate entrance into the gym. He knew immediately why Bix had made the special request, but not the special responsibilities he would have to perform. "Why do you want me to look like an agent? Who do you need me to kill?"

Bix explained, "We say 'neutralize,' or 'remove,' but it's neither in this case. I need you to tell the Bacons to make sure their cell phones are turned off before they enter the building, and I want you to make sure Mayor Bacon doesn't dawdle outside to make any calls. I don't want him turning on his phone at all. That would be bad."

"How bad?" JD inquired.

"Imagine the inconvenience of having to make Christmas packages and schlep them to the post office to mail them to our colleague Ben Oliver in federal prison *every year* for ten years," Bix told him.

"Not to mention Ben rotting in a jail cell," JD said.

"Yes, and that, too."

"That would be bad," JD agreed.

The motorcade arrived at the turreted, gothic Red Schoendienst Gym, which had embraced its cohort of agents and cops and armaments and paramilitary paraphernalia in the style of a Teutonic castle. It head-ed around to the alley, next to the dumpsters and the portable generator. Bix was out of his car quickly, standing at the limo door when The Candidate emerged.

The Candidate spoke his lines. "The Mayor thinks it would be a good idea if we visited the Senior Center on the other side of town, and I agree. Why don't you see if that's possible?"

Bacons were popping out of the other side when Bix replied, "Senator, to be honest, I don't believe there is enough time to visit the Senior Center and make it to wheels-up on time."

The Candidate said simply, "Make time." It was a reading Clint Eastwood would have been proud of. "Let's do it on the way to the college."

Mayor Bacon could hear the entire exchange as JD escorted his wife away, making no effort to coerce her husband. Bix had given JD the heads-up. "If you whisk his wife away, he will follow along. He can't abide the image of a younger, better looking man flirting with her, and if he thinks it's a Secret Service agent he'll be extra-agitated."

It was working. As much as Bacon wanted to hang back closer to The Candidate, he was drawn by an invisible force into following his wife and the good-looking guy escorting her. Bix flashed the mayor a smile and a theatrical "thumbs-up." Bacon appeared grudgingly satis-fied as he walked away, and Bix watched him as long as he could while simultaneously leading The Candidate up the long set of metal fire es-cape stairs, through the fire escape door, and into the spartan, 1899-vin-tage hallway where one small office had been re-purposed as a Holding Room. Philpot followed at a slow pace while Merle remained outside in the alley to smoke a butt.

JD performed his task, admirably in Bix's estimation, shepherding the Bacons to their entrance, admonishing his charges, and handing them off to Miranda. Once inside, she and Freeway ushered them into a tight, stainless steel elevator and up to the overlook, where they found seats on benches next to light trees and sound equipment that had been placed by the contractors. Miranda sat next to them and smiled sweetly. A Secret Service agent stood at one end of the overlook, behind them and to their left, because it was a position from which a bad guy could potentially do bad things to the protectee below. By contrast, Bix had stuck Mayor Bacon into a position from which it was unlikely he could do any harm.

Miranda kept an eye on him and his cell phone to intercept any deviations from that plan, and waited for the time she would spring into action.

Not more than sixty seconds later, in a rare tangible exhibition of precision scheduling, Bix looked like a logistical genius when Senator James Curley of Massachusetts and former Democratic nominee for president, arrived at the back entrance to the gym after a private jet ride from Washington to a small airport outside Scepter. A local supporter and friend of Senator Curley's volunteered to meet him and drive the senator and his press secretary to the gym.

Bix excused himself from The Candidate, left him in the Hold and reunited with JD as they walked down the fire escape to meet their guests. Both JD and Bix had known Senator Curley well after working for him in the last campaign—JD in the Scheduling Office and Bix as his Senior Lead Advance, but it had been three years since that campaign. Both wanted to say hello and re-introduce themselves before the fun began.

Advance people, Bix always taught to those he mentored, are supposed to be prepared for anything, but Bix was not prepared for what happened next.

Walking down the staircase with JD in front, Bix could see Senator Curley and his press secretary, C. Wade Moss, exiting the back seat of a large Chevy SUV. Out of the front passenger side climbed a person who was out of context, unrecognizable as a Curley staff member. It was not a cause for elation when, two beats later, Bix recognized the man as Bob Peem. "Shit," Bix thought.

He had barely gotten the expletive out of his mind when, as he reached ground level, Curley walked over to Bix and hugged him.

"It's good to see you, Bix. You look great."

The delicate circuitry of Bix's beleaguered mind teetered on the brink of overload. "He hugged me, the guy hugged me," he thought over and over. "And he knew my name."

"Thank you, Senator Curley. It's good to see you. Thank you for being here," he said, thinking, "he hugged me." If there had been a place to sit he would have taken a moment to catch his breath. Gathering his wits and girding his loins, he greeted C. Wade Moss, whose nose was perpetually buried in his BlackBerry, and waited for Peem to round the limo.

"Bob," Bix said as they shook hands, "of all the events in all the cities in all of the country, you walked into mine."

Peem, as always, looked at Bix as if he was some demographic that had been eliminated from their targeting data. Overcoming a brief bout of confusion, Peem gathered his thoughts. "I thought you might be surprised to see me."

"Not in the least," Bix lied. "Once I heard that Drule was coming down, I expected you to bless us with your presence as well." It was a whopper. Bix was gobsmacked, more by Curley's hug than by Peem's psychodrama. "How did you manage to connect with Senator Curley?"

"I'm the one who has to approve the campaign's use of private jets, and we use a company out of Chicago. I arranged to get on there before he went to Washington to pick up the senator."

"Gulfstream 450?"

"550."

"Sweet ride," Bix grinned. "Power hasn't gone to *your* head."

"Let's talk when you get a chance," Peem said.

"You didn't come for the waters?"

"What waters?"

"I'll stick my head in the Staff Hold as soon as things get going here."

JD, after experiencing his own hug and personalized greeting from Senator Curley, was equally mystified. They deposited the senator in Hold with The Candidate, showed Peem the Staff Hold next to it, and walked out into the gym, remaining behind the rope lines separating secured versus less-secured portions of the room, to check the crowd, the press and the sound system. Before walking out on to the tiny stage he had jammed into one end of the basketball court, JD composed himself. He had been afflicted with a case of the giggles since the hugging incident. "Did you see that? He hugged me. I saw him hug you, man, and I thought, 'I've never seen him do that. He must really like Bix.' Then he hugged me, and he knew my name. Did you see that? Who was that guy?"

"You've seen plot twists where the evil twin shows up?" Bix said, "That was the friendly twin."

"They always get more personable after they lose." JD waxed philosophic.

Bix just stared at JD.

JD recognized his error, and then he and Bix said in unison, "Except for Al Gore."

Thigpen's crowd of veterans, a little more than a hundred by Bix's estimate, all standing, filled the space between JD's eight-foot by twelve-foot stage and the three tiers of press risers thirty-five feet away. An eight-foot buffer zone directly in front of the small stage made a huge gaping hole in the middle of Tiny Town, the diminutive event space. Standing on the stage looking out at the small-but-high-quality crowd, and watching the traveling press corps as they set up on the press risers, Bix and JD bemoaned the terrible site, remaining distant from the microphone, just in case. Bix, ever the optimist, was grateful for the matched set of six American flags on poles that his contractor, Gershon, had supplied. They always had good flags in stock, which was a major factor in Bix's appreciation for their skills as an event contractor.

Bix instructed JD to choose ten veterans from the rear of the crowd and invite them to stand on stage behind The Candidate and Senator Curley during the event.

"They haven't been vetted," JD said.

"Vet them yourself. Ask them if they are supporters. They'll tell you the truth," Bix said. "Then ask them if they'd like to stand on stage. You'll find eight who will work. Tell them if they screw us, you'll have their veterans benefits cancelled when we come to power."

Kate called Bix on his cell from the opposite end of the minuscule site to tell him the press would be in place in two minutes. She reminded him, "CNN, MSNBC, Max News and Fox News are carrying the event live. The audio guy is confident it will be up and running by then."

Bix waved and gave her a thumbs-up, and then looked up to the bleacher seats in the gallery above. He beamed a wide smile and a thumbs-up to Paula Bacon, who smiled and waved. He cleverly followed this with a smile and thumbs-up to her husband, who showed no hint of emotion, and a wave to Miranda, who was beaming.

In the Hold, Peem, The Candidate, Senator Curley, and Moss talked while they waited for their cue, but not with one another. The Candidate and Peem stood in one corner of the room deep in conversation, while Curley and Moss stood in the center, engrossed in their separate BlackBerry worlds. Rather than rely solely on the spoken word in case the once and future Democratic nominees had erected their respective cones of privacy, Bix tapped each one on the arm to alert them that he required their attention.

"Gentlemen, one word about format before you go out," Bix said. "We are treating this like an overgrown press conference-slash-rally hybrid. As with a press conference, we will have no introductions, no off-stage 'announce,' no voice-of-God. The place is too small and there is literally no need for introductions. Senator Curley, you will take the podium first to read your statement, and *unlike* a press conference, you may expect audience reaction. We have a crowd composed entirely of veterans. They should be your crowd."

Bix motioned for them to follow JD, who led them out into the hallway that separated offices from gymnasium, to a door at the far end where they would enter the gym, at which point the two principals would walk less than five feet and take two steps up to a stage set on twenty-four inch risers. It was a mini-event, and the contrast in scale to the upcoming rally was another source of irritation for JD, who had mentioned it more than once, "The rope line from their point of entry to the stage is less than five freaking feet long; five freaking feet! It's the shortest distance between two points since Mickey Rooney." It was a reference he knew Bix would understand, and understand as well that he wasn't being amusing when he said it.

Bix confirmed with Kate that the press were connected to the audio feed, signaled "OK" to JD when she told him they were ready to go, and JD opened the door into the gym. "The stage is yours, gentlemen." JD figured they could find their way to the stage without being led, with a wall on their left and a rope line on their right. He watched to make sure.

Despite the lack of formal introductions or hoopla, their small crowd exploded in applause. "Good start," Bix thought. He left the building the instant Senator Curley began his remarks, an instinctual behavior for Leads, while JD remained to monitor his event. After the program began, it was on autopilot as far as Bix was concerned. He was in no hurry to visit with Peem in the Staff Office and he knew he'd find Merle in the alley, somewhere near the dumpster, smoking a butt.

Outside once again, standing on the fire escape landing, he first called to check in with Mike at the rally, where Mike was having a hard time hearing his phone ringing through the din of the crowd that had already begun to swell. "I'm in the buffer zone in front of the stage," he told Bix. "Let me walk back into the building."

Bix waited a few seconds until Mike was back on. "I can hear you now. Not one but two of our magnetometers didn't show up," he reported. "Rudd told me a little while ago and it the first time I've seen him smile. The little creep snickered—he actually made 'snick snick' sounds. We've got people lined up all the way back to downtown Scepter."

"Is Thigpen there? Did you spring him from the joint? Is he having a fit?"

"Yes, yes, and yes," Mike said.

"Good," Bix said. "Is the uniformed division being helpful?"

"They're moving the crowd through as fast as they can. It helps that the weather's warm, and Thigpen did a pretty good job of getting out the word not to bring bags or purses, but we are still two mag's short."

"Don't sweat it. You know what happens if we arrive and there are people still waiting in line to get in. How does it look so far?"

"It looks freaking awesome," Mike said.

"Do you have my escort squad in place for our arrival?"

"I've got five Laborers' Union guys ready and waiting," Mike said.

"Have our folks from the senior center arrived yet?"

"The first bus just arrived. We're moving them into the VIP area now. Did you hear about what Ben got for them?"

"He said it was going to be a party, but he didn't say how," Bix said.

"He got a local vendor to donate two frozen drink machines. He's set them up for frozen Margahritas and Mojitos."

"Booze?" Bix asked. He was stunned at the immediacy of his reaction and its resemblance to something his eighty-year old father would say. Again. Twice on the same trip.

"Nope, virgin. But we aren't going to tell them."

"Brilliant. I'll thank Ben in person. Better yet, I'll call him myself to see how it's going. In case I don't get him, let me know when the last bus arrives from the Bacon Center."

"Will do. There's one more thing I have to tell you. Nora called. She said that Shaunesy showed up at the headquarters in Scepter with more than a dozen people, only three of whom are local, and they are waiting there for more to show up. Shaunesy told her they are meeting Drule there, and he will escort them to the college for a meeting with the boss. They are planning to arrive just as the motorcade pulls up."

"Now *that's* brilliant. They may pull it off if Drule arrives in time."

"Do you have reason to believe he may not?" Mike asked.

"Why, no, I have no reason to believe that."

"Just checking. I thought maybe you knew something about that."

"Why, no. I haven't heard. His flight could have been delayed. The airplane may not have been able to take off due to the added weight of his self-importance. Who knows? Call me if you need anything. If not, I'll call you when we have departure."

He immediately called Ben, who was waist-deep in over-stimulated retirees. "Ben, have you achieved your mission?"

"We have achieved lift-off, still climbing to escape velocity," he reported. "The first bus has arrived at the site, and I've asked him to come back in case I can't fit everyone in the next two buses. The second bus is almost filled. It will be gone in less than a minute."

"Good job, Ben. You won't have to get a tattoo now. You've earned your stripes."

"I still have another bus or more to fill. You can give me my stripes when we fulfill the mission."

"I'll confer a stripe and half immediately and give you the rest later. Good job."

* * *

Bix walked back down the iron fire escape to bum a butt from Merle, a practice which had become a minor ritual through the previous months. "It's a lovely day in Charleston," Merle said between drags as he handed Bix one of his cigarettes. "Congratulations on the great press this morning. The boss was impressed."

"He didn't mention it," Bix said.

"He was distracted by this thing with Jamir. I think he's worried that another old friend might become an embarrassment for him. And you *know* he hates having people ride in his car other than his close buds. *That* probably upset him more than the Jamir business," Merle said. "He just forgot about the press this morning."

"For the next leg of the motorcade to Scepter," Bix said, "my Aunt Mabel and a few members of her bridge club are riding in the limo. I forgot to mention it."

Merle pulled out his lighter and handed it to Bix. "He will love it," Merle said as he took another drag.

The phone in Bix's sportcoat pocket peeled annoyingly. "Why don't you change that ring-tone," Merle said. "It sucks."

It was Mike. "We got a crowd!" he yelled into the phone. "All of a sudden they just showed up. One moment no one was there and the next there are thousands waiting outside the mag's. It's incredible."

"Are you moving them in?"

"Yes, we now have a steady stream."

A loud shout of "Bix!" pierced the air from on high. They looked up to see JD standing on the fire escape, motioning at them to come inside.

Bix told Mike he would call him back and handed back the lighter to Merle. He dashed up the fire escape, all the while assuming that auto-pilot had ceased functioning. Merle took a last hit of his cigarette before he put it out and threw it in the dumpster.

"We've lost our audio feed to the press and half of our lights." JD looked sticken. "We're checking all of our connections, but nothing so far."

With that, a man wearing a t-shirt with "Gershon Technical" written across the back raced out of the fire escape door, brushed back JD and Bix, and ran down to the alley, around the corner of the red sandstone turret to the portable generator. After a long thirty seconds he was back up the stairs with the breathless news that "everything looks fine down there," and rushed back inside, followed by JD, Bix, and Merle.

Technician man disappeared immediately to the far end of the gym, next to the press area where the sound booth was located, while Bix moved with grim interest to the hallway door that looked in on the site, where he could watch unseen. Senator Curley, only twenty-feet away, was speaking.

"The P.A. system is still working," Bix told Merle, "so the press can get some ambient sound and Curley can't tell they don't have a feed. And the lights aren't completely embarrassing. It's a small enough room that the other half of the lights are doing an OK job."

"It's still embarrassing," JD said as he began to walk away, defeated.

"I have to agree," Bix said. "At the moment, our home viewers are watching guys with their lips flapping, like a silent movie with no subtitles, in front of a not very inspiring static visual."

"Embarrassing," JD said. "Remember, we're only as good as our last trip."

Merle remained silent for a long time too, preferring to watch the action unfold without any helpful comments.

"I'm going to look around," Bix said. "This can't go on much longer."

Merle broke his silence. "It can't?"

"That wasn't helpful," Bix said.

Another technician was scrambling in and out of the site and down to the Gershon truck parked outside while the first technician hunched-over the soundboard flipping switches and checking wires. JD walked around looking concerned. Bix thought, "What is the stupidest thing that could have happened?" He walked back through the hallway checking electrical outlets jammed with power cords, through the Holding Room where he thought someone may have inadvertently tripped on one of the wires which snaked everywhere, then reluctantly into the Staff Hold where he knew he would encounter Peem.

"Do you have time to talk?" Peem asked when Bix entered.

"Not at the moment," he said. "We've lost power to our audio feed and half our lights."

"So your event is going in the crapper?" Peem said.

"Only so far as there is no audio and their faces are only lighted on one side."

"What are you going to do?" Peem said.

"I'm doing everything I can do. I'm walking around with a concerned look," he said as he continued to scan the wires leading in and the outlets to which they were connected.

"Is that it?" Peem said.

"No, we have other people walking around with concerned looks." Bix noticed a BlackBerry lying on a side table in the corner, next to the couch, half hidden behind Peem, and he saw a wire running from it to the ground. "Personally, I'm looking for a loose extension cord and any bozo or bozos who may be responsible for it." He knelt down next to the side table and followed the wire to its logical conclusion. There he found, below the outlet where the BlackBerry was plugged-in, lying on the floor between the table and the couch, lifeless, a thick extension cord with a three-pronged plug and large strand of masking tape wrapped around it on which something had been written with a Sharpie in large black letters. Bix pulled it out and read it aloud. "Do Not Unplug!"

It was better than a stiff cup of coffee for Bix. Ten thousand cc's of pure, uncut, unadulterated, demon delight.

"This is why you traveled halfway across the country." Bix held up the cord where the words, so carefully labeled by the contractor, could be read clearly.

"Shit," Peem said.

"Mind if I unplug your BlackBerry and plug this back in, or are you not finished recharging?"

"Shit. Plug it back in."

"'Cause I can leave your BlackBerry plugged in if it's not completely recharged," Bix said.

"Fuck you, plug it in," Peem said.

"Next time you want to talk with someone far away," Bix said, "remember that we have telephone machines on our desks now, as I'm sure you must have on yours back at Headquarters. You don't have to leave the office to talk to other people any more." Bix turned and plugged in the extension cord, rose slowly, and walked out into the hallway to watch the scene for a minute before going back into the Staff Hold.

Out in the gymnasium where the action was happening, spot lights and sound feed sprang to life. Television cameras that could once only see dimly could now both see and hear, as could the consumers of their live transmissions. This was propitious, as Senator Curley was completing the last two sentences of his remarks: "I offer my unwavering support and endorsement. Permission to come aboard." After he said it he turned, gave an informal salute, then the two shook hands. It was TV magic. It was *the* sound bite. It was *the* video clip.

The audience erupted in applause once again.

It was the kind of moment that a less experienced Advance man could have taken as a sign that he led a charmed existence, and although Bix took no solace from knowing it was dumb luck, he enjoyed the occasion nonetheless.

JD came bounding back into the Staff Hold searching for Bix, the corners of his mouth extending to his ear lobes. "Did you see that? The press got the ending, and it was perfect. What did you do? Hi, Bob, when did you get here?"

"Hi, JD, didn't you see me? I just rolled in with Senator Curley."

"No, I didn't. I didn't know you were coming."

"No one did," Bix said.

"Ah. So. Bix, did you find a cord disconnected back here?"

It was a tough decision for Bix whether to take the high road, do the noble thing and not "out" Peem to JD in hopes that Peem would be grateful for the gesture and get off Bix's back, or do the petty thing, spill the beans and make Peem look like an idiot. He opted for petty. Peem had surprised him by sending Drule and then surprised him by showing up himself, and Bix disliked surprises, having picked up the prejudice by osmosis from the Secret Service.

"Old Bob decided it was more important to recharge his cell phone than for the national media to be able to hear our event and broadcast it live to hundreds of thousands of viewers. What is truly remarkable is that he flew thousands of miles out of his way to accomplish this," Bix said.

"Bahhhhhhhb, did you do that?" JD asked.

"I didn't know it was one of your extension cords. It's like…the gymnasium is fifty or sixty feet from here. What are you doing running extension cords all the way over here?" he said, balking at the concept of personal responsibility.

"Bahhhhhhhb, you pulled our plug, didn't you?" JD was nearly as incensed and pleased as Bix. "The one marked 'Do Not Unplug' with a big exclamation mark at the end? That's not very collegial now is it? I thought we were all on the same team here."

"Look, I apologize, what can I say?"

"'Goodbye' would be a good start," JD said.

Bix laughed out loud. "Good suggestion, JD. Go on back out there and make sure nothing else goes wrong and I'll stay here and make sure Bob doesn't touch anything." He wasn't about to let Peem off the hook.

JD left to stand next to the sound board in the gym, near Kate and Cornelia, and listen to the remainder of The Candidate's remarks. At Bix's request, he also kept an eye on Mayor Bacon in the balcony.

Once they were alone, Bix challenged Peem. "Robert, you do understand that sometimes we need electricity to power all of those electrical thingamabobs you see out there in the gym and that sometimes we have to go to extremes to find it in a building that was built when Grover Cleveland was president? Did you travel all the way here just to sabotage my event, or were there more items on your agenda?"

"We are concerned about the political situation down here and about the situation with Jamir Parviz, and I thought I'd come check it out myself, that's all."

"Is that the royal 'we'?"

"What?"

"Nothing. I have two suggestions. Number one, as we speak, Mayor Bacon, who I assume is the 'political situation' to which you refer, is upstairs in the viewing gallery. If you are concerned about him, go up there and talk. He would be honored, and we need him to remain off of his cell phone until we reach Scepter College. And B, I leave the Jamir issue to you. When he arrives at the college, he's all yours."

"That's the thing," Peem attempted to glower. "I had to find out from Sophie that she was bringing Parviz to our rally in Scepter and bringing a copy of the manifesto. Why the fuck do I have to find out from Sophie and not you, and who the fuck gave you the authority to expose us to that? And who the fuck gave you the authority to put Bacon in the limo?" Peem decided, two steps after Bix, that the best defense was a good offense.

"Robert, the only reason you're using that kind of language is you know I can't hang up on you in person, so, for starters, fuck you back, and the Gulfstream you rode in on. The reason Sophie had to tell you about bringing Jamir to Scepter is that you don't check your fucking messages, which I left for you at two a.m. and three a.m., informing you what I was doing."

"I didn't get those."

"Because you haven't checked your voicemails."

Peem shrugged.

Bix stayed on message. "And lastly, *you* gave me the authority. You said 'make this thing go away.' I assumed you intended for me to do it ethically, and not 'make this thing go away' like, say, Rambo. Ask yourself the question: Other than showing the evidence, *how* do I make this thing go away? Doing nothing isn't an option. That allows Dick O'Malley to dominate the news cycle for a day or two, even if the story dies quickly from lack of support. Tell me, what would the *big* brains at Headquarters have recommended, unless of course you don't know who they are?"

The question triggered Peem's most basic insecurity. "Where the fuck do you get off talking like that? I can still *fucking* fire you."

"That doesn't answer my question," Bix said, his delivery flat as paper. "As far as firing me, I've never said this to anyone in a position of authority, but I'm going to say it to you. I dare you. I double dare you. I double dare you with a fucking cherry on top." There was not a hint of emotion in it.

Kate walked into the Staff Hold as Bix ended his tirade. "Now, boys, are tempers wearing thin? Do we need to brush up on our Dale Carnegie?"

"Hi, Kate. No, we're fine," Peem said.

"Yes, Kate," Bix said, "Bob threatened to use the immense power in which he is cloaked to terminate my employment, but we're fine."

"Bob, I heard you pulled the plug on us, which is what caused our live TV feeds to miss the first, like, I don't know, *twenty* minutes of Senator Curley's remarks," Kate said sarcastically. "Mightn't firing Bix appear like an asshole thing to do after that? As much as you *think* you know about the situation here, you haven't been here and we have. Isn't that why you sent us?"

"Yeah, what she said," Bix said, still savoring the situation's entertainment value.

"I'm not here to interfere unless I see something happening that I can fix," Peem said.

"Go fix the mayor upstairs," Bix said. "Honor *him* with your presence. We wouldn't be jumping through these hoops if you guys had let me promise him that we'd visit his senior center before the primary."

"We couldn't promise that," Peem said. "And what would the optics of that be exactly? Everyone knows he supports our Opponent."

"We could have contextualized the optics," Bix said. "Now I have to work with an irritated, all-powerful county boss who does not like being challenged on anything, any time, and hasn't had *any* practice at it lately. The last forty-eight hours have been shock treatment for the poor man. Why don't you go stroke him?"

"If you tell me everything is under controlthen I believe you. I don't need to get in the way."

"Your coy reticence would be adorable on a nineteen-year-old coquette, Bob," Bix chided, "but it's particularly unattractive in a campaign manager. And you're being rather selective about what constitutes a political situation down here. I'm *not* telling you everything is under control with the mayor, and you know it. If you would like to mitigate any political damage our Advance and our Candidate's quest for the presidency have caused, go talk with him for thirty minutes. Perhaps then your visit to South Carolina will have had some value. There's a young lady named Miranda sitting with him now, but she could use your help."

"There is no way I'm getting stuck with that guy for *five* minutes much less thirty," Peem said.

"Make it fifteen minutes," Bix said.

"No way."

"Then sit here and please don't touch anything," Bix said.

"How far is it to Scepter College from here?" Peem asked.

"A half hour drive," Bix said. "If you want to go ahead of us, Curley's friend will have to drive you. We don't have a spare car. If you want to go in the motorcade with us, you can ride in Staff 1."

"Is Senator Curley riding in the limo from here to the college?"

"I haven't heard yet. It's the boss's prerogative to invite him."

"Yeah, right, unless you decide it first," Peem said.

"If the good senator threatened to fuck us to death at the next event if he didn't ride in the car, I'd put him in the car. If he wanted to bring his pet boa constrictor, I'd give it an 'S' pin and hold the door for it. And while we're at it, the boss is running for President of the United States, not President of the Vestal Virgins Society. Every once in a while, he might have to interact with one of the great unwashed for more than forty seconds. He knows all politics is local. Well, this was local, but it affected my ability to produce a national media event. Right now I have another national media event to conclude. I have to go snatch *success* from the jaws of the guy who came down here to make sure everything was OK. Don't touch anything."

Bix's aversion to more conversation with Peem was so acute as to cause him to go back into the gym and listen to The Candidate's remarks. Standing next to JD, Kate, and Cornelia at the rear of the room, Kate whispered, "Peem came down here looking for trouble."

"That was my impression, too," Bix whispered.

"By the way, you should know the traveling press have heard that Dick O'Malley will be at the rally in Scepter, and they know he's doing his program live. They're asking about the manifesto."

"How much interest is there at this point?"

"On a scale of one to ten," Kate said, "I'd say it's a five. There is interest, but they know it's a 'Mystery Date,' and they know O'Malley is all over it. It isn't occupying a lot of RAM on anyone's hard drive yet."

"Perfect, thank you. Please let me know if they begin circling in the water, hopefully never," Bix said. "Some interest is good, however."

"Roger that."

Bix summoned JD out into the hallway, asked him to go upstairs and stand near the agent who was standing post in the viewing gallery, look official, and keep Bacon from moving after The Candidate finished his remarks. "Bacon is going to want to get up and leave when our guys are working the rope line. Keep him seated and incommunicado until we're ready to move. Try to look serious, and stick your earpiece back in. That squiggly wire is the best credibility you have. Hopefully he won't notice that you and I are wearing the same hard pin."

"What happens if he asks me if I'm a Secret Service agent?" JD said.

"Ask him, 'Why? Do you want to touch my gun?'"

"What if says yes?"

"Tell him you'll show him in the men's room."

* * *

Despite working the rope line longer than usual, The Candidate finished shaking hands with the audience of veterans and escaped to the sanctuary of Hold, where Peem was waiting for him, long before Senator Curley was ready to stop glad-handing. Curley had not been on the presidential campaign trail for over three years and the man was *fresh*.

Silently counting every second, The Candidate waited with the appearance of patience while his new BFF tarried in the gym with "his people" and Bix briefed him on the rally in Scepter. Two agents stood post in the hall outside the open door.

"Are you inviting Senator Curley to ride in the limo?" Bix asked him.

"I think it would be poor form not to. He's come a long way to endorse me. What's the deal with Bacon's senior center? Am I going to have to go tour this place?"

Peem was already taking up space in the Hold and Bix thought it was a perfect time to invite him to do his duty. "Not if you strongly suggest to your campaign manager that he should go upstairs and introduce himself to the mayor and then escort him down to the motorcade when we call. It would be the least he could do, considering." He left it at that.

"Considering what?" The Candidate astutely observed.

Bix attempted to maneuver him into a conspiracy. "Considering Bob has come all this way at the last minute because of his concern for the local political situation, it would be edifying for him to have a conversation with Mayor Bacon, wouldn't you agree, Senator? I mean, *you* had to take one for the team. I think it's the least Bob could do, don't you? He could even ride in the VIP van over to the college with the mayor and his lovely bride. He'll enjoy Paula Bacon, don't you agree?"

The Candidate willingly accepted the opportunity to pimp Peem, seeing as how it was the manly thing to do. "Yes, I agree. You'll enjoy Mrs. Bacon, Bob, and you'll learn a lot from the mayor. You should ride with him to the college."

"You don't want me in the limo with Senator Curley?" Peem asked.

"I'll be fine. You go with Mayor Bacon." The Candidate was clearly enjoying it.

"It's a long drive," Peem pointed out, hoping the blunt trauma of it would cause him to rethink his impulsive joke.

"How long?" The Candidate asked.

"Bix said it's a half hour. Isn't that correct?"

Bix was stuck. The length of time The Candidate was going to be exposed, un-aided, to Senator Curley mattered. "Approximately. Maybe a little faster in the motorcade with police escort." A little faster was irrelevant. A half hour was approximately twenty-nine minutes too long.

"All right, you come with us," The Candidate told Peem.

It took almost ten minutes for Kate and Cornelia to load the press after Senator Curley completed his comeback tour along the twenty foot-long expanse of rope line, throughout which Miranda kept talking to Mayor and Mrs. Bacon. Jay-Dee continued to stand post even after the real Secret Service agent had left, and Bix forced Peem to accompany him up to the viewing gallery for a few precious moments with the mayor, if only to give Miranda a break for a while. At the appointed time, JD and Miranda escorted the Bacons downstairs to the motorcade and into the white, twelve-passenger, American-made van marked "VIP Guest" on the windshield, back window, and two side windows. Its place in the motorcade was seven vehicles removed from the limo because Bix, ever cautious, had asked Freeway to add a Staff II van, although it was unclear whether they would need it because it pushed the VIP van back one slot farther away from the object of Mayor Bacon's attention.

Bacon inquired another time before JD closed the van door behind him. "Can I turn on my phone now?"

JD had donned his sunglasses when they walked outdoors. They looked too "California" to be real Special Agent sunglasses, but they were sunglasses, and they blocked Bacon's view of his eyeballs. He leaned into the van. "Sorry sir. Not in the motorcade. We've got enough electronics in this motorcade to fry it and your brain." No one asked him to explain the physics and Bacon was sufficiently cowed. Miranda started talking again immediately. JD closed the door.

It was Bix's cue to move the protectee and his special invitee "ride-alongs," Senator Curley and a smiling Peem, to the limo. As they walked, Peem moved up next to Bix, which was disturbing. Bix sensed another dialogue.

"I heard from Drule that you kidnapped him to iguana-town this morning and that he'll be late as a result," Peem said.

Bix could look truly perplexed, with good cause. "Iguana-town? Is that what you said? What are you talking about? I understand the 'kid-napped' part and the 'late' part, but not the 'iguana-town' reference."

"Drule wants me to fire you on the spot. You're batting a thousand on this trip."

"You're not the first one to tell me that." Bix said. "Why don't we talk when we get to the college. You have a nice ride with your two senators. I know you'll be the belle of the ball." It bought him another half hour of peace.

He walked away to take his place in the back seat of the large, comfortable for a change State Patrol Crown Victoria that served as Lead Marked car, and do some business on the phone while Peem did his thing, whatever that was, in the limo, and Miranda chatted up the Bacons non-stop in the VIP van.

He greeted his car-mates, Captain Contarini of the South Carolina Highway Patrol, SAIC Farrow, who sat in the back seat with Bix, and Shane, who was sitting in the front passenger seat.

As the motorcade pulled away Shane turned to Bix. "No surprises, to your knowledge?"

"No surprises yet," Bix said. "I'll ask my cohorts in crime. Have you heard from the agent you sent to the senior center to check it out?"

"Not yet. He'll arrive in another few minutes. He's meeting Chief Fry there." Shane said. "Have you heard from your guy?"

"I asked our Site II, Ben Oliver, to go over there to Advance it. I'll call him."

Bix first called Mike to tell him the motorcade had departed en route to Scepter. "How does it look?"

"It looks awesome," Mike said, "and you know I think that word is over-used. There have to be twenty-five thousand people inside and at least another five thousand people outside the mag's, probably more. There will still be a lot of people who haven't gotten in by the time you arrive."

"I'll tell Merle," he said. It was code for, "We'll get The Candidate to request that the magnetometers be opened and the remainder allowed in, unscreened," which would have sounded snotty if his car mates, all law enforcement officers, were listening, and they couldn't help but listen. "How about our greeters?" he asked.

"Greeters from the college are in place, but I haven't seen anyone from the campaign. I thought Shaunesy might bring the few that he had name-checked for the arrival before he ambushes us with his galloping horde."

"Let it ride," Bix said. "If he doesn't show up, he doesn't. If he does, let him know that you know he's got a large group waiting in the wings, and it might not be a great idea to show up with them later."

"If I see him, I'll tell him."

"I'll call you at Bravo," Bix said.

"Ten four," Mike replied.

Bix turned to Shane. "Mike tells me there are twenty-five thousand people inside and at least another five thousand outside, slowed no doubt by the lack of two mag's which didn't arrive."

"I heard about that," Shane said.

Bix made the call to Ben, who took an eternity to answer, giving Bix a slight case of heartburn. "Ben, how does it look at the senior center?" he asked ambiguously.

"The second bus has left and we are almost finished with the third. I may be able to get everyone into the third bus if I push hard enough. They will be out of here in a couple minutes."

"Anyone squawking?" Bix said.

Shane looked back at Bix and gave him the Sherlock Holmes once-over.

"There are a few who don't want to come along, but no one's squawking."

"Yeah, I heard you're promising them free drinks."

Shane looked at him strangely again.

"Damn, Mike told you," Ben said. "Yes, frozen margaritas and mojitos. I don't even know what a frozen mojito is, but hey, it sounds good. Then Kate and Cornelia can use the machines for the press lunch after."

"It sounds great. Do you have your tarp ready if anyone keels over from virgin mojitos?"

"I've got it."

"Good Advance, Ben. Good job."

"Is this really good Advance or a criminal conspiracy?" Ben asked.

"You gave them credentials, didn't you?"

"Yes."

"Well, then, it's official."

"We made the credentials at Kinkos."

"That's official."

"Just asking."

"Speaking of official, you can expect to see Chief Fry any minute. Be prepared."

"I was a Boy Scout."

"I could tell without asking," Bix said. "Call me when you're done."

Bix hung up and looked at Shane. "My guy just got there and to his surprise there isn't a soul in the place. It's a ghost town. Tumbleweeds." He made no attempt to contain a laugh.

"Does that have anything to do with the availability of free drinks elsewhere in town?" Shane asked.

"Hey, Shane, when you live in a desert you've got to go where there's water."

"Water?"

"That, too, if they want. Chilled."

"So you're calling it? No OTR to the Bacon Senior Center?"

"I'm calling it. If no one's there, why go? You can call the Detail Leader and tell him to tell the boss, who I'm certain will agree with me. I'll inform the mayor when we arrive."

"Better you than me." Shane smiled a cautious smile, looked at his watch, called the detail leader to report that the senior center was empty and the OTR was DOA, and called his site agent to tell him to go to the College of Scepter.

Bix held his breath and prayed, in his way, that the abduction would be complete by the time Chief Fry arrived. There was nothing more he could do to influence the outcome.

Moving to the next drama on his agenda, he surreptitiously changed into his International Advance Man of Intrigue (IAMI) guise and called Sophie for an update on their progress. The ancillary conversation among Bix and his car mates was convivial, disarming almost, but as an IAMI, he had to guard his words. It was at that moment he realized he'd read too much Ian Fleming as a child and drunk too many shaken martinis as a young adult.

Sophie fumbled with the phone after accepting his call, during which time Bix could hear the sounds of an automobile traveling and eventually Sophie's voice in the distance projecting over the noise, "I'm giving the phone to Hani."

"Hello, Bix, it's Hani. Sophie is driving and we are having a very enjoyable time."

"This wasn't supposed to be fun. Are you going on a picnic?"

"No, we are on our way to Scepter. Everything is fine. Jamir found a copy of the article that he and you-know-who wrote, and we are on our way to meet you. Sophie?" Hani turned to her and spoke so Bix could hear. "How long until we arrive in Scepter?"

She spoke loudly, "A little over an hour."

"She says we will be there in a little over an hour," Hani said.

"How does Jamir look?" Bix said.

"You can ask him yourself. I'll hand him the phone."

The next voice Bix heard was Jamir's. "Bix, hi. What did you want to ask me?"

"I wanted to know how you look."

"I look like a Republican. Does that work?"

"As long as it isn't Elizabeth Dole I'm good with it. Any problems?"

"None, really. Abia and I passed a large van that must have been the Max News people you told us about. They flashed their lights at us like they wanted us to stop, but I drove by and kept moving. Abia has a BMW. They had no chance of catching us."

"You made it home safely?"

"Yes, but not very long after we arrived the same van drove up and parked outside our house. Abia's car was parked in the garage. They cannot have known whether we were at home."

"What did you do?"

"We were trapped. We couldn't go out without being seen. We were hoping they would get tired of waiting and go away in the time it took me to shave and find that article, but they didn't. When Hani and Sophie called and told me they were a half an hour away, I told them to meet me at a market two blocks away from my house and I snuck out the back door and through some neighbors' yards. That is how we connected."

"Exciting," Bix said, "and you got some exercise."

Jamir laughed. "That would have been the best part, but I am wearing a suit and did not need the exercise."

"Thank you for going to all of this trouble," Bix said. "Hopefully it will be worth it, and you can go back to growing your beard tomorrow. By five o'clock in the evening, you'll be sporting a full one again."

"Abia said to say thank you again for that. She tells me I can't grow it back."

"Thank Dick O'Malley and Max News. If it were up to me she'd still be out in the woods enjoying her privacy and hating your facial hair.

While I have you, Jamir, can I ask about the manifesto? What is it, and why does it have the Young Republicans at Stearns U riled-up?"

"It isn't a manifesto," Jamir said. "It's an article we wrote entitled 'Manifesto of Misperceptions' about U.S.-Iran relations, and how ignorance of each other's cultures and intentions is driving so much of both country's foreign policies. It was printed in an alternative college newspaper, and we didn't use our real names because I was worried about my family members who were still in Iran. I didn't want them blamed for something I wrote that might offend the ayatollah."

"How did you sign it?"

"We co-wrote it as 'The Great Satan' and 'Jihad Joe,' playing off stereotypes.

"No wonder no one could find it. What's the date?"

"February 16, 1981."

"What does it look like? I mean, is it old, yellowed, wrinkled, tattered? Is it a flat version of me?" Bix said.

"I have a copy of our original. It looks like it was typed on a typewriter in 1981, and the paper looks old but it's not in bad shape. Why?"

"I would like to make copies for the press, and I'm thinking we should make color copies to capture as much of its ancient-ness as possible."

"That's a good idea," Jamir said. "If we pass a place where we can make color copies, we'll stop. How many do you need?"

"Thirty copies should be enough. They're primarily for the traveling press." Bix thought about what he'd said for an instant. "You know, you really don't have to do that. We can send someone to make copies when you get here."

"We will be happy to stop. It isn't a big deal," Jamir said.

"To me, it's a big deal. I'm sending a college professor who is a former high-ranking State Department official, the deputy foreign minister of an important U.S. ally, and the executive assistant to our campaign manager out to make copies. It feels like power to me."

That got Shane's attention. He looked at Bix oddly once again but squelched his investigatory instincts.

"Be certain you use it wisely, my friend," Jamir said, "and always for good."

"Let me get back to you on the wise and good thing. I may have to tell you to go home," Bix said.

Shane looked over again, seemingly concerned.

"I'm making the Secret Service nervous, Jamir. I should go. Please ask Sophie to call me when you are a few minutes away from the college and tell her to look for Freeway. He'll meet you at the security perimeter and show you where to park then bring you in."

Having exposed his car mates to the conversation, Bix felt he owed them an explanation. "In case you're wondering, gentlemen, we will be visited today by an old friend of the senator's who is accompanied by Bob Peem's A.A., Sophie, and the old friend's brother-in-law, who happens to be a government official from another country."

"What country?" Shane said.

"Uuuuuh, it's located east of 35 degrees east longitude on a map. Does that help?"

"Not really."

"I can vouch for him, I know him personally and they're here at the request of the campaign."

"As long as you escort them," Shane said.

"Either me or someone with a staff pin will be with them at all times."

"We're good then. By the way, we are coming up on the county line. Chief Fry should be waiting for us up ahead. He wanted to lead us once we were in Scepter County," Shane said.

"And you let him?" Bix asked.

"We know the way," Shane said, and smiled.

Bix watched ahead with interest. Chief Fry's appearance at the county line could signal "mission accomplished," at the senior center, unless Ben was in the back seat of his car in handcuffs, in which case it could signal something completely different.

"I have to ask," said Shane. "I'm assuming you evacuated the senior center. How did you do it?"

"We offered them a better party than the one the mayor offered, along with a ride there and back, that's all."

"That's why you wanted the mayor off his cell phone," Shane said.

SAIC Farrow observed candidly, "He's going to be hotter than a whore house on nickel night when he turns it back on. He'll have a hundred messages waiting."

"A," Bix said, "we will have achieved our common goal of *not* going to the senior center, and two, he'll be angry at first, but I will bet you my nickel that he lightens up by the time we leave."

"Good luck with that," Shane said. "He can still cause you a lot of trouble. You're plunking him down in the middle of dozens of local and national newsies. If he's pissed off, he might say something."

Bix smiled. "I'd better get him to lighten up quickly."

"That will be a neat trick."

Chief Fry was waiting in his cruiser on a gravel road not three feet from the Scepter County line as the motorcade passed. Bix spotted the car, pivoted in his seat for a longer look and was relieved not to see any perp's in the back seat.

Once the motorcade passed, Chief Fry turned on his emergency lights, threw his gear shift into Drive, spun his wheels on the gravel and sped off to catch it.

"That butthole is going pass the entire motorcade on this little two lane highway," Shane said. "Where did he get his training?"

"At the Close Cover Before Striking Correspondence College of Law Enforcement Knowledge, followed by post-graduate work in the Brother-in-Law Academy," Bix said.

Fry waved as he passed the Lead Marked car and kept movin'. "He has to be going ninety," Shane said. He then instructed Captain Contarini, their wheelman, to maintain his speed no matter how fast Chief Fry went."

The chief eventually settled in fifty yards ahead of the Lead car and kept his position, proudly displaying an artistic array of emergency lights in hues of purple, green, and white. Bix, having lost confidence in his ability to identify colors, asked SAIC Farrow, "Am I seeing that correctly? Do those look odd to you?"

"They sure do," he said, "but he's a city chief. He can do whatever he wants."

"It's like a Christmas tree vomited on his car," Bix said.

He was an appreciative audience, as were Shane and Contarini, which was Bix's intention—he wanted a few more chits in the "Bank of Cooperation and Good Humor." It was important to have them on his side because, just minutes hence, "amusing Bix" would become "bad guy Bix" when he planned to have their magnetometers shut down, allowing the remaining crowd to pour in dirty. Dirty crowds always made unhappy agents.

Bix looked out to see Chief Fry making a left turn onto Highway Road T, the wrong direction for a motorcade headed to Scepter College but the right direction if it was headed for the Bacon Senior Center.

Shane strained forward in his seatbelt and stared. "Where the hell is he going now?"

"He wants us to follow him to the Bacon Center," Bix said.

"You're right. He expects us to follow him. He can't be that dumb."

"Nah, you're right, he can't be," Bix said.

"What an idiot. I ought to arrest the son-of-a-bitch."

"For what?" Bix said.

"For taking up space on the planet, or breathing air that could be put to better use by someone else."

It was turning into an amusement ride, and Bix knew it had reached its apogee before the inevitable two hundred foot vertical drop. "If Mayor Bacon saw that, and I think Mayor Bacon probably saw that, he *just* found out that we aren't going to his senior center. Oh my god, poor Miranda, what have I done to her? What's he going to do? The horror."

Shane offered encouragement. "I bet it's not pretty back there in the guest van right about now."

"Should we stop and, like, run to her aid?" Bix said.

"It's too late now," Shane said. "Whatever was going to happen has probably already happened, and if it hasn't, it probably won't. Besides that, his wife's in the van. I assume that's why you invited her."

"The dame's got class, I give her that. Her presence will calm the savage breast."

"Don't you mean 'beast'?"

"No, but that, too."

"You think he'll be calm when we arrive?"

"Not necessarily, but I have a Plan B, and after that I've got a Plan C. After that, I always have ritual suicide."

"That will be interesting to witness," Shane said. The other two occupants agreed.

* * *

It was not a mayor but a human dance inferno in a scruffy tan suit that exited the VIP van at Scepter College. It was a barrel on stilts hopping up and down in short successive beats, doing his utmost to keep his composure, spitting small curses under his breath, turning on his cell phone the instant his feet hit the ground and holding it up to his ear while it cycled through its power-up.

Mike Pitcher was at the arrival point, the door of the limo, watching his five out-of-state union boys fifty yards down-motorcade splay out a temporary, movable, walking rope line. They would prevent anyone from the back end of the motorcade, specifically the VIP van, from walking up to the front, and reinforced a hard line of metal barricade directly from the VIP van to the door of McBride Hall.

Once Bacon entered McBride Hall, he couldn't turn back. He could no longer access secured areas where The Candidate was insulated from danger, or return to the motorcade. McBride Hall was out of the view of press or public view, and Storie would be on-hand to swoop him into her attentive care and distract him all the way to the VVIP area.

After Bacon entered McBride Hall, it would be one less concern on Bix's checklist. Before he entered McBride Hall he could cause a nasty scene where the press might see him, or maneuver to reach The Candidate with an inside run straight up past the motorcade on the opposite side. Either of these would be preferable to causing a scene directly in front of the press, who were camped out just a hundred yards away waiting for news to occur. While they expected to be covering a rally, they would have been more than content with news of a large angry local mayor/county boss having a meltdown.

Immediately inside the Admin building, President Gerta Gilliman waited with her greeting party of eight college luminaries, including the chairman of the Board of Regents, who stood holding a handsome tan leather doctor-style valise, embossed with the College of Scepter logo, to present as a welcoming gift.

They were gracious and welcoming and well behaved, due in some measure to the presence of overwhelming authority. As educators they understood the concept of maintaining order in the classroom and caused no trouble and attempted no OTRs of their own. Gerta could not help but blurt an invitation to drop by the reception she was holding for college VIPs after the rally. The Candidate graciously told her he was at the mercy of the schedule that day and he thanked them for their gift, organized a group photo as the college photographer snapped away, and then followed Bix and Mike, or pushed them to move on, always with his contingent of mobile Secret Service agents, past the official greeters to the event that awaited.

Mike briefed Bix as they led The Candidate, Senator Curley, Peem, Moss, and Peaches to the Holding Room, where Bix turned around immediately to go back outside. "Brief the boss," Bix said to Mike "I'll be back in a couple of minutes." On his way out, he asked Merle to wait before going outside to check the site. "Give me two minutes and then we'll go with Mike to look at things. We still need a few minutes for the press to set up."

It was time to face the music. Bix walked out of the Admin building, past the agents standing post and the clumps of agents and cops and dogs and paramilitary, down-motorcade to take his beating from Bacon, who would have found out the total truth, the whole scam, by that time. Bacon had not entered McBride Hall. He was standing outside, halfway between the motorcade and the building, screaming into his cell phone, attended by his wife, Miranda, and a phalanx of very tastefully attired young labor union members spread out and holding a long piece of heavy duty rope to guard against the possibility of a mayor who might attempt to lurch. It was almost high noon, literally and metaphorically, and Bix was Gary Cooper.

Or Cooper-ish, because Cooper didn't have Miranda, and Mrs. Bacon, and Storie, and clumps of law enforcement officials, to protect him.

Bacon spotted Bix only after Bix had closed within a few yards, and he pounced verbally, like a tiger that had been startled, but thankfully had also been chained to a post. This particular tiger did not abide constraints of any kind, and the situation was not only especially constraining, it was humiliating for good measure. It was more than he could tolerate. He exploded at Bix.

"You son-of-a-bitch," he said, his diction perfect, as Bix looked down on him, remaining emotionless. "I see youah fuckin' goons heah with that rope tryin' to tie me in an' keep me from goin' anywayah, an' Ah know what youah did with ma senia centa. You Nawthenahs come down heah an' think you can fuck with us but this is wheah we live boah, an' this is ma caountah. Ah'm gonna see to it that you pay foah this. Youah boah ain't gonna win Sceptah Caountah, Ah can tell youah that riate now. An' weah may take the whole o'the state a'South Carolina with us."

It was Bix's moment of decision. Was it apologize and retreat or was it attack? Bix needed to resolve the situation in thirty seconds, and reasoned the mayor wouldn't respect him if he backed down. "Now wait a minute Mr. Mayor," Bix inched closer to him, "these perfectly handsome young men are not goons. He looked around at them and shouted, "ARE YOU?" up and down the rope line. "ARE YOU GOONS?"

"*Noooooooo*," was their response.

Bix continued his polite harassment. "And before you get your freaking undies in a bunch, you don't have one clue what I did to your senior center, not one clue in the world! Do you?"

It created doubt in the mayor's mind, the pause that asks, "What does he know that I don't?"

Bix blathered on. "Why don't you check your hostility at the door and go find out what you don't know. Right out there." He pointed to the door of McBride Hall. "And guess what, if you still hate us, the national press is right out there, too. You can tell them directly. You can wait two freaking minutes, can't you?"

"Boah, youah pushin' youah luck."

Storie had inched outside of McBride Hall, where she had been watching from afar, to a place where she could hear but stand unseen behind the shrubbery. Bix saw her and shot her a quick nod, found inspiration in her smile and decided to amp up the theatrics.

"No, sir," Bix said, "I'm not pushing my luck, because you're the man, but you used to fight the man, but now you *are* the man. So what kind of man are you going to be?" It was complete nonsense, gibberish. Storie stifled her laugh. "Give me two lousy minutes, *then* you can bust my chops, or are you the man that you always hated, the man you always fought against?" Bix didn't wait for an answer. "Miranda, please escort Mayor and Mrs. Bacon to our VIP section. Mr. Mayor, I will meet you there after I get this rally underway."

Storie scurried back inside, surprised the Bacons when they saw her there in enemy territory, and accompanied them through the building, through the great hall to an exit on the south side where they could see part of the crowd and hear all of the noise, which was loud. With the aid of speakers the size of buses blasting from carefully mapped locations, the Scepter College Quickly-Cobbled-Together Marching Band played in the distance from the opposite side of the crowd, between two buildings on the crest of a hill in front of the far-off "First Amendment Area" and nearly thirty-thousand people filled the Green in front of old Administration Building. The crowd required no amplification.

As they followed the walkway through a rope and stanchion chute to the VIP area, Mayor Bacon had to yell to be heard, which fit his mood, which was irritated. Distracted by Storie's sudden appearance, he was suitably impressed, but deterred only slightly. "Young ladah, how in the wahld did ya'll find yoah way intah this den a'criminals?" he roared. "I wouldn't expect yuah to be keepin' sech compny."

Paula Bacon interceded. "Eugene, be kahnd. They ah ouah guests whahl they ah heah." Her voice cracked slightly at the higher decibel level.

"Yes, deah." The mayor said the words but could not suppress his state of physical agitation.

"Why, you invited me, don't you remember?" Storie said. "You said, 'You ought to come along and watch this rally that your opponent is having in my town,' and I said I'd be here."

"Ah remembah the convasashun, but I didn't believe youah be able ta jes show up," he shouted.

"When I told them you invited me, they couldn't say no," Storie hollered back.

"Yes, Ah think theah may be moah to it than that."

Paula again felt the need to express restraint. "Eugene, be kahnd."

The mayor tried to repress himself. He talked as he walked and twitched in anger, his eyes darting from Storie to sidewalk and back every two seconds. "In case yoah friends with anah of those boahs with yoah opponent's Advance team," he told her, "Ah'm about to show them who runs things heah in Scepta Caountah. That Bix boah cannot come in heah and get away with takin' advantage of my good naycha. Weah gonna see who makes the news t'day. Yoah kin tell yoah friend Bix that he has failed, and he done so igno*min*iously."

"How did he do that, Mr. Mayor? By doing his job?" Storie said.

The question stumped him. He "harumped" as he walked the path, grumbling to himself. Storie looked back at Paula Bacon, who smiled and said nothing. She was finished raising her voice.

The happy little crew, including Miranda, who walked a few feet behind out of spleen-venting range, rounded the last tall shrub and entered the bike-rack reinforced, specially secured, close-up seating: VVIP-land, where new surprises awaited.

* * *

Sophie and her group were still a half hour away from Scepter when she called Bix, who answered as he walked briskly back from the scene of the showdown in front of McBride Hall. "Hi, Bix," she said. "I'm a little perplexed."

"Great," he thought.

"Hi, Sophie," he said, "I don't like it when you're perplexed, because you're one of the least perplexed people I know." Up to that moment he was beginning to feel good. So far everyone had survived. But the good feelings felt by a neurotic Advance man could be swept away with little more than a "Bix, I'm a little perplexed" when the right person said it.

She followed up with, "I'm not sure what I should do here."

Bix looked around to see if anyone could hear his conversation, although it would have been difficult to eavesdrop on the fastest moving object among all of the animate things in secured area. He had stepped back inside the Admin building when he asked, "What's the problem, Sophie?"

"Peem just called me and told me to take my time getting to Scepter."

"OK, that's news. Did he explain why?" Bix asked.

"He said they weren't sure it was a good idea to bring Jamir to the rally."

"By 'they,' did he mean our boss and him?"

"That is what I was led to believe."

"Did you tell him how good Jamir looks?"

"I did. I told him he looks like the spawn of Omar Sharif and Elizabeth Dole."

"He didn't care?"

"It went over his head," Sophie said. "He doesn't care anyway. They're worried about what he represents, not what he looks like."

"What does he represent?"

"He represents controversy, and you know how they feel about controversy."

"Yes, they recoil. Me, too, but Jamir represents a lack of controversy. On substance, he's a distinguished professor and former State Department official, and on cosmetics, he looks the part, so you come right ahead. Peem didn't tell you not to come. He told you to take your time. Well, you've taken your time. I will have Freeway meet you at the security perimeter on the south side of campus so he can show you where to park and escort you in."

"What if Peem calls back and tells me not to come at all?"

"Remind Bob that I didn't force Jamir to shave his well-earned beard only to tell him he isn't needed. If Peem can cite one political crisis in American history that has been resolved by hiding some or all of the facts, tell him you'll drive Jamir to Tahiti and drop him off there. By the way, is Jamir with you? Is he hearing all of this?"

"No, I'm in the ladies room in a gas station. I pulled over to call you in private after Peem called. You've convinced me. There is no reason not to come to Scepter. Jamir presents very well, and this manifesto is a big nothingburger."

"If Peem gives you any trouble, tell him you drove around as long as you could."

* * *

Back in Hold, Bix rounded up Merle and Mike for a quick walk-through. He darted a glance at Peem and said, "We'll talk once we get this thing off the ground."

"Merle, now's the time to ask the boss to ask the Detail Leader to open all the magnetometers and let the crowd in. We still have a few thousand people waiting outside because two of their mag's never showed up."

"That's a good enough reason for me," Merle said. He went over to The Candidate and spoke briefly. The Candidate beckoned Detail Leader Caputo, Caputo beckoned Shane, Shane spoke into his sleeve, and then the mag's were ordered open to any and all.

Mike, wearing a head-set with microphone to communicate with his contractors, led his Lead and the Trip Director out a covered doorway on the ground floor level of the Admin building. They walked through the buffer zone on the ground next to the catwalk, past a long line of linked bike racks forming a metal barricade to hold back the masses that pressed up against it, to a set of stairs directly to the stage, where their appearance sent a sudden ripple, then a roar, through the crowd of over thirty-five thousand enthusiastic souls. After modestly waving off the unintentional attention, they checked the lectern, the microphones, the angle of the teleprompters, the audio feed to the mult-box, and the appearance of the crowd, which was overwhelming.

It was a living organism, a great hulking monster stretching out several hundred yards in some places, its tentacles reaching out farther in others between buildings. It was eighty-thousand eyes and eight hundred-thousand teeth, breathing, undulating, joyful, and instantaneously uproarious with the least provocation, ablaze with American flags along the distant perimeter. Two official campaign banners, horizontal in nature, and hundreds of colorful hand-made poster-board signs all miraculously clustered within the areas that could be seen by television cameras. More than a dozen two- and three-foot-diameter helium balloons or various colors were tethered to the ground at irregular intervals and heights far out into the crowd, "to give a sense of perspective on-camera," Mike said. It was a Mike thing.

Looking out from the stage, the crowd became faceless after the first twenty-five yards, where the topography began to rise slightly, offering a good view for those who stood at a distance. Bix's eyes went quickly to his VIP section, tucked away nicely next to the press riser, separated by ten feet of lighting and mechanical equipment and nearly impossible for the press to see. There he spotted Mayor Bacon engulfed in adoring constituents and Storie standing nearby giving Bix a "thumbs-up." Bix had taken it upon himself to rename the VIP section, with appropriate signage, the "Mayor Eugene V. Bacon Senior Center VIPs." The large horizontal hand-made sign was all but invisible to the press or anyone outside the VIP area, but it was visibility for the good mayor and Bix had a hunch he would like it.

Behind the stage, five hundred people sat stacked on three twenty-foot long sections of twelve-foot tall bleachers built upon the cistern, comprising a steroid-enhanced version of the cookie-cutter visual demanded by Headquarters. While impressive, the real visual was beyond and above the heads of those seated in the bleachers.

Mike moved around to the side of Merle as he was sizing up the crowd from the podium. After first placing his hand over the microphone, he leaned in to Merle, saying, "Look behind you."

Merle turned around and saw, for the first time, their massive vertical banners soaring sky-high behind the bleachers in front of the Administration building. The forty-foot tall palmetto trees in off-white stood in perfect equipoise with the fluted limestone columns that framed each one. The last banner on the left was breathtaking, its upper quarter carrying the state's signature crescent moon with the three-foot tall word "Liberty" written within. The remaining three quarters of the banner was solid indigo.

In total, it was the perfect combination of art and political symbolism, colossally photogenic, instantly recognizable—or so Storie had told Bix, and he believed her.

Merle's eyes rose to the top, his jaw slackened, his mouth agape. He was almost unintelligible but he was eloquent. "That's the coolest thing I've ever seen."

"You're right, it is," Mike said. "It's our tribute to Mark Rothko."

"Who's that?" Merle said.

"Never mind, but if you say his name in front of the press they will think you're educated," Mike said.

"It's impressive, whoever it is," Merle said.

"Obviously, it was Bix's idea," Mike said.

"And Mike's execution, so to speak," Bix said.

"Only if I screwed it up," Mike said.

Merle was appropriately astounded. "It's magnificent. It has the Bix touch all over it."

"I washed my hands first," Bix said.

"As you always do," Merle noted.

"If you gentlemen are satisfied," Mike said, "Kate tells me the press are set up and ready to go, and our travelers are already suitably impressed."

"Let's start this thing," Bix said. "Is Ben with the sound guy?"

"He's waiting for my cue," Mike said.

"Let's go get the boss and Senator Curley," Bix said. "You are doing the off-stage announce, I assume."

"Be happy to," Mike said.

Retrieving The Candidate and his recent endorser from Hold, leaving behind Peem, Moss and Peaches, Bix brought his two principals to the exit door where Mike awaited with a hand microphone.

Ben was on alert outside to cue the entry music, another cacophony on the "approved music" CD from another briefly famous garage band, when he heard Mike's voice over the loud speakers.

Bix pulled an index card from his pocket and handed it to The Candidate. "Your call on this, but it may be advantageous to add this to your acknowledgments."

The Candidate examined it as if it might contain anthrax dust, and read it aloud softly.

"I would like to thank Mayor Eugene Bacon for his hospitality, and honor him for his years of courage and service to the citizens of Scepter County and the State of South Carolina. I respect his decision to remain neutral in this primary election, and not bring to bear his immense power and influence for any one of the candidates, and I know he will be a force for good for our party's eventual nominee, whichever one of us it is."

Bix waited to hear his reaction.

"Yeah, I can do that, or something close to it," he said.

It was then that Bix spoke. "Yeah, it's kind of ragged at the end, now that I hear it." It was good to show humility.

"I'll clean it up," The Candidate said.

Bix was certain he would, whether it was needed or not. He cued Mike.

"LADIES AND GENTLEMEN," Mike said, then paused for a moment, and said it once again, "LADIES AND GENTLEMENT, PLEASE WELCOME THE NEXT PRESIDENT OF THE UNITED STATES," then he dropped his inflection to say his name, so as not to sound too triumphant, then it rose again, "AND U.S. SENATOR JAMES CURLEY."

Bix was reminded that the roar of a tornado is generally described as being similar to that of a freight train, and it occurred to him that the sound of forty-five thousand people screaming their lungs out might arguably be described as similar to a whole lot of freight trains. The ground trembled.

Ben cued the music and The Candidate and his new BFF were out the door, shaking hands for a few seconds with a few of the closest people straining at the bike rack, then four steps up to the catwalk where everyone could see them and vice versa. The crowd became louder. They walked the fifty feet of raised walkway reaching down shaking outstretched hands and feeling the sound of the crowd in the vibrations under their feet.

Curley was obviously overwhelmed. He had had some very great events four years prior, but only a few like this, a fact with which Bix was familiar because he was the one who had produced those events four years prior.

After several minutes of steady applause, the crowd settled down and Senator Curley began his remarks, which would conclude with an introduction of the main speaker. Merle walked out to the buffer zone to watch the speeches and Bix began to leave when Mike grabbed him.

"Nora called me a little while ago," he said. "She's being held captive at her campaign office because Napoleon Dynamite is there with Nurse Ratched and twenty-five guys waiting for Drule to arrive so he can escort them over here. She told me only a few of those people are from this district, and Shaunesy won't let her leave to come here."

"Does she know who the rest of the people are?"

"She said they are friends of Drule's and Shaunesy's from New York, and they flew down here because Shaunesy told them he'd get them an introduction and a photo with The Candidate," Mike said.

"They're friends with both Drule *and* Shaunesy?" Bix said.

"That's what she said."

"Am I wrong, or does that seem outrageous to you?"

"Outrageous."

"Have you heard from our driver with Drule?"

"Manny called over an hour ago. I estimate he will be here in about twenty minutes."

"Thank you for the update. Now I'll go update Peem, but I have to decide where I'm gonna do the *updating*."

"Update him where the sun don't shine," Mike said.

* * *

Bix did not beat around the bush when he arrived back in Hold. "Let's go outside and speak privately," he told Peem. Leaving Moss and Peaches alone in Hold, they walked outside to "clarify matters at hand."

"Baahhhhhb," Bix said lyrically, "is there anything you would like to tell me?"

"About what?" Peem said.

"Don't be cute, Bob. You tried it once before and it didn't work."

"What's your question, Bix?"

"You could put all the categories on big spinning wheel and throw darts at it to see which one or in what order you need to explain to me what the hell is going on. Let's begin with our international issues. Why did you tell Sophie to stay away? What do you fear from Jamir's appearance here today? Is it that our boss doesn't want to see him? If so, why? Is there something embarrassing in that article? Is there something you guys know that I don't? On the domestic front, why did you sent Larry Drule down here to escort more than two dozen un-vetted and un-name-checked out-of-towners into my event? Who are these people? Why weren't they vetted? If they were vetted, who vetted 'em?" Bix was relatively certain that Peem knew nothing about the Drule deception, but he thought a little assumptive guilt by association would throw Peem off kilter.

"I don't know anything about that," Peem shot back. "It seemed like a good defense at the moment."

Bix wasn't fond of his answer. "You don't? You sent Larry Drule all the way down here and then you arrived on your magic carpet, and you don't know anything about that? 'That' as you say, is a relatively big deal. Your deputy campaign manager and his special friend the RFD are about to escort God-knows-who into the back door of our event to get them a grip and a pic with the next President of the United States, and ultimately, you're the guy who authorized Drule's hard pin."

"I'll look into it," was Peem's shortest distance to "let's move on to the next subject."

"All right, next subject. What's your fear about Jamir?" Bix said.

"The boss just doesn't want to see him right now."

"Pardon my ignorance. Is there something deeper about this?"

"No. He simply doesn't think it's a good idea. Maybe we shouldn't feed the story."

"Bob, that train has left the station. Dick O'Malley is doing *The O'Malley Intrusion* live from here in a little over an hour, and he'll be filling airtime with rumors and gossip. If our only response is 'starve the story,' this is the type of creature that can survive a long time on stored-up bigotry, combined with the photosynthetic effect of klieg lights. Instead of a big story about a ground-breaking kick-off rally in Scepter, you will have a news cycle dominated by the basest form of innuendo."

"And if Jamir shows up they will have a face to go with a name, neither of which are likely to get us any votes," Peem said.

"True, but they will find a picture of Jamir somewhere anyway, and they *will* choose the *least* complimentary one, and it will appear on broadcasts, newspapers, on-line, and in our opponents' TV commercials. Jamir will come across much better live than in an old government ID photo, I promise you," Bix said. "Those things make everyone look their worst."

"You almost had me, up to the point where you promised me. It's more of a story with Jamir here. You're going to need more than that to convince me or the boss."

"It's more of a story if you let people's imaginations, people's *paranoid* imaginations, run wild rather than showing the boring truth. You *want* Jamir on those TV cameras. You *need* Jamir on those TV cameras. Who's going to go out there and take the bullets from the press, you, Bob Peem, or you Lieutenant Wineberg?" Bix looked past Peem as he said it.

Peem looked around. He didn't understand what Bix was talking about, but assumed that Bix was jerking his chain.

Bix was inspired. "We use words like message, visuals, spontaneous. We use these words as the backbone of a life spent manipulating media coverage and public opinion. You use them as a punch line, and I have neither the time nor the inclination to explain myself to a man whose campaign rises or falls under the blanket of the very news coverage that I create."

It was all lost on Peem, who was confused. Bix was happy with that outcome.

"My plan is to dump Jamir on the entire press corps at the same time, hand out copies of the article to everyone, and let him answer any questions. He is a pro. He will handle them well, and Dick O'Malley won't have a scoop so he'll have nothing to talk about. And mark my word, Jamir will get offers to host his own cable TV news show. Anyway, Jamir and Sophie and Hani will be here in a few minutes, and Hani will be more than content to hang out inside the Admin building until the press leaves."

"You had better be right is all I can say," Peem said.

"You go find out why Drule and Shaunesy are marching on our rally with a ghost army. That poses more of a threat than Jamir. And please let me know what you find out. No surprises."

"Same here, no surprises," Peem said.

"I just told you everything I plan to do," Bix said, "and you know who I'm bringing to the party. Now I need to go keep the party going."

Bix walked back to Hold for a fast check with Moss and Peaches, who were carrying on in the exact manner they would if they were anywhere else doing anything else—they were engrossed in their hand-held electronic devices, mesmerized, interacting with the outside world."

He walked behind Peaches, who was splayed out on a couch, and saw that he was playing a startlingly graphic video war game with tiny little female warriors who had stuffed their muscular physiques and ample breasts into armor-clad bustiers that didn't appear to offer much protection or freedom of movement.

"Peaches—glad to see you're using this time to think of ways of improving your mind. I know the campaign will benefit greatly," Bix said.

Peaches went on offense. "This is educational. It improves your strategic and tactical thinking. It's designed to show how strategies can be applied to business as well as war."

"As long as your business is battling large-breasted Amazons in tight metal bustiers," Bix said. "I dropped in to see if you gentlemen are comfortable, and you appear to be."

"Don't let us hold you up, we're fine," Peaches said. "Say, you want that leather bag that the greeting committee gave the boss?"

Bix was a little surprised. It was a nice bag. "Doesn't he want it?"

"Nah, he isn't going to want that. You can have it."

"You don't want it?"

"Nah, I don't have anywhere to put it."

"Done," Bix said. "I'm finally coming out in the black on one of these events. I'll grab it when we're ready to leave. Thanks."

* * *

Walking out of the Admin building to hit the VIP area and ensure that Mayor Bacon was under control, Bix heard another staggering roar from the crowd as Senator Curley introduced the main attraction. Chief Fry happened to be hanging out near the motorcade talking with a few of his local cops, avoiding Secret Service agents as much as possible, when Bix spotted him and made a beeline.

"Chief Fry," Bix extended his hand, "this has been a great experience, and I wanted to thank you before we got so caught up that I forget. Thank you for everything, and don't worry about the Secret Service. Sometimes they get mad, but a lot of times they don't do anything about it."

"Did theyah say somethin?" Chief Fry asked.

"Come with me to the VIP area, we can talk with the mayor there, too."

As they walked toward McBride Hall, Fry voiced his concern. "Ah don't think thah mayah is goin' to be feelin' verah happah riate about nah. He mayeh be someone yu'all miate wanta avoid."

"Not at all, not at all. Let's go see him. I think everything is OK. And we can talk about how you can square it with the Secret Service. It was a cold motorcade driving over here after you pulled-off on County Road Z. My Lead Service counterpart, Shane, you met him I'm sure, was piiiisssed-off. He wasn't just venting. He said he wanted to arrest you. He wanted to pull your license to practice chiefing. I know hundreds of agents, and I know when they're venting and when they're serious."

"Wahl, thas jes' terrible. Cud this be serious trouble?"

Bix nodded, tilted his head, gave him the eyebrow, "Yes, it can be. They're Federal with a capital F."

"What should Ah do? Do Ah need t'go apologize? Ah could tell'im that my boahs had discova'd some dangerous lookin' chahactahs roamin' 'round down the road a piece, an they looked lahk a secuahty risk."

"Definitely don't tell him that. It will make him angier. But yes, an apology will help, but how you explain it will go farther to keep them from being mad at you."

"Whatch'all think Ah oughta say?"

"My suggestion is tell him the mayor told you we were going to the senior center, that simple. Don't tell him the mayor said to lead the motorcade away or that you were trying to get the motorcade to at least drive past, and definitely don't tell him you were avoiding a potential security risk. He'll clap you in irons for thinking he was that stupid."

Walking through the Great Hall of McBride Hall, Chief Fry looked up and inspected its tall ceiling, with its heavy oak buttresses, each adorned with a gargoyle where the beam arched down gracefully into the wall, each gargoyle a cleverly hand-carved little monster, each one different. "This is jes incredible," he said. "Ah had no ahdeah."

It was a little surprising to Bix hearing the chief admit he'd never set foot in one of the main assembly halls in the college, but Bix was in a generous and diplomatic mood and for once he showed the good judgement to zip his mouth. As far as he was concerned, once The Candidate hit the stage, it was all down hill from there, and everyone was his friend. "Yeah, it reminds me of the dining hall in Hogwarts," he said.

"Where's zat?" Fry said.

"In England, sort of."

They reached the Eugene V. Bacon Senior Center VIP area and Chief Fry became noticeably nervous. Bix reassured him. "The mayor will be in a good mood, trust me. He won't be able to be mad."

"If that's true, an' Ah believe ya'll, then he'll be mad that he cain't get mad."

"Good point, Chief, but he won't get mad in front of his people who are having the time of their lives because of him. He will have to defer his anger until later at least. Plus, we have Mrs. Bacon, and she will calm the savage breast."

"Don't ch'all mean beast?"

"That, too."

Storie was standing to the rear of the VIP area, near a tree behind most of the Bacon Center seniors who were comfortably ensconced in chairs closer to the rope line sipping large frozen specialty drinks in plastic cups and watching the speeches. Most of them exhibited unmistakable signs of thoroughly enjoying themselves. When Bix entered with the chief, a few of the seniors noticed and raised their cups in a "welcome" toast. Chief Fry tipped his chief's hat.

Storie was smiling approvingly and Bix saw a moment too late to do anything about it that she was standing next to the mayor and his wife, who were seated in chairs. The mayor glanced over at Bix but did not get up. He nodded slightly and continued watching the speech.

Mrs. Bacon smiled demurely and flashed an equally demure, semi-secret "thumbs-up," her hand closest to the mayor hiding the other hand's gesture. Bix loved the compliment. He smiled, bowed a bit and mouthed the words "thank you" from ten feet away.

Storie took Bix's arm and walked him a few yards farther away from the others. She spoke close to his ear to be heard over the loud speakers without yelling. "Do you want to hear what Bacon said about you?"

"Do I?"

"Yes. After we arrived he was overwhelmed with thank-you's from all of his senior citizens, and a couple of bus loads of veterans you sent from the last site were all thanking him, too. Bacon said 'Ah gotta hand it to that boah. He knows what he's doin'.' And after he heard your boss acknowledge him from the podium a few minutes ago he said, 'Ah gotta hand it ta that boah. He's a slick one.'"

"Did he mean it in a positive way?"

"He did. It was grudging admiration. I think he senses there is something between you and me, 'cause he told me, "If Ah had ah dahta, Ah think Ah wud not be displeased if she mahried a boah lahk Bix."

"He said that?"

"Yes, but then he said, 'But if he was ma son-in-law, Ah'm afraid Ah'd have to shoot the son-of-a-bitch at some poahnt soona or latah.'"

"You do the accent well. Thanks for letting me know. What do you think of the event?" He heard himself asking the question and it sounded a little needy, but Storie's opinion counted, and he could count on her to be honest in her glowing approbation.

"Brilliant. Genius. The press will eat this up. I can see you took a huge risk. This is a big site. You could have gotten ten thousand people and it would have looked empty. It paid off. And you controlled the mayor and made him happy about it, which isn't an easy thing to accomplish. Not bad for a day's work."

"Thank you for your objective assessment," he said. "If you see anything else that might incentivize you to proffer more compliments, give me a few days and then tell me after the glow is over and I need another bump in my polls."

"If I am so incentivized, will we still be communicating in a few days?"

"Yes, but only by code or courier."

"Or you could just roll over and whisper in my ear."

"That could be a problem because if I rolled over and whispered, it might annoy my pet pit bull Fluffy, who always sleeps with me."

"Yeah, right, not only will you not sleep with livestock, you won't even have them in your house, and you probably won't even sleep with me if I haven't bathed first."

"Ms. Toller, this is hardly the time or the place," Bix said. "Why don't you meet me behind that tree over there and we can discuss this in a more appropriate setting, where people can't see the little beads of sweat appearing on my upper lip."

She laughed her hearty laugh, loud enough for a few of the seniors seated nearby to hear above the loudspeakers, and she swiftly stifled herself into a smile. "You're getting moist."

"Don't say that word," Bix demanded.

"Moist."

"You said it."

"Moist moist moist."

"I must leave now. I have a rally to produce, and more crises with which to contend. But first, I must go to Hold and find a cold can of pop to put in my pocket. This was most unkind of you, young lady, although I know you meant it in a nice way, all you did today was weaken a nation."

"A nation, or you?"

"Well, me, but not all of me, just my knees."

"Then go. Go and chill your nether regions." She shot him that sly smile that no one outside of a hundred foot radius could have seen.

* * *

Bix pulled Chief Fry aside and asked him to walk over to the edge closest to the press area, separated from it by space and equipment but accessible to it through one piece of unconnected bike rack in a strategic location. Bix lifted and moved the bike rack at one end and ushered Fry through.

"Chief, how was the mayor?"

"You wah riate Bix, he was fahn. All of those folks from down theah at tha seniah centah are havin' a reeel gud tahm, an' they ah all votahs."

"That's great, Chief, I'm glad to hear it. Say, I was wondering about your opinion of the rally. Have you ever seen a crowd this big since you've been chief?"

"Noah, Ah don't s'ppose Ah have."

"So would you say this is the largest crowd you've ever seen in Scepter, for anything, or just for a political event?"

"Ah guess Ah'd say this is the biggest crowd Ah've seen for anathing."

"Could I ask you if you would say that to the press, just like that?"

"Yes, Ah cud do that."

Within seconds they were standing in the press area, where Bix had escorted Chief Fry behind the main press riser to find Kate, Cornelia, and Philpot, who was in the vicinity somewhere Bix couldn't see. Kate and Cornelia were immediately there for the hand-off. "The Chief says this is the biggest crowd he's ever seen for any event in Scepter, and could be the biggest in their history. Am I getting that correctly, Chief?"

"Yes, that'd be about riate," he said.

"He said he'd be happy to tell the press, if you would like him to do so."

Kate was as happy for the quote as Bix. "Yes, that would be great. Chief, let's go talk to some of our national press. They will love meeting you. I'm sure you already know the journalists from your local news outlets."

"Ah shuah do young laydah." He straightened his hat and his tie and walked away with Kate and Cornelia.

As they walked away, Bix saw Dick O'Malley at the rear of the press area, fidgeting, looking at his watch, paying no attention to the speech, punching numbers on his cell phone and holding it up to his ear, then pushing "end" and holding it down without putting it away.

* * *

Bix dashed back outside, walking not running, through Hogwarts Hall, past the motorcade and the agents and cops, through the Admin building and fifty yards of secured hallways dotted with more post-standers, out of the covered walkway to the rally and the chute next to the stage where Merle stood watching. He hoped he was compensating for the lack of an official workout that morning, and maybe the previous morning as well. He couldn't remember.

"On which side of the stage does he exit?" Merle said.

"The far side," Bix said. "I was headed over there to give him the heads-up."

"That's OK, I'll head over there and lead them off the stage. It will be like old times with JC. He'll look for me."

"Have at it, sir," Bix said.

Merle walked around the front of the stage in the buffer zone, stooping low to remain unseen on-camera, and waited at the foot of a set of stairs on the opposite side.

Bix remained stage left near Mike, who had settled in after an active fifteen minutes of moving around the site, in and out of the buffer zone, back into the Admin building where he could hear people talking to him on his headset, directing the last few moving parts. Soon, the only thing left to do was to cue the rope line music, which should by all rights be an easy thing to do. Thinking rationally, Bix mused, it shouldn't require a cue, merely an individual who could discern when The Candidate has finished speaking and be able to push a button on a CD player when that happens.

It was a constant source of amazement to Bix how often it didn't happen quite that way, the number of times it took an agonizingly long time to start the music after it was clear that The Candidate had stopped talking. Mike never allowed that to occur. He ran his sites with the precision of a Swiss watch and loved spectacle done well.

Part of the spectacle that Mike arranged as a fitting climax to the rally was a deal he cut with a local fireworks vendor who, for a modest sum that was categorized on Mike's site budget as "Decorations," had agreed to set off a brief display, beginning with two substantial reports and several star-bursts, from a park they estimated to be about five hundred yards from the Site.

Mike had asked for Bix's approval early the day before, which he received, and the vendor had gotten the appropriate city license to shoot fireworks in the park. Bix promptly forgot about it.

As they stood in the buffer zone, near the covered walkway that served both as entrance and exit, listening to the last few words of The Candidate's stirring speech to over fifty thousand wildly enthusiastic people, Mike turned to Bix and asked him a question: "Did you tell them about the fireworks?"

The Candidate finished his remarks and Ben Oliver, ever vigilant, standing next to the sound technician, cued the rope line music, and Mike cued the fireworks vendor.

Bix turned to Mike. "Oops."

With that, the sound of two large explosions, resembling something one might experience standing on the deck of a battleship during target practice with the 20-inchers, ripped through the air and shook the stage, the equipment, the crowd, everyone's eardrums, the ground and, of course, the two men for whom it was meant as a salute. Senator Curley, a Vietnam veteran, was visibly shaken, almost taking a dive but quickly composing himself. A true veteran.

Mike looked at Bix. "That was a big oops."

The Candidate, also startled but quickly composed, stepped back from the podium to shake hands with Senator Curley and wave to the crowd one more time before walking down the six-foot length of stairs to the buffer zone, where they would shake hands for the next ten or fifteen minutes.

Bix was devastated. "I'll take the heat for that. I forgot to tell them. I forgot you were doing it at all. I'll tell them it was my fault."

"Don't worry about it," Mike said. "I knew you wouldn't remember that one detail. I only mentioned it once to you, and you had everything else to think about. I told Merle and he mentioned it to them in Hold."

"So you undermined my authority?"

"Absolutely."

"Thank you. I still messed-up and you saved my ass."

"Hardly. As forgotten details go, this one is rather small, I reckon. It was really my idea and my lookout."

"I'm getting old, I'm losing my touch. This is merely the first manifestation."

"You're not getting old—you've gained wisdom. You've learned how to prioritize. You know how to marshal your troops and how to trust them to do their jobs. This was too unimportant for your gaze, too fleeting, an unimportant detail."

"You spin well, my faithful New Zealander companion."

* * *

It seemed as if half of the entire 55,000-person crowd was jammed up against the metal barricade around the stage, within handshaking distance, crushing those in front. Bix noticed two young children in danger of being squeezed into four-and-a-half-inch strips by the weight of people straining forward, their little faces compressed sideways against the bars, their little eyes fixed in terror. He rushed to rescue them and was quickly joined by one of the Secret Service agents who helped him shove back a portion of the crowd and pull the children out and over the barricade and into the buffer zone.

Bix hauled out the one he rescued high over his head when he pulled her free, then, after placing her safely on the ground, reassured her with a hug. After a quick three-sixty, he realized that it was unlikely any of it was caught on camera and he commiserated to the agent, "another thankless bit of heroism."

The agent was sympathetic. "Happens to me every day."

"Even if no one else noticed, thank you for your heroism just now," Bix told him.

"And thank you. You noticed them first."

"But what good was it?" Bix asked. "None of the TV cameras caught it. What was the point? Other than saving a couple of kids. I mean, they can't even vote yet."

"I agree. Welcome to the world of unsung heroes, my friend."

The two children remained where they'd been placed, near their mothers still on the other side of the barricade, and were rewarded with hugs from both The Candidate and Senator Curley while the moms clicked away on their digital cameras. One of the moms pointed to Bix after her little girl had received her hug and shouted to The Candidate, "He saved their lives. If it wasn't for him they would have been crushed to death. He saved them."

"That's a nice endorsement," Bix thought. He looked around again. Still no TV cameras. "Another endorsement lost to the ages."

The Candidate was his usual effusive self. "That's great," he told her. "Congratulations."

"Congratulations?" Bix thought. "Congratulations that your children didn't die?" There was definitely a disconnect somewhere.

The Candidate hustled through another several hundred handshakes and Bix and Shane led him and the gaggle of agents back through the covered walkway to Hold, where they waited for Senator Curley to complete his handshaking tour.

Bix feared the "Dreaded Candidate quiescence"—there was a TV in Hold but no basketball, golf, football, or tiddlywinks games anywhere on the dial—but he placed his confidence in Curley's promptness. Curley needed to fly back to Washington to meet his wife for a flight to their vacation home off Barbados, and he would *not* keep her waiting.

Within two minutes, Senator Curley strolled into Hold smiling a smile that Bix couldn't remember having seen during Curley's presidential campaign, chatting a chat that was completely uncharacteristic. It was like the good old days they'd never had.

Curley pulled his cell phone out of his inside coat pocket and called his wife, keeping her updated on his progress. "It's like a Curley presidential campaign reunion here," he told her. "Bix is here, Mike Pitcher, Kate Hillhouse is doing Press, Merle's here somewhere, and I heard that Thigpen is doing Crowd. They did a great job and it's been a lot of fun."

"A lot of fun?" Bix thought. "Where was that guy four years ago? And he remembers our names?"

Curley listened to his wife talk for a while and said, "I'll tell them. I'm sure they will appreciate it. I'll call you from the plane before we leave."

He looked at Bix and The Candidate and said, "Margurite watched the event on CNN and she said it was beautiful, very moving."

Bix was forced to respond, "Mrs. Curley has one of the finest analytical minds in the Western Hemisphere, if I may say so, Senator." He was taking a chance that Curley would be in the mood to get the joke.

"Just this hemisphere?" Curley asked, laughing.

He got it. "It's only because I don't have a great deal of experience in the Eastern Hemisphere, so I can't really say."

"That's understandable, then," Curley said. "I was about to consider it a slight that you included only the Western one."

Curley, Merle, Mike, Peaches, Bix, and even Moss were in the most hospitable of moods, as was The Candidate before he lost interest.

Curley's departure coincided with that moment perfectly. "I have to go catch a flight," he said before walking several feet across Hold to where Bix stood. "Thanks for everything." With that, he swooped over and hugged Bix, who was once again shocked into near- speechlessness.

It was only through years of professional Advance experience that Bix was able to gather his wits and find the right words. "Today was a tour de force." Bix assumed Curley would like hearing his triumph described in French. Bix then stood back and said, "Thank you for everything, Senator," and shook the senator's hand, to get it on the record that he was still a handshaking kind of guy, too.

Curley hugged, in succession, Mike, Merle, and then Thigpen, who had arrived in time to pay his respects before Curley left. Merle had received the hug treatment before, but Mike and Thigpen certainly logged it in their book of memories. Curley walked to The Candidate, they did the "man hug," which started with a handshake so they were not touching chest to chest at the end of it, and he left with Moss, who had taken his BlackBerry away from his face long enough to shake hands with everyone before departing furtively.

* * *

"Take him to the gym," Bix told Mike.

"You've got a gym?" The Candidate perked up.

"Would I leave you waiting in a desolate Holding room while the press filed their stories and ate their sumptuous luncheon feast?" Bix asked him.

"I don't know, would you?" he asked.

"Only if I could get away with it," Bix said, "which I can't, so we have a gym in the next building over. Mike will be happy to show you. Thigpen probably, too."

Bix turned left out of Hold and everyone else turned right on their way to twenty minutes of R and R, nearly one of which was wasted walking through the first floor hallways of the Admin building to an underground tunnel connected to Crump Hall, a.k.a. the college gymnasium, next door.

At the North security perimeter of police, sawhorses, and metal barricades, Drule and his unknown horde arrived on foot, followed by Shaunesy and Nurse Ratched protecting the rear. At the same time, Sophie, Jamir, and Hani drove up to the south perimeter, where Freeway was already waiting. Bix stood outside of the Admin building watching it all converge on him, weighing the few options he had with regard to Drule and Shaunesy. His fantasy options were violent and inappropriate for the occasion. He called Mike and asked him to come or send Ben with twenty-five of their special VVIP badges, so as to honor them appropriately.

Freeway had been given his marching orders regarding Sophie's escortees and their designated Holding Room, where they were to be taken first. Bix decided at the last second to stash the horde in McBride Hall, where several VIP signs pointed anyway. He walked out to meet Drule and his guests as they walked through security screening.

Ben arrived at the same time with a fistful of handsome VVIP credentials and handed them out to the unknown guests who obediently slipped the strings over their heads and around their necks.

Bix handed one of the VVIP badges to one of the Agents who was standing post and asked him "Do you know what these mean?"

"Yes sir, we've been briefed by Mr. Emory."

After the last man was wanded and passed through security, the unknown horde picked up a Secret Service agent escort.

Although Bix admitted to himself that he may have been biased, Drule's guests looked like shady characters to him. Shady characters in expensive suits. He decided the agent was his ally.

With little fanfare and less pleasantness, Bix introduced himself to the agent and said to Drule, "I'm taking all of you to our VIP Hold."

Drule and Shaunesy were left with no options. Drule asked tersely, "Where's the boss?"

"He's in the bathroom at the moment. Go find him if you want."

Drule was apoplectic. "You sonofabitch. I'm going to have your ass fired for this."

Bix assumed Drule's anger was genuine and that he was showing off for his guests, and Shaunesy, Ratched, and Nora, who lagged behind the horde looking embarrassed. He had run out of diplomacy, but not eloquence. "Look, pencil dick, you couldn't have an intern fired, and how dare you blame me for your own stupidity."

Several of the horde laughed audibly.

"I'll escort you gentlemen to our VIP area," Bix said, "while Mr. Drule here decides what he wants to do next."

The Secret Service agent/baby sitter was pleased to have a destination for the large unexpected group. He helped herd the horde as Bix led them to the Hogwarts Hall, an auspicious site for an auspicious group. When they entered the door, Bix turned to Drule and Shaunesy. "If we'd known you were coming we would have had refreshments," and he said it loud enough for a few of their guests to hear. Then he said, "Wait here," as Nurse Ratched walked-in and Bix left immediately, secure in the knowledge that the agent would remain behind, keeping an eye on them. A few seconds after he walked out of McBride Hall, Bix saw Drule leave with his "all access pass" hard pin to start wandering around, without his guests.

By this time, all the comings and goings were attracting the attention of more agents and cops, part of whose jobs was monitoring the situation around them. They watched with interest but remained silent. Shane stopped Bix briefly as he walked back into the Admin building, not with a question but with a statement: "You're bouncing around here like a pinball."

"Do I look frantic?" Bix said.

"No, just busy," Shane told him.

"Good. By the way, I need an 'S' pin and a couple of 'G' pins."

"I can give you three 'G' pins. You'll have to get an 'S' pin from Agent Rudd."

"*There's* a name I was hoping never to hear again," Bix said. "I wouldn't say it's likely he'll give me an 'S' pin, so give me the 'G' pins for the moment, and if you would, please get an 'S' pin for the campaign manager's AA, Sophie."

"I'll try," Shane said.

Bix scurried off, hurriedly but calmly, to find the traveling trio of fresh media meat and settle the case of international intrigue. They waited for Bix in their own Hold, the Jamir Hold, a small dark-paneled private office on the ground floor of the Admin building in one of the secured hallways. They appeared remarkably energetic, even buoyant, for three people who had been chased and chasing across half the state over the previous thirty hours.

The magnitude of their exertions was not lost on Bix. "I feel responsible for everything you've been through, for some reason."

Jamir and Hani, both of whom appeared to have been recently been clipped from a Polo ad in *GQ,* assured him they were aware of his complicity but did not blame him for the situation.

"Oh, Bix, don't think for a moment that you aren't," Hani said in his clipped Jordanian/British/South Georgia accent. "But that isn't necessarily a bad thing. I find it all quite stimulating." It was as if he was on a day trip out of Harrow.

"We paused and observed your rally for quite a while before we came here," Jamir said. "It was invigorating. We could see the whole thing, and our boy did a very good job from the podium. It was a rousing speech."

Bix felt he was in a scene from a Gilbert and Sullivan production of Lawrence of Arabia. "I wouldn't use the word 'boy,'" Bix said.

"Oh yes, quite right. Cautionary tale," Jamir said.

"It was a rockin' rally," Sophie said. "Has my friend Nora been having a good time?"

"I'm not sure she is," Bix said. "She's in the VIP section. Come with us when we go and we'll find her."

Sophie reluctantly demurred. "I don't want to leave Hani alone, and we all know he can't go out there just in case."

"No, no, no, please do not not go because of me," Hani said. "I'm truly having a wonderful time, I don't mind in the least. You go see your friend. Just don't leave me here when you leave."

"Really, you don't mind?" Sophie said.

"Not at all, you go."

"Thank you, Hani. I won't be long."

It dawned on Bix that they were missing a small child. "Would it be rude to ask about Chelsea? Did we leave her somewhere?"

"We dropped her off at my aunt's on the way here," Sophie said. "She lives in Charleston. Nice of you to remember, though. Shows you care about your people."

"If I cared about my people," Bix said, "I'd let my people go." He thought his two Middle Eastern friends would appreciate the biblical pun. They did. Then they showed him the color copies of Jamir's article, slightly weathered in its original 1981 form, entitled "Manifesto of Misperceptions" with the by-line, "Great Satan and Jihad Joe." Bix laughed. "I love it. No wonder no one could find it."

"I had forgotten," Jamir said. "It was actually published in a small campus newspaper with a circulation of two. Someone would have found it eventually."

Scanning its paragraphs Bix could see it was a competently written treatise on American-Iranian relations, not a call for jihad or a knock on the sacred U.S. of A.

"Allow me to excuse myself for a few minutes while I track down my intrepid leader and his intrepid senior staff and present them with the next phase options, as I see them, if they are interested," Bix said.

He headed off on another hike through the underbelly of the Admin building, down through the tunnel connected to Crump Hall and up to the gym where The Candidate, Merle, Peaches, Thigpen, and Philpot were shooting baskets and seemingly reluctant to think about anything else. Bix felt he had to pry the big boys out of their b-ball zone.

He held up a copy of the manifesto as he stood on the sideline, and when a ball bounced his way he put his foot on it and didn't send it back onto the court.

The Candidate, Philpot, and Merle reluctantly moped over to him. "Here's your manifesto," Bix said, "and we have Jamir and his brother-in-law Hani, who went out of his way to help us find Jamir. My plan is to take Jamir out to the press area with several dozen copies of the article and expose this story for what it is before Dick O'Malley does his program, then I would like to bring Jamir and Hani here so you can thank them yourself. Is that cool with you?" He said in a way that may have been perceived as confrontational, even accusatory.

"That's a lot to consider. Do I want to do this?" The Candidate asked Philpot.

"As Bix said, we might be able to put this to rest, depending on how Jamir performs," Philpot said.

Apparently it was the answer to the wrong question. "Should I see him? What about that?" The Candidate said.

"Is there a question about seeing him, especially in private?" Bix interjected. He hadn't intended to air his astonishment publicly, but there it was, a major faux pas on the level of discussing your case of crabs at a cocktail party.

"I know you've got a dog in this fight," Philpot said, "but there's more at stake here than just seeing someone."

"Yes, there's the whole question of right and wrong, and whether you do the right thing or the wrong thing," Bix said. "Friendship trumps bullshit." It sounded less like common sense and more like disdain by that point.

"Bix is going to guilt us into this thing," Merle said.

The Candidate spoke directly to Philpot. "No, you're right, we should see him." Then he turned to Bix. "You can bring him here when you're finished outside with the press."

Bix's mind wandered. "*We* should see him?" he thought. "The royal 'we' again?"

Bix nodded, acknowledging what he believed to be the only ethical answer to his question. He asked Philpot as he walked out, "Are you going to join us in the press area?" and Philpot toddled along behind Bix.

While on the move, he called Kate to tell her they were on their way. They schlepped back under Crump and up through Admin to the "Jamir Hold," grabbed up Sophie, told Hani they would return shortly, and walked with Jamir and Philpot to the press filing center under a large square tent in the press area.

Kate strategically informed the traveling press, then the local press, then Max News by way of senior producer Adam Strayberg, who was supervising the set-up of O'Malley's live shot from a location on the other side of several oak trees, just past the press area in front of the Max News truck.

She took an uncharacteristically sarcastic tone, "Adam, I understand you've been looking for Jamir Parviz."

Strayberg was laconic, barely making eye contact with Kate as he worked. "We're collecting information like every other news organization. There's a story there and you know it."

By that time Kate could see that Bix, Jamir, and Philpot were nearing the press area, carrying a stack of copies. "I certainly hope there is," she said, "because Jamir will be giving it to your colleagues in the press in about a minute."

Like a prairie dog on alert upon sensing danger, Strayberg sprang to life. His head swiveled, his feet tapped. "What the fuh—?" He didn't finish his expletive before running off, not in the direction of Jamir but toward the Max News truck.

"Hey, they're over there," Kate called out.

Strayberg didn't bother to answer.

* * *

The news of Jamir making news was not received well inside the Max News truck. O'Malley, dining alone in the spacious environs of his truck rather than among his colleagues at the luncheon buffet, almost created a new skylight when Strayberg broke the news to him with an obscene lede. O'Malley didn't like Strayberg's lede.

"*WE'RE* fucked?" O'Malley shouted at Strayberg. "No, *you're* fucked. How could you let this happen? You let those fucking bastards get away."

"How could *I* let this happen?" Strayberg's tolerance for all things O'Malley was long gone, but the money was too good to quit his job. "Well, since you hadn't handed the keys to absolute control of the fucking universe over to me, I would have to ask you the same question. How could *you* let those slimy bastards slip away? No wait, excuse me, how could you let those slimy *fucking* bastards slip away?"

O'Malley ignored the remark. "So what the fuck does the manifesto say?" he wailed. "We're out on a limb here."

"How about if I send a *fucking* intern over to get a fucking copy and find out what the fuck it says, although I doubt there's room in this fucking truck for that piece of paper and your fucking ego at the same fucking time. You may have to step outside into the daylight and risk fucking spontaneously combusting."

"What the fuck do you mean by—" O'Malley didn't finish before Strayberg walked out, slamming the door behind him.

O'Malley raced out of the news truck, physically grabbed the first Max News camera crew he could find and ran to the press filing center to confront Jamir, the fugitive terr-symp.

* * *

Jamir's appearance and his manifesto were greeted enthusiastically by the traveling press, many of whom appeared oddly giddy. Bix took Kate aside when she arrived and asked her if he was reading the room correctly.

"You got it," she said. "They all know that this was O'Malley's big 'get.' They know he's been chasing this white whale for a few weeks and he's got his entire production staff tied up in it, not to mention his ass, and now he's tangled in his own ropes on the back of that whale and it's going down into the abyss."

"Very poetic."

"It was your reference, not mine," she said.

"So O'Malley is Ahab."

"That's one of the nicer things they call him," Kate said.

"I'm just happy that he's Ahab and not me. There was a while there..."

"Nope, you played this right. The press loved loved loved the event and the visuals. They all used the cherry picker to shoot a lot of footage and stills and we had camera crews moving to every angle we gave them. They got some incredible over-the-shoulder shots that show the whole crowd. It looked like a freaking million people. And now they know that O'Malley won't get his big story and can't step on their big story. It's a win-win for them. And Jamir isn't half bad. He's a handsome man."

"Which proves my point," Bix said. "Whether it's Barnum and Bailey or Broadway or broadcast, it's all theater. If O'Malley had gotten video of Jamir twelve hours ago it would have been death. He'd have used that visual as a cudgel to bludgeon us with."

"Big beard, huh?"

"We're talking caves of Tora Bora big."

"Ouch. Glad you got to him first. This is why you're the man," she said.

"There's been some doubt in that regard too," he said.

"I didn't say '*A*' man, I said '*The*' man."

"Either," he said.

* * *

Jamir's availability to the entire traveling press began civilly, conversationally, as two or three journalists at a time talked with him and a couple of still photographers took some casual, almost distinerested, photos. He was standing in a small group when O'Malley crashed the scene.

First O'Malley entered the filing center, set up under a tent at the rear of the press area, with none of his troops in tow. He was huffing, frenetic, anxious to inflict himself upon Jamir. Then he waited, and waited, for his camera crew to arrive and then hook up a microphone as Jamir and members of the press corps watched and waited with him. The entire time O'Malley seemed to be snorting.

Once wired, O'Malley inserted himself among his colleagues, looked over to see that the camera was rolling, stuck the microphone in Jamir's nose and barked, "Why were you in hiding?"

Jamir backed away a few inches, looked at O'Malley and smiled. "Well, I wasn't aware that I was hiding. I was on sabbatical writing a book, but if I'd known you were going to do this I would have been in hiding, certainly."

Laughter erupted from members of the press who had moved closer to watch the drama.

O'Malley was unaffected. "What were you hiding? The Manifesto you wrote in support of Iran? You were obviously hiding something."

"Other than my disdain for you, and this pathetic attempt to manufacture a scandal?" Jamir said.

More laughs from the audience.

O'Malley showed true courage or desperation in the face of overwhelming odds. "How do we know that document you brought is even real or not doctored?"

"It's real," Jamir said, "which is more than I can say for you. Have you even taken two minutes to read the article? You should—you might learn something."

"Have you been in Iran or in contact with people from Iran any time recently?" O'Malley fished for any quote he could use.

"If you are asking if I remain in touch with my family members who are still in Iran, yes I do from time to time, but not enough. Are you asking about my views on American-Iranian relations, economic embargos, relationships in the Persian Gulf? Anything of substance?"

"Why don't you come on my show," O'Malley said, "and we'll discuss all those things. I'm going live in less than a half hour and you can discuss anything you'd like."

Jamir looked to Bix, standing a few feet away from the gaggle. Bix shook his head "no" almost imperceivably.

"How about we let a few of your distinguished journalist colleagues ask a few questions and you take a few minutes to read the article that we wrote twenty-seven years ago," Jamir said, "and then come back with any more questions you might have."

"I know you were hiding out for some reason," O'Malley swore, "and I'm gonna get to the bottom of it." He threw his microphone to, at, one of the production assistants and walked out."

"Who was that gentleman?" Jamir said.

More laughter erupted from members of the press.

* * *

After seeing the press corps' lack of continuing interest in the story of Jamir and the manifesto, with the exception of two persistent female correspondents who apparently found his story to be most interesting, Bix turned his attention to Drule and Shaunesy's un-vetted and un-name-checked VIP greeting committee and to finding a strangely absent Bob Peem. He asked Sophie to escort Jamir when they were finished, pick up Hani, and take them to visit The Candidate in the gym. Then he called Mike.

Mike was directing the tear-down, bopping around the site in his fork lift, moving metal barricade in stacks of ten to the truck that would take them away. He was in his element after the pharmaceutical-grade high that came after a monster blowout rock and roll show such as the one that had just occurred.

"Mike, where are you in the process?" Bix asked.

"I'm finished here. The rest is just clean-up. What do you need?"

"Meet me in Hogwarts Hall. We have to deal with our intruders."

"Roger that," Mike said.

"And see if you can find Bob Peem along your path. He's disappeared."

"Roger."

"And pick up Nora in the VIP area and bring her with you so we can get her a photo with The Candidate before we leave."

"I'll bring her."

Bix began to leave the Press area en route his nemeses, Drule and Shaunesy, when he was stopped by Cornelia, who was accompanied by a woman he recognized immediately as nationally syndicated *New York Times* columnist Rhonda Dodd. Dodd didn't appear happy. For some inexplicable reason he didn't assume the worst, possibly because he had supreme faith in Cornelia's competence. He trusted her more than he trusted himself by that point.

"Ms. Dodd and I just had something odd occur," Cornelia said. "I was escorting her into the Admin Building to use the restroom and Agent Rudd stopped us and told us we couldn't go in. Am I wrong or is that not supposed to be the way it works?"

Bix noticed that Cornelia hadn't bothered to introduce her famous escortee to him, nor he to her, and he was impressed by her judgment. Dodd seemed like a nice enough woman, but she wouldn't care who the hell he was. It was just someone Cornelia was asking for help. Neither did Bix deem it appropriate to ask why they wanted to use the indoor facilities when the outdoor port-o-lets he had provided offered such sumptuous amenities, and very little odor compared to things that smelled much worse.

"*Let's* go find Agent Rudd," Bix said, as he turned on his toes and headed to the Admin Building for another date with destiny.

At the entrance, where The Candidate had already passed many, many minutes prior and would never, ever under any circumstance, emergency or otherwise, ever pass again, stood Agent Rudd, along with the ever-present Knuckles, and a gaggle of agents in dark suits, black shoes, white shirts, dark ties, squiggly wires, and sunglasses—in Rudd's case, super swept-back Hollywood secret agent sunglasses. They were talking in low tones amongst themselves and appeared to be waiting around for the next threat to appear. As it turned out, that was Bix, who was amazed that Rudd hadn't been shunned. Maybe it was professional courtesy alone that maintained unit cohesion. Shane was nowhere to be seen.

"Agent Rudd," Bix began as he approached with his escortees in tow. "Cornelia is going to escort Ms. Dodd inside." He was polite but direct.

"I can't let her do that. We have very restricted space in the hallways and if there was an emergency they would get in the way." Rudd was equally direct but less polite.

It was clear he was yanking Bix's chain.

"Agent Rudd, with no due respect, your protectee isn't even in this building and you know it, and in an emergency you aren't even in the right place to respond, and Cornelia has a Staff pin and she can escort anyone she wants anywhere she wants." Bix raised his voice, a lot. "This isn't a police state yet, despite *your* best efforts, and unless you tell me there is an emergency at this moment we are going to function like we always have, under the rules as they have always been observed."

"I will arrest you," Rudd said.

"Agent Ruddd, I've always avoided saying anything such as this to officer of the law, but I'm going to say it now. I dare you. I double dare you. I double dare you with a cherry on top." Bix then held out his wrists and fixed his eyes on Rudd's. "It's still a semi-free country, unless you weren't aware." He wasn't sure whether he had overplayed his hand.

He had. Rudd was stuck. A bad case of short man's syndrome had trapped him between his insecurity and his desire to screw the hell out of Bix. Bix assumed that getting "screwed the hell out of," in Rudd's mind, would include an arrest and an accidental trip down a flight of stairs.

Rudd pulled out a pair of handcuffs so quickly it looked like he'd practiced in front of a mirror, no doubt at the same time he practiced his quick-draw. He almost yanked Bix's arm out of it's socket and began to slap on the cuffs when fate stepped in once again.

The Advance gods smiled upon the noble and worthy Bix when his old fitness center friend and dinner buddy, Special Agent Guy Mann of the USSS Counter Assault Team, stepped up in his camouflage black uniform and black baseball cap, with his 9MM laser guided pistol slung low on his right thigh in its camouflage holster, to offer a solution before the situation came to blows.

"You can put the cuffs away Kurt," Mann said. "I'll escort the ladies. If there's trouble I will take responsibility for them."

"Thanks, Guy," Bix said. "There's an ambassadorship in this for you."

"It's my pleasure."

Kurt didn't speak.

Bix turned to leave as the ladies and their armed escort walked inside, and he spoke to Rudd as he walked past. "I'm telling Shane," he snarked, and kept moving, not wanting Rude to see him grinning. "Now you're really gonna be in trouble."

* * *

Cutting back around the stage as it was being dismantled, around the cistern toward Hogwarts, Nora and Mike caught up to him. "You're gonna want to hear this," Mike said. "Nora knows what's going on."

"Then why is she hanging out with the likes of us?" Bix asked him.

"Good point," Mike said, "I walked into that. Nora, tell him about our trusted colleagues from Headquarters."

"That group of distinguished gentlemen, except for the few local men who were name-checked, are from New York and they're business aquaintences of Shaunesy's father, who's big into New York real estate. Apparently daddy is trying to do a deal with these guys and Shaunesy promised them a handshake and photo with The Big Guy. And he promised Drule a piece of the action. Apparently Bob Peem invited one or two of them too. This is completely off the books."

"Why?" Bix asked. "Why would they care whether there's a record of this?"

"Because they aren't really raising money," Nora said. "None of these guys are raising funds for the campaign. They're making some small personal donations, but they aren't raising funds and they certainly aren't bundlers. This way Peem and Drule can say they're money people, but no one can check to see if they really are. Everybody is cutting some personal deals here."

Bix assumed that was the case before she mentioned it. She was definitely the main attraction in the Scepter field office. It came as no surprise they opened up to her.

"All of these guys talked to me when we were in the office," Nora continued, "and they're only interested in real estate. They're just here because they were promised a picture with the senator that they can put on their office walls. If any of this has anything to do with the South Carolina primary, or the campaign for that matter, I'll eat my hat."

"And Peem knows about this?" Bix said.

"Does Peem know? They're in cahoots. He's cahooting with Drule—he's the head cahooter. Before he decided to send Drule, he told him there were a couple people he needed him to take care of, so it worked out that Drule and Shaunesy had cover for their own personal connections."

"So Peem was into this two days ago," Mike said. "What a lovely fellow."

"And there's someone else coming," Nora said, "some celebrity who hasn't arrived yet, but I can't find out who it is."

"Is this Peem's person?" Bix said.

"I'm not certain, but I think it's a Peem invitee. It's a Mystery Date."

"OK, we'll keep our eyes peeled for ambient celebrities of unknown origin," Bix said. "If Mr. Peem is partially responsible for this group, I think I know where he will be found."

Bix trod the historic walkways of ol' Scepter College one last time before departure for the airport.

Inside the great hall, under the massive dark brown oak beams and carved gargoyles, Peem was entertaining a few of the shark-suited, French cuffed, diamond cuff-linked, pocket-squared variety of surprise guest. The image of these refugees from an open casting call for *On the Waterfront* inside Hogwarts' hallowed great hall was a shock to Bix's system. It was very nearly a desecration, and he realized at that moment that he couldn't remember the real name of the building. He'd called it Hogwarts so often he had forgotten. As they walked toward Peem, he asked Mike, "What's the name of this building?"

"McBride," Mike said.

"Thanks," Bix said. Looking around at the clusters of intruders sprinkled around the large room he didn't see Drule. Shaunesy and all two-hundred-and-seventy-five pounds of Nurse Ratched were deeply involved in animated conversation with several of their unannounced guests, while standing on a far side of the room were three less-flashily attired gentlemen off to themselves, looking like the only ones who weren't out of place, which made them look out of place.

Nora pointed out the locals to Bix and Mike. "See those guys over there, the ones who look normal, the ones who are standing by themselves? They are the local co-chairs of our campaign here in Scepter County and they have done us a lot of good, but no one's paying attention to them. Peem and Shaunesy are entertaining the out-of-towners."

"Where's Drule?" Bix said.

"I think he is out looking for the big guy," Nora said. "I'm going over and keep them company? They're kind of my team."

"Yes, please, go talk to those poor gentlemen before they leave," Bix said, "and when I come back with The Candidate make sure they aren't thrown under the bus. I want to make sure they get their photos. Tell them to get rid of those VVIP badges. I'll look to you as my wrangler."

"I'll take care of both them and you," she said.

Bix asked Mike to find Drule, probably with The Candidate in the gymnasium, and relay a message to Merle to have his own camera ready to take a group picture. "Come back after you find Drule and talk to Merle, 'cause we need to organize this little photo op."

"Got it, boss."

"I will call Kate in five minutes and ask her to begin loading the press," he told Mike.

"How do you intend to organize this photo op?" Mike asked through a wide smile.

"Dunno yet, but having control of the one and only picture of it will be a good place to start." Mike knew what he meant—no free floating cameras, one group shot. It would work because The Candidate was usually happy to do his part, i.e. shake everyone's hand, give 'em each about three seconds of the old Candidate charm, help organize the group into a group shot, not give anyone the chance to take an individual photo, give Merle ten seconds to take the photo and promise to email it to Shaunesy so he can distribute it, and bolt out the door after another three seconds of that old sincere appreciation and a smile and wave.

Bix immediately inflicted himself on Peem and his guests with the ardor of a fraternity Pledge Committee chairman. "Why gentlemen, I've never seen a more distinguished group of VIP guests," he said, then walked into the circle to shake each man's meaty hand. "I'm Bix," he said to the first few, then it was just "Bix" as each one told him their names. He remembered there were two Sal's, one Vinny, one Lou and a Milo. Milo looked like a cartoon character with bad skin. "Is Bob here showing you a good time?"

They all grumbled in agreement. Bix got the feeling they would have been happier waiting for the big moment sitting at tables with drinks and cigars.

"I hope so," Bix said. "Bob and Larry tell us you're going to be raising a lot of money for the campaign."

The group of big-city Visigoths reacted as one, subtly but perceptibly, as if repelled by a foul aroma emanating from the center of the circle, but compelled to remain cool. They all took a half step backwards in their Gucci loafers and stopped, their heads bowed toward the ground, shrugging and grumbling something sounding close to quasi-agreement.

Peem took absolute control. "These men have already done quite a bit to help us win this campaign."

"Their mere presence among us is inspiration." Bix remained in Rush Week mode. "Well, thank you for being here, and thank you very much for everything you have done and will do for our campaign. Bob, may I speak with you for a moment?"

He led Peem away, and then farther away, then back outside to the quad, the rally site where the tear-down was still underway. "Did you happen to see the rally?"

"Yeah, I got a chance to see it," Peem said.

"Busy with your guests?"

"Sort of, but they aren't your concern," Peem said.

"This isn't the first time you've told me that I should ignore some aspect of what normally would be my job. Why the secrecy? Why didn't Shaunesy, or Drule, or you provide us with their names. Why didn't you want them name-checked? Why haven't they been vetted?"

Another dim lightbulb went on in his head. Some, or all, of these guys might not pass vet. Some, or all, of them might have criminal records.

"They've already been vetted by headquarters," Peem said. "There wasn't any need to go through you."

"You realize of course that you will have to provide their names to the FEC if you take their money. At some point they will be identified, unless they do it through others, which I'm sure you know would be a federal violation. Any way you slice this soiree, it smells of subterfuge."

"You're overreacting. This is fucking outside your lane."

"It's outside my lane up to the point where something bad occurs and everyone asks 'Where was the Lead? Why didn't he know about this?' when a photo pops up on the Internet of the future former next leader of the free world standing next to a guy who's been indicted on twenty-three counts of corruption and endangerment to society. So it really isn't fucking outside my lane, although I've never fucked outside my lane."

"This from the man who brought a foreigner, an Arab, a senior official from an Arab country, to this event, and has to stash him in a holding room," Peem said.

"Point well taken, except for two things," Bix said. "Hani is here because he was helping to defuse a potentially disastrous situation for the campaign, and there will be no photo of him with our fearless leader. And there is only one of him. I bet you can't point to anything your guests have done or will do for the campaign, at least not publicly."

"Neither can you, at least you better not. None of your escapade can ever be made public, and if I ever hear of you telling anyone I'll have you driven out of politics," Peem said.

"Don't try to put me in a good mood, Bob. If I thought you'd drive me out of politics I'd hold a press conference this afternoon. But I will mention these gentlemen to our boss if you haven't. He might want to know there could be some question as to who he's entertaining."

"Larry is briefing him now. It won't be a problem."

The reason for Drule's absence was clear. If he had found the gym where The Candidate was shooting hoops, he had already planted the story of "money guys for a quick handshake."

Bix left to retrieve Jamir and Hani for a quick meet and greet with Jamir's old close life-long friend, The Candidate, and begin the process for departure. He called Kate to ask if the press was ready to begin gathering their gear for departure and she told him they would be on the buses in ten or twelve minutes.

Bix gathered his entourage, Jamir and Sophie, and then Hani from his holding room in the Admin building, and met with Mike along the way to basketball world as Mike was headed back to McBride Hall. Mike confirmed that Drule was in the gym trying to talk with The Candidate when he arrived. "But Drule wan't having much success. When the boss doesn't want to be bothered he doesn't want to be bothered, and when the boss is shooting hoops, he doesn't want to be bothered. Finally Drule gave up and tried to shoot some baskets but he couldn't get the ball to reach the rim."

That comment elicited a big laugh from Sophie. "I can picture that. He reminds me of Neeble, one of the worm guys from outer space. I can't wait to meet his friend, Napoleon Dynamite Shaunesy."

"You will recognize him immediately," Bix said. "When you meet him, just say 'I've heard about you,' and leave it at that. If the putz is capable of worrying about the impression he's left behind, I'd like him to be worried."

"I could say worse things than that," she offered.

"At your discretion. You're hearing the same things I am. He likes to throw his weight around. His problem is that he's practically weightless both physically and politically."

Mike pointed out a contradiction. "His AA however, Ratched, is another story. You will recognize her immediately, too, other than the fact that she's the only female other than Nora in the room, but you won't be so sure at first. You'll have to look hard to be certain."

"Mike, when you go back in there," Bix said as if he was sending his friend into a flaming building, "decide how we should do the group photo so we can roll, excuse me, wrangle these guys when we bring in the boss. We will need to work fast because we will be running late whether we are or not. I will call you when we leave the gym."

"We will be ready."

"And pull those three local gentlemen," Bix said. "Have Nora escort them to the motorcade and we'll take them with us to the airport and do individual photos with them out there. They'll love the motorcade."

"Nora will appreciate that. Will you do her photo out there, too?" Mike said.

"No, I'll instruct her to remain in the VIP van and hide her face when we arrive at the airport. Of course I'll introduce her and get a photo, then I'll invite her out for a drink to talk about our memorable day."

"That's right," Mike said, "you'll bigfoot me with your stories of leading White House Advance teams around the world going back to Harry Truman, and you'll introduce her to The Candidate like you're his closest personal friend, and you'll make it sound like you're personally responsible for ending the Cold War, and she'll go all googly-eyed. I think I'll ride along in the motorcade and do the introductions myself."

"You'll also have to pay for her drinks yourself," Bix said.

"I've been saving my per diems," Mike said.

"I'll be back in a few minutes with my close personal friend, The Candidate."

* * *

Bix and his entourage moved quickly through Bix's secret passages, dotted with post-standers at key junctures, to the gymnasium, where Shane and the Secret Service detail awaited departure.

"I heard you had another run-in with Agent Rudd," Shane said as Bix approached.

"News travels fast over those squiggly wire things. I'll tell you about it in the car," Bix said. "These nice folks are guests of the campaign, with the exception of Sophie here, who is no guest. She's Headquarters staff."

"Nice to meet you Sophie," Shane said. "Gentlemen. You know we have the law enforcement photo-op out here on departure?"

"Yes, we'll do the cops in the hallway here, and then I have to call an audible. We may have to go back to the Admin building via the tunnel and go over to McBride Hall for an unscheduled handshake with the VVIP's who arrived during the rally."

"I understand. We can do that. It's all secured." Shane nodded to let Bix know that he knew who they were.

They entered the old gym to the sound of basketballs bouncing off of backboards and floorboards and then echoing against the walls and ceiling. Suddenly the noise died down as the balls stopped dropping and The Candidate did what he did best—he looked genuinely happy to see Jamir and meet Hani. It didn't hurt that Sophie, one of his favorites at Headquarters, was with them.

"Sophie, Jamir, so good to see you." He hugged her first, then moved to Jamir with a handshake and a man-hug and an introduction to Hani, the full introduction including Hani's current position in the Jordanian government. The Candidate appeared impressed. He looked at Bix, "You talked *him* into this too?"

"He volunteered, Senator," Bix said. "He wanted to help his brother-in-law and you, but mostly you."

"Thank you, Hani. I appreciate you coming to help." The Candidate shook Hani's hand again, this time accompanied with the full smiling Candidate sincerity treatment.

"My pleasure, Senator," Hani said. "I'm very happy that it all worked out, and my brother-in-law is not in the middle of a major scandal."

"Me too," The Candidate said. "Me too. Jamir, you look fantastic," he said. "Speaking of your lovely wife, how is Abia? Did you bring her?"

"She is good, she's back at home. She's happy that I was forced to shave my beard."

"You didn't have to do that for this," The Candidate said. Everyone in the room knew it was complete b.s., and they knew that he knew it was complete bs. He made statements such as that infrequently, but they happened often enough for Bix to make a mental note. He planned to someday ask a professional what it all meant.

Jamir called him out on it. "Oh yes, I certainly did have to shave it, and you know it. You would not have been pleased."

Judging by The Candidate's reaction, it may have been one of the reasons why he didn't hang out with Jamir much any more. Too much bald-faced honesty.

The Candidate, after losing facial expression and taking a half-step backwards in his sensible Johnston & Murphy black tie-ups, then glancing quickly around the room for a possible exit, moved on to another topic. "I understand we rousted you from your secluded hideout in the woods."

"I had no idea that I was hiding out until Bix found me last night," Jamir said. "It was my intent merely to remain out of the way if by some chance the media came around campus during the Primary to ask about your college days. This level of interest was a surprise, but I suppose that muck-raking journalists, like nature, abhor a vacuum, and I had left a vacuum."

"Your intent was noble," The Candidate said, which was a true sentiment. It was so extremely true that it almost made up for the b.s. about Jamir not having to shave his beard. The best thing that his old friends could do was disappear off the planet with no comments, no statements, no pictures, no video, no audio, and no paper trail. He felt the strongest sentimental attachment to those who were never heard from again, by anyone, including him.

"Please tell Abia that I send my best, and thank you for your help in putting this issue to rest," he told Jamir. "We couldn't have done it without you."

Bix was rocked on his heels. It was the kiss-off, the end of the conversation. After their extensive labors to save The Candidate's candidacy, Jamir and Hani were about to get the cursory howdy-do.

Sophie headed it off before it became an insult. "You know Chelsea and I spent so much time in a car with Hani and Jamir over the last two days that she started calling them 'daddy.' Hani's been chased by Max News from Dulles to National to Columbia Metropolitan airport and halfway across the state, and then he and Jamir and Abia were chased across the other half of the state."

"And you and Chelsea along with them," Bix said.

"I didn't know all that," The Candidate said.

"Yes, Senator," she said, "and a lot more. Can't you give these guys some kind of medal when you're elected president?"

He laughed, "That's definitely worth looking into," he said. "Seriously, I appreciate everything you've gone through. I had no idea it was so arduous for all of you, but this could have been a big deal potentially, and you sort of made it go away."

Crickets.

At that moment Sophie showed more moxie than Bix, who wanted to scream. She also knew she wasn't risking her livelihood. "Why don't we take them with us to the airport, then you'd have time to talk."

The Candidate's face was emotionless. He looked to Merle. Merle looked to Bix.

Jamir was gracious. "No, he doesn't have to do that, and we couldn't go anyway because the press might see us."

"You could go, Jamir," she countered. "The press has seen you. They know why you're here and that you're an old friend of the senator's. And Hani and I can stay here until you've left, and then we'll follow behind and pick you up. We have to drive in that direction to take you home, anyway."

The Candidate had no choice. His personal space was about to be intruded upon. "Sure, yes, Jamir, come out to the airport with me. They'll make sure you get home."

"Hani, once again, if you don't mind," Jamir said.

"Of course not," Hani said. "My role here is one of discretion."

"In that case," Bix said, "Senator, we are ready to depart when you are. I'm sure Mr. Drule has briefed you on the people he has waiting to meet you two buildings over."

"He said they were fundraisers and then he tried to shoot some baskets." It was a good dig at a person who deserved it.

"Mr. Drule would know, because I don't," Bix said. "As far as I know, John Wayne Gacy could be in there somewhere. They haven't been name checked through me or the Charleston Secret Service Advance."

The Candidate looked to Drule, who was standing off-court. Drule began to walk toward them, "They were vetted through Headquarters. Bob Peem is with them now," he said, then wiped his mouth. It was his "tell." He wiped his mouth every time he lied, and he was always wiping his mouth.

"If Larry says they've been vetted and Bob is escorting them," Bix said, "then it's your call. The only thing I can promise is that they have been mag'd, so they aren't carrying weapons. Other than that—"

"Let's go down," The Candidate said, "and take a look at the situation."

No one in the room knew what that meant, or everyone knew what they thought it meant. Would he walk in, take a look at the group and decide to turn around and leave? It didn't seem likely to Bix.

"In that case, let's hit the road," Bix said. Peaches handed Bix the leather valise with the College of Scepter logo embossed on it. "It's yours," Peaches said.

Bix thanked him and called Kate to tell her they were leaving the Hold, then called Mike to let him know they were on their way.

"I think our celebrity just arrived," Mike said. "They say it's some athlete. He looks like a short stocky guy to me."

In the hallway of Crump Hall, The Candidate stood at the end of a line of local law enforcement officers, chosen by the Secret Service, who walked up to him one at a time and had their picture taken by a police department photographer with military efficiency.

"Did you get a name? Or a sport?" Bix asked as he waited.

"It's Sookie something, and he plays for a New York team," Mike said.

"Could it be hockey?"

"Not likely."

"Could it be Sookie Smith, the baseball player?" Bix said.

"That sounds right," Mike said. "They all seem to know him."

"Is it the same Sookie Smith whose wife just accused him of domestic abuse in their divorce?" Bix said.

"Google that before you arrive here in Hogwarts," Mike said.

"I don't have to," said Bix. "I just read it last week. Do you have a camera, in case we need it?"

"Yes."

"Be prepared to hand it to Merle if he isn't carrying his."

He hung up and after another round of thank yous and goodbyes, walked out of the front hall directly in front and to the left of The Candidate. He was soon surrounded by agents. Bix leaned over as they walked and spoke softly to him. "We're entertaining a popular baseball player who I believe is Sookie Smith, Golden Glove winner and accused wife beater. We might want to organize this photo-op as a group shot. You know, we *are* running quite late anyway. It's a lot faster to take one giant picture rather than twenty-five individual ones."

"Twenty-five?" The Candidate saw the situation in a new light. "I didn't know there were twenty-five. Let's do one photo with everybody in it. That's why they created the Internet."

Bix turned around and, walking backward and seeing that Drule was lagging behind, caught Merle's attention and motioned to him to move up into the bubble. "Do you have your camera with you?"

"No, I didn't bring it."

"Mike will hand you his when we get into the great hall. We're organizing a group shot, and that photo may need photoshopping before distribution. Got it?"

"Got it," Merle said. "You may want to Stalinize some people before it's made public."

"If only," Bix said. "If only."

As they walked through the underground tunnel to the Admin building, Bix moved forward ten feet ahead of The Candidate, his usual placement in the line of march, to speak with Shane. "You remember we're going to McBride Hall before we go to the motorcade."

"Yes, that's cool, the route's secured. As long as that's the only OTR you have planned."

"Nope, no other OTRs. You know we need to be on-schedule for wheels-up."

"Just checking."

"I understand."

* * *

The Protectee and his personal crowd—his protective detail, the Lead Advance, the trip director, the press secretary, the body guy, and other additions to the entourage—burst into McBride Hall as a stampede. First, Bix spotted Sookie Smith, the man who could not be pictured next to the next President of the United States. He pulled Mike aside and told him to give his camera to Merle.

The Candidate bounced into Hogwarts and past Bix and began shaking hands with the "money guys" before they knew what hit them. After the quickie hello, smiles and light banter with many of them, with Peem, Drule, Shaunesy and Ratchel standing-by waiting for their moment to introduce The Big Guy individually to each and every one of their invitees, The Candidate stood back and utilized his skills in community organizing. "We're running late, we still have to fly to L.A. today and get there by four o'clock, so let's do one big group shot, then you can distribute it to everyone. Isn't that why they invented the Internet?"

Bix and Mike began directing traffic. Peem and Drule, with Shaunesy and Ratchel watching helplessly, began stutter-stepping around The Candidate, attempting to re-direct his energies toward a more personalized approach. He rejected their entreaties to introduce him even to one man.

Bix and Mike continued herding their grumpy guests into a pod with the verbal encouragement of The Candidate.

It was a rare occurence when Bix's interests and tactics coincided with The Candidate's, whose lack of enthusiasm for extended interaction was an advantage, unchallengeable, and useful to Bix in his risk-averse world of Advance, on the road, in public, where the uncontrollable can happen because people try to get away with shit.

Peem's team was clearly flabbergasted. Bix and Mike and The Candidate all ignored Drule's and Shaunesy's weak protestations as if they weren't in the room, and soon all twenty-something guests had been assembled into a scene that was one part high school home-room class photo and one part "Sopranos" reunion. When one of the gentlemen offered his camera for the photo, Bix declined. "Merle here is paid to do this, and it's a union thing." He figured the money guys from New York would understand that logic.

Bix walked to Merle as he began to set up for the photo with Mike's camera. "Watch me," he said softly. "When I do my thing, take the shot. Just let us know when you're ready to go and then give me one second."

Merle had been down that path before with Bix. "Got it. You're going to pre-Stalinize somebody."

As the scene began to calm, Peem, Drule, Shaunesy, and Ratchel slowly edged themselves into the photo op, and Mike helped The Candidate create a space in the middle of the first row. Bix moved next to Sookie at the end of the second row, with Sookie on his right. Merle backed up until the viewfinder contained all of the usual suspects and told the group how good they looked. He finished with, "Ready?"

Bix took it upon himself at that moment to be surprised to be standing next to a big sports star. He moved forward and looked at him in the eyes, "Aren't you future Hall of Fame baseball star Sookie Smith?"

Click. Merle took the shot, with most of Sookie's face covered by Bix's head and left shoulder.

"I got it—that was a good one," Merle piped up cheerfully.

Sookie began to protest, then Drule began to say something, then Bix began to thank everyone in his loudest voice as he made a fast get-away around the group to the side of The Candidate and the protection of his Secret Service bubble. The Candidate stepped out and away from the class photo and turned around, providing no dead air in which social interaction might begin, and spoke immediately. "Thank you, gentlemen, for coming out. I appreciate what you're doing for the campaign." Bix thanked them again as he began to walk away, his shoulder bag over one shoulder and his new leather valise in his hand.

Mike was already walking out the door to his place in the VIP van next to Nora and her three county co-chairs. Bix did a one-eighty, paused for less than a second to make certain he had The Candidate in tow. The Candidate shook hands with the men standing closest to him, then followed Bix. The Detail moved in along in front, sides and rear, the entourage took up the far rear and the unfortunate money guys and Peem's team, sans Peem, were left in a cloud of dust.

Peem bade his VIP guests an uncomfortable farewell and followed along, abandoning Drule and Shaunesy to deal with the fallout. The motorcade and the plane were his only way out of town.

No one looked back. Bix reached the limo first and waved Jamir to the non-protectee side where one of the agents opened the door. Bix walked past and up to the Lead Marked car, Peem sprinted to the Staff 1 van and Freeway, standing eight vehicles away next to the VIP van, flashed a "thumbs-up" over his head. At that instant, the press buses appeared from around the corner behind Freeway, timed to fall in line as the motorcade pulled away en route Charleston airport. Bix could see Kate through the windshield of the first bus next to the driver, steadying herself at the safety rail with one hand and directing him with the other.

The protectee's butt hitting his seat in the limo was the Secret Service's cue to move. Within a half-second, Shane was urging Bix to get in the car. "We gotta go." Bix took once last look to see if anyone was about to be left behind, but didn't hold up the parade.

"Let's go," Bix said as he stepped in and closed the door with his extra luggage, almost falling into SAIC Farrow, who was already ensconced in the back seat.

The line of cars moved ahead slowly at first, down tree-lined College Avenue, past still-cheering and waving crowds walking to their cars or their dorms or to their homes. It picked up speed as they drove farther from campus through a quaint old residential section of Scepter that spoke to its post-Civil War rebuilding and prosperity.

"This is a beautiful drive through this part of town," SAIC Farrow commented.

It was a cue, too. If the Secret Service was relaxed, it was definitely time for Bix to consider doing the same. The trip was essentially over. The rally had been a monumental success. They had dodged all of the bullets; the media coverage was all-rally all-the-time, punctuated with the Curley endorsement and double-punctuated with images of those epic banners which screamed South Carolina; the unprecedented crowd had helpfully screamed "We love you;" and it was all sweetened by the O'Malley cock-block. It was time to relax.

"Yes, it's a beautiful neighborhood," Bix said.

Shane and Captain Contarini agreed.

It was time for a little motorcade humor. The agents loved nothing more than a harmless practical joke, as long as it was played on Staff Advance. Jokes played on the Service were seldom amusing, and only funny if they were truly funny and very, very short lived.

Bix answered his cell phone as if it had gone off in "vibrate" mode, pulling it from the inside breast pocket of his navy sport coat. "This is Bix," he said, then paused, then continued with his Bob Newhart impression while Fed's remained quiet out of courtesy, and then out of interest. "Yeah, Merle, what can I do for you?" Pause pause pause. "OTR?"

Those dreaded initials, that loathed abbreviation, not really an acronym as far as the Secret Service was concerned, more of an opportunity for someone to get killed, received the instantaneous reaction that Bix expected. The car got real tense real quick. Shane turned in his seat and looked at Bix. So did Farrow. Bix was thankful that Captain Contarini kept his eyes on the road, but then he saw Contarini looking at him through the rear view mirror.

He continued. "Yeah, I know the Charleston Convention Center, the one near the airport." Pause pause pause pause pause. He looked at Shane and mouthed, "I don't know," and then held up his right hand palm up to accentuate his innocence.

"Yes, Merle, I know, the Sons of South Carolina Gun and Knife Show is there. I understand our need to reach out on that issue. We could do it, there's a back entrance."

Shane couldn't help himself. After the evening before he had expected the worst, but this was worse than the worst. "What?" he said out loud. He and SAIC Farrow almost reached for their side arms as they both agitated in their seats. Farrow muttered under his breath, "What kind of idiot thought that one up?" as he turned his head away from Bix and looked out the window. Shane turned and stared out the windshield, wordless.

Bix became concerned that someone might start sweating profusely or have a heart attack or find it less than humorous if he dragged it out any further.

"Both Special Agent Emory and SAIC Farrow think the idea blows big time, so you should tell Renegade that they refuse to do it," Bix said into his phone. "They've had it with his bullshit. Tell him exactly like that." He punched the "end" button and looked at his car mates. A large grin crept on to his face.

A classic double-take later, Shane and Farrow realized they'd been had and, happily for Bix, their review of his one-act play was positive. Spontaneous laughter ensued. "You really had me going," Farrow said between laughs. "That was a good one. I'll remember that."

Shane was laughing as well. "That was good. There was just enough reality to it to be true. And no one got hurt. I was about to shoot you."

"No Advance people were hurt in the making of this gag," Bix said. "That'll please the animal rights people."

It was all merriment and mirth in the Lead Car, men of action enjoying a thankfully boring end of a very long day and long night before. Bix's phone rang, for real, which sent up more laughter. "Tell them we can do an OTR to the Hell's Angels convention down at Harley's Pool Hall," Farrow said.

It was Bix's new, dime-a-minute, off-the-grid flip phone ringing, and he didn't recognize the number. "This is Bix."

"Bix, this is Bill James at William and Mary," the voice growled. "Janet Townsend gave me your number. Are you busy?"

"Dr. James, not at all, this is a perfect time. It's always good to hear from you." James was an old friend and one of the rare former professors from his undergraduate days who had had a positive opinion of him.

The car went quiet again.

"Bix, Janet contacted me about the issue you were having with our mutual friend Jamir Parviz."

"Yes Bill. We found him and the article that had caused the rumors."

"I saw it on CNN. After the report on your rally at the college, they did a short story about the controversy, and that it turned out to be nothing. The reporter read a little part of it on the air."

"How did it sound?" Bix asked. "Did they try to make it sound more controversial than it was?"

"No, it wasn't that," James said. "They read the title, 'Manifesto of Misperceptions,' and a few lines from the first couple paragraphs. It didn't sound controversial."

"Was there a problem?"

"The problem is that I wrote an article with the same title, and the opening sentences sounded very similar to what I remember writing. Very similar. I'm trying to find the article, but the real problem is that mine was published in *Middle East Monthly Digest*, and it was two years earlier than the date I heard quoted on CNN."

"Oh. Really?"

"Really," James said.

"You know what they say about the sincerest form of flattery," Bix said.

"Hey, I'm flattered. But if someone looks that up and finds my article and it compares *too* flatteringly, you're going to have another problem on your hands. I thought you might like to know."

"Thank you so much for the heads-up. It's good to have the bad news as soon as possible. I appreciate you letting me know." Bix thought the last comment sounded frighteningly like The Candidate.

After hanging up, Bix reassured his car mates that, while there might be some cause for concern, it wasn't their concern. "This one is political, gentlemen, not life-threatening." Their faces relaxed and good nature again reigned for the last few minutes of the journey to Charleston Airport.

Before the motorcade stopped completely, Bix was out of the car like a spry youth. As he walked past the limo, he was pleased to see The Candidate and Jamir in animated conversation. Catching their attention he gave them a signal, "Give me one minute." The Candidate knew what he meant. The traveling press was still unloading from their buses and loading on to the plane.

With his shoulder bag and his brand new leather valise Bix looked like he was loading on to the plane as well. He walked quickly to Staff 1 before Peem was able to get out and board the plane. "Don't get on the plane yet, Bob. I need to talk with you."

"What about?" Peem asked as Bix walked back to the VIP van.

"Please stay here. We need to talk."

Encouragement—drill sergeant-style encouragement—was needed to move *his* VIP guests, the ones who deserved it, from the van to the side of airplane in something less than all day. The group was milling around, talking casually, moving slowly toward plane side.

"Mike, Freeway, Nora, let's get everyone up to the stairs. Our distinguished co-chairs first, then Nora and Miranda. Freeway, get your drivers. Let's move. We need to have wheels-up today people. Nora, I will introduce you and you can introduce our VIPs. Mike, I assume you're taking pictures."

"I'm ready when they are."

Bix herded the good VIPs into position at the foot of the stairs. Freeway added his motorcade drivers and Mike found his spot to shoot the pictures. Seeing that his departure handshakes were in place, The Candidate was out of his limo, followed by Jamir.

"Take a picture," The Candidate said as he waved Jamir to his side. Mike complied. The Candidate gave Jamir one last man-hug then moved to the line-up at the base of the stairs. Jamir stood aside as Bix introduced Nora, and Nora introduced her three co-chairs. The Candidate appeared happy to stand with them for what was, by his standards, an extended and serious conversation before posing for photos with each one. He was especially pleased to pose with Nora, and also took his time with Miranda and the motorcade drivers, who posed as a group.

Then, like Santa Claus going up the chimney, he started up the stairs in a flash, but halted abruptly and shouted to Bix.

Bix saw The Candidate pause mid-staircase and look back down to him. For a brief instant he was expecting to hear a "job well done" or "thanks for everything" or "that was a hell of a rally." There was a first time for everything.

"Hey, I want that leather bag," The Candidate said.

"Peaches gave it to me," Bix reacted instinctively.

"Well, I want it," The Candidate said, and waited.

"Your official spokesman presented to me as a token of your deep gratitude," Bix said.

"Gimme the bag." The Candidate walked down the stairs to the tarmac and waited.

Bix handed it over. The Candidate started back up the stairs. "You know it isn't real leather," Bix called after him. "It's pleather."

The Candidate stopped dead in his tracks. If it were true, he couldn't be seen using such an abomination. "Why do you say that?" he asked.

"Because it's true. It's a genuine imitation leather bag. And now you own it. Enjoy."

The Candidate disappeared from view into the cabin of the plane, inspecting his new acquisition for authenticity as he walked away.

Peem had also disappeared from view, causing Bix's gorge to rise, almost self-destructively. His gut told him to go up the stairs into the front cabin and drag Peem by his ear back to the tarmac, and his gut was always wrong, so he waited. After a few seconds Peem appeared at the door to the plane and waved to Bix to come up.

Bix waved for Peem to come back down. Peem walked down.

"What's this about?"

"How very kind of you Bob, you're welcome," Bix said. "Yes, it was a great set of events today and all credit goes to the team. They worked their asses off and did a superhuman job. I know you will want me to pass along your appreciation for a job well done."

"Is that what this is about?" Peem said. "Well, fuck you, I can tell the team myself if I appreciate the job they are getting paid to do. If they don't like it, you know there's a thousand people for each one of their slots who will be happy take their places."

Peem started to walk away as Bix piped up. "You invited that baseball player—what the hell was that about?"

"Well, he's a friend, and I just found out about his wife's accusations on the ride out here. He won't do anything with the picture."

"You hope," Bix said. "That's why we vet people. You'd fire anyone on the staff who did the same thing."

Peem continued trying to separate himself from the conversation and Bix. "Yeah, well, it's none of your concern," he said as he inched away. "Unless there's something else."

His dismissiveness was a tonic for Bix's troubled mind.

"No, not really, just one more thing, Bob."

"Yeah, what the hell is it? You're holding up the show."

"Terribly sorry, I'll be quick. During the motorcade out here I got a call from a friend, a professor, who saw the coverage of Jamir and the manifesto on CNN."

"So what's the problem?" Peem continued to walk on the snide side.

"The CNN reporter read the title of the article and a few lines from the first few chapters, and according to my friend, whom I trust, it was the exact title and the same opening sentences as an article he had written for *Middle East Monthly* in 1979."

Peem stopped and gave Bix his full attention. "Does he have the article?"

Bix began to try to separate from the conversation and especially from Peem. "He's finding it."

Peem stood on the staircase looking after Bix like Juliet beckoning to Romeo. "Will you send it to me?" he said as Bix continued to back away.

"It might be Google-able."

The flight attendant called down to Peem, "We need to close the door."

"Does this mean there could be a charge of plagiarism?" Peem shouted.

Bix had almost reached the edge of the taxiway. "It might," he yelled.

Peem walked up the stairs and back into the airplane and the flight attendant closed the door behind him. Five minutes later, they had wheels-up on-schedule en route to L.A., and Bix called his counterpart, the Lead Advance in L.A., to let him know.

He emailed his team in one group hug of thanks and congratulations for an extraordinary job under very difficult circumstances, spent ten minutes shaking hands and thanking every conceivable colleague and collaborator and volunteer on site, retrieved his car from the line of vehicles that twenty minutes before had been a motorcade and now was just a bunch of rental cars waiting to be returned, and drove back to the Hotel Marianne to luxuriate for one night in his suite and await Storie's return. He would decide the next day how to respond to Egan's latest email, which he hadn't read except for the subject line: "Your next trip."

The End

O Me! O life!...of the questions of these recurring;
Of the endless trains of the faithless—of cities fill'd with the foolish;
Of myself forever reproaching myself, (for who more foolish than I, and who more faithless?)
Of eyes that vainly crave the light—of the objects mean—of the struggle ever renew'd;
Of the poor results of all—of the plodding and sordid crowds I see around me;
Of the empty and useless years of the rest—with the rest me intertwined;
The question, O me! so sad, recurring—What good amid these, O me, O life?
Answer,
That you are here—that life exists and identity;
That the powerful play goes on, and you will contribute a verse.'

Walt Whitman, *Leaves of Grass*

ABOUT THE AUTHOR

Steven Jacques grew up on Southside ward politics in the City of St. Louis. He started volunteering at the age of eleven and by the age of twenty-three was serving on the White House staff. He has led hundreds of White House Advance teams throughout the U.S. and abroad and led thousands of presidential campaign Advance teams over thirty-six years in national politics. He served as a presidential appointee in three Administrations, on the White House staff and as a senior official the U.S. State Department and U.S. Department of Commerce.